Praise for Maureen

'The portrayal of abuse is sensitiv[e]
Tess's escape is often thrilling. The characters are vividly real,
and there is a beautiful sense of place … *Stay With Me* is a
powerful and sympathetic story that will speak to many older
YA readers.' *Books & Publishing*

For *The Convent*:
'An absorbing tale, full of buried secrets and family drama
… adults are likely to get as much out of it as teenagers.'
Australian Bookseller & Publisher

For *Somebody's Crying*:
'Maureen McCarthy's books are engrossing because the
protagonists' lives ring true and she articulates the feelings
that most people leave unsaid.' *Weekend Australian*

For *Rose by any other name*:
'McCarthy is so very good at emotional authenticity … most
especially we're drawn to Rose, prickly and delicate as her
namesake.' *The Age*

For *Queen Kat, Carmel and St Jude Get a Life*:
'I first read *Queen Kat, Carmel and St Jude Get a Life* when
I was fourteen, and felt like I was reading my own future.'
Lili Wilkinson, author

Also by Maureen McCarthy

The Convent

Somebody's Crying

Rose by any other name

Queen Kat, Carmel and St Jude Get a Life

Careful what you wish for

Flash Jack

Chain of Hearts

When you wake and find me gone

Cross my heart

Ganglands

In Between series

Stay with Me

MAUREEN McCARTHY

ALLEN&UNWIN
SYDNEY · MELBOURNE · AUCKLAND · LONDON

This project has been assisted by the Australian Government through the Australia Council, its arts funding and advisory body.

First published in 2015

Allen & Unwin
83 Alexander Street
Crows Nest NSW 2065
Australia
Phone: (61 2) 8425 0100
Email: info@allenandunwin.com
Web: www.allenandunwin.com

A Cataloguing-in-Publication entry is available from the
National Library of Australia
www.trove.nla.gov.au

ISBN 978 1 74331 688 7

Cover design and photography and text design by Astred Hicks, Design Cherry
Photograph of girl by Luisa Brimble
Set in 12/17 pt Bembo by Midland Typesetters, Australia

The author would like to acknowledge that the extract on page 86 is from John Gillespie Magee Jr's sonnet *High Flight*.

Printed and bound in Australia by Griffin Press
10 9 8 7 6 5 4 3 2 1

The paper in this book is FSC® certified. FSC® promotes environmentally responsible, socially beneficial and economically viable management of the world's forests.

I shall always be near you
in the gladdest days and in the darkest nights ...
always, always,
and if there be a soft breeze upon your cheek,
it shall be my breath,
as the cool air fans your throbbing temple,
it shall be my spirit passing by.
Sullivan Ballou, 1861

For my grandmother
Lillian Josephine McCarthy
1887–1924
— you are not forgotten

Dated this 21st day of November, 1928,
in Melbourne in the state of Victoria

Name of the patient with Christian name at length:
Therese Mary Josephine Kavanagh

Sex and age: Female, 32 years

Married, single or widowed: Married

Number of children: 5

Age of youngest child: 14 months

Previous occupation: Home duties

Habits of life: Clean

Previous place of abode: Mayfield near Leongatha

Whether first attack: Yes

When and where previous under treatment: No

Whether subject to epilepsy: No

Whether suicidal: No

Whether a danger to others: No

Supposed cause of attack: Shock

Facts observed by myself:
On admission she was very violent and required
restraining. She was constantly calling to Jesus
Christ to spare her and thought the devil was
persecuting her. She now thinks she is insane and
is frequently out of bed praying. She claims she is
a very wicked woman.

Signed *Charles Mc ...*

Bruises on back and arms.

My great-grandmother was an ordinary woman, married to an ordinary poor farmer. She had no one to speak for her. Her husband was the only person who could have helped her, and he was the one who'd decided she was mad enough to be put away. No one in her life thought they might know better. Not her mother or father, or her two brothers, or any of her four sisters, three of them alive and living nearby.

She died in the Kew Asylum two years later, aged thirty-four, without ever seeing any of her five children again. The youngest was only three.

You can be old when you're still young. Even at thirteen you can feel like life has not just passed you by, but that it has nothing more to offer and never will. The threads holding you to the earth seem as thin and delicate as gossamer, so utterly arbitrary that they might as well not be there.

I'm twenty-one now, and everything that has happened to me seems completely random, and yet at the same time as inevitable as if I'd planned it all myself.

How could I have known while I was lying in that hospital bed with beeping monitors and drips in both arms that within only a few short days I would wake with a fierce desire to live?

It was my great-grandmother Therese, I'm sure now, hovering over me for those first twenty-four hours as I cruised between life and death. Standing behind my left shoulder keeping her eye on the plastic tubes and glass bottles, the beeping machines that kept me in the land of the living. It might have been the drugs they'd pumped into me, but I'm sure I felt her lean in close at one point.

Keep breathing, she whispered. *Stay with me.*

one

It's around three a.m. I can't be sure exactly, because I'm hiding under a house, ten minutes' drive out of Byron Bay, off the Old Bangalow Road. If you wanted to find us you'd turn off the main road and go over the railway line, then take a right into Cemetery Road and follow that road past the cemetery into the hills where it becomes a dirt track. We're right at the end, halfway down the hill in a small wooden cottage on stilts, hidden in among heavy palm-tree foliage.

I'm scared of snakes, and I hate crawling insects, but it's the smell that really gets to me. The dank dark smell that makes me feel as though I'm already in the ground, waiting for dirt to be shovelled in on top of me.

I'm not cold. It's still summer – just. Still the season for tourists, and surfers, and girls my age in skimpy halter dresses walking up and down the streets licking ice-creams, their shoulders pink from the sun and their voices careless with hilarity and boredom. I see them sometimes when we go into town, and it's as if I'm watching a movie about a different species. It's hard to remember that I used to be one of them.

I hear the soft sound of a radio playing old rock classics directly above me, then footsteps going down the hall. A door creaks open. He'll be checking his email for news of that container which has failed to arrive. The footsteps come back and I hear coughing and then the creak of bedsprings. It won't be long now.

Time passes in chunks of stale sponge cake, then stretches out in sticky grey lines, like chewing gum. The radio is switched off eventually, and under all the other night noises around me, the scratching wombat and the scurrying mice, I hear that low even rumble. He doesn't usually snore, except when he drinks, which is what he was doing earlier with his brothers.

I crawl out from under the house and go back inside. I go to the bathroom, clean my teeth, take off my clothes, then creep through to the bedroom and slip under the covers beside him.

He puts one hand on my hip and buries his face into the back of my neck and mumbles something like, 'You good now, babe?'

'Sure,' I murmur. 'I'm good now.'

But I'm not good. I'm so far from good it doesn't matter. Every cell in my body is on stand-by, a red-hot alert signal is swinging before my eyes like a neon strobe-light at a fairground. On and off it goes, and I'm half-blinded by its brightness.

He runs his hands up and down my legs a couple of times, turns me around and breathes his sharp vodka-fuelled breath in my face, squeezes my breasts, then he's on top of me, parting my legs with both hands, pushing himself in roughly like he has every right. It hurts like crazy. But I'm glad. Really glad, because some-times when he's been drinking he is too tired. Then he wakes after a few hours, thirsty and discontented. Now his sleep will be deep and trouble-free and that's exactly what I need.

Try and leave and I'll find you. No woman messes with me, babe. I mean it.

But you say you love me.

I do love you.

He does mean it. There would be all kinds of ways of disposing of a body on this property. No one in town knows me anymore. His mother and two brothers would die rather than snitch on him. For all I know he might mean the loving bit as well.

I lie quietly beside him and before long he is breathing deeply again, not snoring now but taking deep even breaths. *So far so good.*

I can hardly believe what I am about to do. It feels as unreal as if someone else has moved their bits and pieces of machinery into my head and pushed the green button on the wall. Red and orange lights flicker as the pistons and levers slowly come to life.

I ease my body out of bed, pick up the pile of clothes I left carefully on the floor – jeans, T-shirt, pullover and jacket – and tiptoe out. Once I'm dressed, I creep down the hall to the end room.

She is lying on her back, arms spread out in her little bed as though she has only just finished playing. Barry, the homemade orange-tartan bear with two odd brown-button eyes, a small peaky snout and a sewn-on yellow hat is lying alongside her. He is a cumbersome, ugly thing, probably the worst-looking kids' toy I've ever seen, but Nellie loves him. She picked him from a table of other used toys at a street stall last year, and he rarely leaves her side. My daughter is three years old, speaks as clearly and precisely as a grown woman, and can already write her name and read a bit. I lean down and whisper her name now and she lifts one plump arm to my neck and mutters something about a green frog. She is tall for her age, sturdy too, with masses of wild black curls and a face sweet enough to break your heart. Just this morning she told me that she planned to marry our dog Streak one day. When I asked why, she said, 'Because I'll be able to go on long runs with him at night.'

'Okay,' I said, 'but what if you get tired?'

She had to think about that one for a while. 'If I get tired I'll climb on his back and tell him to bring me home.'

I have to get her away.

Her arm pulls me nearer, her other pudgy hand is wandering dreamily over my face and hair as she mumbles more about the frog. She puts three fingers into my mouth and when I suck them she giggles in her sleep as though she knows exactly what game I'm playing. I pick her up and settle her heavy head on my shoulder, reasonably confident that she won't kick up, because I slipped a bit of a pill that I saved from hospital into her drink. I grab Barry by one of his fat legs and make for the door.

My things – the stroller and the canvas backpack containing two hundred and forty-three dollars stolen from his jacket, spare clothes for her, a light dress, jeans, two T-shirts, a cotton jumper, underpants, a packet of tampons – are already waiting under a tree nearby.

I settle her into the stroller, wrapping the bunny rug tightly around her, and throw Barry across the handles. It's only then that I remember the old journal hidden under Nellie's mattress, and my breath drops away. *How could I have forgotten it?* The battered black book from my previous life, every page filled with close teenage scrawl. There's my father's Django Reinhardt CD tucked inside the front cover and a few photos stuck in the back. A head shot of my great-grandmother aged fifteen that my mother gave me before she left, one or two of my parents and another not-very-clear one of my brother and two sisters. I purposefully left it until the last minute, thinking that if he caught me leaving then at least he wouldn't get that. It's the one thing I've managed to keep hidden.

I stand still a moment, my heart thumping with the enormity of what it would mean to leave that book behind. He'd find it eventually. I imagine him pulling the room apart looking for clues, and then those long, strong, guitar-playing fingers picking it up and slowly turning the pages, studying the photos, reading every last word of my ramblings. He has the rest of me in place, and now the final piece of the jigsaw. Once he finished he'd turn it over to his mother and brothers. *You were right, mate. One crazy little bitch!*

I was seventeen when I came up here with a couple of friends for a good time. Had some part of me known that I would not be going back? Why else would I have brought that book and those photos?

One crazy little bitch. That's who I am now.

I leave Nellie sleeping in the stroller under a tree, creep back inside into her bedroom that smells of her, and lift up the mattress. When my fingers touch that hard shape, my soul floats above my body for a few seconds. I tiptoe out again through the back door, the lightness still bouncing around my head as I make my way back into the darkness and to Nellie.

Keep breathing. That soft voice in my head steadies me a bit. *Stay with me …* It's so easy to lose sight of what I've got to do.

I make my way gingerly through our front garden of ferns and trees, towards the track leading down to the main road. I can hardly think, I'm so afraid. Every noise, every rustle in the dark makes me more aware of what I'm doing.

The stroller wheels crunch loudly on the rough gravel. I consider folding up the stroller and carrying Nellie in my arms, but with the bursting backpack I know she would quickly get too heavy. There is no other way but this. Every time I hit a stone or a rut the extra noise jolts me to the bone, makes me stop and turn around. Would that one have woken him? I'm expecting him to appear, to hear his voice calling me. And once he catches sight of the stroller and backpack it will be all over. My heart races with the enormity of what that would mean. *Over.* I picture the look on his face as the pieces slot into gear in his head. Will he strangle me here in front of Nellie? No. I don't think so. He'll lock me in the shed and break me to bits first, and then he'll call his brother over; they'll finish me off together.

Think of now. Only now. One foot in front of the other … Or I will freeze to death with fear.

In the distance, the goods train thunders by, making its way down towards Sydney. That means it must be close to five a.m.

I close my eyes and imagine the might of all that iron and steel roaring through the night.

For the last five mornings, that same train has jolted me awake, the loud lonely whistle cutting through my sleep like a blade, making my blood rush in panic, scared that I've said something in my sleep, or that he will see by my face that something is going on.

Before long I am over the track. I edge my way to the smoother part on the side and begin the downward slope at a faster pace. There are hanging branches and deep shadows on both sides, but I know I'm not safe yet. If he were to look long enough through the front window he would be able to see my moving figure, and he might … he just might be doing that right now. A terrible fear grips my insides and I feel light-headed, as though I'm not getting enough oxygen. The air surrounding me is thick and dark, heavy with the scent of bush. I can't really breathe properly until I am over the small dip in the track. Then at least I'm not visible from the house.

Even then he only has to wake and realise I'm not there and it won't be long before he comes looking, and the more I think about that, the more I believe it might be happening. The drinking and the sex give me the best chance I can realistically hope for; even so, I am running now. *I will get there*, I tell myself, over and over. *I'll get there and those people will be waiting for me.* I have to believe it.

But I don't know them! I can't even remember their names. It was five days ago. Why would they put themselves into a potentially dangerous situation for a stranger? Turn back now. Put Nellie back to bed. You have time. If he wakes, tell him that she had a bad dream.

I keep on, one step after another. It's as though my legs and feet don't know how to go any other way. Under all my fear, I know that this might be my last hour on earth, so I drink in the surrounding night. I think of my dead father, my missing mother, my elder sisters and my shy sweet brother. Yesterday evening rushes at me, Nellie and I together on the verandah, with Barry between us, watching the shell-pink and pale gold sky before the sun finally sank. The brilliant mornings here, first light on the leaves and wet grass, birds chirping away in the trees – my love for it all sings alongside the low strident buzz of dread eating at my insides, slow and constant as a hungry rat gnawing through a wall. *Nothing good can come of this … How could it? A massive blunder that will cost … your life … Go back!* The bright morning sun, the frosts and fogs, the wind and the rain – I will die thinking of them. While he is killing me I will think of them. I will die free.

Keep breathing. Stay with me.

Normally, he never lets me out of his sight when we go into town. But something has been going on with the avocado farm he runs with his mother and two brothers. For the last couple of weeks there have been a lot of phone calls and low-level anger directed at the youngest brother, Travis. Just a few days ago, on the steps leading up to the front door of the library, he waved me inside because there was someone coming out he needed to talk to, and he didn't want me to hear the conversation. Whatever they're doing is dodgy. They keep buying more land. The farm brought in virtually no income last year, so where is the money coming from?

I noticed the girl first. She was dressed in a mauve shirt with torn-off shorts, and had the long silky blonde hair and golden skin that I used to dream about – my skin being so pale and my hair almost pitch black. She was sitting on the floor with her legs poking across the aisle. Next to her was a thick-set guy in a bright green Hawaiian shirt, with short curly dark hair and fair skin, who was sitting the same way, except that … one of his legs was missing. There was no right leg sticking out from the faded board shorts. I took a second look and saw his left hand was damaged too. The last three fingers were all caught up in a bunch. I blushed with embarrassment when he glanced up and caught me looking. A prosthetic leg complete with matching sneaker was propped up against the bookshelves opposite. I noticed that he had a scar across his forehead and one eye had a kind of milky film over it.

I motioned that I needed to get past them to the kids' section, and the girl looked up and pulled her legs in immediately. I saw then that she was extraordinarily beautiful. A model's face, with perfectly even features, a big wide mouth with full lips. It was hard to turn away from such beauty. Nellie held out her hand and the beautiful girl took it straight away.

'Hey, little one,' she said. 'What's your name?'

'Fenella,' Nellie replied. 'What's yours?'

'Julianne. But I get called Jules.'

'Well, I get called Nellie.' Nellie puffed out her belly importantly, squinting at the girl. 'And I've got a dog.'

The girl flashes me a quick, gorgeous grin. 'Have you now?'

'Yes?' Nellie went all shy and hid behind my legs, but she watched the beautiful girl from behind my right knee. There was something ethereal about her that must have been obvious even to my three-year-old. The huge grey-green eyes with the paintbrush black lashes, the bone structure that made every time she turned her head a cause for wonder.

'What is your dog's name?' the girl asked.

Nellie took a moment to think. 'Streak,' she said, looking up at me for confirmation. I nodded. 'And Mamma sometimes paints my toenails pink,' she added quickly, as though anxious to keep the conversation going. She held out one small grubby foot inside its plastic sandal for the girl to admire, then looked up at me. 'What else?'

'Lots of things,' I say, feeling the familiar rush of tenderness shoot straight through me. Nellie's existence has complicated my own life almost out of existence, and yet even in my darkest hours I can't honestly wish she wasn't around. 'What about the chooks?' I suggest.

She takes a deep breath. 'And I can feed the chooks if Mamma lifts me up to unlock the gate,' she whispers shyly.

'You live on a farm?'

'And we've got two goats.'

'Wow! You have so many interesting things in your life!' The girl had a lovely light laugh that had the odd effect of making me want to cry – the way it just bubbled out of her so sweetly, like music.

The guy was the same, both of them friendly and full of fun. I could see under the damage that he'd been good-looking. He still wasn't bad, with a square chin, a straight nose, wide smile full of straight white teeth. They talked to Nellie about how old she was and what kind of books she liked, and they both tried to include me a few times but I held back. My hair was tied up with an elastic band, my jeans were shabby – straight from Vinnies – and my faded red top had stains down the front. My feet in the rubber thongs were grimy as well. I was conscious of the rough red patch of skin under my eye and around both ears. Since the stint in hospital I'd become very thin as well. Just that morning, Jay had taken a long hard look at me when I came out of the shower.

'Do something with yourself, why don't you?'

'What do you mean?'

'Eat, for a start!'

'I do eat.' But the truth was I barely ate. Food had lost its attraction.

'Too skinny,' he grumbled. 'Fucking you is becoming a chore.'

The insides of my elbows were particularly itchy that day at the library. I needed a fresh tube of the ointment I'd used in hospital, and I was building up to ask Jay if we could stop at the clinic for a prescription on the way home. I stood rubbing the skin, trying not to use my nails, as I listened to the couple chattering to my daughter. As I moved along the shelves picking out books, reading the blurbs and putting them back, I took quick glances at Jay through the glass door of the library, enjoying my momentary freedom as he talked to the bloke on the stairs outside.

But when I heard the girl tell Nellie that they'd be driving down to Melbourne in a few days, a strange tingling sensation began in my toes even before the idea came to me properly. It rose up to my knees and then into my gut and I forgot about the itching. I edged my way closer to where they sat, aware that something was bouncing back and forth in my head, like a giant moth bashing itself against a hot bulb. Back and forth it went, singeing its wings and refusing to give up.

I'd been out of hospital for a few months. Looking back, I see that I'd been waiting for this moment, or one like it. I became quite close to a nurse in there, an older woman who didn't mess about being polite. When I tried lying about the bruises she didn't buy it, and I opened up a bit. Not that I told her everything, but she knew. She told me that I would know when to make a move, an opportunity would present itself, and if it felt right I should grab it with both hands.

When Nellie wandered off to the kids' section I walked back to the young couple. I could still see Jay through the door – he was standing on the steps, deep in conversation.

The amazing thing was that they seemed to understand instinctively when I told them I needed to escape. I don't know if they noticed the red-raw patches of skin on my arms, the fading bruises around my neck or the desperation in my eyes, but they didn't ask many questions. Luck was on my side, because we got nearly ten minutes to work things out. They had come up to Byron to visit the beautiful girl's sick grandmother and would be driving back down south in a few days. They planned to leave very early in the morning – before daybreak – and they would be happy to give me and Nellie a ride. They knew our road, and suggested a meeting spot under the trees just before the dirt track hits the main road.

By the time Jay walked in through the glass doors they'd disappeared behind some shelves, and I was shoving children's books into my library basket.

....

And so here I am. I tell myself that if they don't turn up then I'll move to Plan B. I'll walk the extra stretch to the main road, we'll hitch into town, and catch the seven a.m. train. I shudder, because realistically I know that waiting on that platform will be like waiting on death row. If push comes to shove, I'll probably decide to go back. If he hasn't woken I might be able to drop the backpack and make up something about Nellie being fractious.

How far now? How far? Surely over this rise I will see the trees that tell me I've reached the cemetery, and from there it's only a little way to where they'll be waiting under the clump of trees.

My heart is racing as I come round the corner. I see a car. Do I automatically assume it is theirs? They told me that they'd be driving his mother's grey BMW, but it's too dark for me to tell the make. This one looks *ominous,* waiting in the dark under the trees, as if it might contain one of Jay's brothers …

I approach tentatively, then stop mid-stride when I see movement. The driver's window comes down.

'Tess?' comes a deep male whisper.

'Yes.'

Elation rips through me, until I see that he is alone. *Where is the girl?*

The door opens and he gets out. He must have his fake leg on, because he moves easily enough in his jeans and windcheater. He smiles and squeezes me briefly around the shoulders, as though this might be some kind of adventure that we can both enjoy. I move away.

'Come on then.'

'But where is … your girlfriend?' I gulp, bending to look into the car in case I've missed her. No one else is there. He's on his own. I try not to panic. I stand still and try to think. What can it mean? Is something dodgy going on?

'Where is she?' I ask again, more sharply than I intended.

'Her gran took a bad turn yesterday,' he tells me. 'She decided to stay an extra few days and then fly down.' He must see that I'm completely unnerved by this turn of events, because he steps back and holds up both hands in a kind of surrender gesture. 'There was no way to let you know,' he says. 'I'm sorry.'

I stare at him, trying to see into his eyes, but it's too dark.

'It's okay,' he adds softly. 'Honestly.'

I hover for another moment before I jump. It's not as though I have a lot of choice. I must trust him or … go back. We stow my bag in the boot and he takes out a blanket. I try to get Nellie out of the stroller, but my hands are trembling so uncontrollably that he has to push me aside to unclip the straps. We fold it up together. Every minute counts. Was that a light? My head jerks to look back up at the track. Nellie wakes up and stares around her, but doesn't cry. Bless her! The guy holds open the back door for us.

'Jules combed the op-shops for a car seat, but nothing doing,' he whispers. 'Sorry.'

'It's okay.'

I climb into the back seat and settle Nellie on my knees and she immediately falls asleep again. The guy shuts the door quietly on us and climbs in behind the steering wheel. The car smells new, seats soft and expensive. He slips the key into the ignition and starts the engine. I take a sniff of the comforting leather and settle back, until I hear the soft click of all the doors locking. Fear rises in my guts again. *Of course they would have contacted Jay after meeting me the other day, just to check out my story! They probably talked it over and had second thoughts. Then decided to betray me. Maybe the girl didn't want to be there when it happened. Jay can be so plausible, handsome and friendly if he feels like it. Instead of going back out onto the road, this guy is going to drive the car back up along the track where I've just walked and deliver me back to Jay. They have it all planned. With Nellie on my lap, what will I be able to do?*

I imagine this so well that it feels as if it's already happening. I tentatively try the doorhandle but it doesn't open.

'I've locked it,' he calls from the front seat. 'Just in case.'

'Okay,' I nod.

Jay will come out to greet us – give the guy one of those quick conspiratorial male smiles. 'Thanks, mate!' He might even chat awhile to make everything seem normal, invite the guy into the house and offer him a drink. 'Tessa's hold on reality is a bit weak,' he'll say apologetically. 'She tends to get confused, you know.' And I'll smile and nod my head because … it might save my life.

But no, the young man is turning the car and driving down the road towards the highway. Relief washes through me when I see the Ballina sign. *So far, so good …* I see his profile in the dark occasionally when he turns his head. His jaw is set and he is concentrating on the road. Once out on the highway he picks up speed and relief floods through me again. I want to ask him if he can see out of his dodgy eye, but I don't.

'Thank you ... er ... I'm sorry, I've forgotten your name.' Since being in hospital I'm like an old person; people's names sit on the tip of my tongue, refusing to step up. I have to wait for my brain to catch up.

'Harry.' He laughs.

'What time is it, Harry?' I ask.

'Just on five a.m. Jules sends her love, by the way.'

'Oh, thanks,' I reply. What else can I say? *Love?* I try to imagine being loved by someone as beautiful as her. 'I forgot to ask, are you planning to go straight through?'

'See how we go,' he says. 'We'll head south until Grafton, then go west to Glen Innes, maybe head down the New England Highway to Newcastle and the coast road. Then I've got a mate in Gosford.' He smiles and turns around to look at me. 'Might stay a night with him. You okay with that?'

'Yeah.' But I'm not taking any of this in. *Just get me away.*

'Bit longer, but figured it'd be good to see some coastline,' he says easily.

'Coastline,' I repeat stupidly. 'Okay.'

I try to remember a life where I might consider travelling the coastline for the pleasure of it, and I can't. I can't even imagine that kind of life.

'So your name is just Tess, or is it short for—'

'Just Tess,' I cut in.

He catches my sharp tone and shuts up, and I'm grateful for that. The soft purr of the fancy engine is all the noise I need. I peer out the window into the darkness. The traffic is mainly coming the other way. Huge trucks roar towards us and are quickly gone. All good.

An hour goes by and Ballina is behind us. He is following the signs to Grafton as he said. The jackhammering in my chest slows even further.

'How old is she?' The voice in the darkness startles me.

'Three,' I say.

'So how old were you when you had her?'

'Eighteen.'

'Wow.' He whistles, but doesn't say anything else for a moment. 'You must have wanted her bad,' he mutters.

I don't reply, but I smile to myself in the darkness. Eighteen years old. Why would I want a kid? Why would I want someone kicking around inside me, sucking at me all hours of the day and night? Why would I want someone relying on me for food, warmth, comfort and security, only to blame me later when things go wrong?

Beth, Marlon and Salome blamed our mother for *everything*. For what happened to Dad, for our lack of money, for the way the neighbours stared at us in the street. Mostly they blamed her just for being who she was, her wacky clothes and posh voice, her wild temper and the way she sang French songs in the mornings. They missed her, of course – we all did – but unlike them I *got* why she had to leave.

We travel for more than an hour through the darkness with barely another word between us. My arms are numb and aching from holding Nellie, but I don't care. At Grafton Harry takes a right turn towards Glen Innes. These places mean nothing to me, but I'm glad to see the signs, because they show we're heading somewhere. He has the radio on now; its low hum is comforting, going from the news and weather reports to classical music, some guy with a plummy accent making snooty little jokes in between. The darkness is comforting too. Harry drives at a steady speed, except for when we hit sudden patches of fog and have to slow right down as we descend into a hazy gloom. This freaks me out a bit. The huge trucks thundering towards us from the opposite direction are like animals from another age, brainless monsters, rushing out of the darkness and stirring up the panic just under my skin, reminding me all over again that anything can happen … at any time.

At last the day begins to break. I stare out at the faint wash of pink light spreading across the tips of the mountains in the distance, the red sun slowly easing its way over one peak like the mournful eye of a sad god, gradually burning away the fog before us. I'm thinking of Jay waking up and finding me gone. He'll get up, bleary-eyed and start calling out.

Tessa, he'll yell. *Where are you?* He'll be annoyed because there will be no answer, and imagining that makes me want to laugh. No answer, and no smell of coffee in the kitchen, and the fire won't be lit. Nor will I be down checking that the foxes didn't get into the chook pen overnight. And I won't be sweeping down the verandah, either, or making sure the dogs have fresh water. A shot of wild elation mixes with the pool of terror in my gut as I see him moving quickly from room to room, disbelief and fury rising in him like hot steam. *Tess!* My heart pounds as I picture it. Eventually he'll walk into Nellie's room, see the empty bed. *What the hell?* But eventually the penny will drop. And then? How long will it take before he starts thinking straight?

Not long. It won't be long at all. He'll call his mother first off. She lives up the hill from us. *Hey, Mum! Tessa up there?* When she tells him no he'll laugh to hide his humiliation. *Well, what do you know?*

She done a flit, has she? The old bag will be dragging on her first fag for the day. I can see her. The tea in one hand, the fag in the other; her scrawny old neck hooked over the grimy green telephone. *Taken the kid with her, has she?*

Yeah.

Then you'd better go find her, son. Ring Nick and get onto it now. She won't get far.

Of course not.

······································

Calm down. I am sitting in a car that's moving at a hundred and ten kilometres an hour *away … away* from him and his family and the last few years of my life. It's going to work out. It has to work out.

'So, how long were you living out there in the hills?'

'Three years.'

'You came up with him?'

'I met him in Byron.'

'Any family up here?'

'His. Two brothers. Mother.'

'Why?' he asks simply.

'Why what?'

'Why did you go for him?'

'I don't know.'

Trying to think up answers is like wading through swamp water. I want to go back into my own head, to the racing tunnels of thought whirling and dodging each other like cars at an inter-section with faulty traffic lights. I have to keep my wits about me. Words are the last thing I need.

'You must have loved him?'

'Yeah.'

He gives a sudden low chuckle as if I've just said some-thing funny.

two

It's hard to even remember myself at seventeen, all wide-eyed and furious, waiting around in cafés and on street corners for something to kickstart my life. My eldest sister, Beth, had moved us to the city within the first year of Mum clearing out when I was thirteen. With great difficulty, she'd got Salome and me into a good high school near the University of Melbourne, where she and Marlon were studying. But I was the one who couldn't even pass exams, much less come top of the class like my three older siblings. I was fifteen and about to start VCE, Salome had already won her place at the Sydney Film School. Each term she came home with tales of the people she was meeting, and the films she was working on, and how brilliant it all was. Within a day of being back she would be at me, demanding to know what my plans were. Why were my marks so poor? Why hang out with losers? Where was my ambition? Always, there was that underlying assumption that we had a duty to show the world how tough and smart and cool we were in spite of … everything.

Not only was I not doing well at school, my social life was a disaster zone. My best friend, Zelda Coleman, had more or less given up on me. Not her fault; I was always letting her down. Nothing was said, exactly. In the end I just bowed out. Friendships were for other people. At lunchtimes I sat with dumb Chloe and silly Nicky Wentworth. Neither of them did anything or went anywhere and they didn't demand anything of me either. Turned out it was easier all round for everyone. At home I spent a lot of time in my room. But instead of schoolwork, I read thrillers from the library – the more ugly, gruesome and bloodthirsty the better.

But I wrote stuff too. I don't know what I wrote, because once it was on the page I never looked at it again. I wasn't writing it to be read anyway. It was more a matter of letting the words out. They clambered and pushed at me through the night and in the early morning before anyone else woke; I'd open the floodgates and they'd all come roaring down my arm and onto the page. I wrote on whatever I could find, spare bits of paper, used envelopes and half-finished exercise books. They piled up under my bed in shoeboxes, like the small skeletons of birds that had started out bright and healthy but had died through lack of nourishment. That I kept them at all in those shoeboxes is kind of interesting, I suppose. Maybe I wanted some kind of record. *This is me. I was here.*

Salome found everything and read it, of course, Salome being Salome. After a wild catfight complete with a blood nose (hers), smashed crockery and a lot of screeching, she managed to convince me that not only was it all a crock of shit, it was the reason I wasn't getting anywhere. I was (to quote her) going *absolutely nowhere.* Did I want to end up like our mother? Vague, irresponsible, discontented and … out of control?

No. I certainly did not.

We ceremoniously burnt it all out the back of the rented Brunswick house, in a rusty old bin. Then we poured a slug of Dad's whisky down our throats – even though we both hated it – and hugged each other to prove that we were still sisters. I promised to get tough and try harder.

And I did. For six months I tried very hard. It was my last year at school, after all, and I knew that if I wanted any kind of future then I was going to have to get an education. At that school, no one was just left to their own devices if they were doing badly. From the start of the year the teachers had been onto me, calling meetings and offering catch-up classes. But I'd left it too late. Or it was beyond me. When push came to shove I couldn't really concentrate. Nothing made any sense. I couldn't get it together.

The results came through and I'd failed everything. Even English. Christ that hurt. I had managed to mess up the English exam in spectacular fashion by choosing to answer questions on books, poems and films that we hadn't studied, and that for the most part I hadn't read. Why did I do that? I still don't know. It made me the only one in the whole of Year Twelve who failed everything. I remember coming down the hall and overhearing Beth and Salome in the kitchen having one of their *concerned* conversations about me. I could tell that the humiliation was blinding them as well. I was their sister, after all, and it reflected on them. What the hell were they going to do with me? What was I going to do with myself?

But that very evening I got a call from Zelda. She must have heard about the results and felt sorry for me. Her grandmother had an apartment in Byron Bay. It would be free for a week in January. Did I want to come up with her and a couple of others for a break? Of course I did, as long as I didn't have to live at close quarters with her new best friend Katie Maitland. I loathed Katie for her shining good looks, her peachy skin and mop of golden locks, her ability to get top marks even though she'd always been totally stupid. Most of all, I hated her for her sunny personality, and all that fake kindness to me even while she was shoving the knife in. Wasn't it enough that she'd supplanted me as Zelda's best friend? Did she have to pretend to *care* at the same time?

'That sounds good,' I said slowly. 'So … who else will be there?'

'Katie, and Sue Butler,' Zelda said casually.

I took a deep breath and tried to think of how to wriggle loose, but Zelda had second-guessed my reluctance.

'Now listen, Tess,' she went on in her bossy way, which I usually found endearing but on this occasion made me want to grab her by the throat. 'Both of them know the results, okay? And we're all sorry. We all understand that you've had a terrible time. No one is going to mention your results or anything else … Okay? Just take the chance to come up with us and chill out.'

'Right,' I said, glad she couldn't see the little daggers I was drawing around Katie's name on a scrap of paper. Having to put up with fake sympathy from Katie Maitland would be excruciating and yet … I knew I would go. The alternative would be another week at home listening to Beth and Salome harping on about TAFE courses.

Zelda genuinely wanted the best for people. She was the first girl I met when I landed at University High in Year Nine. I was pretty spaced out, what with the move to the city and all that had happened to my family. For the first couple of years I did well enough at that school probably because Zelda took an instant shine to me. She showed me around and introduced me to people and did her best to shield me from the curiosity of classmates by telling lies on my behalf. A true friend, in other words. Sue Butler wasn't a bad girl either.

'Okay, thanks, Zelda,' I said. 'I'll see if I can talk Beth into letting me go.' Everyone said that Byron Bay was fantastic. Maybe something good would happen there.

'If money is a problem, don't let it be. We'll help.'

'It's okay,' I said stonily. *Like I'd let them pay for me!* Who wants sympathy when you're seventeen? Or when you're thirteen, or ten for that matter. When Dad died, everyone in the town we grew up in knew what had happened within a day. When Mum disappeared three years later it was worse. People we barely knew would point us out in the street. Teachers and other students felt free to approach me in the playground and corridors while I was playing netball or eating lunch. *Have they found your mum yet? Has your mum come home? Does she call? Write?*

I could feel people watching me as I walked into the supermarket. They were appalled, sympathetic and gleeful all at the same time. You could see it in their eyes.

Surprisingly, Beth was right behind the idea of me going north to Byron.

'You need a break,' she said. 'We all do. You go up there and have a good time.'

In fact, money *was* tight. We'd been relying on government benefits and whatever cash Beth and Marlon could pull in from part-time jobs. But Beth being Beth always had some stashed away, and she gave me quite a lot without ever suggesting that I take care to spend it wisely.

Oddly enough, the week didn't turn out so badly. Katie and I kept out of each other's hair. Every morning I got up early and went for a long swim. Katie and Zelda and Sue were absolutely hell-bent on having something exciting to talk about when we got home, and that meant going out to bars and meeting guys. They were already over eighteen. I was nervous at first, but we plastered on the make-up, stuffed our feet into ridiculous shoes and our bodies into short tight dresses, and I was never asked for ID. I really loved dancing, so apart from one night when I drank too much and got sick, I had a good time.

If I wasn't as interested in meeting guys as the others, it was only because I had the rest of my life to distract me. Also, I suppose I wasn't as confident. My face is okay, I think. My figure is like my sisters', small and neat. My hair is long and thick and curly, and everyone comments on my big blue eyes. But I was shy and terrible at flirting. Once I asked Zelda what I was doing wrong and she told me that I tended to come across as sort of preoccupied, as though I'd rather be somewhere else. That sent a shudder of recognition through me. It was exactly what people used to say about my mother.

Your mother was never quite ... with us, was she? She always seemed to be thinking about something else ... Did your mother ever seek help?

Even at thirteen I knew these questions were polite code for things more sinister. *Your mother was weird, wasn't she? Your mother was unstable, untrustworthy ... crazy?*

I made a point of never answering when people made these kinds of insinuations, even though I knew what they said was probably true. I would stare straight back at whoever was talking, and took pride in never so much as inclining my head to show I'd heard.

Sue was the quiet one of the group, but the first to have a bit of luck. She met a guy the second evening, stayed out all night on the beach, and came back in the morning looking pretty pleased with herself. But he was going back to Victoria the next day, and although he'd promised to ring, he didn't.

Katie had a boyfriend back home, so she was on the phone half the time placating his fears that she might run off with someone else. As much as she protested that she wasn't looking for anyone, we all knew that if some rich good-looking guy turned up she'd be into it – she admitted as much when she was drunk one night.

On the third day, Zelda met a cool older guy in a bar. He was tall, his face all angles like a movie star's, hazel eyes just the right side of too big for his perfect head. She brought him back to the apartment for a meal, but he got very drunk and although he ended up sleeping in her bed I don't think anything happened between them. He took off the next morning in a foul mood, and although Zelda didn't say anything I think she felt humiliated by the whole episode.

I met Jay the last full day we were there. I've often thought since that if only I hadn't gone back to that café the next morning, my whole life would be totally different. When I look around for when it all started, I have to come back to that day. I see myself in that short yellow dress, with my long dark hair tied up on top of my head, actually going back to that café *looking for him*.

It would be funny if it wasn't so sad.

three

Full daylight is on us now. I make out trees and isolated farmhouses in the distance. We've been travelling for nearly four hours. A few cars flick by, but there isn't much traffic going our way. Even so, I keep looking back for Jay's big silver ute, waiting for it to bounce up over a rise, headlights flashing in our mirror, and I'll know it's him before I even see the make of the car or his face, because he'll roar up behind us and flash his lights. Then he'll move alongside, blasting his horn. Harry will panic — anyone would — and pull over onto the gravel. Nellie will wake up freaked out, and my pathetic little half-baked enterprise will be … *over.*

'Hey, Tess.' Harry cuts in on my thoughts. He must have caught me looking back yet again. 'We'll be okay. I promise you. Remember, I've got my phone. We'll call the cops if we need to. We'll get a restraining order.'

'Right.' I try not to laugh, because it's sweet in a way. Imagine believing that a restraining order would stop someone like Jay. I could have told Harry that the cops had proved worse than useless on more than one occasion, but that would probably mean telling him how and why and what happened, and as far as I'm concerned there is no point going over that stuff. If I concentrate on the past, I'll lose my nerve.

'Hey, I need to take a piss,' Harry declares suddenly. 'What do you say? Stop at Glen Innes, we'll grab a coffee, something to eat?'

I desperately want to keep going because I figure that these first few hours will be crucial. The more distance we get in before Jay works out I'm gone the more chance I've got.

'Okay,' I say.

We stop at a roadside café. Nellie wakes, and I feel guilty about having given her that drug, because she is still dopey and sluggish. When I ask if she wants the toilet her head rolls back as though she is about to sleep again, so I get out and carry her over to the big glass doors and we go together into the toilets. I manage to change her clothes with some difficulty. I make her drink some water from the bottle in my bag. I buy some milk and a few of the chocolate-coated muesli bars that she likes and carry her back outside. I offer her the milk and the muesli bar, but she turns away disdainfully. I try to hold her hand, and she won't have that either. She still hasn't said a word, just stands determinedly by herself as though she doesn't trust what's going on.

I lean against the car and look around. Quite a few people have stopped for their breakfast – truck drivers, families in big four-wheel drives with caravans attached. I turn back to Nellie in her pink cord pants and bomber jacket with the fake white fur around the collar. She seems dazed more than anything, walking about in circles, saying nothing. Then she crouches down to stare at a line of ants coming out of a crack in the cement, until some chattering children walk by with their parents. She stands to stare at them, a look of such longing on her face that I almost come to pieces inside. *What am I doing?* I'm too edgy to kneel down and reassure her. With each minute a fresh barrage of terrible thoughts dashes through my brain. This guy Harry has been in the café too long. There is a friendly-looking man in a nearby campervan, waiting for his wife to put on her seatbelt. They might be heading south – should I pick up Nellie and run over? Or maybe I could just pinch Harry's car. I can drive a bit, although I haven't got a license. I could sell it. I peer in to check if the keys are still there.

Stay with me!

The words slide into my head unannounced. So fleeting and faint they barely register. I bend to pick up Nellie and kiss her neck in just the way she likes … but she rears away from me suspiciously and doesn't even smile.

Harry limps out of the café, smiling, laden with paper bags and coffee. He gives a small package to Nellie, who grabs it eagerly. We both smile when she wriggles free of me and squats down next to the car to carefully unwrap the bright cardboard and paper as though she's expecting to find some treasure inside. When he hands me a burger along with a coffee my hands are trembling so badly that the coffee slops and I drop the food. He bends to pick it up but doesn't say anything.

'Thanks …' I mumble.

'It's nothing,' he says. 'Jules made us sandwiches for later, but I thought we needed some hot breakfast first.'

'Thanks,' I say again. It's all I can manage.

Once I actually start eating, it surprises me to realise that I am hungry.

Although Nellie still hasn't said anything, she eats every bit of her burger and seems a bit brighter as a result. The food makes me feel calmer too.

'I noticed an op-shop across the road.' Harry is screwing up his rubbish and looking around for the bin. 'I'm going to see if they've got a car seat.'

I immediately panic. 'No need, really! I'm okay holding her. And I don't think they're allowed to sell them anyway. Seriously, we need to go!'

But he waves away my protests. 'No harm in having a look.'

I watch him crossing the road, feeling utterly exposed. It wouldn't have taken Jay long to figure it out. Which way would I go but south? Every minute is important and this guy wants to waste time looking for *car seats.*

'Where is he going?' Nellie says forlornly, putting her arm around my leg. 'Are we going to stay here?'

'No.' I look down at her little face staring up at me. 'He's going to try to find you a seat.'

'What kind of a seat?'

'Car seat.'

'Do we have to drive more?'

'Bit more.'

'I've got a car seat at home,' she mutters miserably, her lip turned down.

A family walks past carrying coffees and packets of food, obscuring our view of Harry. The mother is elegant, with short, well-cut blonde hair, dressed in close-fitting pastel pink pants, high-heeled sandals and a pretty linen top. The chains of gold around her neck and wrist look real. The father is a big man but not fat, dark-haired and confident. Twin boys of about sixteen are jostling each other and laughing as they juggle their various packets of takeaway. They must be just setting out on some big road trip, because they all look fresh. There is a younger girl trailing behind them, a sister to the twins by the look of her, thin and awkward with long dark hair tied up in a ponytail, carrying nothing. She reminds me of myself at the same age.

'I'm not hungry!' I hear her hiss defiantly at her mother. 'Just leave off! I'm thirteen years old!'

I have one clear memory of myself at thirteen. Most of that year is a jumble of foggy sounds and blurred images, people moving in and out of rooms, doors slamming, telephones ringing, voices calling out. But this one memory comes back to me now, as fresh and clean as a starched sheet.

I was sitting at the old kitchen table. Beth, nineteen years old and home from the city having completed her first year of medicine, was helping Marlon, who was in his last year at the local high school, with his maths homework. Both of them were deeply absorbed, murmuring to each other in what seemed to me to be a secret language, their two heads colliding occasionally under the hanging ceiling light. Fifteen-year-old Salome was sitting next to them, drinking cocoa and staring intently at the figures and calculations that were tumbling from the tip of Beth's pen onto the page. I was scratching away at my own homework, but really watching them: the delight on Salome's face as she grasped concepts way ahead of what she was doing at school made me envious. Salome is like Beth – clear-headed, sharp and clever.

It was still light outside, and warm. The windows must have been open, because a gust of breeze fluttered the thin pages of paper in my notebook when our mother floated in. I use the word deliberately. She did a lot of floating after our father's death. She floated about like a ghost, her spark lost in the general gloom and shabbiness of the house.

She was wearing one of her long, worn dressing-gowns, her feet bare on the grimy floorboards. Her faded red hair, threaded through with grey, was pinned up under a silk scarf. Small red-glass earrings glittered in her earlobes like bright drops of blood. I didn't tell her that, even though I knew she'd probably enjoy it. My big mouth had cost us enough already.

She sat down at the table and clasped her hands in front of her, as though about to address a meeting.

'And so to your *names*,' she said.

My two sisters took up identically pained expressions. My brother sat back. He gave one of his awkward *I-don't-really-mind* smiles, but anyone could see he was pissed off. Our mother's need to make drama out of everyday stuff drove them all nuts. Not me, though. I secretly relished the theatrics.

Beth was really Bathsheba and so a queen, of course. Mum couldn't stand anyone within a three-kilometre radius of herself being ordinary. And Marlon was named after the best actor in the world – 'They just don't make them like that anymore, darling' – and would someday prove himself equally outstanding in whatever field he chose. Salome had purity of purpose, a fire in her belly as well as a good brain, and so her fate would be to pursue some extraordinary goal even if a few heads were lost in the process. That was *life*. Mum threw her arms out wide at that point and closed her eyes. 'Life,' she whispered again to make sure we all got the point. 'In life, heads do have to roll.'

My sisters' eyes narrowed mutinously across the table at each other, the scorn virtually setting the room alight, and Marlon gave one of his nervous *come-on-everything-is-alright* shrugs and turned to the window where night had begun to fall.

Mum's eyes were half-closed, her thin white hands clenched on the table in front of her.

'But never forget that whatever hardships you go through in life …' Her voice drifted away before coming back hard and fast to her theme. 'Stay true to who you are!' She slapped the table for emphasis. 'And the whole of humankind will benefit from your endeavours.'

The Whole of Humankind was another favourite theme.

By this stage, Beth had shrunk down in her seat. Her eyes had glazed over and her mouth was screwed to one side, as though she was sucking on a sore tooth. She was flicking the top of her biro in and out, making that awful clacking sound that drives teachers spare.

Beth was an almost exact replica of our mother at the same age: mid-height, straight as a pencil, clear light-brown eyes and fair skin smattered with freckles. Her wonderful hair was caught in an elastic band and fell down to the middle of her back in red curls. She is extraordinarily good-looking, without being at all pretty, if that's possible. Like Mum, Beth takes life very seriously, but where Beth's seriousness translates into being canny and smart about the ways of the world and how to operate within it, Mum's involvement with the outside world was naïve at best. We were used to making allowances for her wild enthusiasms and sharp temper, but I think a lot of people around that town thought she was crazy. I have no way of knowing if it was true or not.

Marlon and Salome are like Beth, clever, competent and ambitious. They both have the lightly freckled skin and bright brown eyes, but their ordinary brown hair makes them less eye-catching.

I'm different to them all with my dark curly hair and blue eyes. At thirteen I had no idea whether I was crazy or not, but I knew I was definitely not clever or competent or ambitious.

When my turn came, Mum reached across the table with both her fine-boned hands and brushed my hair back from my face, leaving one hand at the nape of my neck. I edged closer, suddenly breathless with anticipation.

'And you, Tess, were named after your *great*-grandmother.'

I tried not to show my deep disappointment. I'd been told this before and had forgotten. How come the others got famous people and grand schemes while I only got some old relative I didn't know? *Tess Browne*. I'd always hated my name. So boring compared to the others, and now I had further reason to think so.

'My grandmother,' Mum explained breathlessly. 'Your grand-pa's mother. She was Therese Mary Josephine and so are you.'

'But why?'

'To keep her memory alive.'

'Why?'

More than anything I wanted to please my mother. We all did, even Beth, although she pretended she didn't, and so I tried to appear cheerful. But it was hard for me to believe that our grandfather, that sour, half-deaf, arthritic old grouch, even had a mother.

She slid a black-and-white photo across the table to me.

'See,' she smiled. 'You even look like her.'

I picked up the photo. It was true. Even I could see the likeness. A dark-haired girl of about fifteen, the long ringlets held back from her broad forehead with a ribbon tied in a bow on the right, her head falling shyly to one side as though she wasn't completely comfortable having the camera's attention on her. Not a beauty by any stretch of the imagination, but the big eyes under dark defined eyebrows had depth. She was lovely in her own way. I put the photo down and looked at my mother.

'So this is Grandpa's *mother*?'

The very concept was awe-inspiring, in some weird way. Mum ignored the question. She picked up the photo and addressed it softly.

'Therese Mary Josephine, you are not forgotten.'

Beth gave a deeply contemptuous sigh, and Marlon smiled, shook his head and cleared his throat.

'Wasn't she the one who went mad?' Salome snickered softly.

Mum ignored Salome and gave the photo back to me. 'It's yours now. Keep it safe.'

'They had to put her away?' Salome persisted coolly.

'Yes, Salome,' Mum said softly. 'They put her away.'

No one said anything. Mum hit the table sharply in exasperation.

'What happened to that woman explains everything about this family!'

Beth's reaction to this piece of information was to emit a long, high-pitched gasp of indignation and throw her head back to stare at the ceiling. When she straightened up again she stared at Mum, as though daring her to say another word.

Meanwhile, I was feeling worse by the minute. I already knew I was a *lovely little surprise,* in other words *an accident,* and now my mother was telling me all over again that I had a hand-me-down name from some mad relative.

Mum stood up abruptly. 'I'm off to bed now.'

I could tell she had a lot more to say, and that she was miffed that no one seemed particularly interested in hearing it. The others mumbled goodnight.

Is that all? I was on the point of yelling after her. *Is that all I get?*

But before she closed the door, Mum turned. My face must have showed some of my frustration, because she laughed and came back into the room, took my chin in one hand and leant in close across the table.

'Every family has a storyteller, Tess,' she said. 'You're ours!'

The words stung although even then I knew she didn't mean them to. *Storyteller!* She might as well have said *troublemaker, fool … liar.*

Beth sighed again, and Marlon looked away. Salome shook her head and went back to what she'd been doing. I knew what they were all thinking, but what could I say? Mum kissed me hard on both cheeks and left the room.

I picked up the photo and stood.

'Off to tell a few stories, are you, Tess?' Salome asked airily, and the sarcasm reverberated through my body like a cluster of jarring chords.

But once alone in the blue room that had become mine that summer, the clanging of her words faded. I taped the photo to the mirror near the small window and stood there awhile, comparing the long-ago face with my own, thinking how strange it was to look so much like someone who was already dead.

'Therese Mary Josephine, you are not forgotten.' I repeated my mother's words in a whisper, and they felt so right and important that I said them again, this time in a normal voice. *Therese Mary Josephine, you are not forgotten.* Was it some kind of premonition? Some sixth sense that things were about to change? Because straight after that I thought, *I will remember this day.* Like the way old people remember where they were when Kennedy was assassinated or when the twin towers came down in New York, or when they first heard their father had died.

The very next day, we found a short note on the kitchen table when we got home. My mother's handwriting was in black ink, a dense, spiky scrawl of words that suited her personality perfectly. She said she'd be *gone for a bit, but would be back as soon as she felt able …*

There were the details of a bank account that would *tide us over* until she got back. Right next to that was a page of instructions about what bills needed to be paid, council rates to be seen to, where we should buy our groceries, how we should divide up the housework. Practical issues that were at odds with her vague, impractical personality. No one said much, but when Marlon left the room, Salome turned on me.

'You and your big mouth,' she spat ferociously.

Blood rushed to my face. I stood rooted to the spot and said nothing.

'Cut it out, Salome!' Beth said sharply. 'It's not her fault.'

'Well!' Salome huffed angrily. 'Think about when all this started!' She flounced out of the room, leaving Beth and me to read the note again.

four

'Hey, Nellie. Look what I've got for you!' Harry is beaming with pride as he holds up the car seat. 'She gave it to me.'

It's old and worn, but all the straps are good and the clip works. Nellie's worried little face opens up with a smile. She jumps into the car and tries to help him fit it to the seatbelt in the back seat. It turns out to be quite a difficult business, and an old guy standing nearby comes over to help. It takes forever, and I'm getting edgier by the minute as I stand near the car looking this way and that for danger. The road into town is filling with traffic. We're wasting precious time. When at last they're through with it, I'm so tense that I'm screaming inside. I scratch behind my ears, knowing it's the worst thing to do. I'd been holding off on that spot for days because last week it bled a lot. The skin breaks so easily. Now I won't be able to stop.

'Okay,' Harry yells over to me. 'We got it. You want to ride in the front?'

'Okay. Yeah.' I get in the front passenger seat. When I turn around, Nellie is grinning proudly, happy with her seat. The old guy who helped has given her a fancy computerised keyboard to play with. He's been camping with his grandchildren and they left it in his car. Nellie bangs the keys, making an awful racket, but I don't care, anything to keep her occupied. I'm not game to ask Harry if he feels the same.

'You feel a bit better with some food in you?' Harry asks easily.

'Yep.' I try to smile. 'Thanks.'

We travel on through the morning. On both sides the land is hilly and green. Grey clouds mass at the horizon. Nellie spots a group of kangaroos in the distance. Grim-faced drivers pass us in both directions. The roadside stops are filled with caravans and four-wheel drives.

On the outskirts of Armidale, Harry turns to me.

'What do you think will be happening back there?' he asks quietly, so Nellie won't hear. 'He'll know you've gone?'

I shrug and look at my watch. 'Yeah. He'll know I've gone.'

Harry grins. 'You've got a few hours on him, I reckon.'

'Yeah.'

'Will he go nuts?'

I nod and try to return his smile.

Jay's hands won't be trembling. I know that much. He'll have his mother and eldest brother, Nick, with him and Nick will be giving the orders. Nothing happens in that family without Nick's approval. Everything – houses, cars, money, who does what and when and with whom – it's all got to go through Nick.

The younger one, Travis, isn't as bad. He's kind enough in his own dumb way, certainly easier to get along with. But I overheard Nick fuming about Travis yesterday. He'd apparently messed up something big and had been sent away to fix it.

So it will be just Jay and his mother and Nick sitting out on the verandah, planning how to find me. Old bat-faced Glenda will be fuming righteously. My refusal to tell her details about my former life, along with my 'hoity-toity ways', grated on her. At the same time as trying to work out how to find me, she'll be sliding the knife into Jay about how he should never have got involved with me in the first place, and Jay will have to suck that up because he needs her. The family has money and he wants part of it. Jay almost burnt his bridges with them years before when he left town to try his luck on the road playing music. When he came back with nothing after eight years, then stuffed up managing the club, Nick wanted him out for good. But on Glenda's insistence he was allowed to stay ... as an underling. Needless to say, Jay chafes under his older brother's authority. There's only eighteen months between them.

It won't take them too long to get on the road and by that stage I will be ... where? Somewhere safe. Out of his range. They could be anywhere by now but I have to believe it. Jay has only met one member of my family properly, my eldest sister, Beth, once – mutual hatred at first sight, of course – and he doesn't know the state of Victoria at all. I never told him about where I grew up, mainly because he never asked. My previous life barely interested him. *Like it's going to take him more than ten minutes to find that address ...* But by then I might have some kind of plan in place. *Yeah?* the mocking voice in my head jeers. *And you were always so good at plans, weren't you, Tess?*

'Will he panic?' Harry's voice breaks into my thoughts.

'No.'

'You sound sure about that.'

'He never panics.'

If I'd left Nellie with him, they might have decided that I wasn't worth the trouble. It wouldn't take him long to pick up some other little fool, but as it is he will come after us ... I know it for certain.

'What's your guess?' Harry asks. 'I mean, what do you think he'll do?'

'He'll be trying to track me down somehow.'

'Is he dangerous?' he asks, and when I don't answer he grimaces. 'Tell me more about him.'

I hesitate. This guy might get cold feet and decide we aren't worth the trouble. He might dump us out here in the middle of nowhere.

'He'll want the kid back?'

'Yeah.'

'Did you ever think of leaving her?' he asks. 'With him, I mean?'

I jerk around in surprise. 'Strange question.'

In fact, I *did* think seriously about leaving Nellie. I figured it had to be quite possible to love your kid and decide never to see her again. After all, my mother did exactly that, my father too in his own way. What future can I give her anyway? I'm twenty-one years old, no money, no qualifications and no place to live. I mulled over all that. At least Jay and his family have money. Dodgy money, but still it is … money. His brothers' wives are nice enough. Travis's wife, Judy, is particularly kind and she dotes on Nellie, who is the only girl among the five cousins. And Nellie loves her cousins. She had a life up there in the hills. Of course, the other reason I gave it serious thought was because I knew it might save my own life.

'Yeah,' I say after a pause. 'I thought about it.'

'So, what made you decide that you couldn't?'

I suddenly resent these questions. This guy with the expensive teeth and half-missing leg has agreed to give us a ride down to Melbourne, but I don't remember signing on to be his new best friend.

'Can't say, exactly,' I snap.

'Try.' He throws me a smile.

'Why? You planning to have kids?'

'God no!' He laughs. 'Maybe you didn't want to leave her with him?' he suggests gently. 'You say he's dangerous?'

'Did I say that?' I snap.

'Well, you implied it,' he returns mildly.

'It's hard to talk about,' I mumble grudgingly. And when I don't say anything else he winds down the window.

'Fair enough,' he says, 'but this is going to be one long trip if we don't talk.'

Such a crumpled-up little thing she was, when she was born, not at all beautiful, her skin as red as a beetroot, her body as scrawny as a rat. When I first saw her I was totally flummoxed. *So this is a baby?* I'd hardly even seen one before. Not a newborn. Not close up like that. And Jay didn't bother to hide his disappointment. He'd badly wanted his firstborn to be a son. When the nurses put her in my arms I felt all over again the absence of my own mother. It was a raw, terrible feeling that I'd managed to paper over for years, and it tore straight through the middle of me like a blunt axe. Panic rose like a high-pitched scream through every cell in my body. When a smiling woman came in offering tea and biscuits, I shoved the baby back to one of the nurses, took the tea and tried to think seriously about how I might make a run for it. I remember propping myself up on my elbows to check where the door was. But the birth had been fierce, and I had so many stitches that I could hardly sit up properly, much less run. So I lay down again and closed my eyes and pretended that what had just happened was a figment of my imagination. It worked … for maybe three minutes.

But a few hours later when Jay had gone home to get drunk with his brothers, I inched off the bed and stood to take another look at her lying on her back in the plastic see-through cot, all swaddled up like a tiny Egyptian mummy. I bent low over her small bony head and breathed her in, and I had a flash of my father listening to country music in the garage. *Islands in the Stream,* that Dolly Parton song that she sings with Kenny Rogers, was one of his all-time favourites. Sometimes I'd sneak out at night when I was meant to be in bed. He liked being alone when he was working, so I'd sit on the round block of wood just out of view, and I'd listen to the words. Once he found me, and I remember him sitting down next to me and laughing softly. He put an arm around my shoulders and we sang the line together, *Sail away with me …*

The words pumped through my brain as I looked at my tiny girl. I put one finger inside Nellie's fist and right there and then she became mine, like my eye or my hand or my foot. Not cute or pretty or perfect. *Mine.* Who would willingly pluck out their own eye, or hack off their foot? Who would cut out their own heart?

'You belong to me,' I said aloud, amazed that such a bizarre thing could actually be true. But having said it I knew it *was* true. I didn't take the words back or doubt them for an instant. The nurse who had come in smiled as though I'd said something sweet and motherly. But those words had been wrenched from the deepest part of me without warning, and they freaked me out almost as much as the baby herself, because even then I had a sense that they might one day mean my life.

I stare out at the passing countryside, glad for that memory in spite of its bitter thread. Over the last year my brain has lost its sharpness. The memories come in blurred clumps, faded of colour, like old cushions left out in the weather too long. Everything that has happened is inside me somewhere, but it has become increasingly remote and frighteningly hard to access.

'Is Harry short for something else?' I ask, trying to soften my earlier surliness.

'How do you mean?'

'Like Harold?'

He shakes his head and gives a deep sigh, and I wish I hadn't spoken. Maybe I've touched on some kind of raw nerve? People get stroppy about the weirdest things. 'You don't have to tell me,' I add hurriedly.

'Helsinki.'

'I thought that was a place.'

'It is.'

'So how come?'

'My parents met there in the Easter of 1986. They're musicians.'

'Cool.'

'Not really.'

'They still around, your parents?'

'Yeah.' He seems surprised by the question. 'Definitely. Yours?'

'Ah … not really.'

'Oh?' He waits for me to tell him more, but I don't.

We drive on a bit, and I frantically search my head for something else to say that won't involve any more difficult questions.

'What kind of music do they play?' I ask.

'Classical,' he says shortly. 'Oboe and flute.'

'What about you?' I ask. 'You play anything?' Then I remember the damaged hand and wish I hadn't. But he's smiling a bit now as he swerves around a huge transport vehicle.

'Yeah.' He turns to me, the smile even wider. 'I was what you might call a *gifted* child.'

'Is that right?' I smile back at him.

'Oh yeah,' he laughs.

Over the next hour I hear about the two classical musicians with their adored and spoilt only child who was destined to surpass them in the music stakes. All those lessons and exams! He tells me about being ten and wetting his pants in front of some big-time professor who'd come especially to hear him play. I hear about the tests he had to pass to get into the top school in New York. I've only vaguely heard of the place, but apparently it's really something. The six, eight, sometimes more, hours of practice a day. How he had the flight booked and bags packed when it all fell apart. I figure that is where I should ask him about his missing leg and damaged face, but I don't. I figure if he wants to talk about it he will.

'So who looked after you when your parents were on tour?' I ask, to change the line of chat a bit. I've got enough bad karma in my life already without hearing about other people's shitty life-changing experiences.

'My gran,' he says. 'I lived with her a lot of the time.'

'How was that?'

'Good,' he says quickly, and then hesitates. 'Do you miss your parents?' he asks gently.

I shrug and look out the window and mutter 'yeah', or something like it. He has a nice easy way of talking, I'll give him that. I miss Dad, of course, but even at the time he died I knew my grief didn't match my sisters' and brother's. They *really* missed him. My grief was all mixed up with the guilt I felt about the part I'd played in his death. They were older and knew him when he was different, when he was really someone around town. In his heyday he was considered the best maths teacher the local high school had ever had. He used to train the local footy team too. *Hey, your dad was the best,* strangers would sometimes come up to tell me. *Your dad changed my life.* I didn't really know that successful person too well. I was ten when he died, and for the last couple of years of his life he had been drinking heavily. Maybe things were already on the rocks with Mum by then and he didn't want to admit it. Who knows?

It was Mum leaving that really cut my life in two. There's before she left and after, and that's the way it has always been for me. Even meeting Jay and all that has happened since fades into second place alongside that. I wonder if maybe everyone has a before-and-after line. Before *this* happened I was like *this,* and *after* it I turned into someone else. Maybe there is only one person in the whole world who can draw that line in your life. I don't know.

'Did something happen to trigger this?' he asks out of the blue.

'What?'

'Leaving?'

'Not really,' I lie.

'You just decided you'd had enough, eh?' he says mildly.

'Yeah, something like that.'

How could I tell a stranger? If I began, I'd never know where to stop. And would he even believe me? I'd have to tell him about that dream I had the night I came home from hospital. It was so vivid that even when I was fully awake and out in the kitchen making coffee it was still with me. I was alone at the edge of a clump of dark trees looking for something that I'd lost. Something important. I heard her voice before I saw her. And when I did see her I didn't know who she was. Her face was unclear and her voice muffled. She was in a drab grey dress, her hair was dirty and she was distressed. *Stay with me*, she'd said.

The dream haunted me all that day and the next. And it didn't go away. It sustained me. Fed and watered me. In the end it was as if I was living inside it. I wasn't alone. How much sense would that kind of shit make to a stranger? Even *I* know it's mad! When push comes to shove, Jay could well be right. *One crazy little bitch.*

'Was it good at the start?' he asks.

'In a way,' I say gruffly, trying to remember.

'How did you meet him?'

I laugh uncomfortably and shrug.

'No worries.' He smiles. 'We don't have to talk about anything you don't want to.'

He says this kindly, with real warmth in his voice. So much so that I suddenly feel like telling him everything. But I don't. I found out the hard way that it's just about always better to keep your mouth shut.

Essential Medical Certificates. Dr M. A. Stewart,
Dr C. Osburne
Very violent. Constantly calling to Jesus Christ and
believes the devil is persecuting her. Her head is
full of voices and noises.

26.11.28
Has improved considerably since admission – seems
almost normal. Converses rationally and intelligently
but has few periods of depression. Mental condition
seems the effect of sudden death of sister ...

1.12.28
Got into another patient's bed. Thought it was her
sister's. Has occasional lapses of this kind but
otherwise is fairly clear mentally.

6.12.28
Restless and uncertain. Has to be persuaded to eat and
is erratic in her actions. She doesn't seem to have
sufficient control. Laughs too frequently, but replies
willingly when she is addressed. Somewhat dazed and
distant.

14.12.28
Emotional and unbalanced. Is impulsive – often
puzzled and dazed. Apparently has no delusions or
hallucinations but refers frequently to her sister's
death.

26.12.28
Very resistive to all treatment. Very undetermined.
No decisiveness. Has to be led to meals and away
from them. Will not settle to anything. Can't answer
questions.

five

Imagine me at seventeen, sitting in a Byron Bay café, drinking – I can hardly believe it now – but, yes, it was a milkshake. *Double* choc with malt! I was a kid! Only kids have double malt milkshakes, right? It was late afternoon of our last full day in Byron. I was with Sue and Katie at Jungle Rum, our favourite café, just across from the railway line. It was full to bursting with hordes of people dressed for the beach in thongs and T-shirts and sarongs, talking and laughing and checking phones. The boss was a heavy, friendly, bearded guy in his late thirties, and the main waitress was a tall, reed-thin woman, wearing a lot of silver jewellery and sparkly combs in her red hair. The music was loud, blues fusion interspersed with cool indie rock bands. Loud, but not so loud that you couldn't talk.

From the first day I loved the feel of that place, and I'd go by myself sometimes to read when the others were still on the beach, working on their tans. Anyway, I was drinking my milkshake, thinking about how much I was going to miss it all. I was also pretending to listen to Sue and Katie, who were talking the usual rubbish about guys they met the night before. I was nodding and murmuring agreement, but I wasn't actually listening to a word. I was waiting for Zelda to come back from her foot massage. We'd arranged to go for a long last walk together on the beach without the other two, to 'talk things over'. Even though I knew she'd be trying to talk *sense* to me about my options for the following year, I didn't mind. We were due to fly home the following afternoon.

So we were sitting there, slurping down milkshakes, when three older guys walked in. Cool older guys. I didn't know how old – in their late twenties, I guessed. But they were all lean and tanned, and a bit dirty and messy, and the tall one looked like a rock star. He had studded boots, and a little waistcoat over his torn T-shirt. I watched him survey the room, an amused expression hovering around his eyes and mouth, just as though he'd landed from another planet altogether, where a whole lot more interesting stuff happened at a much faster pace. His gaze swept this way and that, and then hovered awhile across some nearby heads until … it landed on *me*. He gave me a crooked smile, as if he knew exactly who I was and where I was going. I smiled back, and his grin broadened.

There were a lot of people in the café and loud chatter surrounded us. The guys slumped down at a table near the door. They laughed at each other as they read the menu, and when the waitress arrived they started teasing her, but the tall guy was a bit aloof from it all. He didn't look directly at me the whole time, but every now and again he caught my eye, and every time there was that same crooked smile, as if he was telling me that I could join his secret club if I wanted.

I sat there, sucking my straw, eyes lowered, trying not to laugh with the excitement that was bubbling through my veins. I was not used to that kind of attention.

Katie and Sue were too busy checking their phones to even notice.

I risked a look and caught his eye again. A bolt of something strange flashed up my legs. I blushed and laughed out loud. Katie and Sue looked at me as if I'd gone mad, but I didn't care. I took another quick glance at him and saw that he was laughing too.

Katie leant over to show me a picture from the day before of the three of us in our bikinis on the beach. My face was covered by my hat. 'Okay if I post this one?'

I pretended to look at it carefully and nodded.

'I'll go wait for Zelda outside,' I said, getting up. I picked up my bag and walked towards the door. My limbs were on fire, but I didn't dare look at him as I passed his table. When I was right alongside he reached out and grabbed my hand.

'Hello, girl,' he said.

A rush of excitement shot through my arms and into my chest.

'Hello.' Through the window I could see Zelda on the opposite street corner waiting to cross the road.

'Where are you off to?' he asked.

'To the beach,' I replied. 'With my friend.'

'Yeah?' He grinned at me. 'Now say something else.'

'What?' I looked down into his light-grey eyes and a shiver went straight through me. His eyes contained so much of what I wanted: fun and … danger too. Escape.

'Anything.' He smiled at me. 'I like the sound of your voice.'

I giggled, insanely pleased that he had picked the one thing that tended to put people off.

'Most people don't,' I said. 'They think I sound posh, or … like a guy. Too deep.' I rushed forward with the information without being asked, but I couldn't help it. 'But … it's the way I was brought up speaking,' I tell him breathlessly.

'Most people are idiots.'

I giggled again and blushed.

'So your parents taught you to speak like that?'

I backed away without answering. Any mention of my parents made me recoil. It just happened. A physical reaction that I had no control over. Anyway, Zelda was waving at me through the window. The waitress put coffee in front of the guy and he pulled out a couple of notes and handed them to her.

'Thanks, Lily,' he said. So this sleek, red-headed woman whom I'd secretly admired over the past week had my mother's name. For some silly reason that pleased me, and I wanted to tell her, but she had already glided off to another table. He was looking at me again.

'Will you be back here tomorrow?'

'Maybe,' I said.

'I'll be here,' he told me with a wink. 'I like classy girls.'

I couldn't stop thinking about him all evening. *Classy?* Maybe that could be my new persona. Let everyone else be beautiful, smart and sexy – I'd be … classy, whatever that meant.

When I woke the next morning I knew that I would have to go back to the café, just to see if he'd come again. No point, of course, because I was leaving for home that afternoon, but I couldn't seem to help myself.

Back at the café it was unusually quiet. Only a couple of the tables were being used, and the boss was sitting by the window doing the crossword. I ordered a long black from Lily, thinking it would make me seem sophisticated. When she brought it over I took one sip and tipped in three sachets of sugar. How did people drink this stuff? So dark and bitter it was like drinking dam water. My hot drink of choice in those days was chocolate. What if he didn't show? Would I have to order another long black?

I was there for over an hour and ended up ordering two more of the terrible black coffees so I'd have the right prop when he arrived. People came in and out. At one point a couple of guys were giving me the once-over, but neither of them were him. Once I'd read the paper and an old magazine I started playing with my phone, thinking about how stupid I was to still be sitting there. Gradually I became aware of some kind of drama happening behind the counter. I looked over and saw that the owner was on the phone having a heated row with someone. When Lily saw me looking, she raised her eyes to the heavens and smiled. I headed over to pay.

'What's going on?' I asked, handing her the money.

'Staffing problems.' She shrugged as though it was nothing, ringing up my account and picking out my change. 'I'm the old one he can rely on!' She grinned.

'Not so old.' I smiled.

I really liked her dyed red hair, pinned up with combs and jewellery. Her flowing skirt and weird blouse with the blue edging made me feel so ordinary and drab in my short white denim skirt and T-shirt.

'Well, thank *you*.' She laughed. 'But I'm forty-two.'

'Really?' I was genuinely surprised.

'What a sweetie!'

Behind us, the owner groaned loudly and put his head in his hands. Then he got up, pulled a shoebox down from a high cupboard and started looking through the mess of papers inside.

'My mother's name is Lily,' I told her shyly.

'Yeah?' She smiled warmly. 'Lillian or just Lily?'

'Just Lily.'

The boss looked over at me for the first time. 'And what is your name?'

'Therese, but I get called Tess.'

'You want a job, Tess?'

'A job?' I asked.

He nodded.

'Here?'

'Yep. Right here. Two girls have just called in the last hour to say they can't work tonight. This morning, the young guy I was relying on for the weekend took off to Perth.' He blew out in exasperation. 'And I'm trying to find that list of bloody names!'

'I'm going back to Melbourne this afternoon.'

'Why the hell would you go back there?' he muttered sourly. 'Cold, miserable joint. Do you realise that it's actually raining back there? I saw it on the news last night.'

I knew he was joking, but as soon as he'd said it I started thinking exactly the same thing. *Why go home?*

'Is it just for tonight you need someone?'

'I need someone reliable for a permanent position,' he said. 'Hey, Lily, have you any idea where I can find that list of wannabes? There was that young fellow from Sydney. Mick or Nick or …'

'*Tricky* Dick?' Lily offered, and they both cracked up laughing.

'He seemed okay. I need his number.'

'I have no idea! You had it.'

'I want to do it,' I cut in on their banter. 'But I haven't any experience, and I've got nowhere to stay.'

The boss stopped searching through the box and took a good long look at me. 'You serious?'

'Yes.'

'It's just taking orders and bringing out the food and drinks. Reckon you could do that?'

'Yep. But I've got nowhere to live.'

'I've got a place for you to stay.'

'Really?'

'I've noticed you coming in here this past week. You've got a nice look about you.' He looked at Lily. 'Hasn't she?'

The older woman regarded me seriously for a moment. 'She has, yes.'

'If you want the job, there is a little self-contained flat behind my home. You can have it for a very low rent for as long as you're working for me. It's just a kitchen, bedroom, bathroom and living room. But it's set up with everything. We had my wife's mother in there for a few years. It's very safe.'

I nodded excitedly, but he was still looking stern. 'No visitors and no parties.'

'Okay.' I managed to keep calm but inside I was bouncing. 'How much is the pay?'

'Eighteen an hour. Time-and-a-half on Sundays. But I need someone I can rely on. You want to go away for a while and think about it?'

'I'll walk around the block.' I smiled.

'Okay.'

But I didn't have to think too hard. I'd been dreading going back home and this was my way out. As the idea took hold, a heavy burden seemed to roll off my back. On the quick trip around the block I decided that I would make a break for it. Away from family and expectations and everything else besides. I would live my own life. Within five minutes I was back inside the café.

'Okay,' I said, holding out my hand.

He grinned immediately. 'Okay, Tess! I'm Duncan, and you know Lily here.'

The three of us shook hands across the counter and we all laughed. 'I'll show you the flat now if you like. If it's all okay, you can start work tonight.'

'Okay.'

Duncan lived with his wife, Amy, and their three young kids only a few blocks from the café. There was five-year-old Johnny and twin girls, Louise and Jane, who were three. There was a side entrance into the backyard. When he unlocked the flat and ushered me in, I didn't know what to say. It was so small and bright and clean, with chairs and a table, a bar fridge and a stove. Television and radio, pots and pans. So compact and private and so … utterly neat, compared to our rambling, rented weatherboard home in Melbourne. The bedroom was only just big enough to hold the bed and wardrobe. But what did I care? I didn't have much and there was ample room to put the few things I had. And it was a short walk to the beach.

'You can have it for sixty bucks a week on the conditions that I said.'

'That's great.'

'No parties.'

'Sure … I'm not a party person.'

He frowned at me and then looked at his thonged feet.

'Of course I don't mind if you have a girlfriend over for a cup of coffee or something, but no guys. Got me?'

'Yep.'

'I got kids. And they've got to be able to play in the garden. Amy is here all day by herself and sometimes half the night as well. She needs to feel safe. I don't want to have strange guys slinking in here all hours of the day and night. You got me?'

'I've got you.'

The bathroom had a small bath-shower, toilet and basin. Towels and sheets were all I needed. I figured that the money I had left would stretch to get those few things.

'There is linen in the cupboard,' he said as though reading my thoughts, 'and you're welcome to use it.'

'Oh, that's great, thanks!'

'Alright then?'

'Fantastic. I love it.'

'Why don't you go back to where you've been staying, pick up your stuff and come back here and settle in? And I'll see you back at the café at five.'

'Okay.'

The shit hit the fan when I got back to the apartment. The other three were sitting out on the balcony drying their hair from the beach, drinking champagne, and moaning about having to go back home in a few hours.

'Grab yourself a glass,' Zelda told me. 'We're having a farewell-to-paradise drink.'

'No, thanks.'

None of them could believe me when I told them that I wouldn't be joining them on the plane home.

'Have you gone out of your mind?' Zelda said, grabbing me by both shoulders and searching my face. 'What about your plane ticket and your plans for this year?'

'I have no plans,' I said, pulling away from her.

'But you've got a whole lot of stuff to work out!'

'I'll do it here.'

'You can't just … *not* go home.'

'Why not?'

'What will your sisters say?'

Katie had one foot propped up on the side of the big pot plant and was unscrewing a bottle of bright pink nail polish. She looked up with a smile.

'This is about that guy you met in the café yesterday, isn't it?'

My mouth fell open. I had no idea what to say.

'The one who took your hand at the door?' She turned back to her nails, still smiling.

'I don't want to go home, that's all,' I said, but way too loudly.

Katie shrugged slightly and continued painting her nails and I was left staring down at her bent head, feeling slightly foolish.

'Who are you talking about?' Zelda was totally baffled.

But I'd had enough. I was too rattled by Katie guessing part of the truth to stand there explaining. I simply shrugged and went into the next room to pack my bag. I could hear them talking, and I told myself that I didn't care. I did, of course. I cared deeply. But I didn't want to go home.

I didn't see Jay again for over two weeks. And by then I'd almost forgotten him, I was enjoying myself so much. I swam every morning and worked every afternoon and most evenings, but somehow in that town, with those people, at that time of the year, it all felt like a holiday. The café was my centre. Duncan was really kind and easygoing, and back at their house his wife Amy was the same. Their little kids were so sweet too. As long as I turned up for my shifts and worked hard – which I did – I was brilliant as far as they were concerned. 'Wondergirl has arrived!' Duncan would call out every afternoon when I turned up for work. 'The girl I've been waiting for!' He was kidding, but it did a lot for my confidence anyway.

Lily was warm and friendly too, and when I was able to help her out with a couple of shifts we became real friends in spite of the age difference. She took me under her wing. When at the end of the second week it became obvious that I really only had a couple of outfits she invited me around to where she lived with her boyfriend, and hauled out three big crates full of old clothes that she had planned to get rid of. Most of what she had was fantastic and fitted me right too.

Suddenly, I had a whole new look – swirling skirts and tops, diamante-studded T-shirts, tight white jeans and loose summer dresses, short skirts and big wide belts with brass buckles, and bits and pieces of jewellery. I loved wearing all that stuff. Even the chef, Tom, normally so guarded and shy, commented on how great I looked.

Within a fortnight I knew how to make coffee and work the till and even do basic cooking when Tom wasn't around. No one was interested in how I'd failed all my exams; nor were they particularly curious about my family. It wasn't that they were *uninterested* – I told them things and they listened, but they didn't go on about it or dwell on the heavy stuff. They didn't even seem surprised. They were all older and had stories of their own. I wasn't such an oddity anyway. For the first time I realised that difficult, dark stuff happens to lots of people. Tom's mother was an alcoholic who was in and out of rehab and forever hitting him up for money. As much as he loved her, he was also sick of her. Duncan hadn't spoken to his father for ten years because of the way he'd insulted Amy at their wedding. Amy's younger sister had a spending habit that had put her in serious debt. Worse, she borrowed from them and never paid them back. When things got slack we'd sit around and talk. Everyone's past and present was on the table and I really enjoyed sharing my stories with them. By the end of the first couple of weeks, I not only dressed differently, I *felt* different.

When Jay turned up at the café on a motorbike wearing leathers, my heart missed a few beats, but I wasn't as easily impressed as I'd been only two weeks before. He ordered coffee and cake from Lily, and I thought he'd forgotten me altogether. But when I took the coffee over to him, his voice sent a shiver of curiosity through me.

'Sorry I didn't turn up when I said I would,' he said. 'I had to go away on business.'

I shrugged as though it didn't matter in the least.

'I'm sorry you had to wait around for nothing.'

I flushed. Would he know that I'd waited around? I had no idea then just how well-known he was. How there was always someone around to spy for him.

'So you're working here now?' he asked.

'Yes,' I smiled.

'Since when?'

'Nearly two weeks.'

'Anyone ever told you that you have beautiful eyes?'

'Yes,' I said seriously. 'I get told that a lot.'

He laughed as if I'd said something funny.

'So do you have any time off?'

'Some,' I said. 'But not much.'

'Time to come out with me?'

I found myself flushing again, and to my relief the door opened and the place was suddenly crowded. But he stayed for at least an hour, ostensibly reading the paper, but every now and again I felt his eyes on me. When at last he got up to go, he came over to where I was wiping down a table.

'I'd like to take you out to dinner, Tess,' he said formally, but there was the grin playing around the corners of his mouth.

'I don't know.'

'What don't you know?'

We were both standing looking at each other. I could see that he was several years older than me. But there was something about him …

'Why?' I asked softly and looked around at all the people. 'Why me?'

He paused and looked away out the window. When he turned around to meet my eye the grin was gone. 'I like you,' he said softly. 'I like the way you speak. And I like the way you conduct yourself.'

'Conduct myself?' I repeated incredulously.

'You stand straight and you look people in the face when you speak to them. You're intelligent and … very pretty.'

I was flattered, of course – totally – it had been a long time since anyone called me pretty, much less intelligent, but I tried not to show it.

'So, what is your name?' I asked.

'Jay,' he said.

At the end of the shift when I told Duncan and Lily that I had a date the following evening with Jay Hanson they were both surprisingly unenthusiastic, which took the wind out of my sails a bit. Even Tom looked concerned.

'He's the dude who runs that nightclub out on the high-way, right?'

'Yeah.' Duncan frowned and his mouth went tight. 'With his brothers.'

'So what's wrong with that?' I asked. No one said anything. 'What sort of place is it?' I could tell they thought something wasn't right. 'Come on,' I laughed. 'Tell me!'

But Duncan's phone was ringing and three people walked in the door. 'Just be careful, Tess,' he threw over his shoulder. 'He's a lot older than you.'

six

By now it's midday and we are heading down the New England Highway. The clouds are retreating and the sun is actually shining down on us, making the car warm inside. Nellie has fallen asleep again, but I know it won't last. The poor kid has been cooped up in the car for hours now. I look back at her sleeping in the car seat. Barry is sitting up alongside her, with the new computer toy hanging off his fat paw. About an hour ago we had to stop for her to have a pee by the side of the road, and she made it clear that she was jacked off. Next time she'll probably crack it properly.

'You hungry?' Harry asks.

'No,' I say, too sharply.

Please just keep going. Just don't stop. Please …

'Definitely not, eh?'

He flashes me a quick smile and I see that my reluctance to explain myself has intrigued him a bit. I try to smile back. I want to let him know he shouldn't take it personally, and that he should know there is nothing to be intrigued about. Every vaguely interesting thing about me bled out years ago. I'm like last season's bag. It looked nice enough new, but it got shabby quickly and the handle broke. It's at the bottom of the wardrobe now, not worth mending or even picking up. But how do you tell someone *that*? You don't. More to the point, how do you tell someone that you don't care if you never eat again?

When Nellie wakes again, we pull over briefly and I switch into the back with her and let her paint my nails. That keeps her quiet for a bit. Then I let her draw all over my arms with biro. Anything to keep her occupied so that we can keep shooting along this flat road at a hundred kilometres an hour! *Away … away.*

'Well, I'm going to have to stop fairly soon.' Harry looks at his watch. 'Breakfast was ages ago. We'll stop at Tamworth.'

The road curves around the hills and corners, cutting through the red, turned-up earth. On either side of us are clumps of trees and mobs of grazing sheep. Harry is travelling at the speed limit, but I wish he'd go faster. The only time we slow down is when we pass though tired little towns and hamlets, often with only a pub, a post office and maybe one general store or a roadside café. I watch a young woman, not much older than me, pushing a pram down the quiet street. Maybe she's going to pick up an older kid from kinder, or she might have come out to buy some bread and milk.

I try to imagine myself living in such a place, running a takeaway joint on the corner. Why not? I picture Nellie running about these empty streets, playing with whoever turns up. Maybe I should tell Harry to stop the car right now. I could get out and haul my bag from the boot, lift my daughter from the back seat and … *take a chance?* There might be a job going at the post office. I'm good behind a counter. It's about all I'm good for, actually. I know how to smile at people and be polite. I could weigh up the parcels and sell the stamps.

This is a huge, fast-moving world, I remind myself. It's got to be possible for Nellie and me to get lost somewhere.

'At what stage did you start regretting it?' Harry asks me out of the blue. 'I mean, how long had you been there before you started thinking, *this isn't for me?*'

I groan in mock despair. 'Do you ever stop asking questions?'

'Nope.' He smiles. 'Do you mind?'

I shake my head, because instead of being annoying, the genuine curiosity in his voice is sort of flattering. It's been a long time since someone tried to work me out.

'Okay, give me a minute to think,' I say. 'When did I first start regretting it?'

He laughs. 'It's not an exam!'

'I realise that, but ...'

'But what?'

'It's hard. Thinking back. My memory is kind of ... shot.'

'Try.' He grins at me. 'It will help pass the time.'

I know he's right. Talking does help pass the time. More importantly, it might help me ignore the constant pulse of dread in the pit of my stomach. Trying to guess Jay's next move is like trying to work out when a snake is going to strike. Disaster might well hit any time, and I've got to be ready for it.

When did you start regretting it?

Not for ages. I think I had that first summer when everything was perfect. But I'm not exactly sure of the time span. There were months, certainly. There was the beach and the shops, all the friendly shop owners, the floods of tourists arriving in cars and buses and taxis from the airport. There was the job I enjoyed, with people I'd quickly grown to love. Beth rang to rant on about how irresponsible I was being and I hung up on her. I chucked my phone at the wall. It broke and I got myself a new one with a new number.

And there was Jay.

Maybe it was the confidence. Maybe it was the bike and the money. I don't quite know how to explain it, but he made everyone else seem ordinary. To start with, we met in cafés at the beach, and under trees in parks. He liked it that way. Maybe we both did. I can't remember. At first we did a lot of hanging out, swimming, and meals on the beach. We'd go for long drives at night, me on the back of his bike, sharing music on his iPod. We'd stop at different beaches, throw off our shoes and wade in holding hands. He never rushed me.

He told me things about himself, how he'd come back to Byron after years on the road playing guitar in various bands, none I'd heard of – although I pretended I had. He told me about how tough it was in the industry, and how people used him and took credit for his work. I was full of sympathy. Those hard-luck stories pulled at my seventeen-year-old heartstrings and inflamed my indignation. If someone as talented and hardworking and handsome as Jay couldn't make it, then the whole music business must be completely fucked, as he repeatedly told me. Sometimes he laughed when he told me these stories, but I took on the pain and disappointment underneath his words. I wanted to make things right for him.

There was a whole lot of stuff he didn't tell me, of course. His on-again-off-again problem with drugs, for example, or the fact that he'd been married to a woman who'd escaped overseas. These things I found out later, gradually, and usually through other people.

He often sidestepped direct questions, but that didn't bother me much. I'd never known anyone in *business* before – both my parents were teachers – and I was stupid enough to think that all the mystery meant it was somehow much more important and exciting than what they did. *Imports and exports, distribution costs* and *bottom lines* were words I'd heard on the news. They sounded so serious, *real world* stuff that I only had a vague idea about.

Our meetings became more frequent until they were almost every day. When I'd finish work at ten or eleven at night he'd be outside the café waiting for me.

It wasn't hard to fall in love. I was ripe for it.

I remember the moment. Nothing much had happened between us yet. We were still at the beach even though it was past midnight.

He pulled his guitar out. 'I wrote this song for you last night.'

'Me?'

'My blue-eyed angel,' he said, and began to sing.

I've blocked out the words, but I remember being so touched. I was there on the beach, but I was back home as well. Dad was happiest when he was in the garage working on something, singing to himself. He had blue eyes too.

I told Jay these little stories about my father, and he'd listen without saying much.

'So you miss him?' he asked me once.

'Not that much,' I replied. I was on the point of going on to explain that of course I loved my father, but by the time I was growing up he'd become moody and hard to get along with so much of the time. But I never got to finish my train of thought. Jay burst into a shout of laughter and leant across to run one hand through my wet hair.

'You are so *cool*!'

'Why?'

'You tell the truth. I don't miss my father either!' He said this as if it was something to be proud of, a badge of honour, and it made me feel awkward and disloyal. I hadn't intended besmirching my father.

'My blue-eyed angel,' he whispered, and kissed me behind the ear.

How I loved being on the back of his bike. The long rides we'd take along the beach road, the stars above, the soft warm breeze in my face. I could feel myself racing away from the past and into a glorious future. Going for naked swims and drinking wine and having food on the beach at midnight made me feel as if I was the star in an exotic film. Some nights we'd lie back in each other's arms, damp from the water and each other's sweat, and we'd interpret one another's dreams and then fall asleep on the beach. Those mornings I'd creep back in through Duncan's side gate at six a.m. in a state of euphoria, and slide into my bed for a few hours of sleep before work.

When he eventually took me to the club he managed just out of town, I knew I'd made it. I'd been wanting to see it for ages – after all, it was his main job – and up to that point his response to my hints had been to laugh, run his hands through my hair and change the subject, which upset me. Did it mean he wasn't serious? Then I was allowed in. And once I saw the place it all solidified in my head and became real. The long rides along lonely beaches, the midnight swims and lazy late-night picnics had a dreamlike quality to them. The next day it was hard to believe they'd actually happened. But those hard black surfaces and low red lights at the club were real. Totally. And likewise the singers and dance acts, the private drinking booths hedged in around embossed walls, the shiny dance floor and rotating coloured lights. And Jay, so obviously in charge. I watched him overseeing everything, from the staff roster to the lighting, to the hauls of cash in zip-up canvas bags departing and arriving, and I was so impressed. His office was off the bar, big and plush. No one else was allowed in there without knocking.

'Hey, can I dance with her?' one of his friends might ask when Jay left me to go behind the counter and see to the business side of things. Jay would give the nod and I'd be up dancing like something crazy. Never without his permission, though, that went without saying. I was his girl. Everyone knew that.

That place was magic to me in those first few months. The crowds of people dressed up in their best, the pulsating dance music that hit me as soon as I stepped inside, the deference of the door staff and the girls behind the bar. I was the girlfriend. *The girlfriend.* Away from Beth and Salome and my schoolfriends I became aware of myself as never before. I might look too young for him, but people changed their minds about that when I opened my mouth. I *was* classy compared to most of those cashed-up bogans tottering about drunkenly in their high heels, their breasts hanging out of their itty bitty tops. I didn't swear, for starters. And I didn't drop my 'g's or squeal *oh my God* all the time. I never got drunk. I don't think anyone liked me much, but they couldn't look down on me.

Even when I wasn't with Jay, I was dizzy with pleasure. At work I chatted as I made the coffees and took the orders, but another part of me was combing over what we'd done the night before and anticipating our next meeting. Almost overnight the world had become mine, the possibilities endless. What did it matter that I was just seventeen? In the past, people married young. We were a unit. Jay and Tess. *Tess and Jay.* We would grow old together. Love each other ... forever.

So that first summer was ... so very perfect.

Except it wasn't.

When did I start regretting it? More or less straight away, if the truth be told. Right from the start I sensed that I was way out of my depth. Something happened quite early that should have made me consider my situation seriously. It was a very hot evening. I'd done an all-day shift at the café and rushed home to shower and change into a lovely retro blue polka-dot dress that Lily had given me. She'd barely worn it because she thought it was too short for her long legs. It had a lovely wide neck and a very low back. I wore it with a wide belt. It was feminine and sexy and fun all at once. Jay picked me up, and I rode out to the club on the back of his bike feeling very glamorous. We pulled into a small parking space near the front door of the club and got off.

He took my hand and told me that the dress was perfect on me because the blue matched my eyes. I smiled and told him I loved it too and that it had once belonged to Lil. His face closed over immediately. It was just like having a door slam shut in my face. He turned away, pulled out a cigarette and lit it. I knew something was up, but I didn't for a moment think it could be about the dress. Or me, for that matter. He must have remembered something. I watched him check his phone for messages. He sent a text to someone and then leant back against the bike and looked at me as though from a distance. As if he was checking me out for the first time to see if I'd do.

'Lily at the café?'

I nodded, puzzled by his low tone. 'She's given me lots of lovely stuff.'

He said nothing for a bit, then very suddenly he pushed past me and stood with one arm against the brick wall, his back to me. I knew that he had a temper. I took a deep breath and went over and leant on the wall next to him.

'What's wrong?' I asked.

He looked away, took a deep drag of his cigarette and blew it out. Then before I knew it, he had one hand around my upper arm, pushing me up against the wall.

'I don't want you wearing that slut's clothes,' he snarled quietly into my face, his fingers getting tighter with each word. 'You hear me?'

I jerked back in shock, smacking my head against the wall. 'What do you mean?' I gasped, my voice petering out to a whisper.

He gave me a cold hard look, real contempt in his eyes. The pressure of his hand lessened, but he still had me in his grip. 'You heard what I said.' He flicked his ash on the pavement with the other hand.

'What do you have against her?' I was stunned.

'I don't want you wearing her clothes,' he snapped. 'Ever! You got me?'

'But why not?' I said.

He grabbed my arm again in a vicelike grip.

I tried to pull away, but I couldn't, and it really hurt. 'I didn't bring much up here,' I stammered. 'I'm saving to buy some things of my own.'

'I'll get you new clothes.'

'But I like the things she's given me!' I was reeling, unable to quite believe this turn of events.

'I'll get you new clothes.' He let go abruptly. And without another word he turned and walked off towards the club entrance.

The swell of panic that jammed my chest and throat had nowhere to go. I stood staring after him in total shock. Half an hour earlier, we'd been laughing. He'd been so attentive and loving, so *appreciative*, running his hands through my hair, kissing my eyelids. I must have done something terribly wrong to make him like this. *But what?* I just couldn't work it out. I loved him and – this is where I began to sob – I thought he loved me. But I was torn, because by this stage I also loved my workmate Lil.

When I'd dried my eyes I looked over to the club and saw that he was standing with his back to me on the front step … *waiting for me to come to him*. I remember that moment very clearly because it was almost as though I could see myself from above – standing in the car park by myself, him over there waiting. I remembered my father telling me about the blues singer Robert Johnson standing at the crossroads, deciding which way to go. Was he going to stay a good boy and keep singing church music with his family and community, or was he going to make a deal with the devil and start singing the blues? There were two choices for me at that point too. I could turn around and start walking back into town – it was only about a kilometre away and I'd be there within half an hour in spite of my high-heeled shoes. Or I could walk over to where he was waiting for me and resume where we'd left off. Some part of me knew that if I went over to him and climbed those stairs it would mean that I acquiesced to what had just happened. And if I walked back into town it would mean my life in Byron would be over. I would have to get out quickly and go home. No way would I be able to stay after this.

The prospect of going home to Beth and Salome and Marlon, to Zelda and Katie and my nonexistent future was bad enough. Humiliating in the extreme. But a future without Jay? It was too horrible to contemplate. Just thinking about it filled me with dismay. How could I possibly live without him? We were meant to be together, soulmates who shared dreams and secret ambitions. His was to get back into music one day, and mine was to study writing and literature at university. One day, we both agreed, it would all come true for us. It had to, because we were in love. Only the night before at the beach he'd picked up my hand and kissed my fingers as we were drying off after our swim.

'You're the best thing that has happened to me in a long time,' he'd whispered into my ear.

'And you're the best thing that has happened to me *ever*,' I'd replied without thinking.

How could I possibly give up on that?

And so I walked over to where he was waiting for me.

By the time we were seated at our favourite table near the window he was holding my hand and kissing my hair as if nothing had happened. Calling out cheerfully to his brother behind the bar to bring a special bottle of champagne to us. I was so relieved. I told myself that it had been a small hiccup in an otherwise perfect relationship. But I knew …

Some part of me knew.

After my shower the next day, I was in a hurry to get my hair dry for work. I ran back into the bathroom for some moisturiser when I caught sight of myself in the mirror. I stopped in shock to take in the ring of mottled black and blue skin around my right bicep. There was only one explanation for it. *His tight grip caused these bruises.* But I quickly pushed aside the knowledge, at the same time pushing aside the T-shirt I'd planned to wear. I picked out a long-sleeved white top instead. Without making a conscious decision, I realised when I got to the café that I wasn't wearing any of Lily's clothes either.

All that morning I tried to figure it out and before long I came up with a plausible answer. Jay and Lily must have had some kind of intimate relationship in the past. He didn't want to see his new girlfriend wearing his old girlfriend's clothes. That had to be it. Lily and I got on really well. I knew she wouldn't mind me asking.

When we were both sitting outside having a break I asked her if she'd had a relationship with Jay.

'Definitely not!' she said, appalled. 'Why would you think that?'

'Well … he's …'

She was looking intently at me now, frowning as though worried.

'What?'

'He doesn't like me wearing your clothes,' I admitted in a small voice.

Lily gave a deep sigh, reached out and took me by both shoulders and gave me a little shake. 'I used to be married to a guy like that, sweetheart,' she said softly. 'Please be careful.'

seven

When I open my eyes, my arm is reaching across to hold Nellie's leg, completely numb. I look out the side window at the country-side, feeling weirdly disorientated. Then I see the sign saying Tamworth is two kilometres ahead and feel a bit better.

Without saying anything, Harry pulls over into a car park abutting a large green park. He goes to the boot and gets out a couple of small plastic containers. Jules's sandwiches, I guess. Nellie wakes and starts grizzling, so I lean over to undo her seatbelt and we both get out too. I watch Harry walk over to a park bench, pull out a cigarette and light up.

Nellie runs over to him. 'My daddy smokes,' I hear her tell him.

'Does he?'

'Sometimes he lets me light the match.'

'Wow!' Harry helps her onto the seat alongside him and butts his smoke on the ground.

I walk over to them slowly. Harry looks up and holds an open container out to me.

'Egg and lettuce. Tomato and ham.'

'Thanks.' I take one and so does he. Nellie shakes her head. Harry wolfs his down before he speaks again.

'So, where am I going to drop you guys when we hit Melbourne?' he asks matter-of-factly.

I've been dreading this question. I shudder, and see that he notices. I'm embarrassed, but there's nothing I can do to stop these sudden convulsions. They come from deep inside, quite separate to what is going on in my head. I sit down on the far end of the bench and stare around the park as I take a tentative bite of the sandwich. My nerviness is probably freaking this guy out. I imagine him ringing up Jules, when he gets home. *Jeez, thank God that's over!* Or sitting around a café table telling his friends. *I gave a lift to this strange girl with a kid who was trying to escape some maniac. Wouldn't let me call the police.*

'Brunswick,' I say, because I've got to say something.

'Who's there?'

'Family.'

'Oh right.' I hear the relief in his voice.

'Except, I … I haven't been in touch for a long time.'

'How long?'

'A few years.'

'Wow …' He shakes his head slowly as though trying to imagine it. 'No contact at all?'

'That's right.'

'But it's cool for you to go there?'

'I … I don't know … yet.'

He says nothing for a while. We watch the cars cruising past, the people with their shopping. *Normal lives.* What would it be like to have a normal life?

'Listen, we'd better find out,' he says eventually.

'But how?'

'You got a phone?'

I shake my head.

'You remember the number?'

I nod, and before I can say *wait, I'm not ready* he reaches into his pocket, pulls out his phone and hands it to me.

I shake my head and refuse to take it.

'Is there anyone else?'

'No.'

'Then you must try,' he says.

I turn to Nellie, who is watching us as though trying to work out exactly what's going on, filing it all away for future reference. Suddenly she gets off the seat and runs over to another bench not far away. We watch her as she climbs it and walks up and down as though she is practising tightrope walking.

I try to press the number of the Brunswick house into the phone, but my fingers won't work properly. Without a word Harry takes the phone back, and I whisper the numbers aloud. He hands the phone back. It rings twice before a recorded voice tells me the number is no longer available.

'What about mobile numbers?'

I remember the scrap of paper in my journal.

I go to the car and bring back the piece of worn paper and hand it to him. 'My elder sister.'

He punches in the number and hands the phone to me again.

This is it. My heart is going to bounce right out of my chest if this goes on much longer.

The phone stops ringing. 'Hello?'

'Beth, it's me.'

Silence for about three seconds.

'Who is this?' The familiar voice brings me undone. It's all I can do not to start howling.

'Tess,' I say. There is another pause. 'Beth?'

'What do *you* want?'

'I want … to come home.'

'Well, you can't.'

'Why?' I ask stupidly. My throat jams and tears rush to my eyes. I stand up quickly. Harry looks at me, concerned, then he gets up too. He walks over to where Nellie is playing on the other seat. I watch him help her jump down, and then he goes to the boot of the car, gives a box drink to Nellie and stuffs a couple more in his pocket. I turn my back on them.

'The house has gone,' Beth says in that same sharp voice.

'How do you mean?'

'The lease finished and we all moved out.'

'When?'

'Last year.'

'Where do you live?'

'With Douglas. I'm married now.'

Douglas. He flashes into view with amazing clarity. The stooped posture, the shifty smile, those grey jumpers he always wore. Always sniffing, always clearing his throat and blowing his thin nose. The rest of us thought he'd latched onto Beth because he needed someone to make him look normal. *You're way better than him*, we used to tell her. It's what I want to say again to my sister, who I haven't seen in four years. *Beth, no!* It's on the tip of my tongue: *You're way better than ...*

But I'm more bewildered than anything. Whenever I wake from a bad dream I think back to that house with my brother and sisters. It's like an oasis of security in my head. A place I can go to when nothing else is there.

For the past year I've lain beside Jay and pictured the old kitchen, with the stove and the table and the window, and the old dresser in the corner always crowded with things that should be somewhere else. The Italian man who owned it lived only three streets away, and once he had Beth's measure – she would take care of the place and never be late with the rent – he was so kind to us. Brought us over lemons from his trees and sometimes even eggs from his chooks. Said we could stay there forever.

'What about Marly and Salome?'

'What about them?'

'Where do they live?'

'Marlon is in the Kimberley, and Salome is working in Sydney.'

'But what ... what is Marlon doing up there?'

'Teaching.'

Teaching! My brother is a teacher.

'Where do *you* live?'

'What business is it of yours?'

'I just … I want to …' I gulp in air and try to think what to say. The silence is eating away at my ability to think. But nothing seems to work anymore. 'I just want to come home,' I whisper.

'How can you say that, Tess?' Beth's voice is low at first, holding in the anger, but I feel it building like a tornado beginning its spin, catching everything in its path. All the jagged pieces are flying around and around, getting closer to the core every second.

'I worked so hard to see you through school. I gave up doing what I wanted to do so that you'd have a chance. And you … you just waltzed out. Without even saying goodbye!'

'I'm so sorry, Beth,' I manage to mutter.

'I don't care how sorry you are!' she screams down the phone. 'I've got my own life now! I'm doing what I should have been doing when I was nineteen, instead of trying to keep it all together for you, *you brat!*'

'Beth, I know. I'm so—'

She is sobbing with rage now. 'Marlon and I went up there. I knew I had to do everything I could to bring you home. And you … you had … *that creep* come and tell us that you didn't want to see us. You couldn't even tell us yourself!'

'Beth, it wasn't like that. I … He wouldn't let me come and—'

'He came to the motel with a note written by you!'

'I know. But I didn't … want to do it like that. He … he said that you—'

'Not one phone call in four years to say hello or happy Christmas!' She is shrieking now. 'Not one note in four years to say that you were okay. Nothing. What did I do to deserve that, Tess?'

'Nothing … you did nothing.'

'What thirty-year-old goes after a seventeen-year-old school-girl?'

'He was twenty-seven then, but …' *Hey, babe, seven is our lucky number! You're seventeen and I'm twenty-seven!*

'Same thing!'

'Please, Beth. Please let me tell you …' But I'm shaking all over, weak with the shock of hearing her voice after all these years.

She cuts me off again. 'What can you possibly tell me *now*?'

The enormity of my own betrayal hits me, makes me sink to my knees onto the gravel, the phone still held tightly to my ear. Tears are streaming down my face because I'm seeing her: Beth standing by the kitchen table when we finally twigged that our mother wasn't coming home any time soon, her chin up, eyes blazing, telling us that we would survive. That she would make sure we did. *We will survive.* I believed Beth when she said that no government department would break up our family. I believed her when she said that our lives would go on as before, except different. And I was right to believe her. She kept her word. We had a lot of relatives — our mother was one of thirteen kids, she had five brothers who lived nearby, all of them married with kids of their own — but none of them did much for us. Neither did our grandparents. Our father was dead and our mother gone, and Beth got us away from that horrible little town where everyone knew us. She got us to the city and into a good school, and she made sure that rambling old rented house was as neat as a pin. There were no drunken teenage parties at our place. There were meals on the table every night and apples and bananas in a fruit dish in the middle of the table every day of the week. The bath got cleaned and the bins went out. She made sure that we got every bit of government assistance available, that we had reasonable clothes on our backs, and presents for parties and fashionable shoes. And, in spite of topping the whole year in second-year uni, she deferred medicine – the course she'd set her heart on when she was six years old – and went to work for a local solicitor, typing his letters and answering the phone. But that didn't bring in enough money, so she started cleaning houses for cash, so the government money kept rolling in as well, and we didn't have to live like paupers. After two years she started back at university, but only part-time, because three nights a week and every second Saturday for at least four years my brilliant sister caught the tram into the city to clean offices so the rest of us could go on with full-time schooling. If she was bossy, judgemental and sharp-tongued then she was also proud and hardworking and honest. And what payback did she get from me? I ran off with a guy because he looked like a rock star.

Harry is suddenly squatting next to me. He pulls me up by both elbows and we lean against the car.

'Beth, I'm in danger!' I whisper through my tears into the phone.

'You know something, Tess? *I don't care!*'

Her words resound again and again in my brain. *I don't care.* She means it. She really means it. Beth was never one to muck around with the truth.

I take a deep breath. Some part of my brain must be still working, because I realise that I do have one card left. Only one. And it might not work. If it doesn't, then … I don't know. I will be lost on a wild, furious sea of desperation, struggling to stay afloat, trying so hard not to drown. But part of me knows it will only be a matter of time. Nellie and I will go down together.

I will find you and I will kill you …

'I have a kid.'

Silence for a couple of beats as the words sink in.

'*What?*' Beth sounds as if she's being strangled.

'A kid,' I repeat.

'But … How old?'

I hear the curiosity in her voice. Out of all of us, Beth is the natural mother. Her whole face would soften if a neighbour came in to show off a new baby, or if she got a chance to play with a kid. Then, with a sick feeling in my stomach, I remember the diagnosis she got when she was twenty-three. Endometriosis. The devastation on her face when she told us that the doctor said it was unlikely she'd ever be able to bear a child. The way she tried to laugh it off when she'd explained the logistics of it. Nellie might well be the ultimate slap in the face for her, a cruel reminder of her own condition. Who would blame her if she refused to put herself through that?

'Three.'

'Is it his?'

'Yes.'

Beth remains stonily silent.

'A girl.'

There is a gentle tapping on my back. I turn to see Nellie staring solemnly at me. In normal circumstances she'd be chattering away or demanding something, but she is watching me carefully. I lean over and put the phone up to her ear.

'Say hello to your aunt,' I whisper shakily. 'Say, hello, Auntie Beth.'

'Hello, Auntie Beth,' Nellie chants, her voice as clear as a bell. These are just about the first words she's uttered all day. Harry and I look at each other. 'My name is Fenella and I'm three years old and … a little bit.' She holds up finger and thumb to show the little bit. Then Nellie says yes and no a couple of times into the phone and finally, 'Mamma and me are running away in a car.'

My mouth falls open in astonishment. Then Nellie hands the phone back to me. 'She wants you now.'

'Okay.'

'You'll have to come here,' Beth tells me matter-of-factly.

'Where?' I motion for Harry to fetch a pen.

'I'm up at the farm,' she says. 'Clearing out the house.'

'The farm?'

'Yes.'

'You mean Grandma and Grandpa's place?' I'm bewildered all over again. I wave the pen aside.

'Grandma is dead,' she tells me bluntly.

I gasp aloud before I even think.

'Don't pretend you care,' Beth shoots back.

'I'm shocked,' I say shakily. 'That's all.'

'Get ready for another one,' Beth says. 'Grandpa is in the local hospital. He'll be dead any day. He's made me the executor of his will, and he's asked us up here to clean out the house and sort things through for him, and that's what I'm doing.'

'Us?'

'Marly and Salome will be here in a couple of days. He wanted the four of us, of course.' Her voice rises with accusation. 'But we didn't bother trying to contact you.'

'Right.'

'But if you really are running away, then this might be the best place for you.'

'Okay,' I say shakily.

I find it almost impossible to imagine Beth back there in that old house, much less Salome and Marlon. A shudder goes through me. I hate that place. Not just the house, with its dark smelly rooms, creaking floorboards and rotting verandah posts, but the dirt road leading up to it and the dams and the sheds and … As far as I know, my sisters and Marly hate it too. It is where our mother lived as a child. Surely it would be better to take my chances in Melbourne. Just bum around, see what happens. Haven't I done alright so far? I'm still free and moving in the right direction. Then my little girl looks up at me, and I know with everything in me that I have to find somewhere safe for her. Beth is the only bit of safety I know.

'What about all the uncles?'

'He wants *us*.'

'Why?'

Beth gives an impatient snort. 'Why do you think?'

The feeling slams into my belly and roars through the rest of me like a short, violent storm. I go cold, as though someone has pushed me into a freezer and slammed the door shut. I am standing next to all the other freezing people strung up on meat hooks.

'When will you be here?'

I look around to where Harry is lifting Nellie up so she can look at what is inside the big rubbish bin. I want to thank her, but it is so inadequate. *Thank you* is for when someone tells you the time or gives you a present, and so I stumble over the words.

'Tess,' Beth commands sharply.

'Yes, I'm here.'

'Are you coming?'

'Yes.'

'When will you get here?'

'As soon as I can.' I look at Harry. 'Another day, maybe two?'

I click the end-call button and stand there staring out in front of me for some time.

Harry takes Nellie by the hand and leads her over to a patch of grass. I am lost to all but the rush of memories jostling for position inside me. Eventually he leads Nellie back to the car and looks at me.

'Everything okay?' He is rolling a cigarette and trying to read my face at the same time.

'She's on our grandparents' farm.'

'Where is that?'

'Out of Leongatha. It's about three hours from the city.'

'How will you get there?'

'Train and bus from the city, I guess.' I'm trying to keep calm but in fact, getting up there will be a logistical nightmare without a car. It will mean Nellie and me hanging around for hours waiting for a train or bus, and Jay will be working hard on the case. I can see him, his humiliation and anger building by the hour. He knows people everywhere, and he will leave no stone unturned. Melbourne's Southern Cross railway station would be an obvious place to look.

'Nah,' Harry mutters and takes a deep drag. 'I've got an aunt around there. Nice old bird. I've been meaning to see her for ages. I'll go stay a night or two. Give her a thrill.'

I watch the thin stream of blue smoke coming from his mouth. His profile against the sky is like a cardboard cut-out of a Roman senator. He opens the car door.

'What are you saying?' I hardly dare hope that he might mean what I think he does.

'Jules would kill me if I didn't.' He smiles at me. 'Come on. Get in. We'll get you there. Door-to-door service.' He grins again. 'Not sure how long it'll take us. But we'll be there some time in the next couple of days.' He helps Nellie into the car.

'Thanks, Harry.'

....

Our early lives were closely bound up with that old weatherboard house where Mum had grown up and where her parents still lived. It was fifteen kilometres out of the town where we lived and off the main road another couple of kays, the very house where the family had first settled when they came to Australia in the 1880s.

From the original settlers, it was passed down to our mother's grandparents and then to her parents. Freezing in winter and roasting in summer, it was a shambles of small living spaces and tacked-on rooms.

Our mother used to take us out there to see her parents a lot, until my older sisters and brother jacked up. One by one they refused to go until I was the only one left to accompany her.

If you believed the kids at school, grandparents are warm and loving and interested older people who adore seeing their grandkids. Not ours. There were no knitted scarves or Christmas presents for us. No hugs or offers to show us Luna Park or take us on holiday to Melbourne or Sydney. Our grandparents were relics from another age, and I was terrified of both of them.

'Outside. Outside!' Grandma used to push us out onto the back verandah as soon as we arrived. Too bad if it was cold and wet. 'I've had enough of bloody kids ruining all my things.'

This amused us enormously, because everything inside was old and shabby and worn anyway. The furniture with the faded armrests and chipped legs, the cushions with the threadbare covers and torn edges looked as if they'd been rescued from a tip. The rooms were gloomy and grimy, and the dominant smells were of wood smoke and sweat, cooked meat and liniment – in winter the windows were rarely opened.

The strange thing was that we all liked – even loved – our grandparents in a way, in spite of how they treated us. There was something wild and unpredictable about Grandma that never failed to amuse and terrify us. Well into her seventies, she was stocky and fit and as sharp as a tack in spite of having had thirteen children, our mum being the youngest, and one of only four girls.

Once my siblings stopped coming the visits were better for me. I always enjoyed being alone with my mother, and without the others I was allowed inside to sit on one of the smelly old chairs as long as I didn't interrupt.

Occasionally Grandma would notice me there and go quiet. 'Watch out,' she'd say. 'Big Ears is listening!'

But mainly she forgot about me, and I grew to love that cackling laugh of hers and the outrageous, often mean and funny things she'd say.

'Someone should knock him on the head with the blunt end of an axe,' I remember her saying once about Grandpa. 'It's a wonder I didn't do it myself years ago.'

I used to store up all these little scenes in my head to tell my older sisters and brother when I got home. And very occasionally Grandma forgot she hated kids. Once, she scooped my hair up with her big hard-working hands, found an elastic band and a bright red ribbon and tied it up for me.

'See how pretty you look now?' she said, smiling at me.

But it was Grandpa who fascinated all of us, especially me. He was often out working in the paddocks when we arrived. Sometimes three or four visits would go by without us seeing him at all. But when he was there he dominated the room like a colossus. He was at least six feet four, huge and strong, with a massive bald head, long beak-like nose and small bright eyes under heavy brows. His feet in the hobnail boots were like boats, and his forearms reminded me of bristly tree trunks.

He always shook hands with us kids formally and asked the same questions every time. *How is school? Are you doing your best?* This might be followed by a one-minute lecture on the value of hard work and not giving in to distraction. *Don't fall in with the wrong crowd*, he'd tell us. *Time goes very quickly*. How those two things were related puzzled me. Apart from that he rarely spoke. When his spotlight fell on me it felt as if my life depended on getting the answers right.

'How old are you now, Therese?' he would ask, especially if he hadn't seen me for a while. 'Are you trying hard at school?'

I would answer loudly, because he was hard of hearing, and with a forced smile on my face, because he liked cheerful children. I knew instinctively that he wasn't someone who differentiated between a fake smile and a real one. Effort was all that was required. He was terrifying, but we all gravitated towards him anyway, and so did adults. When he came in from outside it was as though a huge mountain had pushed its way into the room, majestic and dangerous, and no one could ignore it.

When I got a bit older, he occasionally asked a question that I both dreaded and longed for in roughly equal measure.

'How about a poem, Tess?'

Although he'd only had about six years of formal schooling, he knew a lot of poetry by heart. They were mainly bush ballads and limericks and famous speeches from his primary-school reader.

When I began my recitation he would shift his chair up near to me and hang on every word. Even though I was good at remembering poetry, I was usually so nervous in front of him that I'd stuff it up. I'd get to the middle of the poem and begin to wonder if I'd be able to finish it, and that worry was enough to make it go out of my head. But when I got it all right I was exhilarated for days afterwards. There was one he especially loved, written by a bomber pilot during the Second World War.

Oh! I have slipped the surly bonds of earth,
And danced the skies on laughter-silvered wings …

'Hmmm,' he'd say, shaking his massive head, smiling and looking at the ground. '*The surly bonds of earth.* Now that's good! See if you can get it word-perfect next time.'

He glared at me when I stuffed up 'At the Sea-Side' by Robert Louis Stevenson for the third time in a row. 'Practice makes perfect. Next time make it right, word for word. Don't give up until you have it.'

'Yes, Grandpa.'

My big moment came when I was ten. I'd been snooping through Salome's homework and found a copy of *Macbeth*. I hit on a small speech with an opening that was enticing, even though I had no idea what it meant. *Tomorrow and tomorrow and tomorrow.* I read it through, somehow sensed what it was about and made it my business to learn it by heart. The next time I went out to the farm I nervously asked Grandpa if he wanted to hear it.

'Shakespeare, you say?' His whole face stilled.

'It's from a play.'

'Well.' He sat down and yelled for Mum and Grandma to be quiet.

'Tomorrow, and tomorrow, and tomorrow,
Creeps in this petty pace from day to day,
To the last syllable of recorded time;
And all our yesterdays have lighted fools
The way to dusty death.'

And so I went on, right to the end of the speech, standing straight in front of him, arms stiff at my sides, pronouncing every word clearly. Word perfect, right to the end. And my grandfather was enthralled. I could see it. He didn't clap exactly, but he rubbed his enormous hands together, and his sunken blue eyes shone as brightly as two pieces of polished glass.

'Say it again,' was the curt order. And so I did.

'Now say it again, but more slowly. And loudly. I want to hear every word.'

By the third time, Grandma was getting irritable. 'For God's sake,' she fumed. 'You're putting ideas in that kid's head!'

But I was enjoying myself immensely, because Grandpa was actually smiling at me.

'My word,' he muttered. '*The last syllable of recorded time!* Now that *is* good, isn't it?'

'Yes, Grandpa.'

'That really puts it all in a nutshell!' He was laughing quietly.

'Yes, Grandpa.'

'No wonder he's famous.'

'Yes.'

'Will you write it out for me?'

'Yes, Grandpa.' I did it on the spot.

Once he had his hands on that small piece of paper he sat down to study it carefully. Every now and again he'd look up into the distance with the same pleased look on his face.

Then he folded it up and put it carefully in his pocket. 'I've got my own bit of Shakespeare now,' he told me seriously. 'I can take it out whenever I want.'

'Yes, Grandpa.'

But the very next time I saw him, the intense shy pleasure I'd begun to take in his company was destroyed. It was a very wet spring and he had to go out to the back paddock to check on some lambing ewes. He was afraid the truck would get bogged if he took it down to where they were sheltering so he asked me to accompany him. My job was to run down to the sheep and herd them out a gate into the next paddock. I heard the horn blast, but wasn't sure what it meant. There were two gates, and I'd opened the wrong one.

When I got back to the truck, excited to have completed my task, he turned on me savagely.

'You stupid girl!' he growled. 'Pay attention to instructions next time! Didn't you hear the horn? You've mixed the ewes with the wethers.'

I remember the trip home with my mother that day, feeling so utterly crestfallen that I wanted to curl up and die. I also wanted to get to the bottom of him.

'Why is your father so mean?' I burst out. 'And what's with that faraway look? What's he thinking about?'

'He's haunted,' my mother said matter-of-factly.

'By who?'

'Madness.'

'Is he mad?'

'Not yet,' my mother said with a dry laugh. 'Not yet.'

'Then why is he haunted?'

'His mother went mad,' she said shortly.

'Do you think he will too?'

She turned to smile at me, then leant across and ruffled my hair. 'You know, Tessie darling, I really appreciate you coming with me to see them. And learning those poems! They don't know how to show it, but they love you coming. I'm so proud of you.'

I was so happy to have pleased my mother that I vowed there and then to learn more poetry so she would be even prouder of me.

DEPARTMENT OF HEALTH DIAGNOSTIC RELEASE

Diagnosis: Recent Melancholia

Prognosis: Bad

Mental and Physical condition:

A recent Melancholia, stupid and confused, restless
and somewhat resistant to treatment. Can give little
account of herself. No definite delusions discerned.
Possible hallucinations of hearing.

Examined under Sec 88

Chief Psychiatrist

eight

'Hey, Tess?'

I stand transfixed, the phone clutched in my hand, thinking about Beth and the farm and everything I haven't let myself think about in years.

'Tess!' A man is walking towards us, but with the strong sunlight half-blinding me I can't make out who it is. I'm in the middle of some town I don't know and a stranger is calling my name?

Where is Nellie?

Harry has her. He's buckling her into her car seat.

Two more seconds and I see who it is. *Travis*. I want to run but I can't actually move. Jay's brother, Travis.

'I thought it was you!'

He smiles as though I will be pleased to see him, and, like a rabbit in the headlights, I find myself smiling back. 'Hello, Travis.'

Harry looks back and forth from Travis to me a couple of times. He must sense the potential danger, because the next bit happens fast.

'Get in, Tess,' he orders quietly. 'Now.'

I bolt to the passenger door to find it's already open for me. I get in and slam it shut just as Travis reaches the car. A bit baffled but still smiling, he pulls on the handle, but Harry has already locked it.

Travis leans down and peers into the car, his expression changing to one of complete incomprehension when he sees Harry. So they haven't told him yet. He must be on his way back to Byron, not looking for me at all.

Harry starts the engine and throws the car into reverse. Travis's hand is on the back door. He stares in at Nellie. For two seconds there is just the glass between us, and I see the penny drop behind his muddy brown eyes. Now he gets it! The car lurches back, jerking his hand away.

'Jay's brother,' I tell Harry hoarsely.

'Right. Thought it might be something like that.'

He guns the car out of the car park and straight into the highway traffic. There are a lot of horn blasts and screeching brakes. Travis is running after us, and my last image of him is standing on the side of the road, his phone to his ear. We roar down the street and through the town. The whole incident probably took less than a minute, but I'm panting with fear.

'You okay?' Harry asks.

'Yep,' I nod.

'You think he knew you'd be there?'

I shake my head.

'Bad luck then?'

I'm finding it difficult to breathe and my whole body has begun to shake. Harry grabs my hand briefly in a gesture of comfort.

'We're away now.'

'But he's seen the car,' I whisper, 'and the registration. He'll tell them!'

'I don't think he got the rego,' Harry says.

'Yes. He will have.'

'I don't think so.'

'What the fuck would you know? You have no idea about people like him!' The words are out before I even think. He jerks around in surprise but says nothing. 'They're just …'

'Just what?'

'They … don't like losing.'

'Who does?' Harry shrugs, breathes out hard and keeps driving.

I'm trying to calm myself, but somehow I'm unable to swallow the fury swamping me.

'Mamma, my boot's fallen off,' Nellie whines from the back seat. 'Mamma ... Who are we running away from, Mamma?' she asks softly. 'Who?'

'No one!'

'I want my boot!'

'Shhhh!' I hiss under my breath. I snap loose my seatbelt and grope around to find the boot.

'Mamma?'

'Shh, Nellie!'

'But I don't want to be in this car anymore!'

'Shut up!' I hiss, holding her leg roughly as I slip on her boot. She pulls away from me, and I turn back to the front seat.

'She only asked who we're running away from,' Harry says mildly, as I clip on my seatbelt.

'She is three years old!' I snap.

'Okay.' Harry is checking the rear-vision mirror constantly. 'Let's get off this highway. We'll go west over to Gunnedah and Coonabarabran and onto the Newell Highway, head down through Dubbo. Be quicker, I reckon.'

I'm utterly contrite now, mortified and humiliated by my own short temper. What must he think of me?

'I'm ... sorry, Harry. Sorry for being a ... jerk.'

'Doesn't matter.' He laughs to ease the tension between us. 'Try not to worry.'

'Yeah, right.' I give a short snort of laughter and my breath gives way completely. *Try not to worry?* I fight it. I fight the panic. I sit back and try to slow my breathing. Breathe three beats out first, and then in and count to three. Next time count to five.

Try not to worry?

'What are you sorry about, Mamma?' Nellie whimpers from the back seat.

'I'm okay, honey.' I unclip my seatbelt and lean back between the seats to kiss her worried little face. 'Mamma says some silly stuff sometimes, doesn't she?'

'Hmmm.'

'Want to play Can You Keep a Secret?' I smile at her.

'Hmmm.' She puts out one hand tentatively, and then giggles when I begin to draw around her palm.

'*Can you keep a secret? I don't suppose you can …*' I keep my voice absolutely serious, but she is already giggling loudly before I get to tickle under her arm.

'Again!'

We play that one a few more times, and then sing the jumping song as I feel around on the floor for her drawing book and pencils.

'Will you do me a picture of a horse, Nellie?'

'Okay,' she sighs, turning to a fresh page. 'You always want horses.'

'Can you make it blue?'

'No!'

'But you do good blue horses.'

'This one is going to be yellow.'

'Okay. But make it big,' I smile at her, 'because I want to be able to ride it.'

Nellie giggles and begins her picture.

Once I've turned around again with my seatbelt clipped Harry touches my hand briefly.

'We'll be okay, Tess.'

I'm calmer now, and so grateful to him. So grateful I'm almost in tears. Who am I kidding? This guy is the one thing between me and total fucking disaster! If I'm going to get away from Jay, then here is my ticket sitting alongside me. A one-legged half-blind ex-musician in his mother's BMW with time on his hands. And I'd better not forget it.

Well out of Tamworth now, we are driving west, heading for Gunnedah. I want to thank Harry, but I can't seem to open my mouth. Nellie is quiet, concentrating on her yellow horse. When I next turn around I see that she has fallen asleep against the side of her car seat. I look at the time and can hardly believe it's still so early in the afternoon. I feel as if I've been in this car, travelling at this speed, forever.

'Have you been on this road before?' I ask, for something to say.

Harry shakes his head, opens his mouth to say something then stops and dives for the radio volume-control button instead.

'Oh shit, I have to listen to this.'

'Okay.' I'm curious. I wasn't listening to the announcement. 'What is it?'

'Tchaikovsky. Violin concerto,' he murmurs distractedly, trying to tune the radio precisely. Once it's clear, he turns up the volume.

'I don't know anything at all about classical music,' I say apologetically.

'This was mine.' He throws me a swift, tense smile. 'I used to play this.'

'Oh wow.' I fold my arms and sit back. 'Okay. Who is playing it?'

'Some Polish dude. They'll tell us again at the end. You mind listening?'

'Of course not.'

Harry turns and gives me such a warm, full-on smile that the dread fades momentarily, and I almost forget where I am and what's happening.

'It was such a prick of a thing to learn,' he mutters cheerfully as he pulls the car out to pass the truck in front of us. 'Playing it was a fucking nightmare.'

The music begins so thin and plaintively that at first I don't know what to make of it. Then it starts to swell in a slow aching way, building up and up, the tune coiling around itself in a whole lot of complex circles only to retreat again and again, back to the beginning. Or that's what it feels like to me. Our mother was a classical music buff, and she played piano too. None of us took much notice of what she listened to. Dad loved those old blues singers along with all corny pop from the sixties, like 'You've Lost That Lovin' Feelin''.

I caught him crying along to that one once. He was trying to fix the cupboard in the bathroom and he'd sent me to get a hammer. The little radio was blaring away. I came back in just as he was pulling out the rotting board underneath and I saw his face in the mirror. Tears wetting his cheeks as he sang along. I put the hammer down quickly and disappeared.

Thinking of that twists me up inside with regret, because I remember exactly why I ran out of the room. Everything about him had become embarrassing – the music, his fat hairy bum hanging out over his crummy work jeans, even the tears made the need to escape sharper and more urgent.

Memories of my own unkindness attack me at odd hours of the night and day. They fly around like fierce wasps search-ing for unprotected skin. Unless I swat them away quickly they burrow in and eat through to the bone. *If only I'd … Why didn't I? Would it have hurt me to put my hand on his shoulder? Killed me to say something?* Jay was right. *One crazy little bitch*, mad and probably bad as well.

But this music that Harry is listening to is something else, so strange, so tense and wild that I get tingles down my spine trying to keep up with it. I'm not seeing even the green countryside or the wide sky outside my window at all now. It's like I'm being pulled against my will into dark swirling shadows that aren't even there. Not what I need. But what can I do?

Harry's damaged hand pounds and caresses the steering wheel as though it's refusing to give up all those long-learned notes. I try to imagine him in his past life learning them all, the pages and pages of music and the hours of practice. The teacher, correcting, praising, insisting that he play each bit through again and again and again, cold fingers on winter mornings, rumbling gut and racing heart as the exams and performances approach, all that drudgery and hard work and then the exhilaration and relief when the performance is over. How good would that be? It would be a lot to lose.

He shifts in his seat, and I note the slight twitch around his mouth, the inaudible drawing in of breath as the music moves off into some new frightening place, and his body sways almost imperceptibly, rocking along with the long, high, drawn-out notes. Is he imagining himself on stage now, in front of a huge audience? Is he missing it so badly that he wants to die? Is he wondering why? *Why me?* I have to clench my jaw against a sudden swell of emotion in my throat. *Why me? Why is this happening to me?*

Half an hour goes by and the thin, jagged sound of the lonely violin gets wilder and more desperate. The sadness intensifies and pierces me like one of those memory wasps, straight through to my bones. I open the window, take a few deep breaths, wishing I had some earplugs, wishing like crazy it would finish.

I'm seeing myself taking off in the rain towards the hill, rushing through undergrowth, falling, sobbing, hysterical and crazy. Nellie was back at the house with him, but I didn't care. It was over. *Over.* I couldn't take any more. I didn't care about her or the unborn one or myself. Yet when I fell and felt what was inside me give way, a terrible wild grief overwhelmed me. I collapsed under a tree, feeling the poor little thing leaking out of me bit by bit. Breaking apart. The blood was everywhere. I could feel it seeping out into my clothing, down my legs; it trickled out the bottom of my jeans and into my shoes. When I took down my jeans and felt for what was happening, my hands came away sticky with thick dark clots of blood. *A boy.* They'd told us the week before that it was a boy. The boy Jay wanted so badly had given up his hold on life … I tried wiping the bits of him away on the grass but more arrived, and then a rush as though a tap had been turned on and everything in me had given way. At that point I realised that I might bleed to death.

By the last movement, the notes are tearing across my nerve endings like electric currents. My fists clench and my jaw feels as if it is cemented in place. And yet I'm high, flying way above my life. *What happened to this composer? What had he seen or experienced that meant he could make up this crazy stuff?* It rolls on and on and then crashes up into a searing climax that has me gripping the edge of the seat, my knuckles white and my heart pounding. Jesus! At last it's over. How are you meant to get normal again after *that*?

Harry switches off the radio and we drive on in silence. I feel as if I've run a race and I'm bending over with my hands on my knees, gasping for each painful breath. I lift one knee up to hide my face, making myself count to five on the out breath. When my breath comes back into normal range I risk a glance at Harry. But his face is rigid, set in stone. He's somewhere else too, out of reach, holding it all inside.

Slowly, slowly, I relax. Very weird. Terrible as it was, I long to hear it again. I want to keep soaring above my life in that way, swooping and diving over the rocky outcrops, the grey airless space and then back into the dark crevices where no one can touch me.

I take a look back at my sleeping Nellie. Her head has rolled to the other side, the horse drawing on her plump knees about to fall and I want to howl. How perfect she is! Those round pink cheeks, the cherub mouth. Most of her hair is pulled back with a pink scrunchie on the top of her head, but some of her tiny dark curls have escaped; they edge her forehead and around her ears like wisps of the finest wool. A rush of hot fierce love fills my head, spilling into the mad rage that I carry within me constantly. *He will not win.*

I watch the little eyelids flutter softly and then finally open. *I won't let him.* When she sees me looking she smiles and lifts the picture up for my approval.

'Oh, Nellie,' I say, voice thick, leaning over the seat for a closer look. 'It's fantastic! The best one you've done. What is his name?'

'Just Horse,' she sighs.

'What about Sunshine?'

'Hmmm … no.' She shakes her head thoughtfully. 'Just Horse.'

'Can I go for a ride on Horse tonight?'

She shakes her head and puts a hand up over my mouth.

'No! Don't be silly, Mamma!'

'Why not?' I give her a mournful face.

'He hasn't even got a saddle yet!' She giggles quietly. 'When he's got a saddle you can.'

'Quick,' I say as I tickle her foot, 'do the saddle now!'

....

I was taken by ambulance to the emergency department of Lismore General Hospital at two a.m. on a cold Sunday morning, almost dead through loss of blood. I was twenty-one years old and having a miscarriage four months into my second pregnancy.

They insisted I stay for a few weeks. Looking back, I think they must have sensed the situation I would be returning to, and were trying to give me some breathing space. But the pit I'd dug for myself was deeper than any of them could guess, and getting out was going to require more than breathing space. Even so, the weeks in hospital were good for me, because apart from the constant kindness and good humour that surrounded me the whole time I was there, I had time to think. Before the drugs kicked in each night I did quite a bit of thinking.

And there was that one nurse who really helped. She was old, well into her sixties, a dumpy woman with very short grey hair with a lick of dyed silver at the front. But when she opened her mouth the tough, mannish appearance fell away. Her smile was so warm you'd swear she'd been waiting all day to talk to me. She asked politely if she might sit down next to me, and her voice was like honey dripping from a wooden spoon. I quickly eased into its sweetness. I watched her pull up a hard chair and sit squarely on it, her knees apart for comfort, the way a man sits, and for the first time in weeks I felt like smiling.

She went through the preliminaries of introducing herself and then asked how I was feeling. When I said I felt okay she looked down at her sheet, frowning a bit, and then took one of my hands in her own in a matter-of-fact kind of way. Her nails, I noticed, were bitten and torn, and that warmed me to her further, because my own were down to the quick as well.

'We just got you through,' she said softly. 'You realise that, don't you? That you very nearly didn't make it?'

I nodded mutely. She wasn't telling me anything I didn't already know.

She looked at her folder again. 'Are you up for visitors?'

I shook my head.

'That's fine.' She leant in closer until her face was only centimetres away from mine, looking calmly into my eyes, and I felt the well of kindness, the lack of judgement. I tried to smile but I couldn't quite get there. 'And you have a little girl, I see?'

I nodded and then seemed to lose balance, even though I was lying down.

'Three years old?'

'Yes.'

The room began to sway, tilting to the left and then to the right, just as though I was lying in a swing or hammock, but all the time slowly and steadily filling with some kind of black oily stuff that would eventually choke me. It was the pudgy hands I was seeing, the brown legs standing up in the bath, the round moons of her bottom. What if they hadn't got me through? What would have happened to Nellie if I'd died?

After a few more questions the nurse got up. 'Do you mind if I ask a few personal questions?'

'Okay,' I whispered.

'Your partner—' She stopped and looked down at her notes to see that she had the correct name. 'Jason, is it? He seems to think that you have, er … mental health issues?'

I stared at her and said nothing.

'That you suffer violent mood swings. Is that true?'

I opened my mouth to speak, but nothing came out.

'That you become hysterical easily and …'

I couldn't move my face.

'Would you like to be referred to a psychiatrist?' she asked, even more gently.

I shrugged and then shook my head.

The nurse frowned. I could tell that she hadn't made up her mind about me.

'According to him, there's a history of mental illness in your family?'

The surprise must have shown on my face, because she waited for me to speak. The idea of Jay filling her head up with his swampy theories about my family was just … *mind-blowing*. The bolt of indignation that went through me gave me the energy to sit up.

'He doesn't know my family,' I spat hotly.

She nodded thoughtfully and said nothing, but when she reached out and took my hand again, I knew that she was someone I could trust.

'He's referring to my great-grandmother,' I whispered. 'She went crazy, apparently – that's what he's talking about.'

'Oh.' She smiled.

'I was named after her.' For some reason it seemed important to tell her this. 'She was Therese Mary Josephine and so am I.'

'How about I come see you tomorrow and we'll talk?'

I nodded and tried to smile back.

At the door she turned back. 'Such a nice voice you have, Tess. Do you sing?'

'I … I …' I felt myself flushing. 'Not really.'

'A bit?' She laughed at my embarrassment.

'I used to …'

'Not now?'

'No.'

'Why not?'

I almost laughed. *Singing.* I hadn't thought about singing for years. Jay was the one who sang and wrote songs and played the guitar. He was the one who'd devoted eight years of his life to trying to make it in the music business before coming back to live in Byron. I was … I was the one who listened.

'I used to sing along with my father sometimes.' I stopped, too embarrassed to continue. But what I wanted to say was … *He used to tell me that I had a good voice.*

She nodded and smiled as though the idea of my singing with my father really pleased her. 'And you've got such lovely eyes.' She laughed. 'But I suppose you get told that all the time?'

As soft and deep as the evening sky in summer, my mother used to tell me, which was nice when you had no idea where you fitted in. I hope it's true, because the rest of my face is pretty ordinary: a longish nose, thin mouth and freckles.

'You're lucky you've got those eyes,' the woman sighed, as though hearing my thoughts. 'And whatever your partner has to say about it, you're lucky to have been named after your great-grandmother. Lucky to have her in your life as well.'

'My great-grandmother is … dead.' I tried to sound dry and ironic.

'Well, yes. But she is … waiting for you.'

'Waiting for *me*?'

'Waiting for you to claim her. Give back her life. Make her live again.'

I stared at the woman. *What the fuck was she saying?*

But my spirits lifted anyway. Maybe I hadn't dreamt it. Maybe my great-grandmother had stood by me and helped pull me through.

'I'll be back tomorrow.' The nurse smiled. 'Goodbye for now.'

'Goodbye,' I said. 'Thank you.'

nine

Outside the car, the day is brighter than ever. Probably hot now. I shift about in my seat. I need to drink some water. Nellie probably does too.

'You liked it?' Harry eventually asks. 'The music?'

'Like isn't the word,' I sigh.

He throws me a quizzical look. 'So what is the word?'

'Jail. It's like being locked up with a madman howling in the next cell.'

Harry erupts into laughter, and I smile, pleased to have made him laugh but a bit unnerved too. I wasn't trying to be funny.

The lovely green country outside has made its way into the car and into my head. The sign tells me that it's thirty-nine kilometres to Gunnedah, but I have no idea what kind of place it might be. I reach back an arm and stroke Nellie's leg, then shut my eyes and lean my head against the window.

'It must have taken ages to learn it?' I say awkwardly.

'Yeah,' he mutters. 'It did.'

'I spy with my little eye … something red,' Nellie pipes up from the back seat.

Harry immediately joins in the game, and he lets her win. Nellie is delighted.

We stop for petrol and to get a drink and go to the toilet. We pull the rest of the sandwiches from the boot and eat them as we travel along.

When the sandwiches are finished and the juice drunk, Nellie suddenly seems to understand that the trip isn't going to be over any time soon, and she spits the dummy.

'No!' she yells at me. 'I want to go home!'

I try to placate her by easing Barry into her arms, but she hits at me angrily.

'We can't go home, babe.'

'Why not?'

'We're going to see your auntie.'

'I've got aunties at home.'

'I know, but this is a different one.'

'When will we get there?' she bawls. *'When?'*

'In a while.'

'I want another drink.'

Harry sings her a funny song about grasshoppers, but she listens for half a minute and then puts her hands over her ears and shrieks, 'Shut up!' Then she starts trying squirm out of her seat.

'We'll be there soon, Nellie,' I say, trying to be soothing but feeling wretched and tense. 'You'll see your auntie.'

'Will Streak be there?' she says in a small voice. 'Streak is my dog.'

'No,' I sigh.

'But there might be another dog,' Harry offers helpfully.

'What is the other dog's name?' Nellie screams, kicking her feet hard into the front seat.

Harry has to think a moment. 'Hmmm … could be Flash,' he offers.

'Flash is a *stupid* name,' Nellie shouts, and pulls off one of her boots and chucks it straight at the back of Harry's head.

'Ouch!' He ducks, and the car swerves, almost ramming a passing truck.

'Hey, cut it out!' I say, leaning backwards. 'Harry is trying to drive!'

'But he's annoying me!' she screams. 'I hate him.'

I make soothing noises and pat her leg from the front seat, but she just gets louder.

'I've got lollies,' Harry declares suddenly, and Nellie's sobs quickly subside. Her bottom lip is turned down and her little face is grubby.

Harry leans over to the glovebox and fumbles around, eventually pulling out a small packet of red jubes that he presses into her hand. 'These are magic,' he adds for good measure.

'What kind of magic?' she says, stuffing three small red jubes into her mouth at once. She is almost never allowed sweets at home.

'You'll see,' Harry tells her mysteriously. 'Start sucking and you'll see.'

This works until there are none left and she starts up again.

'I want to go home ... Where is Daddy? ... I want to see Bennie and Will and ... Nana.'

She is really scraping the barrel. Nana is not a favourite with anyone. Her sons more or less hate her, even as they grovel for her approval. Nellie's whining makes me nervy all over again. Say we do make it to safety, what am I going to tell her when we get there? And what do I say to Beth?

We stop at the next truck siding and let her get out for a bit, and when we get in again I sit with her in the back. Eventually Nellie's crankiness wears itself out. After about an hour she grows quiet and falls into an unhappy sleep.

The afternoon passes and the kilometres slide away beneath us. I stop looking back to see if we're being followed. The wide flat land stretches in front and behind with few cars. I fall asleep again.

I wake to see that the light is fading. It's now late afternoon. The strain on Harry's eye must be bad.

'Sorry I can't help with the driving,' I say when I see him yawning.

'Can you drive at all?'

'Yeah. But I haven't got a licence.' Some of the oncoming vehicles have turned on their lights. Nellie is still asleep.

'I'll be okay,' he mutters. 'We'll stop at the next town. Find a service station, take a piss and wash my face.'

'Okay.' I start to breathe easy again.

....

Jay's apartment was out of town a bit and he didn't take me there often. He resented that he couldn't stay at my flat, but I stuck to the conditions that I'd agreed to with Duncan. When Jay demanded that I give him a key, I refused point blank and he didn't contact me for a couple of days. But even though I was worried sick I held firm. I loved that little flat and I relished the privacy.

One night I woke to hear someone outside trying to get in. Before I could get up and put on my dressing-gown the door was open and there was Jay, smiling at me.

'Hi, babe.'

'How did you get in?'

He held up a shiny blue key and smiled.

'Did Duncan give it to you?' I whispered stupidly, still half-asleep although my heart was racing.

'Don't look so worried.' He came over and took my chin in his hands. 'I made my own copy.'

'From mine?'

'Yes.'

'But ...' I wanted to tell him that he had no right. 'You frightened me.'

'I thought it would be better than ringing.' He was already pulling off his shoes and shirt. 'Come on. I'll be gone before they're up.'

I stood there by the window. 'When did you take my key, Jay?'

'Never mind.'

'Well, I do mind.'

He walked towards me. When he stood straight in front of me I had to really concentrate on holding my ground. But he just walked straight past, sat down at the table and lit a cigarette.

'Am I generous to you?' he asked, without looking at me.

I gulped, feeling the heat rise in my face.

'Do you ever have to pay for anything?'

'No,' I floundered. 'But I thought … you were happy … to do that.' He insisted on paying for everything. I can't say that I didn't enjoy that, because I did, and I was ashamed that I'd come to expect it.

'I am happy!' he said sharply. 'But I can't believe after all I've done for you, all those dinners and drinks and the clothes and the rest of it, that you won't give a little back.'

I felt sick. There was no question that I'd enjoyed all those things. But I was my mother's daughter, and I still had some fight left in me. 'I wasn't aware that paying for my drinks gave you *access rights*,' I said coldly.

There was silence for a breath or two. I stared at him, refusing to give in.

He burst out laughing. 'You kill me, baby!' He got up and grabbed me into a tight hug, breathing into my hair, laughing into my neck. 'I love the way you talk. And I like your pride. But in the end I'm your man, right?'

I said nothing.

He pulled away a bit and made me look at him. 'Right?' he said again.

'Yes.'

'So I have some rights, don't I?' He looked down at me. 'Yes?'

'Yes, but—'

'I'm not planning on staying here every night. Only when I've been out late and I'm too pissed to drive back home. Is that too much to ask?'

'But you've got your own place!' I protested. 'And what about the deal I had with Duncan and Amy?'

'Duncan is … *nobody*,' he whispered hoarsely in my ear. 'As for her!'

'Amy?' I said in alarm.

'Neither of them like me.'

'They've never said they don't like you.'

'So what's the key all about, then?'

'I've told you!' I was nearly crying. 'I get very cheap rent in return for no visitors. She is here every day with her kids. They don't want strangers staying!'

'Believe me, I'm no stranger to her.' He had a smirk on his face.

'*What?*'

'Let's just say she liked the odd visitor or two.'

I gulped and thought of the Amy I knew, the blonde, pretty, plump mother of those lovely kids. She was so kind to me. Sometimes I'd get a knock on the door and she'd offer me a piece of pie or cake that she'd made. She had a shy, sweet aura about her. A few times when she saw me sitting outside reading she'd come over and we'd talk about books and films we liked. We were slowly becoming friends, in spite of the age difference. I couldn't believe what he was saying about her.

'When did you … know her?'

'When she was about eighteen,' he laughed. 'Such a little slut.'

'Don't use that word!' I snapped before I could think.

He stepped back in mock surprise and then laughed coldly. 'Are you telling me what words I can use?'

'Please don't.' I was close to tears. 'I really like her.'

'You don't know her!' He put one hand under my chin and made me look at him. 'You've been here about two months, right?' I nodded. 'Well, I was born here. There is a lot you don't know about this town.'

'Okay,' I said. 'But they're good to me.'

He shrugged as though that was of no consequence and pushed my hair back from my face. 'So am I.'

I said nothing, but tears were spilling out of the corners of my eyes.

'I'm good to you, yeah?'

'Yes,' I whisper.

'Say it, Tess.'

'You're good to me.'

He fell down on the bed and lay there looking at me. I wanted to ask why he insisted on rubbishing the three people I really liked in the town, but I didn't know how to say it without him getting angry.

'Tess?'

'Yes?'

'You're a lovely girl.'

And when he held out both arms for me, I went into them eagerly.

....

When we reach the outskirts of Dubbo, Harry decides that he's had enough.

'Going to have to stop here,' he says.

Initially I think he means another toilet break, but no, he's turning off into a big modern motel. The vacancy sign is flashing in the early evening darkness, just like the panic lights in my head.

'But we've got to keep going,' I say, trying to keep the desperation out of my voice.

'I can't.'

'It would be crazy to stop now!' I add desperately.

'Can you drive?'

'No.'

'I've only got one eye.' He sighs and then he looks at his watch. 'We've been on the road now for over twelve hours. I've got to rest.'

I look around wildly. I'm convinced that Jay has the make and registration number of our car. Harry sees the consternation on my face, but he shrugs and gets out of the car anyway. Nellie wakes up and starts whining but I leave her to it, get out of the car and follow him. 'Harry?' I call after him. 'Please!'

He turns around and comes back a couple of steps. 'What?'

I cross my arms over my chest and try to sound reasonable, but I'm close to hysterical and I think he can tell. 'You don't seem to realise.'

'What don't I realise?'

I wave back towards the highway, then at the car with the tired, cross three-year-old squirming around in her seat, looking out furiously at the both of us.

'What he'll do when … when he catches us.'

Harry walks back and puts both elbows on the roof of the car and covers his face with his hands.

'No one is following us.'

'How do you know that?' I yell.

'I don't, but—'

'Please, Harry, can we just keep going?'

'I can't,' he says simply. 'My leg is killing me and I'm starting to see double. It's too dangerous.'

'You don't even have a fucking leg!' I shout. It's out before I even think. He stares at me for a moment, letting what I've said just hang there in the evening air between us.

'It still hurts.' He turns his back.

'Sorry … but I … I'm just … We can't. Not now!' I watch him head for the office, wondering how I could have said such an ugly stupid thing. Behind me Nellie is screaming blue murder and beating on the window.

At the door he turns. 'Why don't you get her out of the car? She needs a stretch.'

I walk back to the car and open the door. Nellie is beside herself, trying to get out of the seat, making it impossible for me to undo the straps. She slaps me hard on the nose with one of her hot little hands. It really hurts.

'Mummy the moron!' she snarls. 'Shit for brains!'

I recoil in shock. It comes back so clearly that I feel like I'm still there. I see her kneeling by the low table concentrating on her drawing, Barry propped up next to her. *Your mummy has got shit for brains, kiddo* … he said lightly, ruffling her hair. She never looked at him when he said that kind of thing, but went on with her drawing with extra concentration.

At last I have her out of her seat. She stands with one hand on my leg, crying and kicking me half-heartedly.

'Come on, stop it!' I gasp, squatting down to pick her up. But she won't have a bar of me.

'I want to go home! I want Streak,' she shrieks.

'Take my hand, sweetheart.'

'No!' She squirms away from me. But when she spies Harry through the glass door of the office the tantrum suddenly stops. I watch her running over, thinking how small she is, in her little red boots and tiny black jacket. A spasm of guilt coils around my guts, almost winding me. All the stuff she saw and heard. Why did I wait so long to leave? I should have gone well before … this. *I should have … I should have …*

He picked out a tune on the guitar once, wrote a few lines and got Nellie to join in.

Mummy the moron has no brains
Mind like a sieve and voice like a drain …

If my deep voice was what first attracted Jay to me, it was soon what seemed to rile him most. He was forever teasing me about *talking posh. Sounds like you had a bucket of gravel for breakfast.*

Nellie would sometimes look between us and frown, as though trying to understand what was going on. Maybe half an hour would go by after one of his sneering attacks before she'd come and sit on my knee. *Good, Mamma,* she'd whisper in my ear, wiping away my tears with her hands, and we'd smile at each other. *Good girl,* she'd whisper, twisting my hair around her little fingers. She is three years old! She shouldn't have had to hear that stuff or learn to play those games.

I walk over to the glass door, open it and follow her inside. Harry is handing over his credit card and filling in a form.

'You want your own room?' he says, turning to me.

'How much does it cost?'

'Two hundred.'

I pull Nellie roughly away from messing up the brochures on the table. 'That will clean me out,' I say shortly. 'Okay if Nellie and I sleep in the car?'

'I don't want to sleep in the car!' Nellie's face is pinched with fury. '*You* sleep in the car! Me and Barry are going home.'

'What about a family room?' Harry asks. 'There's one with two double beds and a single.'

I hesitate, uncomfortable with the idea.

The sour-faced woman is looking from one to the other of us. 'But I don't have a cot,' she snaps.

'I don't need a cot,' Nellie screams up at her. That's when I decide. Anything would be better than Nellie and me trying to sleep in the car.

Harry picks up Nellie and gives her a couple of brochures from the top of the desk. 'She's okay in a bed,' he tells the woman mildly.

Like he knows.

'There's a rubber underlay in the wardrobe,' the woman says sharply. 'I'd appreciate you using it.'

I nod. Nellie doesn't wet the bed, but I'm too freaked out to bother telling the old bat. The woman gives Harry the key and tells him where to park the car.

We walk out again and Harry turns to me. 'The room is down that end of the building.' He points, and then grins suddenly as though it's all a bit of a joke. 'We'll be able to make a fast getaway if we have to.'

I nod, gulping down the rush of fury that rises in my throat. None of this is real for him. Not serious at all. He has no idea. *And why should it be real to him, Tess? It isn't his business, is it? He is a kind stranger doing you a good turn and you'd have to be pretty stupid to forget that. Pull your fucking head in. Be thankful for what you can get.*

The room is huge, with three beds. It's clean and warm. The heavy lock and chain on the door are comforting. Nellie rushes around looking at everything.

'Bags this one.' Harry dumps himself flat down on the nearest of the big beds, closes his eyes and pretends to snore really loudly. Nellie giggles. I go and lie on the other bed and she races to sit on my belly.

'What about our toothbrushes?' she whispers in my ear.

I open my eyes and smile at her beautiful little face looking down at me. I push her hair back with my hands and feel in my pocket for a hair elastic.

As I'm collecting her hair up, she turns to Harry. 'Me and Mamma have got long black hair,' she tells him importantly, as if it's a special piece of information. 'Like witches.'

'I can see that!' Harry says from his bed. 'And you've both got pointy chins, too. Like witches.'

Nellie and I grin at each other.

'But the thing I really want to know is ...' Harry beats a drum roll on his chest from where he's lying.

Nellie jumps off me to watch him, completely enthralled by his antics.

'I want to know ...' Harry is playing it for all it's worth. 'WHERE ARE YOUR BROOMSTICKS?'

Nellie squeals with laughter and I have to too. It so lifts my spirits to see her laughing. Some of the chilliness inside me melts, and I have a moment of feeling oddly safe in this room with the fake velvet curtains and the huge television and that bundle of energy prancing around on her pretend broomstick. *I can do this. I have to ... I will not fall apart. I will get her there safely, and then ...*

'I'll go get our bag from the car,' I say, sitting up.

'Don't forget Barry,' Nellie orders.

I pick her up and she nuzzles into my neck. 'As though I would, baby girl,' I say softly, rubbing my nose against hers. 'As though any of us would ever forget Barry.'

'Because he's a special bear, isn't he, Mamma?' she says softly, her hands kneading my ears. 'And he knows a lot.'

'He *is* a very special bear and he knows heaps.'

When I look up Harry is sitting on the edge of his bed looking at us. 'I'll get the bags,' he says quietly.

Nellie runs outside after him and I take a peek at the ultra-clean bathroom. I use the toilet and then think about having a shower.

Nellie rushes back in, holding Barry in one hand and her rug in another. 'He was *sooo* lonely out there!' she yells accusingly.

'But he's okay now, isn't he?' I say tiredly.

'He's missing Daddy.'

'Is he?'

She pops the bear up onto Harry's bed, pulls down the bedspread and then settles him under the sheet. 'Poor guy is all tuckered out,' she mutters as she pulls the sheet up to the bear's nose, and in spite of everything I find myself laughing, because it's what I say to her sometimes. *Hey there, Nellie Bellie. You all tuckered out?*

'But maybe Harry doesn't want to sleep with Barry,' I suggest, taking a look at Harry.

'Bears are okay.' Harry dumps my backpack at the end of my bed. 'It's just witches that scare me.'

Nellie and I look at each other and giggle. 'Okay!'

We collapse again on our beds as Nellie explores her new surroundings. She opens and closes drawers and cupboards, peering inside. It isn't long before she discovers the bar fridge under the bench. She pulls out the small bottles of liquor and lines them up under the mirror and then brings Barry over to show him.

'Which one are we going to drink first?' She turns to me.

'None of them,' I tell her. 'Put them back. Those are grown-up drinks.'

'I want the blue one.' She holds up a mini bottle of liqueur.

'No.' I'm yawning now.

'What about Barry?'

'No.'

She gives a theatrical sigh, picks up Barry and takes him into the bathroom. 'And this is the bathroom.' We hear her bossy voice. 'But you can't use it.'

I look over at Harry and we risk a smile at each other.

'Why can't he use it?' Harry calls out.

Nellie pokes her head back out, frowning. 'Because Barry's not a human bean!' she says impatiently, as though Harry has asked the most stupid question in the world.

Harry cracks up laughing and falls back on the bed. 'God, she is such a *great* kid!' he says, rubbing his eyes.

The remark winds me, in an odd kind of way. It's all I can do not to burst into tears. So I just nod and bite my lip and look away, and tell myself to take heart. Apart from coming across Travis, this day has been filled with good luck. Thanks to this guy, this incredibly kind stranger, I'm safe in this room with my daughter. My sister has agreed to have us to stay, and there is a car outside, which, if we survive the night, will take us back to my family. Okay, I'm going to have to eat a lot of humble pie when I get there. Beth will be so … *Beth*. Sharp and judgemental and bossy; she never held back saying what she thought. And Salome will be difficult in her own way, no doubt, but it's the best chance I've got. And that lock on the motel door looks heavy enough and … I have a clean bed to fall into.

'Who does she take after?' Harry asks.

'I dunno,' I say quickly. 'People say she looks like me.'

'She does.'

'But she is tall for her age,' I go on. 'Jay is tall.'

'I really meant her personality.'

'Ah.' I smile and shrug. 'That is harder to say.'

'I guess so.'

The truth is, Nellie is like neither Jay nor me. She's cheerful and loud and seems to have none of my shyness and awkwardness, and none of Jay's dark moodiness either.

I remember standing by the window a few months ago. She'd just turned three and was playing outside with her cousins. Jay came up behind me and we stood together watching her. The three boy cousins were all older than her, and yet Nellie was organising them, lining them up and giving roles to them all.

'Over this way!' Her shout came through the window to us.

Jay put one hand on my shoulder. 'Where did she come from?' he said, real pride in his voice.

I shrugged and turned to smile at him. 'No idea.' We both turned back to watch.

The three little boys were lined up and saluting. Jay began to laugh. Outside, the drizzle was making green leaves drip with water. The boys had their coats and rubber boots on, but Nellie had taken hers off. She was careering around in a T-shirt and trackpants and bare feet.

'Do you think she's normal?' he suddenly asked, frowning. 'I mean, she's ...'

What? I turned to look at him. *She's what?* Three minutes earlier, I'd been in the bathroom checking out the massive bruise running all the way down from my hip to my knee where he'd thrown me up against the wall a couple of nights before. *What is normal?* I wanted to scream at him. *You tell me.*

ten

Harry and I lie back for a bit on our separate beds and listen to the radio that Nellie has discovered on the bench under the telly.

'Was the baby his idea or yours?' he asks.

'His,' I say shortly.

'He's older than you?'

'I was seventeen and he was twenty-seven when we met.'

'Jeez.'

Jay said a baby would cement us. Settle us down. Who was I to say that it wouldn't? Right from the start I saw that he was a jerky, dissatisfied kind of person. But so was I. He told me that meant we were soul mates, and I agreed. I honestly thought we were meant for each other.

'Three sons, Tess,' he said in the car on the way home from the clinic when I first found out I was pregnant. 'At least!' Nudging me in the ribs, as if we were on this great big fun adventure together.

I was so sick those first few months, vomiting all the time, and by this point a good bit of the gloss had worn off being with him too, but I smiled back. By the time she was born we'd moved from his apartment out to the cottage down the hill from his mother's place to save money, and that's when things started to go seriously wrong.

....

Eventually, Harry pulls himself off the bed.

'I'm going out to ring Jules,' he tells me. 'And get something for us to eat.'

I try to ignore the fresh pulse of anxiety that begins immediately behind my right eye. There was milk left in the carton and a half of the egg sandwich that I've kept for Nellie. A couple of packets of motel sweet biscuits with a cup of tea will do me fine.

'You guys hungry?'

'No.' I shake my head too emphatically.

'Barry and I are starving,' Nellie declares without looking at him.

Harry grins and gives her a mock salute. 'I'll take that as a yes!'

'Listen, she's not hungry,' I cut in sharply. 'There is that sandwich left.'

'I am so!' she protests. 'And so is Barry. And we don't like sandwiches.'

I don't bother reminding her that she ate two egg sandwiches with great gusto earlier in the day.

The truth is that I don't want to be left here in this room alone. What if Travis is onto us already? What if he's traced the numberplate? I want to ask Harry if it's possible to do that, but I know it will make me seem paranoid. 'There is also an apple … And really, she'll be asleep soon.'

'I'll get her something.' He looks at me. 'What about you?'

'Well …' I reach for my wallet to hide the fact that I'm panicking, but he waves it aside.

Something about my inner state must tell on my face, because he feels in his pocket for his keys and turns back.

'See the phone?' He points at it on the bench between the beds. 'Any trouble, ring reception. And lock the door when I go out. Pull the chain across.'

'Okay.'

'I won't be long,' he says. 'You'll be right.'

For the first ten minutes I sit tight, nervously watching Nellie messing around with Barry. Then I get up and stand by the window. Every now and again I push the filmy white curtain aside and peer out. There are only two other cars in the car park and one or two people walking in and out of their rooms. I try to think realistically about what Travis might have told Jay by now. For sure he will have the make and colour of the car. The registration is another matter. Travis being the thickest of the three brothers, there is a good chance that he might not have caught it in time.

'I want to watch telly now.' Nellie picks up the remote and waves it at me. Every nerve inside me is on stand-by and I certainly don't want more noise, so I shake my head and try to take it from her. But she squirms away and presses the red button.

'Nellie,' I shout.

The thing hisses to life with some loud talk show with canned laughter. I stand there, watching her little fingers flicking across the numbers on the remote. I have to step back and hold on to myself, because I am at the point of grabbing the thing from her, slapping her even. The noise continues and I break. Almost.

'Not now, Nellie!' I wrench the remote from her.

'Yes!'

'There is nothing for kids now,' I hiss, holding it out of reach.

'Yes, there is!' she screams, jumping up, trying to take it from my hand. 'Give it to me!'

I turn the volume right down, throw the thing on the bed opposite, and collapse facedown on mine. *I won't do that. I don't … I … I won't do that.* Otherwise all this is for nothing. Everything is lost. Jay will have won.

She picks it up and begins to press one button after another and then lo and behold *Peppa Pig* is on. She runs over to me with the sweetest smile. 'Can we turn it up just a tiny weeny bit, Mamma?'

I melt and do as she asks.

'See,' she says triumphantly, sitting on the floor to watch. 'I told you.'

'How did you know?'

'I just did.'

'You're so smart.' I ruffle her hair before collapsing back on the bed. *Shit! What was I thinking? Why would I deny her Peppa Pig after a day in the car?*

It's not long before I see Harry's car pulling up outside. The car door slams and then he knocks.

'Harry!' he yells. 'And I come bearing gifts.'

Nellie looks up from the floor. 'Is that Harry?' she asks.

'Yes.'

'Is he our friend?' she asks.

I crawl off the bed onto the floor, pull her onto my knees, and put my arms around her, trying at the same time to block out the dark fear racing around my head. 'Yes,' I whisper into her hair.

'But does Daddy like him?' she asks softly.

Harry knocks on the door and I get up to unlock it for him.

'Is he Daddy's friend too?' Nellie persists, standing up now and searching my face for answers. But I ignore her.

Harry has five boxes of food and some cans of drink, all of which delight Nellie enormously. 'Are we allowed to have some?' she asks me anxiously.

'I think so.'

'Beer?' Harry throws me a small brown bottle before I can refuse.

I stare at it and then look at him and then at the two cans of orange and lemon.

'Better have the soft drink.'

'Why?'

'I haven't drunk alcohol for years.'

'Suit yourself.' He hands over a can of orange. 'Listen, it's still mild enough to sit outside on the lawn. Otherwise all this is going to stink the room out. There are tables and chairs and …' He looks at Nellie. 'Guess what?'

'What?' she laughs breathlessly, waiting for the big surprise.

'Swings and a slide!'

Her face breaks into a wide smile, and, squealing with delight, she runs for the door.

So that's what we do. We sit out on the white plastic tables in the fading light watching Nellie making two new friends. One is a boy her age, and the other looks to be his sister, who is a bit older. The three of them are climbing up the kids' slide, happily calling out to each other.

'Watch me!'

'Here I come.'

Harry pushes the food towards me, smiling. 'Get into it.'

I take off the lids and position them in the middle. He dives into the plastic bag for serviettes and spoons.

Nellie runs back from the swings every now and again to grab some food. Jay has strict rules about her sitting down at the table while we eat, and I'm getting a weird sort of kick out of letting her do what she wants.

'Barry loves it here,' Nellie yells from the top of the slide.

'That's good.'

'How long are we going to stay?'

'Just tonight.'

'Then are we going home?'

'Not yet.'

'Soon?' She doesn't wait for my reply, but folds both arms across her chest and takes off down the slide.

'I think I will have a beer,' I say suddenly. Anything to calm me down. With no warning at all, my heart has begun to race. These moments hit when I least expect them. It's as though I'm watching myself from above. I'm a bird in a cage, flapping about uselessly, completely trapped with no way out. This time I manage to hold it in and gradually the panic subsides.

Harry hands me a bottle of beer. I watch him cracking open another one for himself with his damaged hand. He takes a long gulp.

'Was he abusive?' Harry picks up his chopsticks and hoes into the food. 'Physically, I mean?'

I shrug and try to smile without opening my eyes. It doesn't seem right to bring up terrible things so I sit back and close my eyes and listen to the children. The warmth of the dying afternoon sun on my face is so nice.

'I'll take that as a yes,' Harry mutters grimly. 'But you stayed anyway?'

'Yeah, I stayed.'

'Why?'

'I'd burnt my bridges by then.'

'Why didn't you go back to your family?'

'Well … that's a long story.'

Harry looks at his watch. 'Do I look like I'm going anywhere?'

That makes me laugh. 'It's sort of embarrassing to talk about,' I say.

'Most stuff is sort of embarrassing to talk about,' he says dryly. He gets up and goes over to push Nellie on the swing.

I drink the whole bottle of beer, and I have to say it makes me feel a lot better. When Harry comes back from the swings, I end up telling him a bit about Jay and he listens without much comment.

'Tell me about you and Jules,' I say. 'When did you meet?'

'The first day at university,' he said. 'We were both eighteen and we just fell for each other straight off.'

'Yeah?'

'I had two legs then.' He laughs in his open, easy way.

'You reckon she'd have gone for you if you'd been legless?'

'Ah … now that is a question!'

'Jules is so beautiful,' I murmur. 'She should be a model or something.'

'Yeah,' he smiles ruefully.

'Is it a problem?' I ask stupidly.

'How could it be a problem?' He looks away.

'You ring her before?' I ask.

'Yeah. She sends her love and says stay strong. She also reckons you've the most beautiful eyes she's ever seen.' He laughs.

I flush a bit, thinking of Harry and his stunning girlfriend discussing me. 'Yeah?'

'Oh yeah, and she also reckons that if that guy comes after you we should kill him.'

I look up to see if he's joking. But he is looking at me steadily with his one soft light-brown eye.

'I don't think so,' I say quietly.

'Why not?'

How can I tell this kind stranger that if anyone is going to die in this stupid little drama, it will be me? Can't he see that? It's as clear as night and day. People like Jay never die.

'I picked Jules as a bit of a hippie,' I say to divert the intensity a bit, and at the same time avoid remembering the fantasies I used to have of killing Jay myself. Terrible fantasies that eased some of what I was carrying around inside. I would imagine smashing his skull in with an axe as he slept. Or getting my hands on some heavy drugs. Once he was out to it, I would drag him out to the car and put a pipe from the exhaust into the window. With a bit of luck it would be written off as suicide. 'I thought she would be all for peace and love and that kind of thing.'

'No, that's me.' He grins. 'I'm the peace-loving one. You got us mixed up. Jules is the fighter.'

'I can't imagine it!'

'You'd better believe it.'

'Wow.'

Right on cue his phone rings.

'Hey, Jules.' Harry turns away to take the call. 'I was just in the middle of telling Tess what a dangerous, violent person you are.'

'I don't like you working there. If you want a job, why not the club?'

'I like my job.'

'Duncan is a moron.'

'He's not.'

'You like him, do you?'

'Yes, I do like him ...' I said nervously.

'He's hot for you, Tess.' Jay's voice was light, but I always knew that when his eyes narrowed he was deadly serious. 'I've seen him looking at you.'

'No!' I'm incredulous. This was *so* not the case that it was almost funny. But not quite ... Initially I was flattered that he was jealous of other men looking at me, but before long it was a big drag. I had to second-guess him and watch myself around guys of any kind.

'I see what I see, babe.'

'But Jay, you imagine it.'

A few days later when he told me he'd be away a couple of nights on business I was secretly relieved. Things had got so tense between us that I thought a break might be good for both of us.

I worked a double shift the first day, and then when Lily asked me to go to the beach with her and a few friends the next day I agreed. They were all older than me, but really nice. There was Lily's boyfriend Ray, Ray's sister Melanie and her husband,

and a couple of other guys. It was the most perfect Byron day ever, hot and bright, the sea as clear as green glass. My fair skin made me wary of the afternoon sun, but I slathered on the sunblock and allowed myself a few hours in the water in the new bikini I'd bought on a whim that morning. One of the guys taught me how to bodysurf and I loved it. Once back on the sand, I donned my wide-brimmed hat, long-sleeved shirt and beach pants. We played beach cricket and then went back to Melanie and Roger's place for drinks and dinner on her balcony.

It was easily the best day I'd had in ages, although admitting that to myself made me feel guilty. I hadn't missed Jay one little bit. I didn't get home until nearly midnight. The sun and the swimming and the wine and food had wiped me out, so when I slipped the key into my door, I was privately glad that I had another night on my own. What did that mean?

He was there waiting for me. Lying on my bed in the dark. I couldn't hide my dismay when I switched the light on.

'What are you doing here?' I blurted out.

He smiled.

'You said you were going to be away.'

'Have I upset your plans?' he said lightly, but there was such coldness underneath.

I said nothing and flounced into the shower. I felt so grimy and tired and totally pissed off. I slapped on moisturiser, praying that he might have left while I was in the shower. No such luck. I came out into the room, my hair up in a towel, and he was in exactly the same position.

'So, what's wrong?' I said, beginning to rub my hair dry.

'I don't know, Tess,' he smirked. 'You tell me.'

I said nothing but sat at the end of the bed and continued drying my hair.

'How was the beach?'

I stared at him in astonishment. 'Have you been spying on me?'

'I came home early and went looking for you.'

'So why didn't you come say hello when you found me on the beach?'

'I didn't think I'd be welcome.'

I looked at him then, thinking that it was probably true. He wouldn't have been welcome with all those people. Whenever Lily heard his name her expression tightened into one of distaste. So I'd stopped talking about him.

'Who were those guys?'

'Lil's friends.'

'You seemed to get on well with them.' So calm and measured, pretending to be light about it, but I could sense the anger and accusation underneath.

'Yes. I got on well with them.'

'I saw them looking at you.'

'Can we talk about this in the morning?' I was nearly crying with exhaustion. The sun and the few drinks and the fun had left me totally depleted, and I had to be up for another full day at work.

'I thought you didn't go to the beach in the heat of the day,' he said, ignoring the question.

'I wanted to go,' I said loudly. 'Is that so wrong?'

'And you bought a new bikini for the occasion?'

'If you don't trust me, then let's—'

'Let's what?'

I stared at him. Right at that moment he seemed so much older than me, and for the first time ever that was a real turn-off. I didn't understand how things had got to this point, but I realised that I was totally miserable. He was on another planet and I couldn't get my head around where he was coming from. Not only that, I was sick of trying. I looked at my watch and actually thought of going out and knocking on Amy and Duncan's door. I'd tell them that Jay was there against my express wishes, and I felt quite confident that they'd understand.

But Jay could read me so well. He had sensed me switch off, felt my retreat, and he didn't like it one bit, so he changed tactics. It was that simple for him. Suddenly all smiles, relaxed and warm, he held out both arms.

'Come here,' he said, all eager and sweet.

'Jay, we need to talk about all this.'

'I thought you wanted to wait until the morning?'

I sighed and went over to him and let him hug me. I knew that I wasn't going to get rid of him that night and that I had to be up in the morning, and so I gave way.

'You're my blue-eyed angel,' he whispered, running his fingers through my hair. 'We're so right for each other, eh?'

I was too tired to disagree.

eleven

Nellie's new friends have been called inside. There is another boy out now, younger than her. Above us, the sky is brilliant streaks of pink and gold. I feel tipsy. Harry is cleaning up the plastic food containers, stacking them inside each other. The three messed-up fingers on his left hand poke up awkwardly, like an old person with arthritis. I wonder if they were burnt.

'What was it like, knowing that you'd never play music again?' I ask shyly.

He looks up quickly. But right at that moment Nellie rushes over to me. 'His name is Jake,' she whispers.

'Good name,' I smile.

'You want more to eat?' Harry asks her.

She shakes her head and goes back over to the swings. I feel vaguely embarrassed. What right do I have to ask questions when I've been so reticent myself through most of the day?

'Pretty bad,' he says, lighting up his smoke. 'I never used to smoke before. It hit the people around me too.'

'Your mum and dad?'

'And Jules.'

'How so?'

'When we met, we were both … at the top of our game.'

'And now?'

He shrugs, pats his fake leg and grins.

'What does she do?'

'She's studying law, but really it's the photographic work that is exciting to her. She keeps being asked to model for this and that. She refuses most of it, but …'

'Why does she refuse?'

'Because up to now she's thought of herself as becoming a human rights lawyer! I reckon it's only a matter of time before she gives up uni.'

'You think she should be a model?'

'She should be whatever she wants to be. She's beautiful. Why not?' He speaks quite cheerfully, but I can feel underlying tension. 'She's also a talented musician.' He laughs at his own boasting. The pride and warmth in his voice is real, though. 'Anything she turns her hand to, really.'

'God,' I sigh. A lawyer, a model *and* a musician! I try to imagine being that clever, beautiful and talented. 'What instrument does she play?'

'Piano.'

'Well, she seems a lovely person too,' I mumble, seeing again that face and the lovely openness of her smile.

'She is.'

I'm not sure how to follow on from this, so I stare over at Nellie on the swing. 'What job do you have in mind now, Harry?'

'I dunno.'

'Teaching?' I suggest, thinking of the music teacher at my school. Everyone loved her. I joined the choir just to be taught by Mrs Hopkins.

'Yeah.' He takes a deep drag on his cigarette.

'Is that so bad?'

'Just thinking of it makes me want to cut my wrists,' he grins.

'My dad was a teacher!' I protest.

'Was he?'

'Maths and science.'

'High school?'

I nodded.

'So did he teach you?'

'He taught my brother and sisters but I was too young.'

We are both quiet and I am aware of the soft rushing sound of water.

'The Macquarie River,' he murmurs. 'We could go have a proper look at it in the morning before we head off.'

'Okay,' I say.

The drink has gone to my head. I've stopped panicking and I don't even know where I am exactly. So much has happened. The day has been huge.

'You reckon we'll be able to pull Nellie away from the swings?' Harry cuts in on my thoughts. 'Because I'm totally wrecked. I'd like to hit the sack, get up for an early start.'

'Sure.' I scramble up and go to retrieve Nellie. It takes a while to convince her to come in, and involves all sorts of bribes about what kind of breakfast she can have in the morning. When I tell her about the little individual packets of rice bubbles she gives in.

'I can't wait for breakfast,' she tells me happily on the way back to the room. 'I don't have to share, do I?'

'Well ...' I grin at her.

'What if Harry tries to get some of mine?'

'We'll tie him up!'

Nellie giggles and rushes in to tell him.

Harry has already had a shower and is in bed reading a thick, battered book. His prosthetic leg is propped up next to the bed.

'I'll get her to the toilet,' I say. 'Then we can turn the light off.'

'Take your time.'

On her way to the bathroom, Nellie spies the leg. She goes to give it the once-over, frowning as she looks from Harry to the leg and then back again.

'That's my leg,' he tells her quietly. 'Helps me walk.'

'Did ... the real one fall off?'

'It had to be cut off. I was in an accident.'

'Who cut it off?'

'The doctor.'

'Did it hurt?' She touches the leg tentatively with one small finger.

'Not too much but … a bit.'

'Is it hurting now?'

'A bit, but I've put some ointment on it.'

'Your hand is all messed up too.' She leans out and touches his wrecked fingers. 'And one of your eyes has gone funny.'

'It was a bad accident.'

'Did you fall off the roof?'

He chuckles, reaches out and pats her head. 'No … I fell off a bike.'

'Oh.' Her eyes are like saucers.

'Come on, Nell,' I say, embarrassed by her questions. 'Quick.'

'Does the leg need a rest?'

'Yep.'

'Which bit?' She points to the prosthetic and then to his leg under the blanket. 'Which bit hurts?'

Harry laughs and touches his stump. 'This bit.'

Nellie is asleep almost before her head hits the pillow. I go for a shower and when I come out, dressed in a fresh T-shirt and undies under the motel towel, Harry is still reading. After checking the chain is pulled across the door I get in beside Nellie.

'Good night then,' I say shyly. 'And thanks for … everything.'

'Night,' he says. 'You sleep tight, okay?' His good hand goes up to turn off the light. 'You enjoyed that beer in the end, I reckon!'

I smile at him. 'I did.'

He switches the light out and I lie there, stiff as a rod at first under the strange sheet, staring around the room. Eventually I close my eyes, and the darkness closes in around me.

On the verge of sleep I jerk awake and then settle when I realise that it's only Harry from the nearby bed.

'You're doing this for your kid, I reckon.'

'Yeah.' I'm touched that he's thinking about my situation, but I'm so tired that continuing the conversation seems too much of an effort. Anyway, what else is there to say? I left for her. It's true. It's about the one thing I can say for sure.

'Will your dad be there when we get you to the farm?'

'No, he's dead.'

'What about your mum?'

'She's gone.'

'Gone?'

'She left when I was thirteen. We don't know where she is.'

Harry says nothing.

The last fifteen hours slide by in weirdly vivid fragments, as though somehow lit from within with bright neon. Snatches of conversation with Harry in the car, the woman in the motel office, cigarette smoke curling up into the air, the car, Nellie at the park on the swing. Up and down she goes! *Higher!* she cries out. But what if she loses her grip and goes flying off into the sky? And I find her little body all broken and torn on the hard ground? Travis is walking towards me in the car park. *Tess.* I relive the trip down the dark track from our house again and again. Here I am, pushing the stroller past the cemetery, the secret humming of the trees closing in around me. I can't hold on to even one of the images long enough to talk myself clear.

CORONER'S INQUEST

**This Deponent: Thomas Kavanagh on his oath saith,
I am a Grazier residing at Eaglewood.**

I remember 5th of Nov 1928. My sister-in-law, Lizzie
Sheehan, was staying at my house at Eaglewood for
about a fortnight. I saw her frequently through the
day and did not notice anything peculiar about her.
About 8.15 p.m., I was in the kitchen and I heard
a noise. Then my wife screamed out. I went into the
bedroom. My sister-in-law, Lizzie, was lying on the
bed and my wife was looking at her. My sister-in-
law appeared to be in a fit, which lasted for several
minutes. She eventually recovered and my wife and I
left the room. Ten minutes later, I heard a similar
noise and my wife and I went into the room again.
The deceased was in a similar fit. She recovered
from that fit but did not speak and I again left the
room. Shortly afterwards, the deceased took another
fit. She recovered and did not speak. My wife and I
stayed with her and she took another fit and died. The
deceased, just previous to coming to my place, had a
severe illness. I did not hear the deceased ever say
anything about taking her own life. My wife told me
she was worrying over financial difficulties. I keep
poison in the house: strychnine. It was kept in the
kitchen. To the best of my belief she knew it was
there. I identify the bottle containing strychnine
as the same that was in my house.

Taken and Sworn before me the 16th day of December,
1928, at Leongatha.
J Wild, Justice of the Peace.

CORONER'S INQUEST

**This Deponent: Thomas William Commons on his oath
saith, I am a Mounted Constable residing at Leongatha.**

On the 6th of Nov last from information received
I went to the residence of Mr and Mrs Kavanagh
at Eaglewood. I there saw lying on a bed the dead
body of a woman whose name I ascertained was Lizzie
Sheehan, a sister of Mrs Kavanagh, and that she had
died suddenly the previous night. I examined the
body, which was undressed with the exception of a
nightgown. I found no external marks of violence on
the body. From inquiries made I ascertained that the
deceased, who lived at 278 Beach Ave, South Melbourne,
was on a visit to her sister after recovering from
a sickness. In a reply to a question Mrs Kavanagh
said that the deceased was in a very depressed state
during the day and had told her that she was such
a worry to her. I said, have you any poison in the
house? She said, yes. I said, what kind is it? She
said, strychnine. I said, where is it kept? She took
me into the kitchen and took from a jam tin a small
bottle, which contained strychnine. I said, did the
deceased know that this was here? She said, yes.
I said, did she ever say anything to you about taking
poison? She said, no. I said, did you leave her by
herself during the afternoon? She said, I left her
for about five minutes to go to the shearing shed.
I said, when you returned did you notice anything
peculiar about your sister? She said, the deceased
then became hysterical and went into a fit. I said,

what time was that? She said, about five o'clock.
I sent for my husband, who was at the shed and he
and I were with her until she died about 10 p.m.
I said, did you find any utensils about the house that
had likely been used for taking poison? She said,
no. I took possession of the bottle containing the
strychnine.

Taken and Sworn before me the 16th day of December,
1928, at Leongatha.
J Wild, Justice of the Peace.

twelve

'Tess! Come on! Wake up! Tess! It's okay!'

I *am* awake. I am. But something is on my chest, weighing me down. I can't move. I'm being crushed. Where is that laughter coming from? Behind the door! It's opening now. I hear the movement of air as another presence enters the room, and my blood freezes. The terror moves across my chest into my arms and legs. *Please, Jay. Don't kill me in front of Nellie. Don't let her wake up to find my blood on the floor.* Ants are crawling all over my skin.

A strong hand grabs my upper arm like a vice. 'Wake up. Come on. It's just a bad dream!'

I stare around blindly in the darkness. *Click!* A yellow light switches on above my bed. *Not Jay.* It's Harry standing nearby, dressed in a T-shirt and underpants, his hand on my shoulder, his half-leg hanging down at the end of his torso. When he sees I'm awake he pulls his hand away and flops down on the floor next to my bed.

'You were yelling out,' he says, his voice thick with sleep.

'Shit. I'm sorry,' I gulp.

'Thought you might wake your kid.'

I twist around and see that Nellie is still fast asleep, her face turned away. 'Thanks,' I say.

'Bad dream?'

'I can't remember.' My voice sounds hoarse, as if I've been screaming. 'Was I really yelling?'

'Yeah.' He leans across and takes the glass of water from the side table and offers it to me.

I take it gratefully. 'What time is it?'

'Three a.m.'

'Oh shit! I'm sorry, Harry!' I gulp down the water, feeling rivulets of sweat run down between my breasts. My hands are trembling, so I hand the glass back to him and hide them under the sheet. 'I'm okay now. Seriously. I am.'

'No worries.' He edges back across the floor to his own bed, hauls himself up and pulls the covers over him.

'Leave the light on if you want,' he yawns. 'It won't worry me.'

'No, I'll be okay now.' I switch the light off and Nellie stirs in her sleep.

'Good she didn't wake,' he whispers across the space between us.

'Yeah.'

'Night, then,' he says.

'Night,' I say, turning onto my side. I stare across the darkness to where his profile stands out against the light coming in through the window.

'You've got a good little kid there,' Harry mumbles sleepily.

'Thanks.'

But my heart is beating wildly and it feels as though my whole life is weighing down on my chest. It's so heavy. A good little kid, but … *what am I going to do with her?* How am I going to manage with a kid? It's Beth who should be the mother. Not me.

'Can you imagine being responsible for a little kid?' The words rush out, half-strangled, before I can stop them.

'No,' he says.

'It's a total freak-out.'

'I guess it would be.'

'I mean, how am I meant to do it … I'm twenty-one years old!'

'You're good at it.'

It was a kind thing to say. So much so that I start crying. He can hear me, I know, but it doesn't matter so much because he can't see me. It's much easier talking in the dark. I don't have to get up and find tissues and arrange my face to look humble or bashful or disbelieving. I wipe my tears and nose on the sheet as I try to take what he has said on board but … I can't somehow.

'I don't know if I do it right, though,' I say.

'You talk to her, hug her and pick her up. What else is there?' He goes on with more force. 'And you're getting her away from that violent arsehole. Having the guts to do that is something, Tess. Don't you forget that.'

I smile through my tears and an easy silence settles in between us.

'I feel sorry for Nellie,' I admit.

'Why?'

'Both parents losers.'

Harry doesn't say anything for a while. 'The world is full of losers,' he comes back eventually. 'It's what you do with being a loser that counts.'

'I suppose so.' I laugh uncomfortably.

'What was he like with her?'

'Okay,' I say carefully. 'Hot and cold, you know.'

'Guys can be like that,' Harry says.

'How do you mean?'

Harry clears his throat and then has a bit of a coughing fit. It gives me time to take a few deep breaths. I deliberately slide myself around the dark stuff and remember the good days, when Jay hadn't been smoking dope or popping pills or drinking with his brothers. On those mornings he'd wake clear and reasonably relaxed and he'd take Nellie by the hand and show her things, flowers and the bark on trees. He might teach her a song or take her over to her cousins' for a ride on their pony. He could be good when he felt like it. She absolutely loved him lifting her onto his shoulders to pull the fruit off the trees. *Don't think of the awful stuff. Think of the good things.*

'Something tells me cigarettes aren't all that good for me,' Harry mutters, after the coughing subsides.

'No kidding!' I laugh, glad of the turn in conversation.

'My father was pissed off with me most of the time,' Harry says suddenly, as though this realisation has only now hit him.

'Really? I thought he'd be proud of you?'

'He was a perfectionist. Nothing was ever good enough.'

'Oh. One of those.' I say it like I know what he's talking about. Then I take a deep breath and realise that I'm actually enjoying this. Lying in the dark talking to a stranger is weird but good. I feel disconnected, free, as though I could say anything. 'What about when you … when you had the accident?' The words are out before I've taken time to remember that he's never told me anything about his accident. I clear my throat self-consciously, wondering how to backtrack. But it seems there is no need.

'He more or less disowned me.'

'Really?' This time I'm properly surprised.

'They were in England, preparing for a series of European concerts, when they learnt that Mr Shit-hot, who was going to make them so proud, was essentially … fucked.' The bitterness lying underneath the humorous tone is so intense that for a moment I don't know what to say.

'What about your mother?'

'They both came home. She was okay. Annoying, cloying and fucking painful, really, but … okay. But my father was so furious that he could barely talk. They were always warning me against riding the bike. Especially him. And the truth is that I rode it to piss him off, basically. To show him he couldn't completely rule my life.' Harry laughs dryly. 'And I came a cropper, just as he predicted.'

'What happened when they got home?'

'On the first day they came to the hospital I had bandages all around my head, and my leg was already off, and what was left of it was hanging on ropes to ease the wound. But when my father saw my hand and the doctor told him it would never be right he just exploded.'

'In the hospital?'

'Yeah.' Harry laughed again, this time as if he genuinely thought it was hilarious.

'In front of the doctors?'

'In front of every fucker around! There I was, half-blind, missing a leg, my hand irreparable, and he goes … berserk! As though I needed to be told that I was stuffed.'

I knew I shouldn't ask more questions, but I was morbidly curious. 'What did he say?'

'Ah, you know. That I was the biggest idiot in the world. Which of course I was, but … anyway.' Harry blew out hard and put on a deep, pompous voice. *'You were given a great gift and you have wilfully destroyed it. You have brought this on yourself. You have let both your mother and me down. Completely. I'm so ashamed of you.'*

'Was your mum there when he said all that?' I was trying to imagine the scene.

'Oh yeah, she was trying to stem the tirade. *Oh please don't, Daniel.* If you saw that scene in a movie you wouldn't believe it! You would think they were overacting to buggery. *Oh Daniel. Oh my love … my dearest, don't do this! Please … my darling!'*

Harry mimicking his mother has me laughing now. We both crack up in that sick, desperate way that goes with describing something so totally off the wall that it barely seems possible. It's only when Harry has finished laughing and is clearing his throat and blowing his nose that I think he might have been crying as well. I know what that feels like too.

'Sorry to laugh,' I say.

'No. No. I'm fine. Christ! What else can you do?'

Neither of us speaks for a while.

'So then what happened?' I asked, wondering why I found it all so unbelievable. It wasn't as though either of my parents were great examples of love and concern.

'He stayed a few days. Just long enough to let me know that he wasn't going to hang around playing nurse to a pigheaded, spoilt ingrate. *I'm going straight back to England, and if your mother has any sense at all she'll come back with me.*'

'Shit.'

'Yeah, well … he was always like that. Hard. Very hard on himself and on everyone else.'

'What about your mother? Did she stay?'

'For a bit,' he sighs. 'But she didn't know what to say or do either. It cut her up to see me the way I was in hospital. In the end I told her to go back and do her concerts. So she did.'

'They both went back to their own lives.'

'Yeah, but … I wanted it that way.'

'And they left you alone in hospital?'

'Jules saw me through it all.'

'What did Jules think of them?'

'Jules *hates* both my parents like you wouldn't believe!' He chuckles. 'She threatened to kill my father once. She came at him with a kitchen knife. Luckily I was able to pull it away from her.'

'What about you … do you hate them?'

'No, of course not. They are who they are.' He seems genuinely surprised by the question.

We are quiet after that. I'm trying to imagine the beautiful Jules threatening the cold, uncaring father. I want to ask Harry more about how it happened, and where, and who said what to whom. But I can hear Harry yawning and, I guess, settling into sleep. I yawn a couple of times too, hoping I'll drop off before we have to get up again. But I'm alive with all he's told me. Buzzing.

I suppose the laughter has done me good. And in spite of being only a day away from Jay, I feel oddly safe. I'm in a motel room with a stranger in a New South Wales country town. I have to smile. I'm in that spacey, half-awake place before sleep when Harry speaks again.

'How you going to deal with all this shit?' he mumbles.

'What shit?'

'All the shit that has happened to you?'

'Assuming I get away?'

'You will.'

'Well then … If I get the chance I'll put it behind me and start again.'

'Good luck with that,' he says, the sarcasm only barely concealed.

I laugh uneasily then I sigh. What else can I do? I have to forget … get on with stuff or I'll sink.

'Tell me something else about him, Tess. I can't get a handle on what it was like between you. How did it get so bad?'

'You really want to hear?'

'Yeah.'

Things got worse after the day on the beach with Lily and her friends. I'd get home to my little flat after work to find that my things had been moved around. My cosmetics were neatly put away in the bathroom cupboard with all the caps screwed on. There was milk in my fridge when I knew there had been none that morning. At first I thought I must have been imagining things. But when the special pink notebook that I left under my pillow was gone it really freaked me out.

I'd got into the habit of writing most days since Mum had left. I found solace in just noting down stuff. I didn't try to write anything polished or formal. I never imagined that I'd ever sit down and write a short story, for example, or do anything longer than a couple of pages. But I liked to notice things and to try to record and describe them – a view of the ocean along the foreshore, for example, or a description of people at the café or an amusing scrap of conversation that I'd overheard. Occasional bits and pieces about my parents.

'I don't like you coming in when I'm not here,' I said to Jay one night when he let himself in.

'You're imagining things.'

'I'm not.'

'How do you know it's not Amy snooping around your things?'

'I know.'

He had his boots and coat off by then and was stroking my hair, running one hand over my belly. I could almost smell the desire on him. That usually turned me on. In his arms my anxieties flew away. His tongue flicking around my neck and ears, his fingers going for my secret places made me feel so utterly desirable.

But that night I was angry and pulled away. 'Why do you do it?'

When I turned to face him again he was lying on the bed looking at me with an expression that I couldn't read. He didn't say anything for some time, just kept staring at me. I stood there in my undies feeling utterly exposed and foolish, but still angry. Why did things have to be like this? I was so frustrated that I started to cry.

'Come here, babe.' He held out both arms.

I held my ground, but it was hard. 'No. I want to know why!'

'Come here, babe.' He seemed more amused than anything. 'Come on and I'll tell you.'

I surrendered because I didn't know what else to do. And I was genuinely bewildered. I went over and sat on the bed next to him.

He took my hand in both of his and rubbed his fingers into my palm. 'I'm looking after you, honey,' he said softly, as though I'd hurt him. 'Don't you realise that yet? You've got to trust me. I'm looking after you.'

....

'And then …?' Harry asks into the silence.

'Not long after that I got pregnant.'

'Then you *were* stuffed.'

I laugh. 'Yeah. I guess so.'

We're quiet for a while, and I'm amazed all over again at how good this feels. Just to be lying here and letting it out to someone. Telling it how it was. Not that I'm giving him all the details. I don't need to. It's good talking to someone who is interested but not involved.

'I ended up in a psychiatric hospital,' Harry tells me. 'That was pretty full-on.'

'When?'

'About six weeks after my parents went back to Europe.' He sounds gloomy.

'What happened?'

'I sort of fell in a heap.'

'Yeah?' I asked curiously. 'What got you out of it?'

'A variety of pharmaceuticals,' he laughs, 'and the lovely Jules.'

'You still take the drugs?'

'Some … yeah.'

I'm wide awake now and deeply curious. But just as I'm trying to work out how to ask him more about his hospital experience I hear his breathing change and I know he's asleep. I switch sides and close my eyes.

·······································

The first time it happened I was just home from hospital with Nellie and I was trying to work out if the vast amounts of yellow poo were normal. I was tossing up whether to ring the hospital and ask.

Jay walked into the living room where I was putting the baby into her bassinet. 'Did they give you stuff to stop you having kids?'

'No.'

'Did they talk to you about it?'

'A bit.'

He looked at me sharply.

'It was just general stuff,' I said. 'Cheer up.'

He went to his place by the window with his beer. I sat watching him, wishing that he'd show some interest in Nellie. *Look at her!* I wanted to say. *Look at her little head and the way she's breathing so softly.*

I went out to the fridge to get myself a light beer. I popped it and walked back in and sat on the couch. I opened the book I'd been reading before I went to hospital. But I couldn't concentrate. So much had changed.

'What are you doing?' He swiped the bottle from my hand and it smashed against the iron table leg, all the fizzy liquid pouring out onto the polished floorboards. I was so shocked that I didn't know what to do. Just stared at him.

'What?'

'You think drinking alcohol and feeding a baby is okay?'

'It's a light beer,' I whispered. 'The nurse said one was okay.'

'The nurse? The fucking *nurse* wouldn't know anything, Tess!'

'And what the hell do *you* know about it?' I shouted back, and that's when he did it. Grabbed me by the back of the neck with one hand, pulling me towards him, and then slapped me hard across the face with the other hand. The ornate silver ring he always wore caught my earring and tore it from my ear. I gasped in shock, unable to say anything. Blood was everywhere. Just at that moment the baby started crying.

'Look what you've done!' he said. Then he stormed out of the house.

I went over to Nellie and picked her up. I don't know if she could feel my trembling, but it seemed so. I couldn't think what to do. She was really upset, but I had to put her down and try to stem the blood that was pouring from my ear. I ran over to the stove and grabbed a tea towel, soaked it under the tap and put it to my ear. So much blood!

By the time Jay came back things were quiet again. The baby was asleep in another room and I'd more or less quelled the blood, though it was still bleeding a little. One of my eyes had swollen up and my whole jaw ached as if I had a bad toothache. I heard him walk inside, and as soon as he did Nellie woke up howling and I went to her again. When I'd calmed her down, I came back into the living room to find him sitting at the table looking about the room as though he didn't know where he was or what to do. But when he saw me he stood up. I was still holding the towel to my ear and there was blood all over my top.

'Can you stop the bleeding?' he said in a subdued voice, taking the towel from me and holding it to my ear. I shook my head, moved away from him and sat down near the fireplace, still trembling. He came over and knelt down in front of me.

'Babe, I'm sorry.'

'It's okay,' I whispered.

'I'll make it up to you.' His tone was pleading. 'Promise.'

When I look back I wonder why I didn't walk out right then when I still had some power. I hadn't yet turned into the blithering idiot I became later. But I was too freaked out to know what I should do. I was so relieved that his anger seemed to be over that I didn't think long-term. I so desperately wanted to believe him when he said he was sorry that I couldn't think straight.

His mother and Nick came to see the baby later on that day and by then I'd been cleaned up. Neither of them asked how it was that I had a black and swollen eye and a thick bandage taped to my ear.

When he got back from shopping in town the next day, there was a big bunch of roses in his hands.

'For you, babe,' he murmured into my neck. He was like that for the next week. Nothing annoyed him. Nothing was too much. I was happy. The baby thrived.

He didn't hit me again for almost a year. By then he knew he didn't have to apologise. By then I knew that I deserved it.

thirteen

I wake up to the smell of toast and bacon and the sound of clanking crockery, Nellie's chatter above it all.

'Can we wake her *now*, Harry?'

'No, let her sleep.'

'But … what if she *never* wakes up?'

'She will. You going all the way with Coco Pops? Or do you want toast?'

'Coco Pops!'

'Please.'

'Please,' comes her sweet, plaintive little voice.

'Okay! Here you go, then.'

'I want the whole packet.'

'Greedy guts.'

I lie still, eyes closed, listening to them, letting the sense of wellbeing take over. I feel rested, as if I've slept deeply. All the events of yesterday feel as though they happened a long time ago. Even the nightmare feels a long time ago.

'Are you going to cut off the other leg too?' I hear Nellie ask brightly.

'Nope.'

'Why not?'

'I like it. You like those Coco Pops?'

'Mmmm, I love them. So why don't you make your fingers go straight?'

'I can't.'

'What if you banged them down?'

'What with?'

'Something heavy?'

'What do you suggest?'

There's a pause while she thinks. I smile to myself, knowing she's frowning as she tries to work it all out.

'A huge hammer?'

'I don't think so.'

'Why not?'

'Might hurt.'

I open one eye. Harry and Nellie are sitting at the table near the window.

'Hey! What time is it?' I ask.

'About nine.'

'You're kidding.' I gulp and sit up. 'You should have woken me!'

'Why?'

'I thought you wanted to leave early?'

'I figured that we all needed the extra sleep.'

I get up and pull on my jeans and go to the toilet. I splash cold water on my face and check myself out in the bathroom mirror. I look half-dazed with sleep, and only vaguely familiar, as if I might be in the process of turning into someone else. I dry my face and move away. About to pull the door open I hesitate and go back to the mirror. I move up very close and look right into my own wary eyes. *Hold steady,* I tell myself. *Don't fall into craziness. The first night is over. It's morning now. You've got a chance.*

'Mamma!' Nellie lunges at me as I come out of the bathroom. 'Harry said if I eat more Coco Pops I might pop out of my clothes!'

'Yeah? Well, it's always a possibility. Can I have this chair?'

'No! It's mine.'

I sit down anyway opposite Harry, and drag her onto my knee.

Harry pushes over a covered plate. 'I ordered you some.'

'Thanks.'

'We'll go when you've had that. Just pull our stuff together and take off.'

'Okay.' I pull the lid off and start to pick at the food.

'You needed that sleep,' Harry says kindly.

'Yeah.' I smile at him.

'I used to have nightmares,' he tells me quietly. 'I'd have these dreams about being lost and not being able to get to the venue for an exam or a performance. Or I'd walk out onto the stage in front of an audience and my mind would go blank. I wouldn't know where Middle C was!'

I nod, but it's as if he's talking to himself.

'Sometimes it was my fingers. They wouldn't work. Stiff as sticks.' He laughs dryly. 'Those dreams might have been premonitions.'

I catch the sad note and it makes my own throat constrict. I want to say something comforting, but it might come out wrong and make him feel worse.

He clears his throat and gives a deep sigh.

'Do you still have nightmares?' I ask.

'Nothing to get excited about these days. Mostly I sleep like a log.'

'Right.' I don't know how to respond to that either.

'What about you? You have them often?'

'A bit,' I say carefully.

I think of the way I'd go to bed exhausted over the last few months, only to wake after a couple of hours in a panic. I'd lie there, plotting and scheming, trying to work out what to do, trying to relax, trying not to think of things. *Nothing can be worked out in the middle of the night*, I'd tell myself time and time again. *Wait until the morning.* But the mad stuff came dancing its way into my head anyway, swirling and shimmering like the flames of a hundred little fires on a hillside. *Kill him with an axe. Set fire to the house. Kill yourself.* Once I'd doused one flaming idea, another would start up. In the end, I'd have to creep out to the kitchen to break the spell, sit in the dark by myself for a while, rock back and forth and listen to the night outside. It was the only way to calm down. On very still nights I could just hear the ocean, the boom and crash, the deep rhythmic comfort of it.

Jay hated me getting up at night. He was a sound sleeper and so mostly he didn't know about my midnight ramblings, but when he did wake and find me gone he'd get up and insist I come back to bed. He'd pull me up close, both arms locked around me. Then he'd go to sleep again, his breath loud in my ear. It was like being in a cage. I couldn't move. I often used to imagine him waking in the morning to find me dead, suffocated in his arms.

Harry's phone rings, but I hardly register it, figuring it will be Jules. I push the flimsy curtain aside and take a peek out the window. Nothing much going on out there, except two oldies walking to their car. But the sky is blue and I can see the roof of Harry's mother's car still there. Nothing terrible has happened yet. Nellie slides off my knee and goes to Harry's vacated chair. We make faces at each other across the table as I eat the eggs. I'm not really hungry, but I figure that I should eat something. I've grown very thin. If we're going to be driving most of the day then I should eat.

'Okay then. I'll get her.'

I look up quickly. Harry is holding the phone out for me.

'It's … a guy,' he says. 'Says he's your brother.'

I swallow a mouthful of toast and take the phone, my heart hammering in my chest. 'Hello?' I say tentatively.

'Hey, Tess!'

'Marly!' Relief washes through me. 'How did you get this number?'

'You rang Beth on this number,' he laughs easily. 'She gave it to me. But listen, are you safe? Who are you with?'

'Safe.' I turn around and smile at Harry, who smiles back and then makes a monster face for Nellie's benefit. 'Getting a ride down with a great guy.'

'And the other guy?'

'Can't talk now, Marly.'

'Beth said you've got a kid!'

'Yeah.' I turn to where Nellie is bouncing on one of the beds. 'She's good.'

'Can't wait to meet her.' Warmth is spilling out down the line into my whole body and it makes me feel so good. I feel like a balloon gradually filling with air. 'I just knew you'd turn up again, Tessie. I knew it! What's your daughter's name?'

'Fenella, but we call her Nellie.'

There is a pause as he registers this, and I hear him take a deep breath. 'Great name,' he whispers.

'Thanks.'

'Really love it.'

We hesitate, then both start talking at once and stop for the other and then burst out laughing. There is so much to say that neither of us knows what to say first.

'We should get to the farm tonight or tomorrow,' I tell him. 'Are you there yet?'

'No.'

'When will you be there?'

When he doesn't answer immediately I know something is up, but I don't say anything. Marly has a slow way about him. 'Don't think I can come.'

'Why not? Oh, please come, Marly!'

I hear him take a few deep breaths. 'I just don't think I can …
go there.'

'Okay,' I sigh.

When Dad died, Marly went out to the farm to tell our
grandparents. He was also the one to tell them our mother was
gone. That place is nightmare territory for him. It was bad enough
for the rest of us, but somehow it was worse for Marly.

'I'm really sorry,' he says softly. 'I was so excited when Beth
told me you were coming.'

'Did you tell Beth that you'd come?'

'Yeah … and I've driven three days to get to the Darwin
airport!'

'Is that where you are now?'

'I just can't get on the plane!'

I'm so disappointed, because of the three of them it's Marly
I'd really like to see. Beth and Salome will be onto me like crows
before I've had time to sit down, but Marly never judges anyone.

'You need money?' he asks.

'Yeah,' I whisper.

'How much? You got any?'

'I've got two hundred bucks.'

'You got clothes and stuff?'

'Not really.'

'Have you got a phone?'

'No … it's better not to.' I laugh grimly. 'I don't have a bank
account either.'

'I'll get money to you, okay, sis? Soon. I'll work out a way.'

'Thanks, Marly.'

I end the call and smile at Harry and Nellie, who are watching
me closely. 'That was my brother,' I explain, on the point of tears.
I feel that my face is flushed as I put my arm around Nellie.
'He's going to give us some money.'

'Yeah?' Harry smiles and leans in closer.

'What?' I laugh and pull away a bit. 'What are you looking at?'

He says nothing but takes the phone out of my hand, stands up, steps back a few paces and lines us up for a photo.

'What are you doing?' I try to cover my face with my hands, but Nellie pulls them away.

'You've got colour in your cheeks and your eyes are bright.' He starts snapping away. 'And I want to show Jules.'

I try to hide my face in Nellie's hair but she pulls away, giggling.

'Don't be ridiculous!' I protest, laughing.

Harry sends a photo, and within about a minute his phone beeps. He laughs before he reads the text out. *'Oh wow!'* he reads, *'I told you she was beautiful! And tell Nellie that she's got a fat belly!'*

Nellie squeals with delight, and Harry and I laugh as she prances around sticking her belly out.

'Sounds like you and your brother were close?' Harry says.

'We were!' I smile. 'We broke the rules.'

'Rules?'

'After we'd moved to the city house, Beth outlawed any talk or speculation about our mother. She was *persona non grata*. But Marlon and I had an understanding.'

'You talked about it together?'

'Not a lot, but ... a bit.'

There is a knock at the door. Harry goes and pulls open the chain. It's the stringy, sour-faced woman from the office.

'Have you seen your car?' she asks, her eyes darting around the room suspiciously, as if she's looking for clues, trying to work out what has been going on in her precious motel room.

'No.'

We go out to see what she's talking about.

All four tyres have been slashed to pieces. Harry, Nellie and I stand in shock, trying to take in the roughly cut strips of rubber. Whoever did it had more than a pocketknife. The back wheels seem to have been hacked at with an axe, and there are lumps of expensive rubber lying like huge chunks of liquorice all over the ground. The beautiful car slumps now, like an old, beaten warrior. The day is already bright and sunny, but I feel cold and ... terrified.

'Who did that?' Nellie whispers, edging over to put one arm around my right leg. I pick her up and hold her tightly, hating the fact that she has to see it. When a moan of desperation escapes from my mouth she wriggles into me even tighter, hiding her face in my neck. We stand there helplessly, watching Harry move around examining each wheel.

'We should go home now,' Nellie whimpers to me. 'My daddy will know what to do.'

'Oh, baby,' I tell her. 'It'll all be okay. Don't worry.'

'But Daddy will fix it,' she whispers.

'No. He won't, sweetheart.'

Harry's face remains expressionless as he goes inside for the keys.

'This sort of thing has been happening a bit around town,' the woman tells us, without a hint of emotion. 'Kids with not enough to do.' She sighs. 'They target the expensive cars.' The judgemental tone makes me look up quickly. I catch the satisfied expression and want to swipe one hand hard across her pursed-up, ugly mouth. She must register my anger, because her eyes dart away. 'They've never come out this way before, though,' she adds. 'I've already rung the police.'

With a sinking heart I watch Harry opening the car door and getting in. What if they've messed with the engine too? But the motor starts straight away. He switches it off and gets out, and that's when I begin breathing again.

'All good on the inside,' he says thoughtfully.

'There's a mechanic in town,' the woman tells him. 'You want the number?'

'Thanks.'

She disappears and, still holding Nellie, I go back inside and sit on the bed. Her legs are around my middle and her face is buried in my neck.

'It will be kids,' Harry says from the doorway, looking at me. 'For sure.' He takes out his pouch of tobacco and begins to roll a cigarette. 'Don't you reckon?'

'How do I know?' I shrug furiously.

'What kids?' Nellie looks from one of us to the other.

I pull her back into me and say nothing.

'Can we go home now, Mamma?' she whimpers as she flops her head down on my chest. 'Please.'

'Not yet, honey.'

Harry comes and sits beside me. He puts an arm around my shoulders.

'Well, that's put the kibosh on things for a bit,' he says softly.

I don't answer.

By the time the police car arrives, I have edged myself back into the far corner of the room, curled up behind one of the beds, my face buried in my knees. I half-hear some ridiculous drama outside between two tow-truck drivers who arrive at the same time. All the shouting and swearing feels as if it's happening inside someone else's life, not mine. I'm in a dark, hidden space unable to even get off the floor, much less think clearly. But after the initial shock, my little girl is taking it all in her stride. The motel door is open and Nellie runs in and out, giving me updates on what's happening. She is so excited about all the drama outside she doesn't seem to notice that I hardly react.

Eventually the tow-truck drivers work it out and the driver who gets the job tells us that it will be a few hours for the tyres to come from another town. Then it will take the mechanic a couple of hours to fit them. We'd better count on not setting off again until late afternoon.

When the car is on the back of the truck and heading off down the road into town, Harry and I are left looking at each other. The motel owner comes by.

'Alright now?' she says.

'Just great,' I mutter under my breath.

'How far are we from the river?' Harry asks the woman.

'Five-minute walk.'

'So let's go have a look at the river,' Harry says. 'Feel like a walk, Nellie?'

Nellie doesn't answer. She runs over from where she's been playing with Barry on the bed and hides her face in my side.

'There's a nice spot further on down that they swim from in summer,' the woman offers, her voice kinder now. She points to the street at the side of the building. 'Head straight down there and turn right. Not too far along. And you can keep the room until five.'

'Thanks,' Harry says.

I get up slowly. Harry puts Nellie on his back and I follow them silently down the side street. At the end there is a dirt path leading down to the river. We follow it through masses of huge trees and eventually come to the riverbank. The wide expanse of brown flowing river gleams in the sunlight.

Nellie wriggles to get down. Normally she'd be off running towards the water but she sticks close, anxiously pulling at my leg. 'Mamma?' she whispers.

'What?'

'Where has the car gone?'

'To get fixed up.'

'Are we going to get in the water?'

'We'll see,' I whisper.

She ventures away from us slowly, making her way towards the bank, looking around every now and again to make sure I'm watching.

'I realise that you're shit-scared,' Harry says quietly. 'But I reckon we've just got to proceed on the basis that it was local kids having a go at a posh car.'

I say nothing and he squints at me. 'Unless you seriously think he *is* behind it?'

I shrug and shake my head.

'Is it the sort of thing he'd do?'

I shrug. 'I don't know.'

'So he might?' Harry is looking at me intently. 'Is he that weird?'

'I've told you, I don't know!' I turn away from his scrutiny.

What if he's playing with us? I think of those ripped tyres and break out in a sweat. *Jay loves a game.*

....

Jay's rearranging my things in the flat became more common-place, and more bizarre. He began to leave out the clothes that he wanted me to wear the next day. He always made a point of dropping by the café to check on me those times, and if I wasn't wearing the dress he'd left out then he was cold and sulky when I saw him next.

It quickly became easier to just do what he wanted. I told myself that it didn't matter, that I was still having a good time with Jay, and it was mostly true. His nocturnal visits were happening more frequently, but I told myself that it was okay because he always did leave early, before anyone else was up. I told myself that it wasn't anything important and I got good at stopping myself from thinking beyond the day. Then, for reasons I barely understood, I'd get so unhappy that I'd have days when I could barely drag myself off to work. I was crying a lot. *Please don't come in here when I'm not here.*

But he'd go all-out on the charm offensive to win me back. Again and again and again! How stupid could one girl be? He'd arrive in the middle of the night with flowers and expensive perfume.

'I'm looking after you, honey,' was what he always came back to. It became his mantra.

Eventually he got caught creeping into my flat in the middle of the night. It's hard even thinking about the shame I felt facing Duncan. It wasn't that he was nasty or even cold. He just told me to leave the flat by the end of the week.

The next day Duncan told me that I could keep working in the café if I wanted but I had nowhere to live. Within a day, Jay was pressuring me to leave the job and move in with him. I loved the job. I loved being among the thick of it in Byron. I loved swimming in the morning. I loved the coffee with Lily before my shift started. And I was ashamed at having to leave the flat. Duncan and Amy had been so good to me, and I knew I'd let them down. But I let Jay talk me into it.

Lily came around the day I moved out. She stood close to me and pressed a number into my hand.

'Who is it?'

'The local coppers,' she said matter-of-factly. 'You might need them one day.'

Flushed with humiliation, I refused to take it, but I didn't know what else to say.

'You don't have to go live with him, Tess,' she said earnestly. 'You could come to my—'

'I'm pregnant,' I blurted out.

She shoved the card back into my hand and closed my fist around it with both her hands.

'And you've got my number on your phone. Ring me if you need to. I'd love to hear from you.'

'Okay.' I slipped the card into the bag that I had slung across my shoulders.

It all seemed pretty unreal. I was a mess. Being sick and pregnant felt unreal, as though it was happening to someone else.

Within a week I had no phone. It went missing two days after moving to Jay's place. At the time I cursed my carelessness and assumed I'd get a replacement. Jay made such a big deal of helping me look for it that it didn't enter my head until much later that he'd probably taken it himself.

fourteen

We head off along the river in search of the place that the woman was talking about. At the bend there is a clearing with green grass, picnic tables and electric barbecues. The few cars in the car park and two separate gatherings of people make me feel easier. I stand alert and survey the scene from the edge before moving closer. But no one looks even vaguely interested in us, much less threatening. One lot is cooking sausages at a barbecue, and the other is a group of teenagers lolling over the table and chairs. When Nellie sees the shallow water with a metre of sand at the edge she brightens up a bit and insists on pulling off her boots and socks. We go down to the water, but it's very cold. I help her roll up her pants and she gingerly puts a toe in.

'So what's on your mind?' Harry asks when Nellie heads back onto the grass and starts playing in the sand.

'I reckon you must be sorry you agreed to help us,' I mutter.

'Nah,' he grins. 'What else would I be doing?'

'What about the cost of those tyres?'

'Insurance.'

'Will your mum be pissed off?'

'She won't even know.'

'It's her car!'

'Mine, really. She never drives it.'

'Come over here,' Nellie suddenly calls out. 'I've built something … awesome.'

We turn to see her jumping up and down near a small sand-castle with sticks stuck in it.

Harry shakes his head and laughs. 'Where did she learn that word?'

'Older cousins,' I explain, but I'm proud. She is smart. And it's not just about her older cousins. When she was a tiny baby I heard on the radio that talking to them was the best thing you could do, so I decided then and there that if I could do nothing else, at least I'd do that. I talk to her a lot, read to her too, and tell her stories.

We're both silent watching Nellie. She is totally intent as she digs a moat around the castle with her fingers. Eventually Harry leaves me and walks over to help her.

I stand in the flowing river for some time, watching the sunshine sparkling on the surface. Then I go back to the grass, lie down and close my eyes, and try to work out what to do next. What is my situation exactly? What is likely to happen? It's hard getting a handle on reality, much less sticking to it. In the background I can hear Nellie telling Harry about her dog.

'Streak can run as fast as the wind,' she tells him seriously.

'Is that a fact?' Harry murmurs. 'What else?'

'Well … he knows when we come home. He starts barking.'

'Yeah?'

After a while they come back over to me. Harry sits on one side and Nellie starts playing with my feet, putting her little fingers between my toes and making me squirm.

'My daddy sometimes hurts Mamma,' she tells Harry, apropos of nothing.

I look up but her head is down, concentrating on pouring sand between my toes.

'Well, that's not good, is it?' Harry's voice is neutral.

Nellie doesn't answer, but she gets up and throws herself down on top of my belly. 'Will he be missing us, Mamma?'

'Yes,' I say.

'What about Streak?'

'What about him?'

'Will he be missing us?'

'Yes, he'll be missing us.'

'Will Daddy feed him?'

'Yes, I'm sure he will.'

Nellie's attention is caught by some older children who are climbing onto one of the picnic tables and jumping off, one by one. She gets off me and moves over for a better look.

'When things settle down, will you let him see her?' Harry asks quietly.

'What?'

I prop on my elbows and look at Harry. How do I explain that *settling down* just doesn't apply? It will never happen. Things will never settle down until one of us is dead.

'The shared custody thing or—'

'No!' I cut him off.

I turn away and say nothing. If I begin talking about this stuff I'll never stop. I have to erase the reality of Jay from my head.

'Sorry,' I say, trying to make up for my sharpness. 'But … I've got this crazy feeling that if I talk about him too much he'll … appear.'

'Ah!' Harry laughs gently. 'Now that *is* crazy.'

'Crazy is in my genes.' I smile at Harry.

'Hey!' Harry puts his damaged hand briefly over mine. 'You're not crazy, Tess. Don't ever think that. *I've* been crazy and I know what crazy is like.'

I sit up properly to get a better look at him but he's still on his belly looking down, concentrating on digging a hole with his hands. 'Yeah?'

'Oh yeah.' He moves onto his back and holds up his good hand like a cop. 'No buts about it! You're the sanest person I know, *and* you're fucking brave.'

I laugh out loud. 'You must know a lot of nutcases, then?'

'I reckon I do.' He grins at me. 'Quite a few, actually. Hey, I'm going for a swim,' he says suddenly.

I pretend not to notice when he pulls off his T-shirt. Swathes of skin all over his back and right arm are shiny red, some of it thick and raised. There is a wide scar down through the middle of it from his left shoulderblade into his left hip. I can't see the end of it because he is wearing long shorts. I watch him limping off to the water. He steps in and then once he's in up to his calves, bends to pull off his prosthetic leg and chucks it back onto the bank. Other people are watching curiously too as he carefully hops a few steps deeper into the water. He stands there on his one leg for a moment looking out across the river before diving in.

Nellie and I go over and stand in the freezing water watching Harry swim. It's too cold for her and so I settle her on my hip, the water up to my knees. When Harry gets back he swims around my legs pretending to be a shark, much to Nellie's delight. She squeals and giggles, clinging to me.

'Okay. I've had enough.' He pushes himself up, then, using my shoulder for support, stands upright and heads back to shore on his one leg.

Once we're all down on the grass I put one hand on his shoulder briefly. 'Burns?'

'Yeah. I slid along the road for a way.'

'Oh.'

'Had a lot of grafts.' He puts a finger on the bruises on the inside of my arm. 'What about these, Tess?'

'It looks worse than it is,' I tell him.

'Yeah?' he says dryly. 'Well, they look pretty bad.'

We sit there awhile until the sun goes behind a cloud. When we stand to go back to the motel, a light, almost euphoric sense of wellbeing fills me.

'What's going on?' He laughs. 'You're smiling.'

'I dunno.' I crane my neck upwards to watch the trees swirling above us. 'For whatever reason I just suddenly feel … okay.'

'Good.'

It's so unreal to be standing here under these big shady trees, watching the light dappling through the leaves. The colours are so vivid and so strong. There is the splash of water and the muted sounds of people enjoying themselves and … what if this guy is right? He might be. What if I really am *the sanest person he knows*?

We meander our way back to the motel, make a cup of tea and eat biscuits. Harry rings up the garage and asks if the tyres are in. Not yet, he's told. He and Nellie watch TV until Nellie gets hungry.

'I might walk into town,' he says. 'Get some stuff.'

'What kind of stuff?'

'Food. We're probably going to be here for a while.'

'My brother is going to send me money,' I say defensively. 'So I'll be able to pay you back.'

'Well, that's good, but … until then.'

'We'll stay here, Nellie,' I tell her, trying to sound firm.

'Noooo,' she yells. 'I want to go with Harry.'

'She can come with me,' Harry says lightly. 'I don't mind.'

I look at him and almost say okay, because the truth is I trust him. Maybe I shouldn't after such a short time, but I do.

'I'll look after her,' he tells me.

I nod and turn away. I'm at the point of bursting out crying. But what if Jay turns up? Would it be better for Nellie and me to be split up? Maybe. On the other hand, what if he saw her with

Harry in town and he called the police, or worse? As the father, he'd have the right to take his child from a stranger, wouldn't he?

I get up and have a drink of water. 'She'd better stay here,' I say hoarsely. 'But thanks anyway.'

'Okay.'

Harry is back within the hour. I sit on the bed watching Nellie helping him unpack the two plastic bags of shopping. There are biscuits and cheese, tomatoes and some soft drink and some kind of cake, but best of all, he has bought Nellie two dolls. One has black hair, the other blonde. Jay never allowed that kind of thing in the house, and Nellie pounces on them in a trance of pure delight.

'You shouldn't have … done that.' I smile awkwardly.

'They were cheap,' he grins. 'So why not two?'

'What names will you give them?' I ask Nellie.

But she is too busy looking up under their skirts to make sure they've got their undies on and taking their tiny white plastic high-heeled shoes off. 'Jilly and Suzie,' she says eventually, almost breathless with happiness.

Harry and I grin at each other. 'How come?' I ask.

'Because,' she mutters, 'that's their names.'

'Okay!' I laugh. 'Jill and Suzie it is.'

'Not Jill!' she snaps at me. *Jilly.*'

'Did you say thank you to Harry?'

Nellie runs over and grabs Harry by the leg and looks up at him, her big blue eyes shining. 'Thank you, Harry.'

'No worries!' He ruffles her hair and grins as she brings the dolls over to me.

'I can't see where they do wee, Mamma,' she whispers as if it's the big worry of her life, so I take a look under the tiny pants.

'I think they might have their own secret way,' I tell her, and that does for the moment.

Harry hauls some fruit from a bag, and then, as though it's an afterthought, throws a brown paper bag onto the end of my bed.

'Something for you,' he says shortly.

When I open it, I see it's a simple black phone.

'Oh!' The slick thing is nestled down in its cardboard box, encased in clear plastic. It's been a long time since I had a phone and the idea of it is so enticing ... but I don't dare take it out. The whole idea was to just disappear. 'Thanks, Harry, but ... I'm not sure I can take the risk.'

'What risk?'

'I don't want there to be any trace of me.'

'It's all set up. There is no way anyone can get the number unless you give it to them. You won't be traceable. Not like it's connected to the net.' Harry takes the phone from me and punches in his own number under Contacts. 'My number is here if ... anything happens.'

'Okay.' But I'm unsure. What will having a phone mean?

He goes back to the bench. 'And how about this?' He throws over another bag. Inside is a black Moleskine notebook in A4 size. Confused at first, I take it out and simply stare at it. Then I look up, but he has his back to me, fishing for something. Eventually he turns around holding a couple of pens. He throws them over too. Biting my lip, I pick them up off the bed and go back to flipping through the empty pages.

'Where did you get it?'

'I was passing the newsagent.'

'But I ... How? I mean, why did you ...?'

I'm not sure I can finish the sentence, because a mishmash of memory and emotion is making me incoherent. I'm back in my flat at Duncan and Amy's, searching frantically for the pink notebook I kept under my pillow.

Sure I took it. What's the big deal? Baby, I'm your guy, right? I need to know what's going on in that little head of yours. What chance have we got if you keep secrets, Tess?

He won that one too. After some discussion, I agreed to quit writing for the greater cause of *keeping our relationship true*. There would be no secrets between us. Except, of course, for the ones he kept from me. But I told myself that they didn't matter too much. Writing in my notebook was something I could easily do without. At that point I still believed in the dream that had brought me to the place where I found myself, my place with him. Of course I could do without writing!

And I stuck to that decision until I started living out on the farm. But with a new baby and no phone or contact with anyone but him and his family, when the opportunity presented itself, I grabbed it with both hands in spite of the promise I'd made.

I was pushing Nellie in the pram across the road from the supermarket in the main street of Byron when I saw it lying facedown in the gutter about six cars down from where Jay was waiting for me. I stopped and picked it up, thinking it would be full of someone else's life, shopping lists, maybe, or business accounts. But it was completely empty. I looked around to see if anyone was watching and then stuffed it inside one of the bags hanging off the handles of the pram. Jay was listening to music as I clipped Nellie into her capsule and loaded the groceries into the back seat. I told myself that if he didn't find it when we unpacked the shopping, then it had been sent to me.

When we got home, he picked up a couple of the bags of shopping and rushed inside, mumbling about needing to see if there'd been a message left on the home phone. The empty black book was in the one bag left on the seat. Another omen. Quietly and methodically, but with a pumping heart, I got Nellie out and carried her and the bag inside. I could hear Jay on the phone in the alcove that operated as his office. I unpacked the groceries and took the black book to Nellie's room and shoved it under the wardrobe.

I decided that I would only write when Jay was out of the house. I stuck to that even though it was sometimes hard. He'd often sit out on the verandah with his brothers drinking and discussing business, and I knew they'd be there for ages, but I didn't give in. It was too dangerous. I would only take it out when he was away all day. But even though I kept the handwriting very small, before a year had passed I'd filled up every single page. I remember feeling so desolate as I wrapped it up in thick plastic and put it into a small, old-fashioned, bright blue kids' case I found down at the tip. It was as if my best friend was leaving town. I wrapped the case up in more plastic and hid it under Nellie's wardrobe and waited until he was gone again for the day. When Nellie was asleep in the afternoon, I dug a deep hole and buried it. I know exactly where it is, behind the chook shed near the gate leading out to the small paddock. I remember once I had the earth packed down tight, I stood a moment and looked around the surrounding hills. I breathed in the soft, fluttery breeze and gorgeous golden sunshine filtering down through the tall palms, and I promised myself that if I was ever allowed to grow old I would come back to that spot and dig it up.

Something came back to life in me the day I found that book in the street. I had the strong feeling that *it had been sent to me* … and since filling it up, I've been unconsciously waiting for the next one.

And here it is.

I look up to see that Harry is watching me carefully. Who is this stranger? This guy who after a day or two knows what I need?

'Thanks,' I manage to whisper.

'That's okay.' He rolls up the plastic bags and stuffs them into the rubbish basket, then pulls a can of lemonade out of the fridge. 'You want one?'

I hold out both hands and try to smile. 'Okay.'

'Write it down,' he tells me seriously. 'All the shit you've seen. The crap you've been through. Just spew it out onto the page.' He grins. 'Can't do any harm.'

I take a swig of the soft drink and lie back on the pillow. Nellie is on the floor playing with her new dolls. Harry sees my tears, but I don't care really. I'm thinking of my mother the night before she left. *You're the storyteller, Tess.*

fifteen

The garage finally calls at nearly six p.m., by which time the day has turned grey and blustery. The tyres have only just arrived and will be fitted first thing in the morning.

'He'll keep the car overnight.' Harry is standing by the door. 'We'll have to stay another night here and take off early in the morning. That alright with you? Hey!' He grins and points to the notebook. 'You've started?'

'Just scribble.' I feel my face flush. 'Can you afford an extra night?'

He shrugs off the question. 'Scribble is where it all begins.'

'So you're a writing expert as well as …?' I joke.

'General therapist to nutcases everywhere,' he laughs, and Nellie wakes.

'Are we going home now?'

'No.'

'When?'

'We're going to stay here another night,' I say, thinking that she'll throw a fit, but she sighs, hops off the bed and, dragging Barry with her, heads for the door. 'Where are you going?'

'Barry needs fresh air.'

'Let's walk to the pub for dinner,' Harry suggests.

'How far is it?' Nellie seems to like the idea.

'Not far,' Harry tells her.

'Can Barry come?'

'No. Bears aren't allowed in pubs,' he tells her seriously. 'Last time one came in for a meal he ate so much that no one else got anything. After that they made a rule that bears had to stay home.'

Nellie thinks about this for a while, then she looks up and sees he's tricking her and giggles.

We borrow a couple of umbrellas from the motel office and walk down to the pub in the main street. The wind sends grit into our eyes and mouths. But the rain holds off. The pub has thick lurid carpet, and rows of pokies. It's full of older people, couples mainly, quietly eating their meals. We choose a small corner table behind a pillar near the window, so we can look out at the approaching storm. The menu is written up on a blackboard.

'I'll pay for this,' I hear myself saying.

He shrugs and then leans forward. 'You look worried.'

'I'm okay.' I move my shoulders around, trying to release the tension. 'Just a bit …'

For some reason, the walk into the main part of town has made me edgy. And now I'm inside, the place is freaking me out. What the hell am I doing here with all these strangers? A group of people in their twenties come in, all dressed up and wisecracking with each other as they push two tables together and start arguing about who is going to get the drinks. Thirty-seven hours ago I was back in the hills with Jay. Am I so dumb that in less than two days I've forgotten what he's capable of? I look around wildly. *We really shouldn't be here.* I look out the window and see rain pelting down, and the panic rises. I've pushed my luck coming to a place like this, and it will backfire. *Something is going to happen.* I can feel it. Fear crawls across my skin. I watch Nellie busily collecting beer coasters from nearby empty tables and piling them up next to me, but she seems so far away now. I'm watching her from a distance on a jumpy homemade film. *How do we get out of here?* Harry is frowning. Every now and again he takes a quick hard look at me and I begin to wonder if I was crazy to trust him. *Who is he? Has he contacted Jay? What if coming to this place is part of the plan they've nutted out together and we're going to be handed over like two bags of shopping?*

'So what do you reckon, Nellie?' Harry asks. 'You hungry?'

'Hmmm.' Nellie goes around to Harry's side. 'What can I have?'

'You like hot chips?'

Her little face breaks out into an excited smile and she comes around to me. 'Can I have chips?'

'Why not?' I say shakily, running my hands through her hair. She immediately senses my panic. Her eyes begin to dart about the room as though she too senses the danger. Something isn't right. *She can feel it too.* Oh Jesus. But how much of this is real? Should I be afraid? Jay was always telling me I was paranoid. Maybe he's right. Maybe this is all in my head. *Where is that voice when I need her?*

Please help me, I whisper under my breath. *Please don't let … it happen … please stay with me …* But I'm on my own. No ghost from the past is hovering around, urging me forward, holding me still. No one is telling me to breathe.

Jay is neurotic about what food Nellie eats. Everything has to be organic and ultra-good for her. She's never allowed to have an ice-cream unless someone he knows has made it, or told him it doesn't contain any dreaded chemicals, the names of which I can't even remember.

I pull her to me with one shaking arm and kiss the top of her head and try to smile at Harry.

A middle-aged waitress comes and Nellie gets to order her chips and Harry orders steak. I order soup and bread, but I'm too wound up to even think about food. Harry goes to the bar for drinks.

We're sitting there waiting for the food and looking out at the dark, wet sky when … it happens. Jay walks in. I see the profile clearly, the long straight nose and high forehead, the ponytail down the back. We are squashed into a corner, not easy to see from the door, but my breath gives way. Everything feels as though it's collapsing inside but at the same time I'm weirdly sharp, coldly assessing my options, checking out just how far it is from the front door and how long it will take us to get there. The alternative is to scramble over to the other side of the table, hide Nellie in some way, get us both behind the pillar, and crawl out under the tables. That might give us a chance. He's not moving. I watch as another man approaches him. They smile and shake hands, turn together and start walking towards us. And that's when I see that it's not him.

Not him at all.

'Will you look after her?' I say, getting up, aware that my voice is shaking.

'Of course.' He takes a closer look at me. 'You okay?'

'Yeah.'

'You look … white.'

'I'm okay,' I mutter.

I wind my way around tables towards the swing doors with the *Ladies* sign. I push the door open, stumble into one of the cubicles and vomit. This has been coming. It's been hanging around the edges all afternoon and now here it is, like a kid waiting on the sidelines for the coach to give him a turn on the field. *Here it comes.*

I try to hang on, but the waves of dirty floodwater are rushing towards me. All the broken toys and sodden shoes, the bruises and kids' bikes, the battered guitars and swarming flies are swirling in. I lose my grip and drop to the floor, then edge backwards on my bum into the far corner behind the toilet bowl. I shut my eyes and bury my head in my knees. *Stay away. Don't …*

Blood is beating its way through my body, getting faster and then ... *faster.* I keep my eyes shut, but I know the walls are inching slowly inwards, towards me anyway. A high-pitched note echoes down the empty corridors of my brain. Someone is screaming. Closer now. I try to draw a deep breath but the air stays in my mouth and won't go down. The ceiling is collapsing, the sound of splintering wood and board gets louder. I smell the dust in the air as it edges downward, hemming me in. I'm caught in here now, like a chained dog who smells the fire but can't escape.

My legs and arms have gone stiff and I can't loosen them. They'll call a doctor and they'll put me away. *Just like what happened to my great-grandmother.* I can see the specialists in their white coats conferring. Their faces are passive and noncommittal, but under the nods and the dry tones, blinks and frowns, there are smirks of derision, an understanding that doesn't need to be spoken aloud. *Better get this little crazy into hospital, eh!* Nellie will be sent back to Jay and he'll be given full custody of her. My fate sits on my chest, waiting for me to unravel, just as Jay used to tell me I would. *You need me, babe. Without me they'll put you away. Just like they did to her ... blood wins out every time.*

'Tess! Is there a Tess in here, please?' There is banging on the cubicle door.

'Yeah,' I manage to croak. 'Here.'

'Are you okay?'

'I'm ... okay ... I think,' I whisper.

'Are you able to open the door, sweetie?'

I think it must be the concern in her voice, the word *sweetie.* Who knows? But my limbs slowly come to life and I'm able to get shakily to my feet, and the relief is enormous. I open the door and try to smile.

It is the middle-aged waitress who took our order, built like a small tank, her arms like loaves of thick white bread, and her face as broad and flat as a pancake. And I've never been as pleased to see someone in my whole life.

She looks at me inquiringly. 'You're Tess?'

'Yes,' I manage to whisper.

'Your friend is worried about you.'

I nod stupidly.

'Are you okay?'

I shake my head and try to smile.

'Too much to drink?' she smiles understandingly.

I make no reaction to this. I see she doesn't believe it either. It's just her way to make me feel normal. 'You do look pale, love.' She takes my elbow.

I let her lead me out of the cubicle and over to the sinks to wash my mouth and then through the main toilet door. When we get there I see that the big dining room is exactly the same as when I left it. Harry and Nellie are standing by the window looking out. The woman guides me over to them.

Harry doesn't say anything. I see that their food has been more or less finished.

'Hey,' Harry says.

'Hi.'

'Mamma!' Nellie grabs me around the knees and looks up, and the anxiety and confusion in her face takes away any of the pride I felt that morning at getting her away this far. I'm not a fit person. I've done the wrong thing. She'd probably be better off with him. 'Where did you go, Mamma?'

'Sorry, sweetie.' I squat down and hug her close. 'I just got a fright.'

'What kind of fright?' But she doesn't wait for an answer. She turns to the waitress, who is asking if I'd like my soup heated up. 'I ate all my dinner,' she tells the woman.

'Good girl!' The woman smiles.

'I ate every single speck.' Nellie turns back to me and runs her fingers through my hair like little combs.

'No, you didn't,' Harry laughs. 'I ate some of those chips, remember?'

I sit down. Keep my shaking hands under the table.

The woman comes over with the soup.

'Thanks,' I say and pick up my spoon, but the idea of putting food in my mouth seems odd, to say the least. I take the first spoonful because Harry and Nellie are both watching me keenly. I smile and put the spoon down. 'Afraid I'm not hungry.'

Harry pushes over his half-finished glass of red wine. 'Here, try this,' he says gently. 'Settle you a bit.'

'Thanks.' I take a gulp and shudder at the strange taste. But when I take another, I decide it's okay; I like the way it spreads through my mouth and slides down my gullet. I look at Harry's damaged face opposite me and wonder how many stitches he had in that gash across his forehead. I don't deserve what he is doing for me. I pick up the spoon again. Over in one corner there are whoops and cheers. Maybe it's someone's birthday. Drinks all around. Ordinary life continues. I take a few mouthfuls of soup and then another sip of wine, and feel the blood in my veins warming. I smile at Nellie and flick her hair around a bit, trying to make her smile. Harry is right, I should eat something. I take the spoon to my mouth and tentatively sip the soup.

'Don't be spooked, Tess,' he says casually. 'You hit a rough spot, that's all.'

'Yes.'

'Be okay now,' he grins. 'Until the next one.'

I smile shakily. I can tell by the way his fingers are playing with the menu that he knows what's happened. The way he's frowning. *He's been here too.* It lightens the load a bit to know that.

He gets up and buys another glass of wine and we sit quietly, watching the people around us. At one point I try to get Nellie to sit on my knee. I need to feel her little body up close. But she rebuffs me. 'I'm going to tell Barry all about this when we get home,' she says sniffily, 'about you getting lost in the toilets and everything.'

'Aww, please don't, Nellie,' I whine playfully. But it pleases me to hear her so chirpy about it all.

On the way back to our room the sky is dark and the wind is sharp. We have to shout to make ourselves heard but the rain holds back until we are just metres from the hotel entrance. Harry puts Nellie on his back and we run as the black sky opens. As he's turning the key in the door I have another moment of panic. What if we're going to find the room has been upturned while we've been out?

But the room is just as we've left it. And when the chain has been drawn behind us I breathe out with relief.

'I'm glad to be here,' I say.

'Yeah?'

'Yeah,' I manage.

Right on cue the rain starts to pelt down again. Thunder rumbles in the sky. We turn off the lights and watch out the window, Harry and me on both sides of Nellie. To have a dry comfy place on a night like this is … I've been lucky so far. If we can get down to Victoria in one piece it might all turn out okay.

'Did he hurt her?'

'No,' I lie. 'Just me.'

After the stint in hospital I wasn't as good at pretending – not that I dared say anything – but against my own best interests I sometimes couldn't keep the irritation off my face or stop my mouth going tight in just the way he didn't like.

Slapping me about, yelling and grabbing me by the neck and pushing me into the wall didn't work as well as it used to. I became expert at not letting it reach me. I'd just let myself fall down into another space inside my head and feel the airy freedom there – and be almost surprised by the bruises on my legs and arms the next day. He couldn't touch the core of me anymore, and on some level he sensed it. He had to find another way to get at me and keep me in his power.

I get Nellie to sleep and then, leaving the door ajar, go outside to join Harry, who is smoking and watching the storm. We sit on the narrow verandah together and watch the rain sloshing down between the cars. My arms are folded against the cool air but I'm relishing it, staring out into the night, wishing I could stay forever. I don't want to go to that farm. I don't want to face Beth or Salome, much less my grandfather. *If only …*

Harry's phone rings and he fumbles around for it in the pocket of his jacket.

'It's your brother again,' he says, handing me the phone. 'Listen, I think I'll go have a shower.'

'Okay.' I take the phone, hoping that Marly is going to tell me that he's decided to take a plane. Better still, that he's already in Melbourne and is about to get a bus up to the farm.

'Hey,' he says. 'Is this too late?'

'No, we had to stay another night. Car trouble.'

'Okay now?'

'Yeah.'

'I've arranged for a thousand bucks to be at the post office when you get there. So you've got something to go on with. I get paid tomorrow, so I'll send more.'

'Thanks, Marly.'

There is some kind of tension in his voice that makes me know he wants to say something else.

'There is stuff you should know, Tess.'

'What do you mean?' My heart dives.

'You need to know this,' he begins again. 'Beth probably won't tell you, so I will.'

I catch my breath. 'What do I need to know?' I wait and he says nothing. Some horrible new thing is going to explode into my life and I … I don't want it. *I won't have it!* I find myself holding the phone away from my ear. There is nothing I need to know except how to remain safe.

'What?'

'Mum sent stuff to you.'

I take a sharp breath but don't say anything for quite a while. *'What?'*

'Yeah.'

'What kind of … stuff?'

'Salome and I both said that we should get it to you some way. It wouldn't have been that difficult. We could have sent it to the post office up there in Byron. Someone could have found you and let you know.'

'A parcel?' I whisper.

'She opened it. It was addressed to you, but Beth opened it.'

'So what was in it?'

Marly makes a deep, exasperated sigh. 'A whole lot of fucking shit about our great-grandmother!' he snorts. 'Remember that photo Mum gave you the night before she went?'

I nod but can't speak.

'It was stuff about her. Grandpa's mother. The other Tess.'

'Yeah, I know.'

'She went mad.'

'I know.'

'Shoved off into a mental asylum.'

'I know that.'

'Do you know why?'

'No.'

'Her sister killed herself out there on the farm and it sent her crazy.'

'Oh.' I had a vague memory of being told this. 'What was the sister's name?'

'I don't know,' he says. 'Lizzie, maybe. Who cares?'

'Okay.' I gulp. *Please, Marly, calm down.*

'*Our* mother was off her tree, right? You know that, don't you? You have to understand that.'

Please, Marly! I'm on the point of begging him now. *Please don't talk to me like this. Please.*

'You were thirteen years old when she left. *Thirteen!* I mean, it was bad enough for the rest of us. I was only eighteen …' His voice is cracking now. 'But *thirteen!*' he gasps. 'What kind of mother does that to a girl of thirteen? And when she eventually decides to get in contact after years away she sends you all this crap about someone who's been dead for so long it doesn't matter.' There is a pause while he gathers his breath a bit.

'What kind of crap was it?' I ask, curious in spite of myself.

'Documents. History stuff. Bits and pieces.'

'Was there anything else? I mean, a note to me or …?'

'I dunno.'

'Does … does Beth still have it?'

'I don't know. But I doubt it. She was so jealous of Mum sending something just to you. We all were. Nothing for the rest of us. Just you.'

I can tell he's crying and I can feel how terribly unfair that would seem to them all. 'Sorry,' he says in a quieter tone. 'I'll ring you again in the morning, okay?'

'Okay. Bye, Marly.'

The truth is that I never really connected with the anger that my siblings felt towards our mother for leaving. Not on any deep level, anyway, although I pretended to. I felt the pain, of course, the sense of total abandonment, desolation and loss, but … not the anger. Their way is probably much healthier.

I just missed her. Terribly. I missed the fun of being with her, the mad laughter, the talk about dreams and politics and who was doing what to who, what Beth should do with her hair, whether meat was really bad for you, or if she should cut down the peppermint gum that she'd planted just because Nancy McCann next door objected to its leaves falling on her side of the fence. I missed the way she'd take my hand when we were out walking. *Watch out for cars*, she'd joke as we crossed the road. On our street a car passed by every ten minutes.

Our mother adored gardening. She had climbing roses and jasmine crawling over the fences, great twisting trunks of wisteria growing on frames she erected herself. The verandah was covered with her pots of impatiens and pansies and petunias, geraniums and roses. On hot summer nights we'd sometimes sit out there and watch her watering with the hose. She'd come over occasionally to squirt our feet. 'I can't believe I have produced such a troop of wonderful human beings!' she'd say to herself, but loud enough for us to hear. 'If nothing else, you lot make me feel I've done something with my life!' The others would all groan and laugh and tease her, but I know they loved it too. They loved being her pride and joy, like I did. *All of you*, she'd sometimes mutter, *every one of you lot, my pride and joy*.

That night I have disconnected dreams which drop away as though into some chasm as soon as I wake. Except for one vivid fragment.

I am walking down by the river with Nellie. And I see a woman sitting on the grass. She turns around and smiles at us. I can't see her face exactly, but I think it might be my mother. She doesn't seem at all surprised to see Nellie. I stand watching her and feel very happy.

sixteen

Harry makes us tea while I shower, and then I wake Nellie. She's grumpy while I'm dressing her, rubbing her eyes and complaining about Barry's behaviour during the night.

'What did he do?' I ask, trying to push one of her arms into her top.

'He is so silly,' Nellie says indignantly as I zip her jacket up. 'He thinks Streak would like to make friends with a pussycat.'

'Hmmm, that is a bit silly.'

'It's very silly,' she corrects me.

But when I tell her she can wear her rubber boots, she cheers up.

The guy from the garage rings at eight a.m. to say he's on his way with the car.

'You sleep okay?' Harry wants to know.

'Yeah, good.' I smile at him. 'How about you?'

'I was playing in front of a huge audience,' he tells me ruefully. 'It was going really well, but I was worried that my hand was going to be shown on TV and everyone would think, *Yuck. Get him off!* So I was trying to hide my hand at the same time as play well.' He laughs and shakes his head. 'A big ask!'

'What were you playing?'

He closes his eyes. 'Hmmm. Dunno. Something light and choppy.'

'Yuck!' Nellie, who'd been listening to every word, pipes up. 'Get him off!'

Harry's mouth falls open in mock anger. He pretends to grab her, which has her squealing and giggling with pleasure.

Half an hour later I strap Nellie into the car seat and slide into the front. Harry starts the engine.

'Where are we going *now*?' Nellie moans from the back seat.

'Down to Melbourne,' I tell her quickly.

It seems to suffice for the moment. She's thinking about it, anyway. As we edge out of the parking space and onto the road she keeps staring back at the motel until it disappears from view.

'Are we ever coming back?' she asks.

'Do you want to?' Harry asks.

'I want to go to Melbourne first.'

Harry chuckles. 'Has she ever been to Melbourne?' he asks.

When I shake my head he laughs again.

The sky is heavy and dark as we head south along the highway from Dubbo, through constant drizzle. The radio tells us the day will clear into brightness by the afternoon, but that seems so far off at this point that it's meaningless. The current reality is wet and dark, but the snug safety of the car hurtling along at a hundred kays is all I need. My little girl is within arm's distance and the kind guy alongside me doesn't seem to mind being there too much. What more could I ask for?

An hour in, red and gold light shoots thick straight lines through the trees onto the road ahead of us and a fresh bolt of enchantment catches hold of my heart. This day is like no other, I remind myself. There is every reason to hope. Recent rain has left swathes of water sitting in giant puddles on both sides of the road. The surfaces collect the pink and gold light, each one a pool of gleaming beauty that disappears too quickly as we shoot by.

We drive straight for about three hours, right into an industrial grey light of an ordinary day in late summer. The countryside seems more or less the same, as we cut our way through it, trees and grass, turned up red earth, grazing sheep and crops. Until another hour passes, and I realise that it's changed without me even noticing.

The bushy mountains and rocky outcrops, the hills and curves, the dips and corners have evened out. The road is straighter now, the country less cluttered, flatter and older too, or so it seems. The leaden sky reminds me of a battered old dinner plate, turned upside down over a delicious meal.

I'm half-asleep when Harry pulls over into a big roadhouse for petrol. *The Coolabah Café* is written in huge letters on the roof of the long building. I lower the window and crisp air rushes in. We're in the middle of nowhere and yet … it's so busy. There are at least a dozen enormous transport vehicles parked along fences at the back and side of the building. A couple of tourists are consulting a map out the front. Radios blare and men walk by in work clothes, rubbing their hands, calling to each other, shouting good-natured abuse, smiling, jumping in and out of trucks, checking tyres and loads, honking their horns as they leave. Nellie wakes complaining of hunger.

Harry pays for petrol and looks in at me. 'Want to get something to eat?'

'Okay.'

He parks the car behind one of the big transports and we all get out. I watch Nellie take his hand. They walk on ahead towards the glass doors of the café and I take a minute to stretch. I count the trucks to fifteen until I get confused as to whether I'm counting some twice. They wait in rows, like huge tanks left to rot after a big battle. The water is everywhere, glistening patches along the cement, deeper puddles in the dirt, birds going berserk with their sudden good fortune. They splash about, fighting for space, fluffing out their feathers, hopping and diving on each other, chirping and screeching.

Once inside, I see Harry and Nellie waiting for me at a table near the window. They wave me over. I'm not hungry, but I point out the egg and bacon roll, thinking I'll be able to save it for later.

Harry leaves his jacket on the chair, stands up and goes over to the counter to join the queue. 'If Jules calls, tell her I'll ring back.' He points to his jacket pocket.

'Okay.'

When the phone rings first I don't get to it in time. When it rings again Harry is in the middle of ordering the food from the woman behind the cash register, so I pull it out and press the green button. Marly. It might be Marly with more to say about Beth and the stuff Mum sent. The line cuts out before I can even say hello.

Nellie is kneeling up on her chair, intent on her game with a dozen or so sachets of salt and sugar. She has them in teams, the sugars lined up next to the plastic sauce bottle and the salts in two straight lines behind a tiny vase full of artificial blue flowers.

When the phone rings a third time I get to it faster. 'Hey,' I say. 'Tess speaking.'

There is a moment of someone breathing.

'Tess.'

My whole being stills. I am suddenly alone in that big, bright, cheerful room. I get up quickly and back up against the nearest wall. A roaring begins around my ears, quickening and expanding each time the glass doors open, the rhythm of it becoming more chaotic. I stare around frantically. Three men eat alone at separate tables and another half-dozen road workers in high-visibility gear laugh and talk over coffee. There are possibly a dozen lining up for takeaway at the glass counters, Harry among them. He's not here. Which doesn't mean that he's not outside, possibly watching me.

'Tessa, where are you?'

I'm only just breathing by this stage, and I certainly don't remember where I am. I watch Harry walk back to the table and hear Nellie's voice chirping away, followed by Harry's deep voice.

How come other people know how to live their lives when I don't even know where I am?

'You need to come home, baby,' Jay says calmly and reasonably. 'You know that, don't you? You and Nellie need to come home. We can forget all this.' He waits for me, but I don't make a sound. 'You had no right to take Nellie, Tess.' His voice is almost caressing. 'You know that, don't you, baby? We'll work it out, eh?' Still I make no response. 'You're acting illegally, Tess. Any judge will tell you that.' Still I make no sound. 'Tessa?'

'Yes.' The ground seems to be falling away from under me.

'You understand what I said?'

'Yes,' I whisper. *Illegal. Any judge ... You need to come home.*

'Tell me where you are and I'll come and get you.' His voice becomes a soft, urgent whisper. 'Because ... I love you, baby. You know that, don't you?'

'Yes,' I whisper.

'So where are you?'

I try to think, but my terror has everything jumbling up in my brain. 'I don't know,' I whisper truthfully, but trying to think anyway. *Where are we?* 'There is a name along the top of this building, but I've forgotten it.'

'So where were you last night?'

I think hard but I can't even remember that.

He sighs and waits a moment. 'But you're still on the road?'

'Yes.'

'So what highway are you on?'

'Well, I ...' I turn to the window automatically to see if there will be something out there that will tell me.

'Come on, Tess,' he says in his cool, patient, calm voice. 'Think.'

'Okay.'

I turn back to the room, to where Nellie, dressed in her pink cords and boots, her hair tied back into a bun on top of her head, is smiling excitedly as the waitress sets down the food. I see how little she is. How very little. I have a sudden flash of finding her that day, locked in the back room.

My little girl, face grimy with dust and tears and the smell of her pee on the floor, and his cool expression as he watched me kneel down and hold out my arms. My little girl, so terrified that she wouldn't move towards me. Those raised red marks on her legs where he hit her. Not with his hands, even, but with a stick. A short, hard stick. His mother was sick in bed and I'd just come back from visiting her. I'd made her a cake, and she'd kept me talking for well over an hour. *I'll just run up and give this to her,* I'd said. *Will you watch Nellie?* Thing is, I could see he was in one of his sour moods and I'd stayed too long. I had to coax Nellie over. But before I got to hold her, he jerked my head back by the hair, twisting me around to face him.

'She has to learn, okay?' He twisted my hair tighter, and I gasped with the pain and kept looking at him blankly. 'Whining and interrupting me when I'm working. She has to learn not to do that.'

I stared at him.

'You understand that, don't you, Tess?' My head was as far back as it would go by then.

'Yes,' I whispered. *Coward Tess.* 'Yes. I understand.'

Now I watch Nellie hop down from her chair and go around to Harry. She takes his crippled hand in her own to have a good look at it, then she puts it back by the side of his plate as though she has finished with it at last. They both look over at me, smiling. It's precisely at that point that I see myself back on that hospital trolley.

Dying. Feeling myself slowly ebbing away. And not minding that much either. And then I hear that voice again, clear as a bell in the cacophony of this busy café.

Stay with me.

So clear! I turn around quickly to see who has spoken. But no one is there. No one has spoken. There is just the hard wall behind me. That's when I come rushing back into myself, gasping as though I'm coming up to the surface after time underwater.

No way will that bastard ever touch her again!

Harry looks over at me. He must be able to tell that something is up, because his expression becomes serious. He pushes free of the table and comes straight over. I press the red button and give him the phone.

'It was him.'

'What? How? Did you say anything to him?'

I can only stare at him in shock. 'No. But he's onto me.'

'Christ,' Harry groans. 'His brother must have got the rego after all.' Harry sits down and sighs. 'The car isn't in my name. Fuck, he must have got in touch with my mother. I should have thought of that … He's fed her some bullshit and she's given him my phone number. I'll change it as soon as I can.'

'But you can't do that!'

'Why not?'

My hands are shaking and I'm speaking too fast. 'What about your family and friends? You can't just change your number!'

'There's my mother and there's Jules and there's … you. I can't think of anyone else who needs it. For the moment I'll just turn it off when I'm not using it.'

We're on the road again, the kilometres disappearing beneath us. The towns get closer and closer together as the morning pushes on into late afternoon. I'm tired, but I'm too on edge to doze. Harry turns every now and again as though to speak and then seems to think better of it. Eventually he switches on the radio. But there is nothing decent to listen to. 'You got any music?' he asks.

I undo my seatbelt, lean back and take my old journal out of the backpack. Inside the front cover is Dad's CD. Its cover is torn and the image old-fashioned, but I'm suddenly curious to hear it again.

'Who is it?'

'Django Reinhardt. Have you heard of him?'

'Vaguely.'

'Gypsy Jazz.'

'Okay!' Harry puts on his right indicator and picks up speed to pass the truck in front. The music explodes into the car, so lively and dark, so full of lovely life. I slump into my seat and throw my head back, clasping my hands over my belly, thumbs bouncing in time, my grimy toes dancing in my cheap sandals.

I'm a girl, maybe eight or nine, sitting outside the garage on a hot night, this music pumping out into the surrounding darkness from the tinny player Dad keeps out there for his own use. I feel myself lifting up, as we drive along, flying out across the sky to meet him. *Hey, Dad!* I look back at Nellie, who is wriggling her toes and flapping her hands around in time with the music for Harry's benefit. *Hey, Dad. Here I am. I got away …*

I played this CD to Jay once. We'd been for a late-night swim and neither of us wanted to go home, even though it was late. So I'd slipped it into the stereo of his brother's car and we left the doors open and leant our backs up against it and listened to it in the warm darkness. Within minutes I was overwhelmed with a flood of memories of my father. It was almost too much. I hadn't known until then how much was sitting there, dense and complex as this music would look written on a page. When the music finished Jay put his arm around me.

'Why are you crying?' he asked, genuinely incredulous.

'My father,' I whispered, taking the hanky he offered, 'that music … it brings him back to me so vividly. I can see him … how it used to be when—'

'He's not worth it,' Jay cut in sharply. 'He let you down.' He pulled me into a tight hug and then kissed me. 'I won't let you down, okay?'

'Okay.'

That felt good. He was older and knew about everything. And he was good-looking and had money, and didn't seem to mind that I was young and pretty stupid. To be told by such a person that he would care for me felt wonderful.

I open the window and lean my head out a bit, letting the breeze take my hair. The notes dip and soar like a flock of birds. Ten minutes in and they've busted straight through into my heart. Except for fear, I've been devoid of strong feelings for so long, and now every funny, sad, painful thing that has ever happened to me is coming together in these riffs and bars of music.

'So what do you reckon now, Tess?' Harry calls over to me.

'About what?'

'Anything.'

'I reckon,' I say, hauling my arm through the air out the window, 'that this is good.'

'What in particular?'

'Being here and … listening to this music again. My dad's music. Getting away!'

He grins at me.

'Thanks to you and Jules.'

'No,' he says. 'You were brave enough to go.'

Almost an hour passes without us saying anything else. Eventually the CD ends and I look over at Harry.

'You like it?' I ask.

'Yeah. Who wouldn't like it?'

'But do you think it's … really *good*?'

'Of course it's good.' He frowns. 'It's fantastic.'

'You seriously think it's really great music or are you just saying it?' I persist.

He takes a long suck of his bottle of water and laughs. 'It's fucking great music, okay … Of course it is!'

'Okay, now let me tell you something. That guy played with only two fingers on his left hand.'

Harry nods, says nothing. I can't even read his expression. It's just his profile staring at the road ahead as he drives.

'Two fingers, Harry!' I can't keep the excitement out of my voice. It seems so important that he knows this. I hand him over the cover with the notes on the back. He nods and puts it on the dashboard.

'Sure, I'll read it later.'

'He was the only European jazz musician that the Americans took seriously.'

'Your point?'

'What can you do with your fingers?'

'Not much.'

'Show me.'

He holds out his damaged left hand. I take it in my own and manipulate the fingers, as though I know what I'm doing. The thumb is fine, so too the index finger. The next one is stiff and bent but there is some movement. The next two are disfigured with no movement at all. 'Have you worked with this hand much since the accident?' I ask. 'I mean, have you had physiotherapy and stuff?'

'Yeah.'

'And?'

'It's become pretty handy for rolling fags,' he grins sheepishly.

'Start tomorrow,' I order.

'Okay!' he laughs.

'You got a guitar?'

'No.'

'Get one tomorrow.'

When Nellie and I come back to the car after a quick toilet stop Harry is reading the CD sleeve notes.

He looks up at me eventually, a laugh playing around the corners of his mouth. 'So you think I should start teaching myself to play with two fingers and turn myself into a jazz musician?'

'Why not?'

He gives in and throws his head back to laugh.

'Do it to piss your father off.'

That idea makes him laugh harder.

'Come on, Harry. Tell me you'll think about it!'

He puts the cover down, starts up the engine, and closes his eyes for a moment before we get back out onto the road. I can tell he's tired.

'Let's hear it again?'

'Sure.'

It is almost nine p.m. when we finally get to the turn-off that will lead to my grandparents' place. My body stills. In my relief at having somewhere to go I'd forgotten how even this road would affect me. How can this be right? It feels like I'm driving straight back into the past.

Harry must sense the change in me, because he keeps glancing over. 'So, tell me about this place we're going,' he says.

'It was where … where my mother … grew up,' I tell him. Then I start to weep quietly in the dark. I can't help it. I don't make any sound, so I don't know why he stops the car.

He turns off the lights and puts a hand on my knee. 'It's gonna be okay, Tess.'

'Yeah. Of course. Sorry.'

'It will,' he tells me again. 'It will work out.'

'Yeah.'

'So this house we're heading for belongs to … who?'

'My grandparents. Only my grandfather now. Grandma is dead. He's sick in hospital and … is dying, apparently.'

'Right.'

'Before that it belonged to his parents. I was named after his mother, my great-grandmother.' I shrug and laugh a bit. 'Not that that has got to do with anything!'

'Okay.'

I fumble around in my pocket for a tissue, but Harry offers me his hanky. 'Go on, take it.'

'But it's ironed,' I protest, trying to give it back.

'That's Jules for you.' He grins. 'She insists on everything being ironed. Even sheets.'

'She irons sheets?'

'I used to think it was crazy too,' he says conversationally. 'But have you ever slept in ironed sheets?'

'No.'

'It's unreal.'

'Is it?'

'Believe me, Tess, it is!'

'I believe you!'

There is a smattering of rain on the window. I peer out, wishing suddenly I *was* Jules. How easy it would be! Born beautiful and talented, she nabs the kindest, nicest boyfriend around. Nellie stirs in her sleep.

Harry leans back against his window and reaches out to take my hand. 'So you used to live here?' he asks.

'No.' I blow my nose. 'But we came here a lot.'

He nods and turns up the radio a bit. 'Bach.' He smiles. 'I used to play this.'

'How old were you?'

'About twelve, I think.'

I'm glimpsing the boy again, Harry and his bouncy curls, carrying his violin to lesson after lesson. Doing his best. Coming back home to his gran, who looked after him when his parents were away on tour.

The shower stops; clouds move across the sky and a half-moon is sitting there amid the bright stars, and I remember how it was before Dad died and Mum went away, and how I loved the sky up here. Mum and I would be coming back from one of our visits to the oldies – sometimes we'd stay longer and have dinner with them, always chops and spuds and sometimes pumpkin and peas – and on warm clear nights she'd just about always stop the car, usually at the same spot about a kilometre from the old house where there is a bit of clearing between trees. The stars were so bright. We'd both get out and I'd lean against the car and watch her turning around on the spot, both arms stretched out, her face turned up to the stars.

Look up, Tessa darling, she'd call to me. *Find your own lucky star!*

'Listen, if this is all too much. If you really don't want to go to your grandparents' place, then come with me. My aunt will put us up for a while. She's okay. She won't mind having your little girl, either. Or we can go back to the city.'

'I told Beth I'd come,' I say. 'I've got to face them sometime.'

'Okay.' He starts the car.

I soon catch sight of a faint light through the trees. When we pull up in front of the house, Harry lets out a long sigh, stretches back and closes his eyes for a minute. I peer out, so grateful to have arrived at last, and glad too that it's night-time so I can't see too much all at once.

We get out into fresh, chilly country air that smells of rain. Harry unbuckles Nellie from her seat and I pull out my backpack. I look up into the star-filled sky and try to make a wish. But the porch light goes on before I can.

Beth's face in the yellow glow is exactly as I remember it. She is in a long wool dressing-gown and slippers. Her red-gold hair is falling loose down her back. She looks like a stern aunt from a BBC adaptation of a Brontë novel. The only thing missing is her candle. She comes closer, and then closer still, takes me by both shoulders.

'Tess.' She gives me a small smile, and kisses me on both cheeks.

I have a mad nervous impulse to make a joke just to see her laugh like she used to.

'Hi, Beth,' I say.

She lets me go, and looks over to where Harry is standing with the sleeping Nellie in his arms.

'I'm Harry. I gave your sister a ride down.'

'Come in, then,' she orders. 'Both of you.'

Once inside I almost keel over. It feels as if it has been waiting for me all along, the worn laminex table, the sagging curtains, the grease-encrusted walls around the stove. The whole place smells of an old man living on his own. And under all that is something else, more powerful, as deep and personal as my own sweat. *Us.* It smells of all of us, my brother and sisters and Mum and Dad. It reeks of the past.

'I've only been here a couple of days.' Beth waves apologetic-ally around the room. 'I stayed in a pub in town last night.' She smiles grimly. 'Didn't quite have it in me to be here by myself. It's terrible, isn't it? The place hasn't been cleaned properly in years!'

'Right.'

'We might have to employ help for some of it,' she mumbles. I watch her taking in Harry's blank eye, the gash across his forehead, the damaged hand, trying to work him out. Then she takes a quick look down into Nellie's sleeping face and turns back to me. 'So this is … the child?'

'Nellie.'

Her whole face stills and then softens. With some effort she turns back to us.

'So you drove, Harry?'

He nods, and I realise that I didn't mention I'd be arriving with a stranger.

'Tea?' Beth looks from me to him.

'Great, thanks,' Harry says softly.

Beth goes over to the electric jug in the corner, switches it on.

'I've made up beds for you and her in the room opposite the bathroom,' she says to me. She looks at Harry. 'I wasn't sure how … you'd get here … but I can easily make up a bed in the sleep-out.' She points outside. 'Just off the verandah.'

'Anywhere,' Harry laughs. 'I'm pretty knackered.'

'Did you help with the driving?' Beth asks me.

I shake my head.

Harry looks around the kitchen, taking in the old-fashioned cooking range, the shabby furniture and grimy windows. Beth brings the tea over in a china pot. Then she sets out mugs and milk and sugar. She lifts a plastic lid off a plate and sets out an iced cake for us.

Harry's eyes light up. 'You made this?' he asks, accepting a slice.

She smiles faintly. 'I thought you might want something.'

'Thanks!'

'You got the old wood stove working?' I smile at her, remembering the time Grandma and Grandpa went to Tasmania to see a dying relative and we all had to move out here for the duration. It was a hot summer and Grandpa wanted someone looking after the place in case of fire. Our mother battled that oven every day, swearing and cursing the whole time, just as I suppose Grandma did, and Tess before her. It's a relic from another age, but on a cool night like this the warmth is comforting.

'It wasn't so hard,' she says shortly. 'Mum always made such a big deal of everything.'

I sit back, shocked at her casual mention of our mother.

'Have you heard … anything of her?' I ask.

'No.' Her face tightens. 'Nothing.'

Liar.

Nellie suddenly wakes up. She pulls away from Harry's shoulder and stares around the kitchen suspiciously. Her eyes rest on Beth for a while and then they go back to Harry's face as though she's trying to work out who he is.

'Nellie, this is your Auntie Beth,' I say.

'Where is Flash?' she asks, struggling to get down. She comes over and stands by me. When I try to pick her up she pushes me away but keeps one hand on my knee. She stares around warily from Beth to Harry and then back to me. 'I want Flash,' she mumbles darkly. 'You said—'

'Who is Flash?' Beth asks.

'The other dog,' she whispers shyly. '*My* dog is home with Daddy.'

'Well …' Beth is confused. She smiles. 'I'm not sure, sweetheart.'

Thankfully Nellie lets it go. Her little head swivels this way and that, taking everything in.

'He doesn't know where you are?' Beth asks under her breath.

'No.'

Nellie climbs onto Harry's knee and reaches for some cake.

It's while I'm drinking the tea that the day catches up with me, hits me between the eyes, making me queasy with relief. I begin to shake. *I've done it. I got away. I am … Where?* The combination of exhilaration and exhaustion is brutal. I try to think, but I can't. *Who are these people?* I know the strange young woman in front of me is my sister. My sister, who I haven't seen in four years! Next to her is the half-blind, one-legged ex-musician who gave me a ride down. Harry. I remember the two nights we spent in the motel. Getting tipsy that first night as we ate the takeaway out on the lawn. I thought I was so smart then, forgetting the danger and the insecurity. I don't forget it now.

This is my child sitting on his lap. *My child? His child. Our child.* Am I for real? Am I going to wake up and find myself back in Byron? Will Jay come in any minute with that wry look on his face? *Nice try, Tess.* Or will it be my mother? *Bad dream, sweetie. Don't worry. Bad dream.*

Mum. I almost say the words aloud. *I dreamt that I had a baby. Isn't that crazy?* Suddenly my teeth are chattering uncontrollably and I can't hold the cup. Hot tea splashes over my knees.

'Tess?'

'It's been a big day,' Harry explains.

'Yes,' Beth says.

Nellie lurches away from Harry and scrabbles onto my knee, kneels up to face me, throwing her arms around my neck. 'Mamma?'

'Yes.'

'It's okay now,' she says softly.

'I know, baby,' I whisper. 'I know.'

'Good, Mamma,' she whispers in my ear.

I hug her tightly. She's three years old! I so hate her having to see me like this. It's my job to look after her. Too often lately it has been the other way around.

'If you've finished your tea I'll show you where to sleep,' Beth says uncertainly. My shakiness has unnerved her.

With Nellie on one hip I follow my sister meekly up the musty old hallway to what was known as the blue room, the one just down from where Grandma and Grandpa used to sleep.

There are two freshly made-up single beds, a cheap dressing table in between, a chair and an old wardrobe. Everything feels so familiar that it's as if I've never left.

'This is just how it was,' I say stupidly. But I feel something waiting for me at the edges of my brain, some unwanted memory about to leap forward and attack me. *This room. I remember this room. This was my mother's room when she was a little girl and she told me …* But I can't remember.

'More or less.' Beth waves around the room. 'I did the best I could.'

'Thanks, Beth.'

'I'll leave you, then.' She smiles briefly without meeting my eyes. 'I guess you remember where the bathroom is.'

'Yeah.'

I lay Nellie on one of the beds and begin to undress her. When she sees the pyjamas she squirms in protest and refuses to raise her arms.

'Not those ones! I want my red ones.'

'Haven't got them, Nellie.'

'I don't want to sleep here!'

'You'll be right next to me.'

Her eyelids are drooping. Meanwhile, I'm finding the buttons challenging.

'Why are you shaking?' she grizzles sleepily, and slaps half-heartedly at my trembling hands.

'I'm just tired,' I whisper.

Her eyes close and she lifts both arms up to my face. 'Don't cry, Mamma.'

'Okay.'

'Will Barry like Flash?'

'I think so,' I say.

I sit there patting her hair and she ends up going off to sleep in just her little singlet and pants, holding tightly to Barry.

As soon as I know she's away I lunge for the other bed, facedown. I'm so wrecked that my eyes feel as though they're on fire. How could I have forgotten? *This fucking room!* How could I be back here? After that day I never ... And yet here I am.

There's a movement behind me. I become aware of Beth standing by the door holding a nightie. She comes over and sits on the end of the bed. When I turn over she hands it to me. *I need to tell her that I can't stay in this room.*

'You want to have a bath or something?'

'No ... I'll go to bed.' I'm trying like crazy not to lose it completely, but I don't know how much longer I can hang on. What if Jay is in the ute right now? Roaring up the track towards this house? The image rushes around my brain like a live scorpion, and I'm tempted to crawl under the bed, hide somewhere. I want to hug someone. I want to scream.

Beth must sense my agitation, because she gets up and comes nearer, takes my elbow and gently eases me off the bed then pulls back the sheet.

'Get your things off,' she orders quietly. 'I'll go organise your friend's bed.'

'There's memories in this room, Beth. I don't think ...'

'Well, forget them!' she says sharply. 'The other bedroom is full of junk and the plaster is falling in.'

'Okay … It's just that …'

'And believe me, you don't want to sleep in Grandpa's room!'

'No.'

So I do what I'm told, get into the nightie and crawl under the blankets. I need to calm down. If only I could. But in spite of being so zonked my mind is racing. I shut my eyes and wild bat-like creatures swoop at me, so I keep them open and that is worse. I feel as though ants are crawling over my lids trying to find a way into my head.

When Beth comes back she is carrying a glass of water and a cup of something hot. She sits on the edge of the bed and hands me the glass. I want to tell her thanks, that it's good to see her, but I can't somehow.

'Is Grandpa's rifle still around?' I ask, my voice cracked and hoarse.

She recoils then stares at me hard. 'Why?'

I gulp and turn away. 'I just want to know. It used to be kept in the old laundry.'

'You feel unsafe?'

I turn back to look at her and say nothing.

'It's still there, I think,' she says quietly.

'Is there any ammunition?'

'You don't need a gun, Tess,' she says, and I understand just how crazy I must sound, but I can't seem to help myself.

'It wouldn't be that hard.' I stare wildly at her, not taking the hot drink she is holding out. 'Just aim the fucking thing and pull the trigger.' I'm still shivering like crazy but my voice is strong enough, except … it sounds like someone else's.

Beth gives a deep sigh and shakes her head. 'Take these Panadol,' she says. Putting the cup down next to me, she feels in her pocket and brings out two round white pills. 'Sorry I haven't got anything stronger.'

I sit up and swallow the pills. She settles some pillows behind me.

'Now drink,' she orders, handing me the cup again. 'The hot chocolate will do you good.' I shake my head, but she insists. 'Milk will help you sleep.'

So I drink obediently, so grateful suddenly for this kindness that I almost grab her hand and kiss it.

'You're safe here,' she says quietly.

'Thanks, Beth.' She turns for the door. 'Are you a doctor now?' I ask.

'I finished last year.'

'Congratulations.'

But she only shrugs and murmurs thanks, then disappears without another smile or word.

Eventually I must fall asleep, because sometime later I wake, convinced that someone is in the room with us. When I look around I see a woman by the window in the chair, rocking. Her profile stands out against the light from outside. I'm not afraid of her; in fact, I'm strangely comforted by this presence. A gust of breeze pushes the blind open and more of the night sky comes in. I turn my eyes away to the door and when I look back the woman is gone. I make myself push off the sheet and go to the window and pull up the sash.

I perch on the end of Nellie's bed, my elbows resting on the wooden windowsill, and stare out at the night sky. So bright with so many stars that it is almost like daylight. The old house is set on a hill, and the back garden slopes down towards the creek and the dirt track that leads up into the mountains behind. I can make out the back fence, the gate leading out to the clothesline and the small chicken shed, and the familiarity comforts me. I remember trailing after my mother and grandma as they talked about plants. How Grandma loved the garden. The original trees had been planted before her time, but she was always planting new shrubs and seasonal beds of colourful annuals. She passed all that on to my mother. I can just make out the row of roses either side of the path, and I see myself as a little kid, walking up and down between them in midsummer, thinking that it must be what heaven smelled like.

Nellie cries out in her sleep and that normal sound brings me back to the present.

'It's okay, Nellie,' I tell her. 'I'm here.' I move away from my position by the window.

'Are we home yet?' she asks me, half-asleep.

'Yes,' I say. 'Home now.'

Before heading back to my bed, I stand and watch threads of moonlight dancing across Nellie's face and allow myself a moment of pride.

We got here, baby. So far so good.

He'd been gone with his brother Nick into town for over an hour, and his phone was sitting there on the table where he'd left it by mistake. I knew that they were going to have a meeting with someone there, so I thought I'd be safe. Besides, I'd hear the car, or the crunch of footsteps on the path outside, or there would be noise of him coming in through the back door.

But I heard nothing.

He'd sidled into the room and must have stood listening to me for some time as I gabbled to the woman. All my breathless, inarticulate, fearful ramblings of why I needed help. I'd been on the point of giving the address when, like in the worst horror film, his hand reached over my shoulder from behind and he took the phone from me. I don't know that I have ever felt such shock as at that moment. Nor have I ever felt such desperate dread. His other arm reached around me to cut off the connection. So I was standing there with both his arms around me, and him breathing heavily in my ear. Then Nellie woke from her afternoon sleep. I slipped out from under his hold and went to her.

Nothing happened until Nellie was all tucked up in bed that night. After that I went out onto the verandah and waited. It wasn't for long. He came out and without a word grabbed me by my hair and pulled me inside and into the bathroom, closed the door and made me undress and get into the bath of cold water that he had ready. Without raising his voice he ordered me to lie down in the water. Then he proceeded to 'drown' me about eight times, only letting me surface when I was about to take water into my lungs. He'd let me breathe and cough and then … he'd do it again. I don't know how long it lasted. Maybe it was an hour, maybe it was five minutes, but by the time it was over I was a blithering wreck, sobbing, gasping, slobbering and agreeing to anything if he'd just stop, if he'd let me live. All the time I was thinking of Nellie and what would happen if I died.

He did stop eventually, left me there in the bathroom. I stayed there naked on the floor, snivelling and crying, my whole body shaking and my teeth chattering even though it wasn't really cold. When he came back he was eating an apple. He stood in the doorway looking down at me.

'Don't *ever* do that again, Tess,' he said softly, and then closed the door. I stayed there for another hour before he came back in. By that stage I'd thrown up a couple of times and pissed myself.

The next time he came in it was with two fluffy towels. He wrapped one around my head and the other around my body. Then he led me out into the living room, sat me on the couch and sat down beside me. I was shivering and shaking, unable to stop, not only because of what I'd just been through but because I knew it might be only the beginning. What if he'd decided to kill me now?

'You know we're going to be alright,' he said in a conversational tone. He put an arm around me and began to run his fingers through my hair. 'We'll get married. What do you think?'

I couldn't even look at him, much less speak or think.

'Come on, babe, you'd like that, wouldn't you?' He kissed my cheek.

I tried to clench my teeth together to stop them chattering, then I stuck both hands down under me to stop them shaking. I had the feeling that I was going to lose control of my bowels any minute, and so I had to concentrate on that.

'Be a good move for us, I reckon,' he went on mildly. 'Make you feel secure.'

I nodded.

'What do you think?'

'Okay,' I whispered.

seventeen

Where the hell am I? Something about the angle of the light falling in around the blind tells me that the day began long ago. It is stifling and my whole body under the bedclothes is damp with sweat, but I'm too afraid to push off the covers. I have a vague idea that I've been in this room before, but I've been waking and drifting down again to sleep for hours now and so it might be an illusion. I fall back into the heat and sweat of sleep.

Later, when I wake properly, I sit up, and then slide back down when I hear voices and the clatter of dishes. A male voice shouts something and then there is a low buzz of chatter. Someone laughs. I'm in some kind of jail. Will they give me water?

I look over at the other bed and see that it is empty and the blankets are rumpled. *Nellie.* I kick off the bed cover. I'm in a long nightie that doesn't belong to me, so wet it sticks to my chest and legs. *Soon*, I think. *Soon I will stand up and go to the window and see if I can open it. Soon this heavy feeling in my legs will lift and I'll call out for a drink of water.* I slough off the wet nightie and pull on the jeans and T-shirt that I wore yesterday. My mouth is dry and my heart is beating hard when I open the blind. I pull up the window sash and breathe in sweet fresh air. This is my grandparents' place, but … I don't remember getting here.

I tiptoe to the door and then out into a musty hall. The sour smell is so weirdly familiar. I wonder if the murmuring voices are real or the beginning of a fresh lot of brain chatter. They get louder. I don't recognise any one voice. I put my hand on the doorknob and push open the door, and there they are: my sister Beth at the table with Nellie, who is sitting on a cushion eating an egg. Next to her on another chair is Barry the bear. Beth and Nellie look up expectantly and solemnly. Neither smiles. Barry stares straight ahead, his mismatched button eyes looking almost intelligent in the light. At the sink with his back to me is a man. He turns around and I see a vaguely familiar face. Oh. Harry. It comes rushing back. I smile shakily and he smiles.

'Well ...' he says warmly.

'Hi.'

'You've been asleep a long time.'

'We might go to the river soon,' Nellie tells me conversationally. 'Me and Beebe and Harry and Barry!'

'Beebe?'

'That's me, apparently.' Beth laughs in spite of herself. 'I've acquired a nickname overnight!'

I see that she doesn't mind this at all. I smile back tentatively.

'And Barry and I are twins,' Harry tells me, putting a hand on Barry's head. 'Although I'm not sure he's pleased about it.'

'And I'm their mum,' Nellie tells me excitedly.

'Can I come?' I ask Nellie. 'To the river?'

She has to think for a moment.

'Alright.' She sighs in a world-weary way, as though doing me a big favour. 'But we have to do cleaning first and then go see my *great*-grandfather.' She looks up at Beth over the rim of her cup. 'He's in hospital, isn't he, Beebe?'

'That's right,' Beth smiles.

'Okay.' I look at Beth. 'How is he?'

She shrugs and puts some orange juice in my hands and guides me to a chair. I guzzle it all down, then get up and go to the tap and drink three glasses of water straight.

'I've told him about you coming and he wants to see you.'

I nod and switch on the kettle. Beth's strong sense of the right thing to do has always intimidated me.

When I turn around, Harry is wiping up the egg on Nellie's plate with a piece of bread. He holds it up and makes the sound of a train as it flies around the air before popping it into his mouth. Nellie giggles with delight before turning to me.

'Are we staying here, Mamma?'

'For a while.'

'Does Daddy know we're here?'

'Ah, not really,' I mumble.

'What is he doing now?'

'I don't know. Maybe feeding the dogs?'

'But that is our job!' She looks at the other two indignantly. 'Streak won't like it much if we're not there. He only likes us.'

'Why is that, Nellie?'

'Daddy growls at him.'

Beth nods calmly as she bends over to cut Nellie's toast into small diamond-shaped pieces.

'Beebe is better than you, Mamma,' Nellie declares gleefully.

'Really?' I smile weakly.

'You never cut my toast like this!' She delicately picks up one of the diamonds and pops it in her mouth. I sit down with my tea and watch them. Nellie is talking away to herself as she pretends to feed Barry.

'How do you want to tackle the house-cleaning?' I ask, for something to say.

'One room at a time, I guess,' Beth says. She takes a deep breath. 'Would you mind tackling his room?' she asks, avoiding my eyes. 'When you're ready, I mean. No hurry. It's mainly a question of clearing out rubbish.'

'You mean …?'

'Grandpa's room.'

I look over at Harry helplessly, hoping he can read my mind. *It was a terrible mistake coming here. We should leave after breakfast. This place is going to tip me over the edge …*

'Sure. I can do that,' I tell her.

'We should go into town first up.' Beth flicks the crumbs off the table. 'Get some cleaning stuff … Maybe go and see him?'

'Okay.'

Suddenly Nellie heaves a deep, dramatic sigh and gives Barry a swift punch in the face. 'Barry isn't getting breakfast,' she says furiously, then pulls his left ear and slaps his face again.

'Hey!' Harry protests. 'He's just a bear. Don't be too hard on him.'

'But he knows better!' Nellie declares loudly, her little face screwed up as though she's about to cry.

'What has he done?'

'Sometimes he doesn't even try to be quiet!' she cries in frustration, pushing Barry off his chair. 'Chatter chatter chatter!' Then she gets down from the table and storms into the next room.

The other two look at each other and then at me.

'What was that about?' Harry asks.

I shrug and shake my head, but I know. It was what Jay would say to her when he wanted quietness. *Shut your chatter, Nellie … I'm working. I'm singing. I'm thinking. Stop the chat.*

Beth looks at me accusingly.

'It's not my fault,' I shoot straight back at her.

'Really?' she says coldly. The pent-up fury of years is flashing behind her eyes. 'Then whose fault is it?'

Harry breathes out uncomfortably and clears his throat, and I turn away to the window, holding tight to my cup, trying like crazy not to lose it.

'What I meant was that I can't help being a bit … a bit nervy.'

'Did he bash you?'

I nod and she groans. She covers her eyes with her small white hands and stays like that for a moment. Then she gets up to collect the dishes from the table and throws them angrily into the sink. I watch her pale face come alive with colour, her eyes flashing angrily in just the way I remember.

'So why didn't you leave?' she rants, her back to me. 'Our family might have been … *fucked*, but we had pride! Where was your pride?'

I feel so winded by this that I can only stare at her rigid back. I think my mouth is open too.

'Not so easy,' Harry chips in quickly. 'With a kid.'

Beth turns and looks at him sharply, then back at me, and finally shrugs as though it is all beyond her and she is already thinking about something else.

Humiliation has many hues and shades. This one is a bright pink flag flapping on a high pole against the grey sky of my life. Beth puts more dishes in the sink.

Behind her back Harry makes a funny face and winks at me with his good eye. 'Okay, then.' He moves to get up. 'I'll get stuck into a bit of that stuff in the shed before I go, shall I?'

Beth turns with a full-on smile for him. 'Are you sure, Harry?'

'No worries at all.'

'That would be so helpful.'

He disappears quietly, and then it's just Beth and me.

'A nice fellow.'

'Yes.'

'He offered to help with some of the heavy stuff today before he leaves.'

'Good of him,' I mutter.

Beth pokes her head around the inside door to check on Nellie, then turns back to me with a smile. 'She's fine. Playing with the cushions. So where did you meet him?' she asks.

I see now that she thinks I've ditched one guy only to take up straight away with another.

'The library.' I shrug. 'But I don't really know him.'

'Oh?'

'I met him and his girlfriend there,' I explain defensively. 'And they both agreed to help me escape. He's not my … boyfriend. I don't know him. He's not *with* me.'

'So where is she?' Beth asks as she gets up and returns to the sink. She doesn't believe me!

'Up in Byron with her sick grandmother,' I snap. 'Coming back this week.'

Nellie careers back into the room, picks up Barry by one leg and scoots out onto the verandah.

Beth stands up and looks out the window after her. 'We're going to have to be careful with her.'

'What do you mean?'

'It's a farm. Someone should be with her all the time.'

'We lived on a farm in Byron,' I say dully. 'I'm used to that.'

I follow her out and watch from the verandah as Nellie settles Barry carefully in a wheelbarrow before running off to join Harry, who is dragging rubbish from the shed into a pile just outside the front fence. She grabs one of the old crates and lugs it along beside him. He laughs as he watches her dragging it through the dirt.

'Well, she's a lovely little girl,' Beth murmurs.

There is such yearning in her voice that I turn, sensing a softening. I want to touch her, hug her, tell her I'm sorry that Nellie isn't her daughter. That she would be a wonderful mother. But I pull back when I see her face. The emotion in her voice isn't for me.

'What about these boxes of material? Looks like old curtains,' Harry calls from the shed.

'It's all got to go!' Beth calls back.

'Out-of-date textbooks?'

'Yep. Everything. We'll have a bonfire.'

Beth and I stand there awhile, watching Nellie and Harry chattering as they drag over bits and pieces of old furniture from the shed.

'Shall we go into town, then … get the cleaning stuff?' Beth asks.

'Sure.'

By the time Beth and I have our things together ready to leave, Nellie is too busy 'working' with Harry to come.

'Don't you want to meet your great-grandfather?' I ask uneasily. Nellie shakes her head importantly, following Harry out with her arms full of newspapers.

'She can stay with me if you like,' Harry says.

I hesitate and look at Beth, wondering if she thinks I'm crazy to trust my child with a man I hardly know. *You're a grown woman,* I tell myself. *She's your child; so do what you think best, for Christ's sake. Stop acting the little sister.*

'Are you sure it's okay, Harry?' I say uneasily. 'We might be an hour or two.'

'Sure.' Harry smiles at Nellie and she rewards him with a huge grin. He looks at his watch. 'Take your time. But when you get back I'll head off.'

'Okay.' I grab Nellie and kiss her. 'Be good now and stay near Harry.'

Nellie squirms out of my grasp quickly, anxious to get back to her work. We get into Beth's silver Honda Jazz, and Nellie waves us off.

I'm okay all the way down the windy track through the trees until the turn-off to the main road. Then I get the jitters. *Why did I do that? Why would I? What if Jay arrived and found her with Harry?*

'Beth!' I say suddenly. 'Please stop the car.'

She pulls over and turns to look at me. 'What's up?'

I draw my knees up and put my head in my hands. 'Sorry, but I've forgotten something.'

'I have money.'

'No ... I need ... I need to go back.'

She gives a deep sigh and turns the car around.

I feel her taking quick glances at me, and it makes me want to scream.

'What's going on, Tess?'

I shrug and say nothing, because I can't speak. I'm seeing Jay there now. I'm watching him picking her up, popping her on the back of his bike.

Hey, thanks, man. He'll shake Harry's hand like they're best friends. *Better be off now. Nellie and me have a big trip in front of us.* I'm hearing it. It's happening before my eyes.

'Tess. Talk to me,' Beth suddenly cries. 'What is it? You're shaking.'

But we're crossing the cattle pit now and moving back onto Grandpa's land and I want to get there so urgently that I'm biting my lip and cracking my knuckles. The muscles in my legs and feet begin to cramp up.

But when we get to the house the scene that greets us is exactly as we left it, except the pile is bigger. Nellie is watching, fascinated, as Harry builds it up. They stop what they're doing to watch us come through the gates.

'You forget something?' Harry asks, and when I say nothing, 'Anything wrong?'

I wind down the window and shake my head. He waits and then when he sees I'm not going to say anything, that I'm actually gasping a bit, he throws his bit of wood down, comes over to my side of the car, puts one hand in and flicks my chin briefly with his damaged hand. 'Don't worry,' he says under his breath. 'Nothing is going to happen to her. I promise.'

'Thanks,' I mutter and then turn to Beth. 'Sorry, I just freaked out.' The words rush out of my mouth. 'Let's go now.'

'Are you sure?' Her mouth is in that grim line I remember so well.

'Yes.'

We hardly speak on the way into town. I can't work out if she's mad at me or if something else entirely is pissing her off. She seems preoccupied, worried, as though she has a lot on her mind.

Apart from wanting to thank her for letting us come and to apologise for being such a nutcase, there are other things I'd like to talk about. But my efforts don't get me far. 'So where do you work now?' I ask shyly.

'St Vincent's,' she says shortly.

'What department?'

'I'm still an intern.'

'So did you take time off for … this?'

'A couple of weeks.'

'What about Douglas?'

'He's now officially a specialist in oncology at Royal Melbourne.'

'Wow!' I'm genuinely impressed.

'He's done very well,' she says matter-of-factly. But there is no warmth or pride in her voice.

The truth is that I'm amazed that Douglas could be a specialist in anything. He is the most unimpressive person I've ever met. 'Will you specialise?'

'Not sure yet.'

Is the wall just for me? Or is it for everyone? I can only tell that it's there and I'm not getting any glimpse behind it. I have a sudden vivid memory of the old Beth, so full of warmth and fun.

And kind. In the weeks after Mum left, she would come looking for me when I was off somewhere hiding from the world. She'd sit down beside me, grab me tightly in her arms and rock me back and forth. *She'll be back, Tessie,* she'd say, pulling me on her knee even though I was a gangly thirteen-year-old. *Our mum will be back and everything will be alright. You'll see.*

At last we reach town. The local hospital is off the main road by only one street.

To think that I came back to this town! our mother used to groan, as though it hurt having to admit it after twenty years. *To this bloody awful town when we could have gone anywhere!*

She'd met Dad at university. Both shy country kids without much confidence, from the same hometown, they'd gravitated towards each other because of their shared background. My father was an only child and his parents were old and frail, so after graduation they came back to be nearby. By the time Dad's parents died, my parents had already moved into their house, and my father was happy in his teaching job and Mum was expecting Beth.

Mum never bothered to conceal the fact that she considered getting married and having kids the worst decision of her life. Her tone was never bitter, just matter-of-fact. *Don't take offence,* she would say. *I'm telling you so you don't make the same mistake as I did.*

Beth points to the end wing as she pulls into the hospital car park. 'He's in there. That last window.'

'What … what state is he in?'

'Well, he's not coming home, if that's what you want to know.'

'I mean … is he coherent?'

'You'd better believe it.'

We pull up near a rose garden. Beth turns off the ignition and slumps forward, face in her hands against the steering wheel.

I'm stunned and a bit frantic, wondering how to ask her what's wrong, when she sits up and stares straight ahead.

'God, I hate this,' she whispers. 'I'm so over it already and we haven't even started yet. I want to go home. I want to get back to my job.'

'Beth, I'm sorry …'

But she ignores me, throws her shoulders back in a gesture of defiance, opens the car door and steps out.

I do likewise. 'We don't have to go and see him,' I say over the top of the car. 'If you don't want to and I don't want to—'

'We *do* have to see him,' she replies, slamming the car door shut. 'Of course we do.'

'But why? He was such a shit to Mum.'

'Oh? And Mum was such an angel?' Beth spits back savagely. 'Such a pinnacle of virtue?'

'No, but—'

'He's our grandfather,' she snaps. 'And he's dying!'

'So?'

'Haven't you learnt anything?'

'What do you mean?'

'That you can't just go around doing whatever you feel like all the time!'

I feel as if I've just caught a knockout blow on the chin, and I wonder if I'll be able to stagger to my feet for another round.

'Believe it or not, I do know that, Beth. I might not have known it before, but I know it now!'

'Good!' She turns to go, but I can't let her have the last word.

'By the way, could I please have the stuff our mother sent to *me*?'

'What?' She stops and looks at me.

'Marlon said that she sent me a parcel.'

'I don't remember …'

I give a snort of laughter, because it is so obviously untrue.

'You know she sent me stuff about Grandpa's mother!'

'You think I could be bothered with *that*? I had everything else to worry about …'

'But it wasn't for you to worry about!' I shout. 'Because it wasn't sent to you, was it?' It's been so long since I've been angry like this that I can't hold back. It's as though I've opened a vein in my arm and hot blood is pulsing out onto the pavement.

'No! It wasn't!'

'So you threw it out?'

'I gave it to him.' She jerks her thumb towards the hospital. 'If it belongs to anyone, it belongs to him. Not you!'

I laugh incredulously. 'It was sent to *me*, Beth!'

'What the hell would you want with it?'

'So what did he do with it?'

'Why don't you ask him?' She fishes her bag out of the car, slams the door and walks off towards the hospital entrance.

'I will!' *You fucking bitch.*

All I can do is follow her as she walks straight in front of a big sedan coming into the car park from the street. The driver blasts his horn and yells something about getting out of the way. Beth stops right in front of the car, gives him a withering look and continues very slowly.

'Get the fuck out of my way, lady!'

She gives him the finger.

'Be warned,' she mutters under her breath when I catch up with her near the front doors. 'He wasn't the least interested in it then and he won't be now. It's almost certainly been thrown out.'

'Fine. I consider myself warned.'

We tiptoe into the single ward. The long figure of our grand-father is lying so flat and still in the hospital bed that he might already be dead. Beth heads straight over to the bed, puts a hand on his pillow and leans over his face.

'Hello, Grandpa,' she says in a false bright whisper. 'I heard you saw Sean and Gerard yesterday.' But he says nothing. His eyes are closed and the breathing is deep and slow. She gently shakes his shoulder. 'Grandpa! I've got Tess with me.'

He wakes, startled, with a full body shudder. 'Tess?' he repeats loudly, as though he's been waiting to hear that name his whole life. 'Therese Mary Josephine, did you say?'

'Yes, Grandpa.' Beth pulls me over and more or less shoves me in front of him. 'Here she is!'

'Ah!' One huge hand reaches out from under the bedclothes. 'Little Tess, is that you?'

I tentatively put my own hand into the rough palm. He pulls me nearer. 'Yes, Grandpa,' I say shakily.

'My mother was Tess.'

'I know.'

'So you came home,' he whispers, his eyes still closed.

'Yes.'

He turns away a bit as though trying to remember. 'You've been living up north?'

'Yes.'

'With some rotter?'

I smile grimly. 'That's right.' I'm oddly relieved. At least I don't have to explain myself. He knows it all. Beth must have told him.

'You've left him for good?'

'Yes.'

'That's good to hear.' He draws me closer. 'We all make mistakes,' he rasps, squeezing my hand, oblivious to my discomfort. He turns towards Beth, his voice hoarse but clear now. 'So you're all here now?'

'Salome will be here either today or tomorrow, Grandpa.'

'What about Marlon?'

'Not quite sure when … he'll be … here.' Beth gives me a hard scowl, and I understand that I'm not allowed to say that Marlon won't be coming. 'But soon.'

'Ah. That's good. Good.'

The nurse comes in and props our grandfather up on a couple of pillows. He has lost a lot of weight. The big body I remember so well has shrunk to that of a normal person's. And the skin of his face is stretched tightly over the bones. But the small eyes are open now. They're exactly the same, set deep under those heavy gingery eyebrows, and they shine with life. I stand nearer so he can see me. Those eyes are searching my face now, and I cringe at the scrutiny. He knows who I am. He can see through me.

'Any news of your mother?'

'No.' Mention of my mother usually sends me into a spin, but this day I stay calm enough.

'You get postcards, though, don't you?'

I look at Beth. *Postcards?* She shakes her head firmly. 'Not for a long time, Grandpa.'

'How long has she been gone?'

'Eight years, Grandpa,' I whisper.

'Hmmm.' He shifts as though trying to get comfortable. 'Well, she might turn up one of these days.'

I smile. Eight years probably seems like nothing to someone who is ninety-three!

He closes his eyes for a minute and settles his head back on the pillow as though suddenly very tired. He turns to Beth. 'So how is she doing now?'

'Who?'

'Your little sister.'

'As you see, Grandpa, pretty good.'

'She's very thin.' He reaches one hand up and clasps my upper arm, then my shoulder, and then my wrist, as if he's examining the condition of a calf or a horse. 'You try and eat up now you're home with your sister,' he orders in his rasping voice.

'Yes, Grandpa,' I say, as though I'm ten years old.

He sinks back.

Quietness descends, giving me a chance to look around the room. The view out the window is nice: a green lawn and flower beds, everything fresh and clean and colourful.

'Your mother was always flighty,' he whispers, staring off into the distance as though musing to himself. 'I thought she'd marry a useless bugger and that is exactly what she did. She never had any judgement.'

Beth stiffens slightly. I look at this old man lying peacefully in his comfortable deathbed, being looked after by the friendly nurses, and I think of our father lying in his sad, lonely grave, and anger pulses through me. I suddenly want to lean across and choke the old bastard with my bare hands. *Just because you're dying,* I want to scream, *you think you can insult my father?*

'It's a very hard thing to lose your mother,' the old man rambles on. 'A very hard thing,' he says again in a soft, meditative tone.

'Yes.' Beth looks at me. I'm taken completely off guard too.

'Do you remember *your* mother?' I ask tentatively.

'Oh yes.' He smiles, as though happy to have been asked. 'I remember my mother!'

'What was she like?' I say, a little breathless now. He doesn't answer for a while. I think maybe he hasn't heard the question.

'I see her sometimes,' he whispers. 'Poor woman.'

Beth turns away.

'*What* did you say, Grandpa?' I ask.

'I see her,' he repeats, and then shakes his head from side to side as though wanting to push the thought away.

'Where?' I ask. 'I mean … what do you mean, you see her?'

Beth shakes her head slightly and purses her mouth, discouraging me from asking anything else.

'Outside, usually,' he murmurs and turns to me. 'Up near the old dam behind the house.'

'Does she speak?' I whisper.

I'm not sure that he hears the question. He doesn't answer it, anyway.

'Always in a grey dress,' he murmurs, his head slumping back further. 'Always a long grey dress, when …' His old voice trembles. 'When she loved bright pretty things.' He grabs my hand and I have to fight not to pull away. 'My mother loved bright things.'

'What does she say?' I try the question again.

But Grandpa only sighs and closes his eyes. 'We loved her stories when we were kids. My sister Cathy and I sat by the window in the dark one night after everyone else was asleep. I was about seven and Cathy was four. We were waiting for the little people to come.'

I edge in closer. 'The little people?'

'She was Irish, you know.'

'Mum sent stuff about her to me,' I say, refusing to meet the daggers in Beth's eyes. 'Have you … have you got it, Grandpa?'

He shakes his head and turns away.

'Did you throw it out?' I persist.

He turns his great head towards me and nods.

'You destroyed it?' I whisper, dismayed, and he nods again.

'Your mother had no sense. No sense at all.'

I don't know what to say to this. It seems such an outrageous thing for him to have done, but how can I say that to a dying man?

'The dead have the right to be left in peace,' he mutters.

Beth and I sit there quietly for a few more minutes, but he seems to have dropped off to sleep. What will they say about me after I'm … after Jay kills me? *She was mad. She couldn't cope. She went there willingly with him, didn't she? She was asking for it … had it coming to her. She made her own bed! So let her lie in it.*

The dead have a right to be left in peace.

'I like to think of you all together again,' he mumbles. 'Beth and Marlon and Salome.' He smiles and reaches one trembling hand for mine. 'And now our Tess is back!' Then he turns away from us and the deep, heavy breathing continues. 'Tomorrow and tomorrow and tomorrow.' He laughs and squeezes my hand. 'You did well remembering that.'

'Thanks, Grandpa,' I whisper, a spurt of warmth spreading through me.

'You were just a little girl.'

'Yes.'

'A little girl with a good memory,' he sighs.

He fades after that. An old man sounding like each breath could be his last.

I stand, letting the worn hand hold mine, not daring to even look at Beth, feeling stunned. I never knew he would get pleasure thinking about the four of us being together again. Much less that I meant anything special to him.

Beth and I stay awhile, watching him sleep. She is first to break the trance. 'We'll get going now, Grandpa,' she says, leaning over to kiss his cheek. 'Be back soon.'

But he doesn't hear us.

We walk out of the ward in silence and into the lovely weak sunshine and get into the car. Not a word as Beth puts the key in the ignition and backs out. I glance at her face and it's a mask of rigidity.

Along the main road heading back to the farm I have to remind myself that I am twenty-one and not ten or thirteen. Why should I care that she radiates such disapproval?

It's not until the car is turning onto our road that I remember what else we came into town for. 'Beth, we forgot to buy the cleaning stuff,' I say. 'And dinner.'

'Oh!' She shakes her head. 'So we did, damn it!' She jerks the car over onto the gravel.

She turns to me and smiles properly for the first time, and I feel the weight between us shift a bit, although nothing is said. She checks the mirror and does a quick U-turn and then drives back into town. She looks at her watch. 'We were only with him about twenty minutes!'

'Long enough!'

At the local supermarket we fill the trolley with cleaning things, fruit, vegetables and meat. Beth goes to the bakery across the road to buy fresh bread while I go to the post office to see if the money has arrived from Marlon.

I make a call on the public phone to thank him. I'm still a bit nervy about using the mobile that Harry got me.

He can't talk for long. 'So how's it going?' he asks.

'Pretty diabolical,' I say.

He laughs dryly. 'Salome will be there soon.'

'Oh well, that should make everything so much better!' I say sarcastically, and he hoots with laughter. Just hearing him do that makes everything seem possible. Everything is going to work out.

'What about ... the other guy, sis? The bloke who drove you down? Is he still there?'

'Leaving today.'

'Hang in there, kid. Speak soon.'

'Okay.'

'I feel like a beer,' Beth says as we slam down the boot on all our shopping.

I nod, trying not to show my surprise at this turn of events. It's only three in the afternoon. I've never known my sister to drink before.

'Okay?'

'Sure.'

She locks the car and leads me up the length of the main street to the old pub our dad used to frequent. The Retreat. Its stained-glass windows, cream-tile façade and wide verandah are picturesque in the late summer light. *A quaint country pub,* some travel writer might say. *Stop here on your way through for a hearty lunch of ... washed down with a glass of ...* When I was a kid, this pub held such fascination for me. It was the place where our father went to live his secret life, away from us. The life he lived with other men amid the deep, jumbled, mysterious sounds of masculine shouts and laughter, fighting and drinking. My mother would send me in to get him sometimes. *Time to come home, Dad.* I would breathe in the pungent foreign smells of hops and piss and sweat, wishing wildly that I could stay there and be part of that alien world even for just a while. The place terrified me and yet I was drawn to it.

But this day the front bar is almost empty, just two old-timers sitting on stools, quietly watching the races on the television in the corner. We buy our beers without saying anything and sit out the front in the main street, just across from the town hall where our mother made her debut. I look towards the other end of the street, where cars come and go from the supermarket, and wonder if I dare ask Beth more about her life. I take a tentative sip of my beer and try to think how best to broach it.

Soft sunshine is playing through the gaps between the broad branches of the street's trees, making moving patterns on the road.

Beth takes a long gulp from her beer, almost finishing it in one hit. I look across at her in surprise as her pretty white fingers fiddle with the glass. Now I'm up close, I see the faint lines around her mouth and eyes. Twenty-seven now and still very good-looking, but the bloom has faded.

'So how is … being married?' I ask awkwardly.

'Oh, fine, thanks.'

'Have you bought a house?'

'In Parkville. Near the hospital.'

'Cool.'

'Douglas is a specialist now.' She finishes off her beer and looks at mine, still barely touched.

'Yeah, so you said. Long hours, I guess?'

'He's at the hospital day and night. I'm going to get another beer. You?'

'No, I'm okay, thanks,' I say. I take another sip. When she comes out again I notice that her shoulders stoop in a way that I don't remember.

'I just lied to you,' she says unexpectedly. 'Things are not fine with Douglas. We're splitting up. We're going to sell the house.'

'Oh.' I nod. 'I'm sorry.'

'None of you ever liked him,' she adds sharply.

'But you did,' I snap right back.

She shrugs as though she isn't so sure of even that and takes a gulp of beer.

'Is it mutual?'

'Well, yes, but … messy.' She gives me a swift wry grin. 'Always messy, I suppose.'

I take another sip from my still-full glass and look around. Walking down this street after school, chatting with my friends and eating ice-cream. This down-home sort of casualness is nothing like Byron, even in winter. Here, the women stepping out of their muddy utes and four-wheel drives, stopping to chat, are dressed for comfort in basic pants and jumpers, flannelette shirts that cover their wide bums, their hair cut in short, practical, nondescript styles. A couple of farmers in rubber boots walk up our way, give us the once-over and nod briefly before heading into the pub. They probably know who we are. *Remember that teacher who died? Those two out there are …*

A couple of the Browne girls are back. And are now drinking in the street. It will probably be all over town by tomorrow. I'm sitting there waiting for my sister to tell me why she split with Douglas.

'Tell me what happened to you, Tess,' she says quietly at last. 'You're so different to … before.'

'Am I?' Her question has taken me off guard.

'Yes.'

'Well, I'm not quite sure where to start. I mean …'

'I suppose having a child would …' She doesn't finish the sentence, but I catch her meaning, and the note of yearning in her tone. *She envies me.* Christ, if only she knew!

Nellie flits across my consciousness. The dark shining curls and those pudgy little hands grasping my neck. *Don't cry, Mamma.* I blow my nose, because I don't want to confuse this first proper conversation with my older sister in four years by acting all sorry for myself.

'Will he come looking for you?'

'Yeah,' I nod.

'So, a real bully?'

'Yes.'

'And you were at his mercy? You couldn't leave?'

I play with my glass. The amber bubbles are still exploding but the head of foam is subsiding. *How much do I tell her?* I toss up whether to down the beer all at once like she did. It might make me relax and feel better.

'So how was it possible this time?'

I look at her and see the genuine curiosity in her face. Harry asked me the same question and I fobbed him off. But she's been honest with me about Douglas, so I decide I'll risk it.

'He did something ... to Nellie. After that, I knew I had to leave,' I say. 'Get out before worse happened.' There! It's out, and I've said it without crying.

'What?' she leans forward. 'What did he do?'

I blow out and look away. 'I can't ...' I shudder. 'Not ... yet.'

She nods and we both sit there awhile in silence taking in the street and the sunshine.

'And you found the strength to leave?' She smiles encouragingly.

'Yes.' I'm able to smile back. 'I did.'

'So tell me about *that*.'

'I was in hospital having a miscarriage,' I began.

'God!' She shudders. 'Really?'

'I nearly died, but ... a woman came to me in the night. It might have been a dream. I didn't actually see her. But she stayed and talked me through it. Then the night after the thing with Nellie she ... came again.'

'You mean a nurse?'

'No.' Even a week ago I couldn't have imagined this. Sitting with my sister in the main street of our hometown, confiding private experiences, *broken marriages, ghostly relatives* ... The sun is shining down on my half-glass of beer and I allow myself a small smile.

'So who was it?'

I shrug with embarrassment but blunder on anyway. 'It was Therese.'

'Therese?'

'Our great-grandmother.'

'What?' Beth exclaims sharply. She pulls back and stares at me in horror.

'Yes.' I smile nervously. 'Therese Mary Josephine, known as Tess.'

'Oh, Jesus, spare me. You're kidding. Please tell me you're joking!'

Her reaction shocks me into silence. My face immediately becomes hot.

'I know it sounds a bit—'

'Crazy?' she cuts in harshly. 'Yes, it does sound crazy! It sounds very crazy. Just the sort of crazy crap that Mum would say. For Christ's sake, don't go down *her* path, Tess.'

'Okay!' I'm desperate for her to stop. 'Sorry. Forget it. The main thing is, I got away. I'm here.'

But she won't let it rest. She leans in closer and stares into my eyes, her voice an urgent whisper. 'He'll get custody. I'm telling you now. Keep up the crazy stuff and he'll get the kid! It's that simple. I'm a doctor and I know how the system works.'

'He's never going to see her again!' I'm so humiliated that I could die. 'Never! I won't allow it.'

'Don't you understand?' she says sharply. 'He will eventually find you. You'll have to get a lawyer and it will go to court. And if you talk crazy stuff like this he'll be able to mount an argument that you're unfit to care for a child.'

'But I'm talking to *you*!' I say loudly. 'Not him!'

'There's no need to shout.'

I sink back in my seat. *No need to shout.* Her words send a dull bolt into the base of my skull. Who am I kidding? Beth is right. *He will eventually find you* … Of course he will. *He'll mount a case that you're an unfit mother and* … He will do that. He has the money and connections and I don't. Do I know one single lawyer? No. It's exactly the sort of thing he'd do if … *if he doesn't kill me first.*

'Okay.' I drain my beer and stand up. 'Let's go.'

'I want to support you, Tess!' she says in a more conciliatory tone. 'I really do. I don't want him to have Nellie.'

'I understand that.'

'But you have to get well,' she says softly. 'And stay well. When you arrived with her last night you … seemed very ill. And today—' she looks at my trembling hands, '—you're a nervous wreck! A mess. You have to get well. You need to see someone.'

'Can we just leave?'

'If you talk about dead people coming in the night to save your life, then I'm telling you that you'll wreck your chances of keeping that lovely little girl.'

'Okay, I've got the message.'

eighteen

The pile of rubbish from the shed has grown huge during our time away, so we're within the fence before I see a motorbike, black and shining in the mid-afternoon sun. Harry and Nellie are nowhere to be seen.

My stomach heaves. Not his bike, but … panic anyway.

Beth is alarmed too. She stops the car and jumps out.

I'm racing up the path behind her when the front door to the house opens and out steps Salome in black leather pants tucked neatly into fancy bike boots and a studded jacket with a red T-shirt underneath.

She comes towards us, smiling, hair shaved up both sides of her head with sandy curls on top. She looks fantastic – lean, sharp and small, her face and skin glowing with good health.

'Beth!' she yells and they hug each other. She lets go of Beth and comes towards me. The smile stays where it is, but something else is happening behind the eyes. 'Well, if it isn't *you*!' she says, hugging me quickly.

'Hi, Salome.'

'Good to see you again, kiddo.'

'And you,' I say shyly. She looks so cool and glamorous. There is no semblance of the country kid there at all. I feel like a timid fieldmouse next to her.

'How's Sydney?' It's the first thing that comes to mind.

She laughs and turns as the door opens behind her. 'Hey, Jack! Come out and tell us all how Sydney is!'

To my amazement, a very heavy woman strolls out the door. She has short hair and none of Salome's elegance or boyish poise.

'The usual nightmare,' she says. 'But we love it!'

'Please meet my sisters. Beth!' Salome fakes a scraping bow in Beth's direction. 'And Tess, whom I haven't seen for a long time.'

'Hello.' I hold out my hand shyly. Beth does the same.

'Hello.' The big woman smiles warmly as she shakes our hands.

'And this is my ... my ... what are you, darling?' Salome is chuckling, her arm around the woman's shoulders.

'Your lover, pet.' The big woman roars with laughter. 'Did you forget?'

'Oh, that's right. My lover!'

Beth and I smile nervously and don't look at each other.

Jack grabs my hand again and shakes it more vigorously this time, as though the first one was just a practice go. 'Your little Nellie is an absolute *doll*!' she tells me enthusiastically. 'We've been having the best time. Wow! Can she talk!'

'Thanks.' I am slightly breathless.

There is no time for things to get awkward. We're all heading back inside. Harry is sitting at the table with Nellie on his knee doing a drawing.

Nellie looks up at me accusingly. 'You were away for a long time,' she says and turns straight back to her drawing.

'But we had a good time getting to know each other, didn't we?' Jack rumples her hair. 'Salome, you and me, Harry and Barry!'

Nellie looks up and starts giggling.

Jack is so very loud. But she's warm, and her boisterousness makes me feel good because there is nothing but goodwill behind it. And it gives me distance to deal with my sisters.

Salome is looking me up and down. 'Jeez, you're thin!'

'Yeah.' I try to smile, but don't quite manage it.

'So where have you been?' She throws her hands up in the air. 'Come on, start from the beginning. I know nothing.'

'What do you want to know?'

'Were you with that same guy all the time?' She makes a flicking motion with her hand.

I nod.

'So this is … *his* kid?' She jerks a thumb towards Nellie.

'Yes.'

'Christ!' she laughs incredulously. 'What the hell were you thinking?'

Salome's cutting smiles were always harder to take than Beth's sternness. She was mistress of the coolly devastating comment and the sarcastic put-down. I look at jolly, cheerful Jack, thinking she's a strange fit for judgemental, quick-witted Salome.

'Tess has been caught up in a very difficult situation, Salome,' Beth says warningly.

Salome looks from Beth to me to Harry for an explanation, but none of us say anything. 'What do you mean by *difficult*?'

Harry shrugs and looks out the window.

'Very difficult,' Beth says at last and indicates Nellie. 'Later, okay?'

Salome makes a face and rolls her eyes at Jack.

The panic I had outside has subsided, but not completely. It's still there. I can feel it buzzing down my legs and into my guts. I look at Harry in desperation, trying to catch his eye. *Come on,* I want to say. *Let's leave now. Take me to your aunt's place for a couple of days.* I need to escape them or I'm going to go under. But Harry isn't looking my way. He stands up and goes outside.

Beth and I go back to the car for the bags of shopping. I'm hauling one out when Beth looks at me sharply. 'Salome is … well, I'm sure you remember. Don't let it get to you,' she says.

I nod. 'Did you know she was gay?' I ask as we head towards the house.

Beth nods. 'It's no big deal,' she says primly.

'I didn't say it was,' I mutter, grimacing behind her back.

'Anyone hungry?' Beth asks.

The old table is cleared. Beth washes the lettuce. I slice the tomatoes.

Nellie stands on a chair between Salome and Jack as they butter the bread, both little hands covered in purple and yellow texta. 'I can help,' she says importantly.

'Of course you can.' Jack hands her a blunt butter knife. 'Just don't try stabbing me with this, okay? Or I might have to turn you upside down and tickle your toes.'

Nellie giggles.

Harry pokes his head in and surveys the scene. 'Looks like the sisters have a system going already,' he murmurs, as though amused. He waits until the others aren't looking and gives me a thumbs up, which makes me smile.

'Hey, Nellie,' he calls, 'you want to come wash your hands with me?'

'Okay.' She hops down from her seat and runs past him and disappears out the door.

He turns to me. 'I've got to go after lunch,' he says quickly. 'I've got about an hour left of hauling stuff from the shed and then I'll be heading off.'

'Okay. Thanks, Harry.' I try to act cool. But the idea of him leaving me here is frankly terrifying.

'So, Byron.' Salome pounces on some of the tomato slices and drops them in her mouth.

'Yeah.'

'Difficult times, huh?'

'Yeah,' I mumble. 'And what about you?'

'Good times all the way!' She looks at Jack and they laugh together, conspiratorially, as though their good fortune is secret and funny and something I wouldn't get in a million years because I'm not on the same planet as them. When the sandwiches are ready we call Nellie and Harry inside. Harry has his shoes off and his jeans rolled up to his knees.

Salome gasps when she sees the prosthetic at the end of his leg. When he unstraps it the knobbly knee bone looks red and sore.

'Shit, I had no idea!' She sits up and looks at him for an explanation. 'I thought the limp was a footy injury or something.'

'Bike accident.' He smiles sheepishly, putting the prosthetic leg to one side.

'Must hurt?'

'Sometimes,' he agrees calmly.

'Mamma.' Nellie sidles up to me, her mouth turned down. 'I don't want Harry to go!'

I smile and put my arm around her and look up at Harry, who is talking to Jack about the kind of paint she should buy for the window frames. 'Me neither,' I say.

But Harry leaves that afternoon. I work hard at first trying not to show how I feel. I don't want to admit even to myself how I'm going to miss him. But I think he knows.

He gives my shoulders a squeeze, picks up Nellie and spins her around. 'See you around, kiddo.'

'Don't go, Harry!' She clings to his leg like a limpet and I have to pull her off, but I feel like doing the same thing. *Don't go, Harry.* He's delivered us to the door of safety and now I don't know how to say goodbye. Or thank you.

'You have the phone? I'll let you know when I get a new number, but if you leave a message on the old number I'll call you back.' He seems worried now it's time to go.

'Yep.' I pull the phone out to show him.

'You call, okay?' He opens the car door. 'For anything at all, okay? Just ring me.'

'Okay. We'll miss you,' I say.

'Yeah,' he says softly. 'We've been through a bit these last few days.'

'I've dragged you into all my shit!' I say. Suddenly, to my dismay, a rush of tears hits me. 'Sorry about everything.'

He is in the car now. He reaches out his damaged hand and grabs mine briefly. 'Hey, you and Nellie have given me more than I've given you.'

I laugh through the tears and take the pressed hanky he's holding out. What have I given him except trouble? 'So, give my love to Jules,' I sniff.

'Shall do.' He waves and then backs the car a few metres. Then, he leans out the window again. 'I think Jules and I have had it, actually.'

I don't catch his meaning immediately, but when I do I'm too shocked to say anything. Harry and Jules. Jules and Harry. The beautiful, talented, law student and the handsome, damaged ex-musician.

'Had it?'

'Yeah.'

'Why do you say that?'

'Ah.' He waves his hand a couple of times as though he isn't sure himself. Then he grins. 'She's always telling me she loves me.'

I look at him blankly without understanding. 'And?' I say.

'And I tell her the same thing back.'

'So?'

'We never used to have to do that! It was understood. Now we're both saying it all the time.'

I have to laugh. 'So it's over because you tell each other that you love each other too much?'

He gives the engine a few loud revs for Nellie's benefit. 'We're turning into a bad American rom-com.' He waves again. 'You take care, Tess.'

'I will. But wait,' I say anxiously, remembering the present I'd planned. 'Can you wait one minute?'

'Sure,' he smiles.

I dash back inside and up the hallway to the blue room, and come back out holding the Django Reinhardt CD.

'For me?' He frowns and hesitates before taking it. 'But it was your dad's.'

'And I want you to have it.'

He smiles at me.

'So you won't forget.'

He stops roaring the engine and looks at me directly. 'I won't forget.'

Nellie lifts her arms to be picked up, and she gives his damaged hand a last kiss. We watch him leave together, and for that half-minute until the car disappears over the hill I feel as though my heart is being ripped out.

....

'Jeez, this place!' Salome is looking around the grimy kitchen. 'What a blast being back here, eh?'

We've finished cleaning up after lunch and it's just the three of us left at the kitchen table. Jack has taken Nellie out for a look at what needs to happen to the old laundry.

Salome has already told us that she won't be able to help with any heavy work. She has a bad back, made worse by the trip down. Even cleaning will probably be too much for her.

She plans to sit out on the verandah and work on her new script. We needn't worry, though, because Jack has agreed to do her share.

'I see.' Beth frowns as she takes this in.

'She's totally brilliant with practical stuff.'

'Right,' Beth sniffs.

'Put her in charge and it will be right. I promise.'

I suppress a laugh. Somehow I can't see Beth taking orders from Jack.

'Anyway, why does that old bastard want *us* to do it?' Salome bursts out. 'Is it extra punishment for having a shit mother or something?'

No one answers for a moment.

'The fact is, he does,' Beth snaps. 'He wants the four of us to get the place ready for sale before he dies.'

'So where's Marlon?'

'He's decided not to come.' Beth's face heats up and she averts her eyes.

'Nice for him!' Salome snorts. 'Always so good at sliding out of everything.'

'I thought that was your trick!' It's out before I think.

Salome turns to me with a withering stare. 'What's that meant to mean?'

'Housework was never your strong point, Salome,' I say, a little alarmed with myself for daring to bring this up.

She sniffs and turns away. 'I don't remember you being any better.'

In fact I was, and Salome knows it. She was the complete slack-arse. Marlon always did his share. Not a shred more, but his share. And I was more or less the same, although I had to be reminded all the time. It was Beth who held the household together.

'I vote we pool some cash and pay professionals to come in,' Salome says. 'They'd get it done in half the time. It won't cost that much.'

'I don't have any cash,' I say immediately.

'Take it from the estate.'

'That's not going to happen, Salome!' Beth says angrily, ignoring me. 'It's not the way his generation thinks. They don't ever *get professionals* in for this kind of thing! Not when there are a whole lot of able-bodied people about to do the work!'

'Us, you mean?'

'Well, yes. Obviously.'

'You sound as if you approve.'

'I'm just telling you how it is.' Beth gives an exasperated sigh.

'So where are the fucking uncles in all this?' Salome persists. 'It's not as though we're the only beneficiaries!'

'It's part of the deal.'

'So the old shit is going to manipulate us right till the end, is he?'

'Get used to it,' Beth snaps.

'What deal?' I ask, but no one answers me.

Salome gets up and pours herself more coffee. Beth looks out the window at Nellie and Jack.

I head outside and around to the back of the house to get more wood for the ailing stove fire. Once there, I stare down the valley at the familiar rolling hills and feel the stillness. Tiny brown birds hop and swoop in playful curves around me as I bend to pick up the wood. I close my eyes a moment to listen to their chatter. In the distance, a chainsaw starts up and I hear the baleful cries of cows calling their calves. I try to imagine my great-grandparents' teeming world out here in this farmhouse, the bright crisp mornings, hot afternoons, barking dogs and crying babies, the dark dense nights. What about all the smiles, the tears, the loads of washing, cooking meals and eating them, the tiny embryos secretly clinging to the thick wall of her womb. The births. The sinks of dirty dishes, the buckets of soiled nappies, the visits from family and neighbours, the favourite sister arriving that day, the poisoning, the dying in the blue room, the chilly loneliness of grief.

'Did you know, or did you just time it right by chance?' Salome asks me abruptly when I come in.

'What?'

She rubs her thumb and fingers together, but I have no idea what she means. My scalp is itchy again and I wonder if there will be enough hot water to wash my hair.

Beth looks at me. 'I must admit, I did wonder that too. Did you hear something about the will before you came back?'

I stare at them. They're both looking at me curiously, waiting for an answer.

'What?'

'Grandpa's will.'

'How could I have ... heard about it?'

Beth nods and I watch the pink seeping into her face. A sure sign she's embarrassed. 'That's what I thought.'

'You told me that you were the executor,' I remind her. I turn to Salome, who is looking at me incredulously.

'So you don't know yet?' she breathes.

I shrug impatiently. 'What are you talking about?'

'She doesn't know!' Salome exclaims. 'Oh, sweet Jesus. Wow! For Christ's sake, Beth, tell her!'

'What?' I snap.

'Surprise, kiddo!'

'Tell me!'

'Grandpa has decided to split his estate up in an unusual way,' Beth explains in her best official manner. 'Our eight living uncles and two aunts get three-quarters of the estate. The last quarter will be divided between us four. Meaning you and Salome, Marlon and me.'

'Oh, that's nice,' I say. A few hundred bucks will come in very useful. Our grandparents were poor. At least, I've always believed they were. Their lives were so confined and so frugal. They never bought anything new and they never went anywhere. This old house wasn't just modest. It was creaky, damp in winter and boiling in summer, cramped and run-down. They'd never had a flat-screen television, a mobile phone or a computer in their house. You only had to look around the room we were sitting in to know there wasn't much money about. Mum always told us that the land would be left to the sons, who were already local farmers. And what was left after that, once it was divided between thirteen kids, wouldn't come to much. Mum didn't seem at all put out by this state of affairs. It was just the way things happened on farms.

'Nice is the word,' Salome chortles.

Beth gives a faint smile before she leans in closer to me. 'Tess, the place has been valued. His assets, which take in this house and land and some shares in a few big mining companies, plus some cash, amount to four million dollars. So divide that into quarters. And then divide a quarter of that into four. Each of us will collect at least a quarter of a million.'

'What?' I whisper. At first I don't understand what she is telling me, and when I do I don't believe it. But very soon after that her words catch fire in my head, and as much as I try to hold firm against the flames, they gather me up in their heat anyway, in a heady mix of hope and excitement. *Two hundred and fifty thousand dollars!*

'He's going to sell up the land?'

'Yes.'

'But how do our uncles feel about that? I mean, Mum always said that ...'

'Mum had the wrong end of the stick, as usual,' Beth said curtly. 'Grandpa was never going to leave them the land. The whole lot was *always* going to be divided evenly between his kids.' She sighs. 'Typical Mum! Grandpa never agreed with that old Irish way of doing things.'

'But what do they think about us sharing *a quarter* instead of one eleventh?'

'Who cares?' Salome laughs. 'It's his money. He can do what he likes with it.'

There has to be a catch, and this weird, shining dream will come apart.

Beth ignores Salome's gleeful tone. 'They're not happy, of course. They've tried to talk him around to giving us just one share. Our mother's share, in other words. But he won't budge. There's nothing anyone can do about it. It's with the solicitors. It's all been signed and sealed.'

'Will they contest it?' I knew a bit about this from being with Jay. When his father died the will was contested. By the time it was finished there was nothing much left. It all went to the lawyers.

'They've all agreed that they won't. The lawyer says they wouldn't get far if they did.'

'Why?'

'Grandpa has written his reasons very clearly.'

'Which are?'

Beth sighs deeply. 'Because of … what happened with our parents, he … wants to look after us.'

I get up and stand near the far wall. 'Quarter of a million dollars, you say?' I ask.

'Conservatively. There might well be a bit more than that,' Beth tells me.

This feels very unreal. I'm in shock, I suppose. My brain goes into overdrive as I consider what it could mean. I could take Nellie overseas. Live somewhere safe. Go back to school. *There is a future after all*. Still, I don't trust it.

'And what is the deal?' I ask.

'Simple. We clean up the place and get it ready for sale. That is all he wants from each of us. It's a matter of turning up and helping out for a couple of weeks.'

'So how long have you both known?'

'Last year Grandpa went through it with me,' Beth said. 'Told me to keep it under my hat. I told Salome last week.'

'It's the only reason I'm here.' Salome grins unselfconsciously.

I swallow and look out the window. Having money will make all the difference in the world. If I'd known this was even a possibility I would have left sooner! I would have … No point going down that path. 'So when were you going to tell me?'

'I rang up the post office and the police in Byron last week. No one had heard of you for a long time. We assumed that you'd left town or …'

'Died?' I snapped. 'Did you think I'd died?'

'Done a flit overseas, more like it, or …'

'Or what?' I say sharply.

'Well we had no idea about you.'

'And what happens if … if our mother comes back?' I ask.

'Like she's going to!' But Salome has stopped smiling. It's obviously something she hasn't considered. She looks at Beth.

But Beth is looking away into the distance, even though we are waiting for her to speak.

'If she comes back before he dies, then the will is reverted to its original draft,' she tells us quietly.

'Meaning?'

'Mum gets an equal share with her brothers and sisters.'

'What about us?' Salome looks horrified.

'Nothing.' Beth looks up suddenly. 'We get nothing if that happens.'

'Oh, Christ,' Salome groans. 'Wouldn't that be just *the pits*?'

'Her brothers would like her to turn up, of course, because it means more money for them.'

'Do you mean they're looking for her?' Salome asks angrily.

Beth shrugs. 'I have no idea.'

'I'll slit her throat before I let her walk through the door,' Salome mutters savagely. I stare at her in amazement, hardly able to believe what she has just said. 'Well, I'm *sooo* counting on this money!' she adds defensively.

There is an awkward silence. I look at my hands and then at my feet and then at her again. *Is she serious?*

'Oh, chill out!' she snaps at me. 'As though you're in any situation to pass up a quarter of a million bucks!'

The door opens and the others burst in. Nellie is all excited because Jack is going to show her how to work the lawn mower.

'What about Marly?' I say under my breath. 'Does he know?'

'Not yet,' Beth says. 'We're waiting for him to come.'

'I think you should tell him!' I lean across and pick up her phone. 'You want to, or will I?'

Salome slumps down in her seat and drums the table with one hand. She throws her head back and looks around at the grimy walls and worn surfaces. 'Anyway, it seems a shame to change anything here.' She laughs. 'This would make such a brilliant set!'

'You're still involved with film?' I ask her shyly.

She nods and looks at Beth. 'Did I tell you that I got finance to work on that new script?'

Beth shakes her head vaguely and I say nothing.

'Don't worry,' Salome laughs. 'It's set in a remote religious community. It's about what happens to a girl when she can't believe in God anymore.'

'Sounds interesting,' I murmur, trying to look enthusiastic.

'Yeah, well, it is. And I've got a lot of interest in it already. We have a pre-sale with a Canadian network set up.'

Beth and I say nothing. Salome sees straight through our silence and goes straight for the jugular in her usual style. 'Oh for Christ's sake, let it go!' she exclaims. 'That film was five years ago! Get over it!'

Beth gets up and starts clearing up the table.

We had no warning. The invitations to the premiere of *Abandoned* arrived in the post. I remember the flicker of disquiet crossing Beth's face as she read it aloud. 'What's Salome up to now?'

Salome rang to make sure we were coming. 'Arrive early,' she instructed. 'I want to introduce you to everyone.'

No warning at all.

Beth and I dressed in our new evening dresses and Marly hired a fancy suit, hoping we weren't overdoing it. But the theatre was already filling when we got there, and everyone was dressed up to the nines. Our clothing and fancy hair was not out of place.

Salome met us on the steps and took us inside. 'These are my sisters.' She introduced us to all her film buddies. 'And my brother, Marly.'

We were so proud and excited for her. All we knew was that the film had got great reviews from some major critics, and it had already been picked for a couple of prestigious overseas festivals. That very day Salome had rung with the news that it was going to show in Canada. But we didn't know what it was about.

The opening shot was of a young girl on a riverbank, hiding behind trees and spying on a couple making love … and it went on from there. A handsome middle-aged male actor was walking towards the railway line, in the distance the sound of a train. Next was a series of short scenes of the same man's funeral. From there it cut to an older woman making her getaway in the middle of the night, leaving four kids behind. The whole thing was our story.

The screening ended with a few seconds of shocked silence, then the audience broke out into thunderous applause. The lights came on and the applause continued. People stood up to whistle and clap their approval.

The three of us sat as wordless as wooden dummies. I so much wanted to get up and run from that place, but I couldn't even move. We were, all three of us, numb with shock.

Salome was in front of us, her eyes blazing with excitement. 'What did you think?'

I could only stare at her. When I turned to look at Beth, her face under the make-up had drained of colour. She'd aged in the hour it took to see the film.

'Marly?' Salome's eyes were still blazing excitedly. 'I thought you might find it tough. That's why I didn't—'

'Tough!'

'Come on.' Beth led the charge to the door. But people had begun to mill around the doorways and we were caught. Everyone was congratulating Salome, and when they noticed the physical likeness between us, they began to smile.

'You are all here!'

'Are you the little sister?'

'Oh my God!' A woman was leaning into my face. 'My God, what you've all lived through!'

Someone else had me by the arm. 'I was production manager,' she said quietly. 'Salome told the whole crew all about your early life. After that we knew we were working on something pretty special.'

'You guys have done it hard.'

I nodded, my vision blurry. I couldn't see anything properly. *Hang on until you get outside.* I could just make out Marly's tall frame edging his way to the door. With Beth hard on my heels I pushed my way towards him. 'Marlon.'

But he was moving off without us.

Once outside I followed Beth, who'd run down the steps, tears pouring down her face. 'How could she … do that?' she gasped over and over. 'How could she do it?'

'I don't know,' I whispered. 'I don't …'

Marly seemed to have disappeared. Beth caught sight of him first. A tall young man in a dinner suit, his back to us, was bending over as though he'd been shot in the stomach. But when we got closer we saw he was vomiting into the gutter.

nineteen

Jack is leaning her bulky body up against the sink. 'Harry and I discussed a few things before he left.' She is addressing Beth. 'When the clearing out and cleaning comes to an end it really would be worth thinking about a few extra small jobs as well.'

'Such as?' Beth says coldly.

'Pulling up that terrible carpet in the living room and sanding the floor, painting a few window frames and fixing the fence out front. You'll be surprised at how much difference it makes.'

'We aren't planning to live here!'

'You'll get a lot better price if you jazz it up a bit.'

'Didn't I tell you Jack was a genius?' Salome grins proudly.

But Beth is frowning and chewing a nail. And as far as I'm concerned Jack might as well be talking another language. What do I know about sanding floors?

Jack looks disappointed by our lack of response and turns to go outside again. 'It's just a suggestion,' she calls back.

'Feel free,' Beth calls after her. 'Do whatever you think.'

'Will Harry come back and get all the bad people?' Nellie asks sleepily when I'm putting her to bed that night.

'No baddies here,' I say. 'No one is going to get you.'

'You always say that,' she murmurs, her little face puckering into a frown.

'Because it's true.'

'They might get in that window.'

I sigh, and sit on her bed. She is picking up on my vibes, but I have no idea what to do about it.

'We're safe here,' I tell her again and kiss her forehead. I figure that at least that much is true. Jay won't find us here. *Not tonight, anyway.*

'But the wind might blow us over.'

'No, it won't. This house is strong. My grandpa and grandma lived here for years and it never blew over.'

She wriggles away from me and wraps both arms around Barry. 'You can go now,' she says.

'Not till you close your eyes.'

'Go,' she orders, twisting further away. 'I've got Barry.'

I leave her in that bed, in that room, and stand in the doorway, trying to ward off the sense of doom slowly descending on me as I think of what is in front of her. Her friends will have homes in tree-lined suburbs, they'll have fathers and brothers and sisters to play with and learn from. They'll join netball clubs and learn piano and feel secure and part of things. All I've got to give her is my own loneliness and dread and lack of security. *Her* mother will always be on the alert, afraid, on guard. What the hell did I think I was doing, dragging her off like this?

I turn back into the room and see both her arms around Barry, her eyes still wide open. 'Mamma?' I swear she can smell my fear.

'Yes?'

'Are you sad?'

'A bit.'

'Are you missing Streak, too?'

'A bit, sweetheart.'

'Will Daddy know about the buckets?'

'Yeah.'

'Will he know that the blue one is for Streak and the baby goats get the red one?'

'Yeah. He knows that.'

'Did you tell him?'

'Yes,' I lie to her. 'I told him.'

I step out into the hallway and close my eyes very tightly.

I wake that night with the scratching sound of possums scampering on the tin roof above. It tears across my skin like a claw. *I am safe.* Again and again I tell myself that. *Safe.* But I don't really believe it. *Where is he?*

Jay is looking for me. I can feel it in my bones. He is closing in too. *Or am I just imagining that?* I lie there imagining the worst, trying to work out my next move. What's the plan? Where do I go next? The only way I can calm myself is to get up, wrap myself in a blanket against the cold, and go outside to look at the night sky. I walk across the lawn to the back gate. Patches of pale yellow moonlight fall across the grass as I make my way through the deepening shadows and stare around at the surrounding hills. The old woodshed and picket fence, the tank and the windmill and the openness around the house, so different to Byron, give me comfort.

I know all I can realistically hope for is that he will be diverted by something. Work, maybe, or some other gullible young woman. *If only* … How could I possibly wish it upon someone else, to step into the life I had with him? And yet I do. If it would save Nellie and me then I wish for it.

The next few days pass swiftly enough. There's so much to do. Rubbish to sort through, scouring the floors and sinks, and visiting Grandpa with Beth. And I'm so exhausted I hit the sack along with Nellie most nights, and my sleep is deep and dreamless until I wake, usually around two or three in the morning, and that's when everything comes crashing in on me again. I lie in the dark, wondering where he is, sometimes for hours, shifting from one side to the other, scrabbling around in my head for solutions, waiting for morning.

One night I wake after only a couple of hours and wrap myself in the old chenille bedspread and sit on the end of Nellie's bed, aware of voices in the kitchen. I move closer to hear the scraping of chairs, the chinking of mugs. Something drops to the floor, followed by the buzz of low, earnest voices. I creep down the hall to listen.

'She's a mess!' Salome isn't bothering to whisper. 'I saw her sitting out on the verandah last night at about three a.m.'

'I know.'

'So what did he do to her?'

There is silence for a moment.

'The usual. Physical and mental abuse. I see it all the time.' I see Beth's face in my mind's eye and I feel like slapping it.

'What about the kid?'

'She won't talk about it, but … I think so.'

'Why won't she talk about it?'

'Maybe it's too hard,' Beth says in exasperation. 'But I'm worried about her state of mind.'

'Yeah?' Salome asks curiously.

'She could tip over the edge any minute.'

'What the hell does that mean?' Salome exclaims.

Beth gives a big sigh. 'Have a guess, Salome!'

'I mean, what will happen then?' Salome bumbles on.

'I don't know.'

'What plans does she have?'

'None, as far as I can gather.'

'So what are we going to do with her?'

There is a clattering of dishes and the sound of water rushing into the sink.

'How come it's always me that has to find solutions to everything?' Beth's voice is low and angry. 'I'm in the middle of a divorce. Trying to sell a house. Dealing with a husband who thinks he should be compensated for my lack of *empathy*!' She snorts. 'Why don't *you* come up with something?'

'Has she been to the police?'

'Don't think so. No.'

'But that's ridiculous!'

I head back to my bed, hot with humiliation. Why didn't I leave with Harry? I chuck my pillow on the floor, kick off the bedclothes, and lie there in the dark grinding my teeth with anger. Fuck them both! I'll ring Marly in the morning and go back to Melbourne the very next day. I will not stay here under their sufferance! Or we'll hitch up to Darwin and stay with Marly, and I'll get a job and I'll pay him back. I can't go on living here.

And I can't go on sleeping in this same fucking room …

I was only ten. It was just after my father died. My mother had been in quite good spirits when she brought me in to show me where she used to sleep as a young girl. All her brothers had slept out the back, in two specially-built rooms, and her older sisters were in a much bigger room near her parents. As the youngest girl she had ended up the only one with a room to herself, and it used to make her feel lonely. She'd just told me about the way she used to kneel up at the window and pray for a sister her own age to come along. She believed if she prayed hard enough it would happen.

But once my mother sat down on her old bed she forgot about all that. She was staring around the room, chin in her hand, completely distracted by something else. I stood by the doorway, watching her, saying nothing, waiting for her to speak. Her eyes that day were so vivid and blue in the light coming through the window. They reminded me of the ocean on a bright day, almost translucent.

'This is where Lizzie died,' she said quietly.

'Who?'

'Your great-grandmother Tess came in here and found her sister Lizzie writhing around on the floor.'

I stared at my mother, feeling a chill creep over me.

'Why … what did she die of?' I went over to sit next to her. The word *writhing* did something to me. But Mum moved away from me, off the bed and onto the floor herself, flat on her back. She closed her eyes.

'Mum!' I protested, horrified. 'Don't!'

'Shhh.'

'Why are you on the floor?'

'Lizzie took poison,' she said in a hoarse whisper.

'Why?'

'Your grandfather was just a little kid and Lizzie was his favourite aunt. She was musical and kind. They were poor, and Lizzie was the unmarried one who always brought presents for the children. Hers were the only presents they got. They all loved her. Your grandpa was about your age now when it happened. And he saw it all. He and his sisters stood around and watched her die over a period of about four hours. No ambulances then, just a horse and dray and the doctor ten miles away. But maybe there was someone they could have called. I bet there was someone!' she said angrily. 'Over the next few weeks, Grandpa and his sisters saw their mother … go mad.'

I gulped and thought of that huge old man sitting on the couch in the lounge room, how pleased he'd seemed with the latest snatch of poetry I'd learnt for him. Imagining him as a little kid my own age watching someone die like that was impossible. *Writhing* …

'Why did she do it?' My voice was too loud. In spite of the warm summer day outside, there was not much light in that room. Along with trying to picture my grandfather as a little kid standing over the dying body of his aunt, I was wishing that my mother would get up off the floor. I wanted her to start behaving like a proper mum again. Since Dad's death she'd got a lot weirder. My brother and sisters were forever raising their eyes and sniggering behind her back, and I wanted all that to stop.

'We don't know,' she murmured. 'They did an autopsy and she wasn't pregnant. Maybe she thought she was. Who knows? Why does anyone take their own life?'

I wanted to get away, to go back to our house in town with bossy Beth and snotty Salome. How come I was the only one expected to come out to this old place now? I wanted to go back and tell Marlon what Grandpa had told me that day. That being so tall and wiry, Marlon was a natural athlete and so he should try hard and get into a local team and make the most of his talents. That's what Grandpa had said. Most of all, I wanted to get back to where things made sense.

'After Lizzie died, Tess became distraught.' My mother was mumbling to herself now as though I wasn't even there, her eyes still closed. 'And she never recovered.'

'Why didn't she recover?' I asked stupidly.

'People thought suicide was a wicked sin back then. Your great-grandmother would have thought her sister was in hell.'

'Hell?' I whispered in awe. 'Is that a real place?'

'*They* believed it was!' she snapped. 'The bloody priests told them so, and they believed it!'

'But would God let that happen to someone kind and nice who everyone loved?' I asked. But what I was really wondering about was my own dad. If he meant to be killed by that train, would he be in hell too? I wanted to ask my mother, but I didn't dare. *What if she said yes?*

'Lizzie died on the fifth of November.' Mother gave a mirthless laugh from the floor. 'And they had Tess in the asylum by the twenty-first. No mucking about in those days!'

'Mum, get up!' Her loud, sarcastic tone seemed far worse than her soft spooky one. 'Please!'

'Never to come out!' she shouted. The sob in her voice was real and it freaked me out badly. 'They let her die in there!'

When Mum eventually sat up her cheeks were wet with tears, and this truly shocked me. She was actually crying about someone she'd never met. *Crying!*

'It's easy to go mad, Tess,' she said, wiping her eyes on her dress. 'So easy.' She laughed again and held out her arms to me, but I turned away. I wouldn't even look at her as I headed for the door.

'Mum! We've got to go home.'

Sometimes it's the only *sane* thing to do.

The next morning when I go out to the kitchen, Nellie is already dressed and 'helping' Beth and Jack pull jars and tins off the pantry shelves, throwing them into a plastic rubbish bin. Salome is making tea. She has established her work space out on the verandah, and I can hardly bring myself to look at it, I'm so jealous. A silver laptop on a small wooden table pulled from a bedroom, bundles of research notes and booklets in neat piles around her. I duck back to the bedroom and call Marly. He doesn't answer and so I leave a message for him to ring back urgently. Before I have even brushed my teeth the phone is ringing.

'What's up, sis?' he asks.

I burst into a rant about how I hate being here and can't stand another minute with Salome and Beth. I've got to get away. 'So I'm wondering about how to get up there, where you are?' I stop abruptly and wait for his response. *Oh sure, yes. Come up here, Tess.*

You and Nellie. I'll send you the fare tomorrow. I'll make everything right … I'm waiting to hear all that. But he remains silent for some time. He hums a bit, clicks his tongue and clears his throat.

'Hang in for a while, Tess,' he tells me at last. 'You have as much right to be there as the others. Things will work out.'

It was not what I wanted to hear. In fact, I'm so disappointed that I can't even reply. I click the phone off, wash my face in cold water and head back out to the kitchen.

Beth stops and looks up at me carefully with a worried frown. I don't need reminding that I have dark rings under my eyes from last night.

'I'm tired,' I tell her, before she can say anything.

'Not sleeping well?'

'Not particularly.'

'Something worrying you?' Salome calls out from the stove, all sly innocence. *What are we going to do with her?*

'No! Everything is just … so great, Salome!'

'Shit! No need to blow your stack. I was just—'

'Just what?' They are both looking at me now. 'I want to get something clear with you two. I have as much right to be here as you both.'

'Well, of course … you do,' Beth says in a small voice.

'He's my grandfather too. This place is as much mine as it is yours.'

There is silence. They look at me, blank-faced, completely taken aback.

'And I'm not expecting either of you to find any *solutions* for me!'

Nellie looks up from the book she has found, her little face swivelling from one to the other of us as she tries to work out what's going on. 'Barry wakes up all the time too,' she says softly.

I plonk myself down next to her, pull her to my knee and catch her hair into pigtails with trembling fingers.

'I tell him to be quiet.' She breathes out as she flips through more pages of the book, not looking at any of us now. 'But he sometimes just wakes up.'

'I know that,' I say, and look at the other two again. 'I'm doing my share of the work, aren't I?'

Beth nods carefully.

'So leave me be.'

'We're worried about you, Tess,' she says reasonably. 'That's all.'

'Well, don't worry about me!' I snap again.

The truth is, I'm worried about me too. In my darkest moments I know I'll never be free. Even if he doesn't kill me, he will be forever hanging about on the edge of my life, souring any possibility of a future. Grandpa's money is a mirage. One way or another it will slide out from under Nellie and me. The uncles and aunts will join forces and bring on a legal challenge as soon as he's dead. They've probably begun it already. The case will be dragged into the courts and that huge pool of money will be whittled away to nothing.

But the physical work is hard, and there is so much of it that it saves me from dwelling too much on all that might happen. So much rubbish to see to, collect and discard – decades of accumulated stuff from the house and sheds to haul into boxes for the local op-shops, and even more to drag to the pile to be burnt. Then there is all the cleaning-out of grimy cupboards, the scrubbing-down of walls and floors. I don't mind any of it, because it keeps the other, darker reality at bay.

That day passes quickly enough too. Late in the afternoon, on my way out to the back gate with a bundle of junk, I stop to watch Nellie helping Jack with the sanding-down of a partially rotted verandah post. They are making up a song together about biting march flies. It's so funny and clever, and Nellie is so much part of it, that I just have to laugh. That night they stand up together and sing it to the rest of us. The clapping, the laughter and the praise for Nellie, and then the look of pure pleasure on Beth's face when Nellie runs over and sits on her knee!

'Was it a good song, Beebe?'

'That was the best song ever, Nellie,' Beth tells her, caressing her hair and smiling at me. 'The best song I've heard in ages.'

Then later when we are washing up, 'Is this our other family, Mamma?' Nellie asks me.

Our other family? I watch Salome's face soften. Her cool, guarded expression falls away completely and she smiles with a warmth I've never seen before.

'It is,' I tell Nellie. And when Nellie looks around they all nod their agreement.

'And Barry too,' Nellie adds quickly, looking over at the bear lying on his face on the floor.

Salome, Jack, Beth and I all agree in unison. Yes, Barry is part of our other family. We all love him too.

I have to stay. I can't rip her away from all this, can I?

Jack finds me out at the wood heap. I'm leaning against the old saw watching the sunset washing over the deep purple sky. Streaks of gold and pink radiate out from the fast-disappearing red sun.

She parks her large body down next to me and comes straight to the point.

'They can both be a couple of bitches,' she says calmly. 'My advice is just go along for the ride. Don't let them get to you.'

I have to laugh.

'My theory is that the whole business of your dad dying and mother leaving is eating them both up inside.'

'Does Salome talk much about Mum?' I ask curiously.

'No.'

'What about Dad?'

'He's a saint, apparently.' Jack gives me a droll grin.

'He wasn't,' I cut in.

'Yeah, I figured that.'

'Why won't Salome go see our grandfather?' I ask when we're getting up to go in. 'Every time Beth and I go in he asks after her.'

Jack nods in agreement. 'I tell her that if he dies without her seeing him she'll be sorry forever.'

'Salome is never sorry,' I say, 'about anything.'

'Ah.' Jack puts one large hand on my shoulder. 'She's just no good at saying it.'

I'm taken aback by this but say nothing, hoping she'll continue. Instead, she changes the subject.

'Being here with Salome makes me want to know more about her background. Are there photos?'

CORONER'S INQUEST

This Deponent: Harold Thorton Bourman on oath saith,
I am a Medical Officer residing at the Kew Asylum.

I find from the records of the Hospital that the
deceased, Therese Mary Josephine Kavanagh, was
admitted to this institution on the 21st day of
Nov 1928 on warrant now provided. She was suffering
from primary dementia and was in good health on
admission. By December 1929 she was reported as
being in an extremely thin condition. In April she
was admitted to the Hospital Ward as her health was
failing rapidly. She was last confined to bed on the
26th day of July and became weaker so that she died
as I am informed at 5 p.m. on the 1st. She had a sore
on the back of her head that would not heal as she
was continually scratching it. She was attended at
her death by her mother and sister,
Dr Rogers and myself, H Bourman.

twenty

I wake, scratching the new bad patch at the back of my head. My hands wander to my shoulderblades, and then down over the jutting hipbones.

I stand naked in front of the cracked mirror and consider my ribs, wondering how the insubstantial cage of bones could possibly hold all that it has to, windpipe, lungs and heart. What would it take to crack it open? Not much. Not much at all.

Eat and get strong, I tell myself sternly. *Get strong! You have a daughter.*

The next morning, I approach Grandpa's bedroom. Tentatively. Once I'm inside, the smell is even more pronounced than in the kitchen – urine is added to the mix. I open the blinds. The bed is unmade, the sheets are grimy, and his big boots are under the window. There are some photos on the walls, and above his bed a big oval picture of Virgin Mary looking at the child Jesus in her lap.

I make a pile of all the dirty linen I can find, old socks and work trousers, a couple of threadbare, smelly towels and some shirts, and shove them all into one of the thick plastic bags that Beth and I bought at the supermarket.

Then I fold up the cheap multicoloured rug on the worn carpet. I find a heavy porcelain pot under the bed. It is empty, but deep brown stains come almost up to the brim. I try not to think of my grandfather pulling himself out of his bed to piss in the night.

Before taking on the wardrobe, I go to the window. The view is lovely. I can see across the verandah and down the gently sloping hill to the valley where the creek lies. Salome is sitting at the work desk she's set up for herself. I watch her awhile as she bends over the laptop, every now and again looking up to stare into the distance. Nellie is out there too, mucking around with Barry and some old bits of things that Beth must have given her. They don't see me looking at them.

When I slide open Grandpa's wardrobe, jumbled clothes and packets of photos and some of Grandma's toiletries slide out. In the other side of the wardrobe are her clothes. I shove things into plastic bags. There are good-quality jumpers here, and old-lady petticoats, and nice blouses, and lots of shoes. This stuff will go to the Red Cross shop in town. The breeze coming in through the open window is already taking some of the smell away.

At the bottom of a big cardboard box filled with old cards, newspaper cuttings, knobs of wool and wound bunches of string, broken plates and wire coathangers with crocheted covers, I find part of a letter. One screwed-up page. I wouldn't have seen it except that I trip on the carpet as I'm dragging the box over to the corner and half its contents escape. I smooth it out and feel my heart quicken when I see my mother's dense black scrawl. It's not until I'm halfway down the page that I realise she is writing to me.

Remember that it was common for wives and mothers who couldn't shape up to be put away in such places. Such were the rigid ideas about females. You laughed too loud and too often, your habits were slovenly, you got drunk or enticed men by acting lewdly, perhaps you made the mistake of humiliating your husband in public … He might have had his eye on someone else and the asylum was a convenient way to get rid of you. It's all there on the public record for any of us to read. It only took two people to declare you insane. Those places were full of women like my grandmother. Rejected, banished and abandoned.

And so, Tessie, my darling girl, I'm giving all these bits and pieces to you. In a very real sense I'm giving her *to you. These few last records of her life might make the basis of ... something.*

Find out whatever else you can. Don't let her be forgotten. Find a way to

But the page ends. I turn it over. The other side is blank. No ending to the sentence. I get up and tip everything on the floor and begin a frantic search through the box, desperate for the rest of that letter. I turn out all the drawers, examining the contents of cardboard shoeboxes and tax department envelopes, ten-year-old electricity bills, Mass cards and Christmas cards, letters from strangers and aunts long dead. I examine every piece of screwed-up paper I can find and come up with nothing but an old newspaper clipping with a marriage notice outlined in black ink.

GIPPSLAND CHRONICLE 1914

The marriage of Mr Thomas Kavanagh, second son of the late Daniel and Ellen Kavanagh, and Therese Mary Josephine, third daughter of Brendan and Mary Sheehan, was celebrated in the Roman Catholic Church in Leongatha on Wednesday.

The Bride, who was given away by her brother, Mr T. Sheehan, looked very becoming in a beautiful dress of white silk muslin trimmed with Irish embroidery and Limerick lace. She wore a shamrock brooch and carried a bouquet of white orchids and asparagus fern, the gift of the bridegroom. The Bridesmaids were daintily attired in plain white muslin trimmed with Valenciennes lace.

Two separate portraits of my great-grandparents hang side by side on the far wall. Tess, dressed as a bride with curls peeping out from under the veil, and my great-grandfather, Tom, looking rakish with his heavy moustache and starched rounded collar. Neither of them smiling. Her expression is tentative more than anything, as though she might be gearing up for what will happen next. It is a black-and-white head-and-shoulders shot, lightly coloured by the photographer. I like the plainness of the shot; there is no angled pose or fancy lighting effects. The lace of her dress fits tight and high around her neck and there is a cameo brooch at her throat. She is nineteen and marrying a man of thirty-six. Did anyone think that was odd then? Was she warned? I stare at the photos. Was Tess overwhelmed by how handsome and intelligent Tom was? Was he considered a good catch? Did she ever wonder for a minute why he chose her?

I get up and move closer, drawn to it as though by some other force. Those widely spaced eyes are looking straight into my own.

Stay with me.

Thoughts race about my head, like centipedes released from a jar, frantic and angry, unsure where to go. I stare at the photo. That night in hospital, when I was wavering between life and death, I'd been sure that the voice whispering to me belonged to this woman … Her lips are not moving, and yet I can hear her voice. Dead for over eighty years and yet … *she lives.*

A sudden breeze makes the curtains flutter. There is the long, low moan of a cow calling to her calf in the distance, but apart from that … nothing. Silence roars around the room. My mouth goes dry. I look over at the battered old bed and I imagine her in this very room, the night her sister Lizzie died. Lying there exhausted next to her husband, her eyes staring into the darkness, thinking of her sister lying dead in the next room. How did she get through the hours until daybreak?

What happened to that woman explains everything about this family ...

It is my mother's voice I hear now, coming at me from the past, so clear that my heart quickens. I lock eyes with the young girl in the portrait again, realising that at nineteen she was two years younger than I am now.

'Tess.' I reach up and touch the picture, and she gazes back at me. Gentle, hopeful, sweet.

There is a cough behind me and I jump. When I turn I see Beth standing by the door watching me.

'Tess,' she says quietly, her face blank. I feel madness swirling in the air between us like electricity before a storm and it frightens me. 'Please,' she implores, 'please don't go crazy on me.' She turns abruptly, walks out and closes the door behind her.

I slump back down on the floor against the wall beside the old dressing table, draw up my knees and look around. It's so quiet in this room, so very still that I can hear my own breathing. I close my eyes and begin to rock, and that's when I feel them, the ghosts from the past gathering around. They press in close, filling the room with discord. There are deep masculine voices shouting orders. Then someone is blaming someone else, demanding that something should happen. And women are arguing among themselves, shrill and strident. Someone else is crying. Why? What are they saying? Who are they and why are they all so angry and sad? No one can agree on anything. I feel I know them and yet I know I don't.

I know them.

I open my eyes and slowly the feeling of being surrounded fades. The air returns to normal. I scramble up and shake myself and open the window wider. Down the hall, I hear the faint sounds of Jack in the lounge room pulling up the carpet.

twenty-one

'What are you writing?'

I'm so engrossed, head bent low over the page, trying to catch the last light, that I don't see Salome approach until she is up close, staring over my shoulder. Startled, I automatically cover the page with my hand like a kid in school and then feel embarrassed.

I have come out here to the back verandah to watch the sun set and write in the book Harry gave me. Salome has a towel wrapped around her head. The sweet smell of her shampoo makes me think of flowers and sunshine.

'Nothing much.' I close the book. There is no way in the world that I'll share even a word of it with her.

'Can I join you?' she asks. She is dressed in her usual tight jeans and a white shirt. I nod and she settles herself next to me, dangling her legs over the edge of the verandah.

'You always were a scribbler,' she says mildly.

I think of her burning those shoeboxes full of my scrawl, and a burst of the old bitterness flames in my chest again. Why would she do that? I was just a kid. I wasn't doing any harm to anyone.

'So,' she sighs and gives her hair a vigorous rub, 'even if Grandpa dies tomorrow, it will take months for the money to come through. The assets have to be sold. Best-case scenario, it will take a year.'

'Your point?'

'What are you going to do next? You and your little girl?'

I breathe out and stare into the setting sun, trying to stay calm. Has she come out to remind me that I have some decisions to make and a little girl to take care of? Like she would know a thing about any of that. I try to concentrate on the rim of sinking red sun. The blush remaining on the distant mountains is a faint shade of mauve.

'What do you care what I do next?' I say quietly.

'You're my sister! And there's no need to get stroppy.'

'So that's what this is about, then?' I shoot back. 'Me being stroppy?'

'No!' She laughs. 'Not at all.' Her laugher is light and airy and lovely, and yet it grates against every nerve-ending in my body. Salome was always so good at mocking me, making me feel that I'd missed the point in some way.

Maybe half a minute goes by. She's going to hit me with something soon. I can feel it. I go into my head the way I used to with Jay, mentally shutting the doors and pulling down the hatches.

'What do you think of Jack?' she asks suddenly.

'I like her,' I reply, surprised.

'Yeah, she likes you too. And your little girl!' she adds enthusiastically. 'Wow! We both love her.'

So where is this heading?

Salome pulls out a pack of cigarettes from her jeans pocket and lights up. I'm deeply surprised by this. I've never known either of my sisters to smoke. She takes a drag and gives me a quick grin. 'Don't tell Jack. She hates me smoking.'

'Okay.'

'I only have one a day. You want one?'

'No, thanks.' The smell reminds me of Harry. I wonder if he's still staying with his aunt or if he's back with Jules by now.

'You reckon Marlon will turn up?'

'I don't know.'

'I miss Marlon,' Salome says suddenly, and once again she laughs in that same easy way. 'He was always such a *boy*! I really hope he comes.'

'Yeah.'

When Beth rang him and told him about the money he was in the middle of a school day and apparently sounded neither surprised nor interested in the news of his imminent windfall. Since then, none of us have managed to get hold of him, apart from my quick rant about wanting to leave. I've rung a couple of times since and left messages, but he hasn't called back.

Salome's profile is so perfect against the light, the straight nose and curving mouth, the neat crop of thick hair. I feel her sudden hesitation, her stepping forward and then back again, not knowing how to broach whatever it is she wants to say.

'Remember the day you wouldn't go into the chapel to see Dad's body?' Salome finally says.

I stiffen immediately. She's staring out at the darkening sky, as though unaware of me even being there.

'That's going a long way back, Salome,' I say carefully. 'Why are you bringing that up?'

She shrugs. 'I remember that day so well.'

'I was ten years old,' I say.

'I know how old you were,' she mumbles.

I start to panic. What has it got to do with anything? Does she want me to feel guilty about it all over again? I was ten years old!

'I've been dreaming about that day.' She hesitates. 'And I've been thinking a lot about that time. About him and ... Mum and everything.'

'Really?

'It's being here, I guess.'

'Yeah.'

It was a bright, sunny morning when the four of us got out of the car and walked with Mum towards the low, white-brick funeral home. Everything about that place was tidy, from the tightly manicured lawns to the tall palms shielding the place from the street. I remember wishing that our own house was like it.

I fell back when Mum and Beth and Marlon and Salome reached the glass doors of the front entrance. As they began to climb the stairs, something made me stop. I took the first step up and then I stopped again.

'I'm not going in,' I told them.

They all turned to look at me.

Mum, who'd been leading the way, came back down a step. 'But why?'

'I don't want to,' I said, feeling quite odd. I think it was the first time I'd ever asserted myself. Mostly I just took my cues from the others.

'Don't be afraid.' She was holding out one hand to me, expecting I would take it. 'Just come in with us. No one else will be there. We can all say our goodbyes to Dad in private.'

'I'm not afraid,' I said, and I wasn't.

'Dad has gone, darling,' she went on gently. 'It's just his coffin.'

I knew that too. I'd stood outside the bedroom door eavesdropping on her conversation with the undertaker the day before. 'Yes, I understand,' she'd wept. 'A closed coffin. Yes, of course.' *A closed coffin.*

I was only ten, but I had already guessed that there would not be much left of a body after it was hit by a train. So why would I go into that place and stand next to a shiny wooden box containing bits and pieces of my father? Why would I? Having to wonder if they'd been able to stick him back together in any way, and knowing deep down that it would be impossible. The remnant flesh and bones of my father would be bundled up like a bag of meat under all the polished wood, the hush and low light, the candles and soft music. Anyway, why should I go say goodbye to him when he never said goodbye to any of us?

When they saw that I wasn't about to change my mind they left me there, out in the sunshine. I sat on the step for a while and then went over to the grass to watch the birds. There was a man on a mower making slow tracks around the lawn and I watched him. I had to admit I was curious. What could they be doing in there? I started to worry that I might be missing out on something.

Salome came out to check on me.

'You want to come in now?' she asked. Her face was very white and her eyes were red from crying. 'Say goodbye to Dad?'

'No.' I shook my head.

She waited awhile, not knowing what to say to convince me. I wanted to ask her what it was like. Was I missing anything? But I didn't want to compromise my position.

'You were an unusual kid,' Salome says now, flicking her ash onto the ground thoughtfully. 'You always had your own life going on inside.'

'Everyone does,' I mumble uncomfortably.

'I was jealous of you.'

'You were jealous of *me*?' She is still looking out at the darkening sky, smoking determinedly.

'Yeah, I still am, actually.'

A squawk of disbelief rushes from my mouth before I can even think. I want to laugh but actually I'm on the brink of crying.

'Salome, you're the one with a career,' I begin quietly. 'You've got a life with Jack in Sydney in a cool house with loads of friends. A future, in other words. I'm running from a man who will kill me if he finds me. He either takes my little girl or he kills me. Maybe both of us.' My tone is becoming belligerent, so I try to hold back, but I'm breathing hard and I badly want to hit her. Of all the stupid things to say!

'And you're *jealous* of me?' I try to lighten up at this point, sound amused even.

'Yep.' Salome laughs awkwardly. 'All you said is true, but …'

'But what?'

'I'm still jealous.'

'That's insane.'

'It is,' she agrees. 'And I'm trying to get over it.'

I lie back on the verandah, and for whatever reason I suddenly see the funny side. *Salome is jealous of me!* I start laughing, and it becomes like the time with Harry – I can't stop.

Salome used to make me laugh a lot when I was a kid, telling me knock-knock jokes that were so lame we'd both crack up together, neither of us able to speak for minutes at a time. Once, she insisted I come with her to steal lollies from the supermarket. I was the decoy, except I didn't turn out to be a particularly good one and the manager saw her. We ran out of there together, up the street and around the corner, hiding behind cars and shrieking like hyenas as we stuffed the lot in our mouths before anyone could catch us. I was terrified, expecting to be caught any minute, but I needn't have worried. Salome was always too smart to get caught.

She sees me laughing and it gets her smiling a bit too. And it's like being those same kids again and the tension evaporates into the night. Something I wouldn't have thought possible even *ten minutes* before.

I sit up eventually and so does she. The darkness is surrounding us now. I can't see her face.

'When did you know you were gay?' I ask.

'I've always known.' She takes a deep drag of the cigarette. 'Remember that crush I had on Mrs Hodson in Year Six?'

'Oh, I do!' I laugh. 'You kept bringing her flowers.'

'I was totally in love with her.'

'Were you?' I smile.

'And after her there was Maddie Lawson. Remember?' Salome laughs. 'Then I went to film school.' She sighs deeply. 'I've had lots of lovers.'

'Really?' I ask shyly, thinking *I've really only ever had the one.*

'Mostly disastrous,' she adds dryly. 'Until I found Jack.'

In the background I hear Nellie calling for me. She'll be off to sleep in a while and I really should go in, but … I don't want to move.

'Tess, that time I read your stuff and burnt it … I …' She stops, sits up and pulls out another cigarette. 'I still feel so damned bad about that.'

'I thought you said you only have one,' I say, looking at the fresh cigarette.

'Yeah, well, sometimes I bend the truth a bit,' she says. 'Thing is, I knew it was good.'

'What?'

'Your writing.'

'I was seventeen years old, Salome! It was the usual teenage rubbish.'

'It wasn't, though,' she says thoughtfully. 'It was sharp and witty. It had real depth. You were brilliant. Mum knew it. We all did. I was jealous.'

I don't have anything to say to this, but I'm touched beyond words.

'I needed to say it,' she explains.

'Thanks,' I mutter, embarrassed. 'It was years ago.'

'It was on my conscience, I suppose.' She grins at me and stands up. 'What I really came out here to tell you is that you and Nellie are welcome to come live with me and Jack in Sydney for as long as you like.' She looks at me directly. 'We've got a big spare room upstairs – it's virtually a self-contained flat, and you don't have to pay. You can chill out. Find your way into something. Maybe go to university or get a job. It's there for you, anyway.'

This is so unexpected I don't know what to say. I can't even look at her. Me and Nellie living with *Salome*! I try to imagine it and can't. How long would we even survive?

'I really appreciate the offer,' I say after a while. Pretty lame, I know, but it's all I can manage, I'm so shocked. I think Salome is a bit embarrassed too.

'Jack and I have talked it over. We both want you to come. Getting lost in Sydney might be just what you need to do.'

I smile. *Getting lost in Sydney?* I like that idea. It's sounding better by the minute!

'So think about it, okay?' She picks up the towel and is almost to the door. 'We're serious. Jack and me both want you to come.' She turns to go inside.

'Salome.' I call her back. 'There was a note with that stuff.'

'What stuff?'

'The stuff Mum sent me. What did it say?'

She comes back a few steps.

'I didn't really read any of what she sent. Except … the first page.'

'What did it say?'

'*To Tess the Storyteller,*' she says wryly. '*Lots of love from Mum.*'

'Oh.'

'I was so jealous of that too.' She runs both hands through her damp hair and disappears through the back door.

I go inside myself and curl up into a ball beside Nellie, who is almost asleep.

'What were you doing?' she grumbles, her eyelids fluttering with tiredness.

'I was talking to Salome.'

'Do you like being in this house, Mamma?'

'A bit,' I say, running my hand over her forehead. 'What about you?'

'Yes,' she says slowly. 'It's alright.'

'You love Beth?'

'Beebe,' she corrects me, her eyelids closed now. 'And Jack is my best friend now.'

'What about Salome?'

'A little bit.'

twenty-two

I take Jack into my grandfather's bedroom to show her the wedding photos.

'Oh.' She puts her hand over her mouth. 'But you look like her!'

We sit there awhile, in the darkening room across from the two portraits that have taken on a vaguely eerie quality in the fading light.

'You know, Tess, I think you should get the old fella to talk before he dies.'

'He doesn't want to talk about her.'

'He won't answer direct questions, that's all. You have to hang in there and wait. He'll talk.'

'Beth will kill me.'

'He's dying. It's your last chance.'

'But she's already freaked out about me …'

'So go on your own. Don't tell her.'

'I don't drive.'

'How would you go on the back of a bike?'

'Fine.' I grin, remembering how much I loved being on the back of Jay's bike.

'What about tomorrow?'

So that is what we do. We tell them I'm helping Jack with the sanding and we need to go in together to ask the hardware shop about sanders and oils and so on. If Beth and Salome find it strange, they don't say anything. And Beth is only too happy to mind Nellie for me.

Jack's solid presence fills the ward as soon as she sits down. From the start, she calls my grandfather by his first name, and he acts as if that's the most natural thing in the world. Another time I know he would have found it impertinent. She tells him in great detail about how the clean-out of the house is proceeding, the fence that she knows how to fix and her plans to sand the floors.

His face takes on a new liveliness. 'Sounds like you're all doing a good job, Jack!' he whispers. 'Like you're getting stuck into it.'

'Oh yeah.'

'You know what you're doing?'

'My father was a builder, Frank, and I worked for him for a few years. You pick things up without even trying.'

'Of course you do,' he says approvingly.

'Polished floors are all the go these days,' she tells him. 'There's good wood under there, too.'

'Blackwood,' he gasps.

'You have to come out and see it when it's done,' Jack declares matter-of-factly.

The drawn old face collapses into a rough approximation of mirth. 'Ah!'

'You've got to see it,' she insists. 'We'll get you out for an hour, make sure what we're doing meets your approval.'

The audacity of this is actually making him laugh. I can hardly believe it. *Any day now,* they've said. *He'll be gone any day.* The assessment seemed spot-on only the day before. Yet here he is, laughing.

'I'd like to see the cattle sold,' he says after a while. 'Thursday.'

'Thursday.' Jack nods. 'We'll get our heads around that one. Now, Tess needs to talk to you. I'm going to get lost.'

'Okay, Jack,' he says mildly.

'See you outside whenever,' she tells me.

I nod and watch her disappear. I don't think I've ever been alone with my grandfather before. Not as an adult, anyway. Everything I'd thought to say has now gone out of my head and I panic a bit. What was it we decided that I needed to know? How should I approach it?

I needn't have worried.

'Tess,' he says. He reaches out one dry, trembling hand to me. 'I was hoping to get a moment with you before … I die.'

Right now I'm ten years old again, a little girl next to this huge and powerful colossus, flat on his back and dying, but still capable of a knockout blow. I brace myself for the big put-down. The dismissal. What will he say? That I'm a disgrace just like my mother?

'Now, will you have a look in there for a long envelope?' He waves at the steel cabinet next to the bed. 'I think it's in the top drawer.'

I stand up and open the drawer. At the back I find the envelope. It's a bit worn but basically intact.

'It's from your mother,' he says slowly. 'You should read it.'

My mouth goes dry. I look at the front and my hands begin to tremble. Those spiky, dense black words scrawling across the envelope make me weak inside. I feel vaguely nauseous and have to sit down. I peer closely at the stamp so I don't have to keep looking at the familiar handwriting. I can't make out the letter's origin.

'America,' he tells me in a whisper. 'One of the nurses told me it's an American stamp.'

'Oh.'

'So take it out.' My hands are still shaking as I slide the folded pages out. 'And now read it, love.'

Dad,

I want you to know that I think of you often, and that for all the miles I've put between us, you are still here, in my heart. Much as I try to erase you I can't. You won't go away. There are things I need to say that you might not want to hear. No doubt you will console yourself that I always lacked sound judgement and that my hold on reality was always tenuous and that I've proved you right by messing up most things in my life and that therefore I have no right to speak at all. So be it.

I recently had a very vivid dream of your mother. She was wearing a long grey 'Asylum dress' and she told me you were dying. 'Tell Frank not to worry,' she told me. 'It will be a good season. The dams are full and you should get a good price for your lambs.'

In the dream she disappeared into a dark wooded area. I was too frightened to follow at first because I had the strong feeling that I would be led into madness. Always my fear, as you well know, because it is yours too.

But I went anyway and I'm glad I did. After walking through heavy dense bush I came out into a clearing and found her swimming in a big lake of clear water, her dress now pure white billowing out in the water around her. 'Tell Frank it isn't his fault,' she called out to me.

The dream stayed with me for days. Even now I sometimes close my eyes and remember it. It works like rich sweet oil on scaly skin, easing some of the loneliness inside my heart. Did you ever forgive your father for putting her away in that place? Instead of helping her get over the grief of her favourite sister dying in that terrible way, he abandoned her to strangers! His own sweet wife! You've said she was sweet yourself on many occasions, sunny-natured and kind. In your heart of hearts can you ever forgive him for that?

My life is strange now. I have a friend or two. I make some money. I live and I think. But I am a stranger in a strange land. I feel it more and more as I get older.

I hear about the kids from my trusted source and that gives me enormous comfort. That they're doing well, in spite of me, allows me to breathe some relief. I'm told that they never come to see you, but I'm hardly one to judge them on that score.

That Beth is now a doctor and married makes me so happy! She wanted that from the time she was six. And Marlon, teaching in a remote Aboriginal community! I can see him there. His sweet, patient and kind nature would fit in so well. And Salome has made her mark. I saw that film Abandoned *by the way. Did you? The one that won the prize? It was a beautiful film. I could see that, even though my absence was the brooding presence hanging over the story, it was beautiful. I cried all the way through it. I was so proud of her.*

Except for my baby. What has happened to little Tess? It keeps me awake at night. Have you seen her? Has something terrible happened to her? Please let me know. (Get Jimmy to write to me at the Melbourne P.O. box address at the bottom of this page and my friend will get the message to me.) Tell me the truth. Good or bad. I'm in no position to ask for lies. Forget your pious judgement for just one minute and get me word of her.

Little Tess. Named after your mother, of course. She even looked like your mother, and was dreamy and imaginative as well. From the time she was a little girl I felt that she was your mother come back for another go at life. I know you felt the same. You liked her best of all your grandchildren because of that connection to your mother. Don't deny it.

I need to know if she's okay. (I was going to write happy.
But who is happy? Who on this earth is ever happy?) She is
nearly twenty-two now and so, odds on, she's not happy.
That doesn't matter. I just want to know that she is alive.

I'm going now and I won't be writing again – to anyone.
The truth is that I wouldn't have done what I did except I had to.
You might not understand this (men rarely do!) but I was never
cut out for marriage or motherhood, even as I loved aspects of it.
I never truly wanted it and when Eddie died I lost any feeling
for it altogether. Not that he was such a great catch – as you were
so fond of telling me – but he was mine. Can you understand
that? He was mine. And he kept me sane. And when he'd gone
I couldn't see my way forward. Just like your mother, I was losing
my mind.

I had to go and live the life I was meant to live.

I know I was never an easy child, too flighty and
temperamental for most people's tastes, and so different to my
conservative, sensible, smart sisters that I must have seemed like
an aberration to you and Mum. And yet there I was. Yours. I wish
you could have loved me better. That's all.

I forgive you, Dad, and with all my heart I wish you a
peaceful death and a happy journey into the next life.

Your loving daughter, Lily

P.S. Whether you realise it or not, you're lucky to receive this
letter. I very much doubt I will receive any such letter of forgiveness
from my own children.

I sit there in the upright chair next to his bed, warm golden
sunshine pouring in through the window. I read the letter through
another couple of times because it all feels so unreal. As though
I might be dreaming. When I look up he's asleep again.

'Grandpa.' I lean over and take the cool dry hand in my own. 'I've read it.'

'Good,' he mumbles.

'Do you want ... to write back?'

He makes a sound in the back of his throat and then wakes up a little. 'Yes,' he whispers. 'You bring in paper and pencil next time.'

'Okay.'

'And you write it for me.'

'Okay.' I pick up my bag and do up my jacket and walk to the door.

'Tess!' His hoarse whisper stops me in my tracks. I turn around. 'Will this mongrel come after you?'

'Yes,' I tell him.

He waves one trembling hand at me and then his breathing subsides again.

'When Marlon comes tell him to come in here,' he whispers when I reach the door.

'Okay.'

No one has told him yet that Marlon isn't coming.

I sit on the front steps and wait for Jack to come and pick me up. Within a few minutes she comes roaring into the grounds and I tell her about the letter and we decide to go and have a coffee before going back to the farm.

'I didn't find out much but thanks anyway, Jack.'

'For what?'

'Just for being here,' I laugh.

When we get back to the house Nellie is helping Beth bake a cake. I can see that Beth is loving every minute of teaching her.

'It all got a bit out of hand,' she smiles apologetically.

I pick up Nellie for a hug and she puts her sticky fingers in my mouth to suck.

'My dad has long hair,' she tells the others in a conversational tone. 'And sometimes he puts me on his shoulders when he is picking avocados.'

'Does he now?'

'Yep. We've got a farm!' she declares. 'A huge farm! And a dog.' She gives my hair a tug. 'What is Streak doing now, Mamma?'

'I don't know,' I say.

'Can we go and get him and bring him here?'

'I don't think so, baby.'

'But I love Streak!'

'I know you do.'

I leave them to their cooking and go up to the old dam to think about my mother's letter. The calm eyes of the half-dozen cows resting under the trees in the fading light watch my progression up the side of the dam as though they are lost in their own thoughts of her too. It is here, out in the open, that I feel her all over again in the soft breeze blowing through the small clump of trees near the water's edge.

The next morning I get a call from Harry.

'How are things?' he asks.

'Okay,' I say. 'You?'

He tells me about his aunt and the farm. How he's been taking some time to unravel a few things in his head.

'Sounds good,' I say, trying to sound light and carefree.

But hearing his voice gives me a rush of longing to be back in the car with him, on the move to somewhere else, Harry and I and Nellie. Or in that motel room feeling so close and safe, sitting outside on the white plastic chairs watching the rain pouring down. All those quiet times we had driving along, then the abrupt rush of talk, the laughter and questions. The truth is, I miss Harry a lot. I want to ask him if it's really over with Jules.

'So what are you doing today?' he asks.

'Painting the back fence,' I tell him. 'We've nearly finished it. You should see the rubbish pile out the front now. About twice as big as it was when you were here. It's going to be some bonfire.'

'You sound good, Tess.'

'I'm pretty good.' I take a breath, hardly daring to ask. 'You want to come back for the bonfire?'

'Jules is back,' he says shortly. 'I'm heading back to Melbourne.'

'Oh.' I swallow my disappointment. 'That'll be good.'

'Did you see the seven o'clock news last night?' he asks suddenly.

'No. Why?'

'Three brothers living just out of Byron have been charged with manufacturing and trafficking amphetamines.'

'*What?*' My whole world slams into stillness. 'What did you say?'

'The three of them are in police custody.'

'Are you kidding me?' I whisper.

'He was involved with something like that, wasn't he?'

'I'm … not sure exactly. Three brothers! Did they give names?' My voice is squeaky.

'I'd just come in from outside and missed half of it.'

'How do I find out? No internet out here.'

'Go into town and pick up a paper.'

'I will. Thanks, Harry. I'll go right now.'

'Hang on, Tess.'

'What?'

'Just one more thing,' he says slowly.

'Yeah?' I'm virtually jumping up and down at this stage, desperate to get off the phone and go get that paper to check if it's Jay. 'You've got to go to the police.'

'Why is that?'

'Because the guy is a fucking maniac!'

I listen to Harry trying to convince me to make a full report to the New South Wales domestic violence unit, but his words slide off me like water off a duck's back. Every time I even think *police* I feel Jay's hands around my throat pushing my head under the water. *Drowning.* That is what the word *police* conjures up in me.

'He's already left a lot of really damaging evidence on my voicemail.' Harry is still talking.

'Damaging to him or me?' I try to make light of it.

'To him, of course!' Harry says impatiently. 'Those messages will play out very nicely when it comes to court.'

When it comes to court? God, no! Not if I have anything to do with it.

'What ... did he say?' I ask in a small voice.

Harry hesitates, then says softly, 'Just go to the police. Will you at least take down the number of the domestic violence unit?'

'Send it to me by text. I ... I haven't got a pen here.'

'Go get a pen,' he orders. 'Please, Tess. For Nellie.'

So I do. I take down the number thinking he's right. I must do it.

'Take care now.'

'You too, Harry.'

I tell the others about the arrests and they whoop with excitement. Jack immediately hops onto her bike, burns into town and comes back with a paper. My breath gives way momentarily when I see the photo.

'Him?' Salome asks, staring at the photo curiously.

I nod, feeling chilly apprehension sliding all the way down my backbone. 'Yeah, that's him.'

The Hanson brothers. Three separate mugshots. The article states that their mother has also been charged as an accessory to the crime. It's a big bust for the New South Wales cops and they're very pleased with themselves. I allow myself a few seconds of heady elation until I read that the three brothers have already been released on bail. There are strict conditions, but they're not locked up.

Not in jail. I freeze up again.

When Salome has read the article all the way through she looks at me with something like awe.

'Did you have any idea about what they were doing?'

I shake my head, feeling stupid.

'The coppers will want you as a witness.'

I don't reply, but even the idea of standing up as a witness against him fills me with terror.

Beth seems to sense this. She pulls the paper away from both of us. 'That's ages away,' she says, putting an arm around my shoulders. 'Don't even think about it! Consider this the beginning of the end!'

If only she's right!

When the weather forecast comes on the radio, Beth turns to the rest of us eagerly. 'Let's celebrate. Have the afternoon off. All this clearing-out is nearly finished anyway. It might be the last warm day before winter. We'll take a picnic down to the river where we used to swim.'

'Okay,' I say warily.

'You up for it, Jack?'

'Sure.'

I'm not sure if I should be feeling safer knowing the police have him in their sights or … *not*. I try to get inside his mind. What would he be thinking under the circumstances? But it's so hard to know. Still, I reason with myself, this has got to be good news, surely? He's in deep shit. He'll have a lot to think about apart from me and Nellie.

On the other hand ...

Soon we're in Grandpa's dusty ute, travelling slowly along the highway, looking for the turn-off to the river, which will take us to the swimming hole. The sky is as blue as a cornflower, and it's warm. Beth is driving and Salome is sitting alongside her in the front with her arm hanging out the side window, whistling loudly and making Nellie laugh. Jack and I are sitting in the back with Nellie in the car seat between us. We have rugs, a packed lunch of egg-and-lettuce sandwiches in the boot, a bottle of icy champagne wrapped in a wet tea towel, two thermoses of hot tea, and jumpers in case the weather turns. I wind down the window, let in the crisp air and take a few deep breaths.

The beginning of the end?

Finding the turn-off from the main road proves tricky. There are a number of small roads leading off the main one, but none of us can remember which is the right one.

'It's here.'

'It's got to be here.'

'No, we've come too far.'

Right at the point when everyone is getting prickly and dispirited we find it. We follow the rutted dirt track past crops of corn and paddocks of sleepy cattle, great big river gums, and grass so high that it reaches the windows of the car. A truck going the other way passes and the driver, a local farmer judging by the big brown arm sticking out the window, gives us a suspicious look as if we haven't any right to be here.

'Don't look at us like that, mate!' I growl, loud enough for the others to hear. 'This is *state* property.' Beth and Salome clap and burst into laughter.

'Mum used to get so riled up about that kind of stuff!'

'Yeah,' Salome joins in, 'she was a big one for state property!'

When we get down to the riverbank we throw the rugs under the tree and pull out the plastic water container, oranges and dry biscuits. Before the town got a swimming pool, everyone used this spot in the heat. Our mother loved bringing us here because it is where she swam as a kid with all her brothers and sisters.

There is a bit of chat at first about sunburn and what time we'll eat lunch, but after a while we all chill out and become quiet. The sun is hot. About an hour in, the clothes start coming off. Salome is first. She peels off to reveal a bright orange-and-black spotted bikini under her jeans. She flops down on her back to soak up the rays. Beth has red one-piece bathers under her dress and looks magnificent as she settles down on the rug with Nellie. Compared to them, I feel so plain and skinny and wrecked in my faded shorts and singlet. I want to cover up again when I see them noticing the bruises, fading now, but still there, running down both my arms and legs. But no one says anything, and anyway, it's too late to hide. Jack refuses to take off anything except her shoes. She rolls up her jeans and stands in the freezing river.

'Not really one for cold water,' she gasps. 'When are we having the champagne?'

Salome throws her an orange. 'None for you,' she teases, 'unless you go swimming.'

Nellie parks herself on my legs and begins to play with some sticks. 'This is my house,' she says, drawing in the dirt. 'And this is the shed.'

'Which house?'

'My house,' she says, not looking up. 'And here is Streak in the shed.'

I look up and see Salome, who is lying on her towel, gazing at her tenderly. When she sees me looking at her she seems a bit embarrassed. She gets up quickly and edges herself into the water up to her knees and then dives straight under. When she comes up again, both arms waving helplessly, she is gasping. 'Bloody freezing!'

Beth is next but only manages a few strokes before getting out.

Nellie jumps up and stands by the edge to watch them, her little toes in the squishing mud.

'I want to go in, Mamma.'

'It will be too cold, baby.'

'But I want to!' She runs over. 'Please!'

'Wait a bit.' I'm relishing the stillness and the warmth. I fiddle with her hair, kiss her, try to make her sit down with me. 'Let's wait until we get really hot.'

Beth gets up again and takes her hands, smiling at me. 'I'll take her. Come on, Nellie. Let Mamma daydream!'

I sit there in a bit of a daze watching Beth gently encouraging Nellie into the chilly water. The squeals and laughs as she slowly allows herself to be fully immersed make me smile.

'Look at me, Mamma! Look at me!'

'I am looking!' I wave at her and smile.

Eventually I decide I might need some freezing water to clear my head. Beth is due back at work next week. Salome and Jack will be heading up to Sydney around then too. I've got to decide whether to go with them. I know I can't stay on the farm because I don't drive, but part of me would like to be around until Grandpa dies. I know Beth would like me to do this too. There are flats available in town, and she has said she'd help with the rent. I used to be hurt that Jay never wanted to know anything much about my early life, but that's now playing in my favour. Although I told him about my great-grandmother being put in the asylum – information he used against me – I can't remember ever telling him a word about my grandparents, much less where they lived or even the name of the nearby town.

Soon we're all in together throwing a tennis ball around. Nellie is on Jack's shoulders, squealing like crazy. I see that they are all, Jack and Salome included, entranced by this little girl of mine and it makes me proud.

The bright, hot day turns into a peaceful afternoon. We pull out the champagne and the sandwiches. Jack brings up a pile of river stones and shows Nellie how to make a house with the stones and twigs from the overhanging trees.

'Where is Harry now?' Nellie asks.

'He's at his aunt's place. Remember I told you?'

'Are we going to see him?'

'One day. I hope so.'

'I've been having some crazy dreams since being up here.' Salome drains her glass, burps loudly, and holds it out for another. 'Seriously.' She looks from Beth to me. 'I don't know what to make of them.'

Beth gets up from where she is sitting with her feet in the water and wanders over to sit on the rug.

'Me too.' She smiles. 'You first.'

'Last night I dreamt that … *Tess* was here with us.' Salome is frowning.

Beth laughs and points at me. 'Haven't you noticed?'

I feel a shiver through me, because I know what Salome means.

'Our great-grandmother Tess,' Salome says.

'Oh.' Beth shudders and turns away as though she doesn't want to know any more.

But Salome continues anyway. 'She was up at the dam, dressed in this long shabby dress. It's so weird, because I've never thought of her since that last night with Mum, when she gave you that photo.'

'What else about the dream?' I ask.

'She was agitated … as if she had something important to tell me.' Salome shrugs and turns towards the river.

Nobody says anything for some time.

'What about you, Beth?' Jack asks. 'What about your dreams?'

But Beth has turned her back on us. 'Dreams!' she calls with forced carelessness. 'They're just the unconscious mind sorting through the day's rubbish.'

'Really?' Salome shoots back sarcastically. 'Tell that to Jung, why don't you?'

Beth shrugs. Salome, Jack and I smile at each other behind her back. Salome throws a plastic ball at Beth, making her jump.

'Come on, tell me your dreams.'

'No.'

'Why not?'

'I don't want to add fuel to the fire,' Beth says primly.

'Which fire, Beth?' Salome mocks. 'I don't see a fire. Anyone else?' She looks at Jack and me. 'Anyone see a fire?'

But Beth has had enough. She gets up and dives straight into the freezing water.

Salome laughs, lies back, and puts a T-shirt over her face. I sit up, chin resting on my knees, lazily watching Beth's pale, strong arms knife through the water like a couple of sharp blades bent on destruction. In spite of the swift current she is making her way slowly and surely to the opposite bank. Determined, that's our Beth, and a strong swimmer. I smile in admiration, remembering that I used to be a good swimmer too. I was sixteen when I first swam this river. No way I'd attempt it today.

'Does anyone know why her sister killed herself?' This question from Salome startles me, but I don't let on.

I shake my head. Beth has been pulled downstream a few metres but she's over halfway across already. I remembered the way that once you were in the water it always seemed so much further to the other side than it did from the bank and I felt again the twinge of fear I had then.

'She wasn't pregnant,' Salome adds dreamily. 'We know that much.'

'How do you know that?' I ask sharply. But Salome just sighs and shrugs. The T-shirt is still covering her face so I can't read her expression.

'Autopsy report,' Salome says eventually, her voice muffled under the cloth.

'Oh.' I grit my teeth. So they did read through some of what our mother sent before handing it over to Grandpa to destroy.

'Yeah,' Salome goes on, 'there was some story of her being let down by a soldier from the First World War.'

'Was he killed?'

'Apparently not. She thought he was dead but then when she found out he was alive she thought he'd rejected her. There was some kind of tragic misunderstanding and he turned up to her funeral distraught. *Oh Lizzie!* he kept wailing. *Oh Lizzie, why didn't you tell me?*' Salome's tone is flat and without expression but in spite of this, and the pocket of brilliant sunshine we're sitting in, a sudden chill runs right through my body.

'Tell him what?'

'That's what I don't know.'

'Salome!' I can't keep the irritation out of my voice. 'How do you know this stuff?'

'Beth told me.'

'So what else does she know?'

'Ask her!'

'I can't.'

'Why not?'

'She already thinks I'm half mad!'

Salome laughs quietly and sits up, shading her eyes with both hands. We watch Beth emerging from the water on the other side of the river. She stumbles up through the mud and the tussocks in her red bathers and then stands to wave both arms at us victoriously.

'Hey, look at me!' she yells. 'I made it!'

'What a surprise,' Salome says ironically.

But Jack gets into the spirit of Beth's victory by putting Nellie on her shoulders. They wade down into the water to wave back at Beth excitedly. Nellie turns.

'Stand up!' she orders sternly. 'Wave!'

Salome and I do as we're told. Salome edges closer to me at one point and raises her palm for me to slap.

'You write the book,' she says seriously, 'and I'll make the film.'

I laugh and turn away but the suggestion immediately ignites a weird little dream I didn't even know I had until that very moment. *How would I go about finding out what really happened? Where would I start?*

We stay later than we originally intended, and when we get back into the car there is sand in our toes, and Nellie is half asleep in Jack's arms. As we wind our way back along the track I decide it's been the best day I can remember in a long time.

'Is Daddy doing a silly right now?' Nellie asks suddenly. 'Is that why we're here?'

Jack looks over at me for an explanation, but I don't give anything away.

'Yeah, probably,' I say, light as I can make it.

'Beebe!' Nellie calls to Beth, who is driving.

'Yeah?'

'My daddy sometimes hurts my mamma,' she says matter-of-factly.

'Does he, darling?' Beth says calmly.

'He goes silly sometimes, doesn't he, Mamma?'

'Yeah,' I agree. 'He does.'

'And that's when we have to go up to Nana's,' she tells them. 'Mamma and me have to sleep in Nana's spare bed.'

'Is that right?'

'Yes,' Nellie says. 'But sometimes we forget Barry.'

'I bet Barry doesn't like that,' Beth says softly.

Nellie mutters something to herself and Beth puts down the window, letting fresh air into the car.

⸻

I hadn't realised that the drugs were getting a grip on him until his older brother, Nick, approached me at their mother's place.

'You've got to get him straight,' he told me sharply.

We were standing on the verandah, looking down into the valley. Below us, Jay was sitting with his guitar, away from everyone. It was one of those family occasions I hated. The only good thing about them was Nellie getting to play with her little cousins.

'Me?' I laughed before I thought better of it.

'You're his woman. He's too far in. Get him out.'

I said nothing and then nodded. Because that was what you did with Nick. You didn't answer back. He and Travis despised drugs. I knew Jay's days with them would be numbered if he picked up a serious habit. Was that what was happening?

He'd started having people over in the evenings more frequently. I'd be getting Nellie to bed and I'd hear the first bike or truck making its way up our track, and my heart would dive. Within an hour maybe a dozen guys would have congregated on our verandah. At first, the loud voices, the shouting and laughter were easy enough to deal with, but as the night progressed and people got off their faces things became unpredictable. After a bit of forced chit-chat I'd beg tiredness and head off to the other end of the house to where Nellie was sleeping. Jay never seemed to mind my going. I'd just lock us in the main bedroom and wait for it all to be over. I never slept well those nights, but Nellie did and that was all that mattered, really. Sometimes it would be five a.m. before the last guy left or flaked out on our floor.

Over the last few months, the parties had got bigger and rowdier. Women started coming with the guys, and the tone got more aggro and frightening. There were fights, women shrieking and screaming and being sick. Occasionally someone would knock on my bedroom door, thinking that the bedroom was the way back to where the party was, or sometimes a way out of the house. I'd wake and so would Nellie. They were always off their heads on something. One night a woman came right in and started screaming at me for no reason at all, and Nellie got very frightened.

Jay had always smoked a lot of hash, but the pills made him mean and distant. When I got past caring about his insults about my body and my family and my snotty voice and my skinny legs and my lack of decent tits, he began to look for other ways to taunt me.

It didn't take him long to work it out. Nellie was my soft spot. The place he could always get me.

I remember the first night I had to leave the house. There were about a dozen people there. The music was extra loud. Some were out on the verandah and two or three were milling around in the kitchen. Jay was off his head earlier than usual. I had Nellie on my hip and was filling a glass of water at the tap when he came over and tried to take her from me.

'Let me dance with her,' he ordered. 'Come on; let her go. She wants to dance with her daddy. Come on.'

But I wouldn't let him take her, and he found that infuriating, although he pretended that he was cool because his friends were there.

'Hey, this is *my* kid, right?' He was grinning like a madman. His pupils were dilated, and the guys who were standing around watching snorted and laughed awkwardly, their eyes sliding away from mine.

And so we had a tug-of-war over Nellie. She was screaming and he was trying to kick my legs out from under me so he could get a proper hold on her. Fortunately the drugs had taken away some of his agility and I was able to slip around him. Terrified, I stumbled barefoot up the path towards his mother's place because … there really was nowhere else to go. I banged on the door. She answered very quickly, as though she might have been expecting me to turn up.

'What is going on down there?' she snapped, but she let us in. 'I can hear that music from here!'

'Jay has some friends over,' I gasped.

'Can't you get him to turn it down?'

But she made up a bed for Nellie and me.

These kinds of nights became more frequent until it was every couple of weeks. But after that night I decided I'd never wait it out again. The crowds arrived and I'd take off, with Nellie in my arms, for his mother's joint. Mostly he forgot that I hadn't been there.

In the morning, Glenda would lecture me. *Men only play up if you let them*, she told me. I hated her so much for that. She'd seen the bruises, the black eyes and the shaking hands, and she knew he was down there blind on dope and pills, but she wanted to make sure I knew it was my fault.

twenty-three

When we get home from the river, Marly is in the kitchen chopping vegetables. He looks exactly the same, except his hair is much longer. It's tied back into a ponytail with an elastic band. There was no car outside or bike to warn us. It's as if he appeared magically.

'Where have you all been?' he complains as he hugs us one by one. 'I thought I had the wrong house or something.'

'How did you get here?'

'Mate dropped me.'

'Who?'

'You wouldn't know him.'

'We knew you wouldn't be able to stay away!'

'What's with the long hair?' Salome teases, pulling it. 'Finding our feminine side, are we?'

Marlon smiles, and when she introduces him to Jack he hugs her warmly too, just as though he's known her all his life, when in fact he's never even heard of her. This wins her over straight away. Marlon has always been like this. Whatever the situation, nothing puts him out. 'So, the cleaning finished yet?'

'More or less.'

'Good timing, eh?'

'And you're making soup!' Salome lifts the lid and laughs in delight when she sees the stock bubbling away. 'Did you bring the ingredients with you?'

'Of course!' Marly grins. 'I knew you wouldn't have them.' Chicken soup was always the one thing he could do in the kitchen.

'So how come it took you so long?'

'Thought I'd wait until the work was done.' He grins and edges backwards out the door.

When he comes back in again there is a squirming bulge under his old blue jumper. The others are still talking excitedly and I'm the first to notice.

'What are you hiding?'

'Is my niece Nellie around?' Marly calls, pretending not to see her standing right next to me. 'I brought something for her, but I guess I'd better give it to someone else, because I can't see her.'

'Here!' Nellie decides to forget her shyness and steps forward. 'Here I am!' She squirms away from me, runs over and stands right in front of him. 'I'm Nellie,' she yells, looking up at him.

'Can't see her anywhere!'

'It's me!' Nellie roars. 'Here!'

'Oh, there you are!' He pulls a squirming Jack Russell puppy out from under his jumper and puts it at her feet. The little dog looks up, its tail wagging winningly. Then it begins to lick her shoes.

'For you, Nellie,' Marly tells her.

Nellie stares blankly at the pup for about three seconds, then begins to smile. She looks at me. 'Is he mine?'

'I think so,' I say.

'Yep!' Marly grins and then looks sheepishly at me. 'I should have asked you, I suppose.'

'Yeah, you should have.' I laugh. 'But where did you get it? Didn't you come by plane?'

'Yeah.' He smiles, looking down at Nellie. 'My mate's bitch had three and he asked if I wanted one. I took a punt—' he looks at me and makes a scared face '—that it would be okay.'

Nellie is kneeling on the floor staring at the puppy, who is jumping up trying to lick her face. 'He's got spots!' she squeals. 'And his tail won't stop moving.'

'He is actually a *she*,' Marly bends down to tell Nellie. 'She's a girl, so what will we call her?'

'Flash.' Nellie doesn't hesitate. 'We've been waiting for Flash for ages, haven't we, Mamma?' Nellie says. 'For ages and … ages!'

'Yes.' I take her on my knee and gather her hair up into a bright elastic band. 'We have. For ages.'

'And now she's here.' Nellie wriggles free and lies flat out on her tummy, her face nearly in the bowl of milk Beth has brought, watching the puppy lapping away, the tail wagging wildly. The satisfaction in my little girl's voice makes me so happy I could cry. But I don't.

'The best present ever,' I tell my brother later, as we are eating his soup. And I mean it, even though I'm trying not to think how difficult it will be managing a dog if and when we are obliged to escape quickly.

He shrugs. 'No worries, Tess.'

....

The next night we decide to light the bonfire. Jack and Salome ride into town for beer and meat. When they come back, they marinate the meat in lemon and garlic and salt. Marly makes a gridiron with some wire he's found. Beth finds an old billy in the pile of rubbish, and Marly shows us how to make damper. Nellie and I get the job of making salad and wrapping the potatoes in foil to cook in the coals.

When evening approaches, Nellie is allowed to throw the first match. She takes this job very seriously. It takes a while to catch, but once that happens the whole thing is alight and glowing within a minute. After that it becomes *her* fire.

'Can I throw these bits into the middle, Nellie?'

'Hmmm!' she says. 'If you're very careful.'

'What about Beth? Will we throw her on top?'

'Nooooo!' Nellie giggles.

We pull chairs from the verandah, grab our drinks and watch the day slide away in the force and beauty of the big fire.

'So what has been happening with you, Marly?' Salome asks casually.

'Not much,' he says and we, his three sisters, laugh because it's what he always says. *Not much. No problem. No big deal. No worries. No dramas.* Even as a kid he always downplayed whatever was happening, even when those events were big and involved him. He rarely got excited or made much of them. When he won the under-fifteen state cross-country championship we heard about it through someone else at school. And when he broke his leg climbing a tree out on the farm he told no one for about four hours. Only when he couldn't stand the pain any longer did he tell Mum that he *might* have done something to his knee.

And so he tells us about his tiny community school in his calm easygoing style. About the kids who turn up and those who don't, about the number of languages spoken, and about the problems with getting in supplies when the wet season begins. Of course, we want to know everything. What is his life like up there? Are the crocodiles really that numerous and dangerous? When exactly does the wet season start? What does he do when he hits Darwin? Is he still playing guitar? What about his band? We find out that the band dissolved a couple of years ago because they could never get together to practise, but that he still plays guitar. We find out that he had a girlfriend called Lizzie for two years. Is it over? But he only grins and says he's not sure. He loves his job and he's learning the local language. He likes living alone. The Kimberley is in his blood now, he tells us, and he wants to live up there forever.

The food is cooked and we eat it, the dark night surrounding us alive with the bright sparks and glowing embers.

'This food is very good,' Marly teases, 'but not as good as Beth's stir-fry.'

Beth laughs and picks up a twig to throw at him.

Stir-fry was pretty much our staple diet after Mum left. We'd come trooping into the kitchen after school and Beth would be at the bench chopping vegetables. Looking back now I think it was the only dish she knew how to make. But it filled us, and I think we were all glad of it, and in time she taught herself others. I smile at her now through the sparks and flames of the raging fire, wanting to tell her how comforting the sight of her was during that terrible time. Marly must be thinking the same thing, because he has his arm around her shoulders. They are talking quietly and intensely together, and I wish I had the energy to get up and join them, but I'm loving sitting here on the opposite side of the fire, just watching.

'Hey, we need some music,' Jack suddenly declares. 'Badly.'

'Anyone got any music? CDs?'

'I don't think our grandparents believed in music,' Salome says drolly.

'Better not wake Flash.' Nellie is sitting on a rug on the ground, the pup curled up into a little ball next to her. 'He might be having an important dream,' she adds seriously.

I watch Marly smile and see that he loves her already. *He loves her already.*

Beth backs her car near to the fire and turns up the radio. Golden oldies hits. Buddy Holly is singing.

'I'm wondering what it was like being the only male with your parents gone,' Jack says to Marly.

'You want the two-minute version or the five-year one?' he quips.

The rest of us laugh uneasily.

'Oppressive, is my guess,' she persists, and then grins.

'Beth got us to the city within a year,' Marly begins carefully.

'Three cheers for Beth!' Salome mutters.

Marlon ignores her. 'And being the cowardly male, I aligned myself with whoever was winning the war at the time,' he adds.

'The war?'

'Beth and Salome were in combat pretty much constantly.'

'You too, Marlon, in your own sneaky way,' Salome shoots back.

'How sneaky?'

'So quiet and passive, but you always ended up getting your own way.'

'What a load of bullshit!' he protests, laughing.

Then it's on. It's as though someone has unscrewed the top of a gas bottle; it's leaking out into the air around us, hissing loudly, and dangerous too. We are all laughing, taking it in our stride, shouting, but listening to each other too. I look at Jack, so glad she's here to ask awkward questions. God knows we all need her to loosen us up.

'Marlon was a history student with zoological tendencies,' I explain, remembering all the animals that he used to bring home and try to keep alive in his room.

'Hence, Flash.' Jack smiles, looking over at Nellie, who is now at my feet asleep, the little pup in her lap.

'God, this place is … Well, it's full of ghosts!' Marlon says when there's a lull in the conversation. 'I walked into the lounge room before and I thought I saw Mum over near the china cabinet. Seriously, I almost called out to her.'

'I saw her too,' Salome pipes up. 'Yesterday, sitting on the verandah in a red dress. Least, I thought it was her. It wasn't any of you!'

'What about you, Tess?' Marlon calls across the fire.

I smile at him and say nothing.

The good thing about sitting around a fire is that you don't have to talk. You can just tune out and listen to the roar of the crackling flames and pretend you don't hear the teasing conversations around you. You don't have to pay too much attention to the busy, disjointed chat going on inside your own head, either. The unresolved disputes about where to go and what to do, the regret, the plans and the fears, slide away for a while. In front of a fire, you smile and laugh but you stay apart, and wonder at the history behind all the bits and pieces of wood and cardboard going up in flames. The remnants of old tables and beds, rotted-through fence posts and baby cots, fruit boxes, half-complete packs of playing cards and board games are being changed into some other matter now. That's what happens.

You can think of your grandparents and all their children, the days and nights lived right here in this place on the hill above the creek, with the big trees all around. And your great-grandparents … You can think of Tess coming here as a newly minted bride of nineteen, then each of her five children arriving over the next few years. You can think of her sister coming here one day and taking her life in this very house right behind us. What made her do it? Did she have any idea that it might send her sister mad with grief? You can think about Tess being taken away from here, down to a huge place with cold baths and enormous wards and brutal staff. Never to return.

I shudder. Do the dead really die?

'We're all here together; we should talk about Dad,' Marlon suddenly says quite loudly.

I jolt out of my private reverie, immediately alarmed.

'I mean the night he died,' Marlon continues blithely, 'and what happened before.'

Oh jeez. I look at him and shake my head. *Come on, Marly! I'm not ready for this.*

I look at the others. Beth is sitting up rigidly, hands in her lap, waiting to see what is coming next. Salome, who's been bent over happily tending the fire with sticks, stands up and goes over and sits down on the ground, leaning her back against Jack's legs.

'What about it exactly do you want to talk about?' she asks him.

'Tess's part in it,' he says simply.

'Not a good idea,' Beth says sharply, not looking at me. 'Better to leave it.'

'I don't think so,' Marly says mildly. 'Better to talk about it.'

I gulp, glad they can't see my face in the half-light. I can't look at any of them. I contemplate making some excuse about needing to put Nellie to bed, but it would be too pointed.

'Okay.'

Salome looks over at me.

Marlon gets up, comes around to where I'm sitting. He knows he has a certain power over the other two and he's going to use it.

'She was ten years old,' he says, 'and she had no idea what she was saying.'

'But I did,' I say, loud enough for the others to hear. 'I did know what I was saying.'

'No, you didn't!' he declares scornfully, looking around at the others. 'You were *ten*!'

Beth nods in agreement and, to my relief, so does Salome.

'I blamed it all on you for years, Tess,' she says quietly, 'but Marlon is right. You *were* just a kid.'

'What the hell are you all talking about?' Jack looks at us as though we've all gone crazy. 'I can't take this shit for one minute longer. Get a grip, the lot of you.'

We all laugh. But I'm a bit choked up too.

'Okay,' I say to Beth and Salome. 'Thanks.'

I was ten years old the day I took myself off for a walk down by the river before heading home. I knew I shouldn't. It was not considered a suitable place for a young girl to walk on her own at any time, especially in the winter at dusk. And especially further along, where the houses and lights give out and the river turns under the bridge and the trees grow more dense and the dark spaces more numerous. All kinds of strangers set up their camps under the trees out there, mainly to fish the river and enjoy the quiet; families in the school holidays, travellers, tourists, but oddbods, too, just passing through. Groups of young rowdy local men went there as well, to light fires and cook their steaks, get drunk and fight. It was a place where girls were often said to 'get into trouble'. And yet there I was, on my own, defiantly deciding not to go home after my music lesson and ... *there they were.*

Our mother and my father's boss, Gerald Wilson, were lying together under the trees on the riverbank, about a kilometre out of town. They were sitting close and laughing together and drinking from the same red plastic beaker. From my hiding place in the shadows of the trees I watched as they progressed to kissing and fondling each other. Dumbfounded and amazed, I crouched spying on them for over an hour. I can't remember much about my own feelings as I watched. But even at ten I knew this was dynamite. On the way home, I promised myself that I would never ever tell a soul about what I'd seen. Not my mother or my father.

Especially not my father.

And yet, that very night when the six of us were sitting down to eat the special curry that Mum had made earlier that day, in honour of Marlon's birthday, the fateful words came spilling out of my mouth. We'd finished the first course, I remember. Salome was packing up the plates. Beth had made the cake and she was carefully placing bright pink candles in rows along the top, making the number fourteen. Mum was looking on, her usual dreamy self, putting her hand on Dad's shoulder every now and again as she retold the story of the day Marlon was born. How they very nearly didn't get to hospital in time. They'd barged through red lights and up one-way streets to make it. There was much laughter and joking. I remember looking across the table at her flushed face, wondering if I'd imagined that scene down by the river just a few hours before.

'Those candles really are awful, Beth,' Mum said suddenly. 'He's a young man. He doesn't want pink! I'm sure I've got better ones in the pantry.'

'*Now* you tell me!' Beth protested loudly.

Mum got up, still laughing a bit. 'It's not right to subject a fourteen-year-old boy to rows of bright pink candles, darling.' She kissed the top of Beth's head. 'Let me just go have a look-see.'

'They're totally fine, Mum,' Marlon told her impatiently, rolling his eyes at Beth. 'I have to be at practice in an hour. Come on, sit down!'

But Mum was in the pantry already, standing on a stool, her legs and feet the only part of her visible. 'I have black sparklers in here somewhere,' she called. 'Hang on!'

'Okay, who's got a story?' Dad loved to have us all there at the table at the same time. Eating together every night had become a thing of the past. Even when we managed it, it was usually rushed, because someone had to be somewhere, especially my older siblings. There was netball practice, music lessons, football training, along with outings with mates and sleepovers with friends.

I looked around excitedly, hoping that one of the others would take the baton. For years the deal had been that when we ate together in the evening everyone had to tell a story about their day and then a vote was taken as to whose story was the best. Dad kept a score on the fridge and at the end of every week, whoever had won the most got a prize – an extra scoop of ice-cream, or a chocolate frog. The prize didn't matter, but the competition did. I was still young enough to love it even though I rarely won. Apart from a chance to show off and have everyone's undivided attention, it was also a chance to find out about my older siblings. Their lives seemed so exotic compared to mine. I relished whatever snippets they deigned to share. What they did, who they hung out with, what they found funny, important and worth talking about was all fascinating to me.

'Come on!' Salome said, calling to Mum, still in the pantry. 'I've got loads of homework.'

'Me too.' Beth sighed in exasperation. 'Who cares what colour they are?'

'But I've got the container!' Mum called out victoriously.

'Who wants to go first?' Dad said hopefully, trying to keep the good vibe going. Mum often upset the easy running order of things like this without seeming to realise she was doing it. It was more that she went off down her own track without seeing how irritating it was for us all. I usually didn't mind. But this night I did mind. I suddenly understood for the first time why the others got so exasperated with her. Beth had made and decorated the cake and now Mum was taking it over and that wasn't fair.

Dad nudged Marly. 'Come on, birthday boy. A quick story!'

'Sorry, Dad.' Marly sighed impatiently and looked over at Mum. 'I've got to get going.'

Clearly disappointed, Dad turned to me. 'What about you, Tessie?' he said, digging me in the ribs affectionately. 'Got one?'

'Okay,' I said, searching my head frantically for something that would catch their interest. But the others weren't even looking at me as they waited for Mum, who was still inside the pantry, huffing and puffing about the stupid candles. A flash of intense malice ripped through me.

'I went down to the river after school,' I said.

'Who with?' My father's face immediately became serious. He didn't approve, but he wasn't going to lecture me on Marlon's birthday.

'On my own,' I said.

Dad's frown grew deeper and he shook his head at me. Marlon had his elbows on the table. Beth was drinking tea, tapping impatiently with one foot. Salome was painting her right thumbnail with silver varnish. Not one of them, apart from Dad, was paying me any attention.

Even Dad was tapping his fingers on the table, waiting for Mum. I took a look behind me. She was still on the stool looking through a box.

'I saw Mum and Mr Wilson,' I said.

Dad's smile and cool raised eyebrow told me my meaning hadn't sunk in. Yet.

'They were lying down together under the trees near the bridge,' I burst out breathlessly, before I could even think. Salome looked up. Marlon stared at me. Beth put her cup down and turned around. *At last!* I had their attention. No one said a word. But they were all looking at me, waiting for me to go on. Dad's head jerked back as though he'd been shot, his face shifted sideways a little, the expression weirdly unreadable. Even so, he was still smiling when he looked over at Mum.

'What do you mean?' His voice sounded odd.

'They were kissing and ...' I grinned around at the others, who were staring at me, open-mouthed, '... he had his hand up Mum's dress!'

There was a thump behind us. Mum appeared, her face flushed and smiling. She held up a dozen sparklers. 'More the thing for a guy!' She chuckled, rumpling Marlon's hair.

He moved away sharply and stood up. His chair tipped over and clattered to the floor. He was staring at her in a kind of horror. Mum looked at him and then around at the rest of us, her expression one of pained incomprehension.

'What's the matter?' she whispered. 'Only took a minute.'

'Tess was down the river this afternoon,' my father said, staring at her.

At that moment I understood that I'd unleashed something truly terrible. And as every second passed I could feel it building into something bigger and more terrible.

Dad was putting on his jacket and picking up his car keys. His face was drained and his eyes were glazed as they stared at Mum.

'Where are you going, love?' she said softly.

'Out.'

'Oh for God's sake!' Mum exploded. 'Stay and … please!'

'Stay?' he cried out, anguish in his voice. 'Why would I do that?'

I was suddenly completely overcome with fear. I surged to my feet.

'It's not true!' I shouted. 'I made it up! Really I did. It was just a story!'

But no one was paying me any attention now. I'd lost my audience. Dad left the room. We all sat in silence and listened as the car started outside.

'I was just being stupid,' I whispered. 'Really! I didn't mean it.'

Mum sat down and buried her face in her hands as we watched. When she leant across the table to try to touch Beth's shoulder and then Marlon's hand they both pulled away. Salome sat where she was, just staring blankly at Mum. Eventually Mum got up and fetched a knife and began to cut the cake.

'Who wants some?' she asked in a shaky voice.

'It's not yours to cut!' Beth snapped coldly. '*I* made it. It's Marlon's birthday!' She got up, pushed her chair into the table and walked out of the room. Very soon after that the other two left and it was just Mum and me sitting together at the table. I wanted so much to tell her I was sorry. But every time I opened my mouth sawdust flew in and I couldn't work my tongue around it to make words.

She gave me a piece of cake and I ate the icing and left the rest. In the end I couldn't stand being there in that silent room a moment longer and so I got up too and left. At the door I turned around and she was there looking down at her cake with all the dirty dishes spread around her.

It seemed then as though things couldn't get much worse. But they did, and very quickly. That very night things got a lot worse.

The police apparently came by at about two a.m. None of us woke, but when we got up to go to school we found our mother in the kitchen, sitting on the floor. She stood up to tell us to forget about school. Dad had been driving back home at around midnight. He had failed to stop at the rail crossing and was hit by the goods train coming through. She'd already given a statement to the police and had been waiting for us to wake so we could go down to the hospital together. *The hospital? Does that mean he is alive?* But I was too scared to ask.

It was on the news all day, and of course in the local news for much longer than that. There was no alcohol in his blood and the crossing lights had been working. An unlucky accident or … *suicide*? Either way, he had apparently died instantly. I can't remember any particulars about what came next. It's all a blur.

When our mother disappeared three years later, Beth and Salome remained unperturbed about it for some weeks. Or pretended to. Marlon kept his own counsel. None of us ever knew what he really thought about anything.

'She'll be home soon,' Beth declared. 'After all, where else could she go?' We knew she hadn't run away with the principal because he was still running the grammar school.

I seemed to be the only one of us who knew that she wouldn't be home any time soon. Not that I said anything. A week went by, and then two, and then a month. When she still didn't show we called the police. A detective came by. *You waited a whole month?* His perplexed ruddy face told us how amazing he found that. 'Most people would be reporting it after a few days!' We tried to look unconcerned, but his reaction unsettled us all. Was this the outside proof that there was something wrong with us?

Within a few days the same detective came back. Mother had taken a plane to Paris two days after leaving us, and three days after that had gone on to Cairo in Egypt. *Cairo!* The French police had been cooperative, but their dealings with the Egyptian authorities had got them nowhere. Their conclusion was that she either didn't want to be found or that she had met foul play in some way. But until they had something new to go on ...

Decided that she didn't want to be found? Foul play? Both scenarios seemed too terrible to think about and yet ... they were about the only things I could think about. What had happened to my family wasn't my fault and yet ... *it was all my fault.*

Nellie and Flash are wrapped in a blanket by the time we all head indoors. After we've made a small nest on the floor for the puppy, I put her to bed.

'Will Flash be here in the morning?' Nellie asks when I kiss her goodnight.

'Definitely,' I tell her, and she smiles.

'Flash is our lucky dog,' she murmurs, her eyelids closing.

'How do you work that out?'

'Because she flashes like a star,' she says impatiently, as though I might have worked that one out myself.

She's asleep, but I stay there awhile, her hand in mine.

I come back out to the kitchen to join the others for some tea around the table. Marly flicks on the late news and we all groan. No one wants any politics or bad-news stories after such a fantastic evening.

The second news item begins with a headshot of Jay.

One of three brothers apprehended for drug offences in Byron Bay last week has absconded. Yesterday, Jay Hanson failed to meet the strict bail conditions laid down for him by the court. Police want to hear from anyone who knows his whereabouts.

My heart stills for the couple of seconds when I see his face up there on the screen, and I'm left chilled to the bone.

Everyone is quiet for a second.

'What does it mean? Absconded?'

'He's done a bunk.'

I close my eyes and try to get inside Jay's mind. Where would he go? Maybe he plans to change his identity and start again. A lot of people head west or go up to Darwin or overseas to do that. Would he be one of them? I tell myself that it's probable.

At the same time I don't believe it. Not really.

twenty-four

I hear the rasping breath before I even get into the room.

'I'm here, Grandpa.'

He is lying on his back, eyes closed, but my voice gives him a start.

'Tess?' One trembling hand reaches out.

'I've come to help you write the letter.' I take his hand.

He tries to sit up a bit, without much success. I pull a few large pillows from a nearby chair and settle them behind his head and shoulders. He has become weaker since the last time I saw him. I sit down and pull a pen and the notebook from my bag.

'Alright then.' He clears his throat a couple of times. 'Well.' But his eyes remain closed and the long rasping breaths continue. Has he gone to sleep?

'Grandpa?'

'Oh, yes. Yes,' he whispers. 'Just say … Well, just say …' But he doesn't go on. He reaches for my hand again and stays quiet for some time.

'What do you want to say?'

'Tell her I got her letter. Tell her that I want to see her.' His voice is thick and rasping.

'Okay.' I write it down and wait.

When I dare look up, I see he is staring into the distance. 'Tell her that her little Tess is alive and well and is writing this for me.' He reaches for my hand again and squeezes it. 'And tell her to come home and see her grandchild.'

I write all that down as simply as he has said it.

'Is that all?'

'Yes,' he rasps. 'That's all.'

'Love from Dad?' I suggest tentatively.

'Love from Dad.' He sighs. The hand is more feeble and the breath less stable, each one an effort. 'When are you going to bring her in?' he gasps.

'Tomorrow?' I smile. 'Wasn't sure you'd be up for a noisy three-year-old.'

'My eldest sister was named Nell,' he whispers, 'and she was noisy.' He laughs. 'She was a force of nature.'

'Mine is too,' I say, my throat thick with feeling for him.

'Beth told me,' he whispers.

'Goodbye, Grandpa.'

'Goodbye, Tess. Send the letter to the postal address she gave me.'

'Okay.' I go over and get the letter out and take down the address.

'Get it off as soon as you can,' he barks. I turn to go and that's when he begins to talk.

I walk back to his bed to listen.

'My mother didn't want to go,' he mumbles. 'We couldn't find her. Uncle Con was going to take her down by train, but she … We couldn't find her. Eventually we did. She was hiding under the house. *Don't take me away*, she was crying. *Don't send me away.* When the train came she grabbed me. *Stay with me, Frank. Don't let them take me, Frank.* I was the only boy, you see. I had four sisters and I loved my mother. I clung to her. I believed that no one would ever get me away from her. But they did. They did. They got her on that train. She was standing at the window, clawing it with her hands … Her face! I will never forget. Already she looked like someone else.'

'Did you ever see her again?'

'No.' He held out one trembling hand and I took it. 'I suppose my father didn't know what to do with her. She was grieving, you see. I don't blame him. He wasn't to know she'd die there.'

'Yes,' I whisper.

'He thought the doctors would make her better.'

'Yes.'

We sit quietly for a long time.

Eventually, I get up to leave. He stops me at the door again. 'Tell Marlon the rifle is behind the door in the shearing shed.'

'What?'

'Tell him to clean it with a bit of rag. Tell him … the oil is in a small tin can near the side door. He needs to oil it. The cartridges are there too, I think.'

'Okay.' I take a deep breath.

'Marlon is a good shot,' my grandfather goes on in his breathless rasp. 'You tell him to aim at the legs.'

'The legs?'

'Marlon is no fool,' Grandpa whispers. 'Disable the mongrel.'

....

I jerk awake to the unmistakable sound of gunshots. *One two three* sharp cracks. I don't move. It's as if someone has put those bullets straight into me. I lie like a corpse waiting for the pain to set in. When it fails to arrive, I'm left wondering if I'm dreaming. But not for long. I leap out of bed and run out, letting the door slam shut behind me. *Nellie! Where are you?*

I find her calmly eating her breakfast in the kitchen. The little dog is curled up asleep on the floor next to Barry, and Beth is clearing the table.

'Can we go to the library today?' Nellie asks bossily. 'I need some new books.'

'Okay. But afterwards we are all going to visit your great-grandfather.'

'Oh goody!' She looks at Beth. 'I'm going to see my great-grandfather!'

'What's that noise?' I ask Beth, trying to seem calm.

'Rifle practice,' Beth says, handing me a cup of tea. 'Marlon is going to take Jack spotlighting tonight in the ute.'

'Rabbits,' Nellie adds excitedly. 'They're going to shoot rabbits.'

'Oh.' I sit down and breathe out.

On her way past with the plates, Beth puts a hand on my shoulder. 'Did you think it was something else?'

I shrug and sip the scalding tea.

'Don't worry. They're down at the old yards. Well away from the house.'

'Finished, Beebe!' Nellie pushes her bowl away and hops down from her chair and comes over to me for a kiss.

'Good girl.'

'Now I'm going to take Barry to school.'

'To school?' Beth laughs in pure delight.

'And Flash too.' The pup looks up and cocks her head at the mention of her name.

'Both of them?'

'They both have to learn to read.'

'Of course they do.' Beth wipes Nellie's mouth with a wet cloth. 'And I can't think of a better teacher than you.'

I watch her trying to make the pup stay still next to the bear on the old fruit box Jack gave her. Beth is laughing softly.

'Beth ... if something happens to me ...' I begin.

She turns, frowning, folds her arms and waits for me to speak, suddenly stern as a headmistress.

'If something happens to me, will you ...?' My voice chokes and I have to look away.

'Will I what?' she frowns.

'Nellie loves you ...'

My sister's stern expression collapses. She presses her lips together as though trying to catch hold of some unruly emotion that she can't control.

'And I love her,' she says softly, looking down at her hands as though she doesn't quite know what to do with them. 'I really do.'

Those words are all I need to hear. I slump down at the table, fold my arms tightly across my chest and begin to sob. I don't hide my face, nor do I try to stop the tears. Her hands are on my shoulders now, kneading them hard.

'Nothing is going to happen to you, Tess,' she says. 'The police will find him. They always do.'

'No, they don't.'

'He'll be so busy hiding from them, he won't have time for you.'

'But if something does happen ... You'll do it?'

'I will,' she says gently. 'Of course I will.'

I turn then, grab one of her hands and look into her face. 'You'll guard her with your life?'

'Yes.' She smiles down at me.

'I'm telling you – after he kills me, he'll try to take her. She won't be safe.'

Beth smiles. 'If that happened he'd be in jail!'

I shake my head. 'I know him. He'll have it all worked out. He might go to jail for a while, but he'll have his family in place to take her. They'll make all kinds of statements about what a shit mother I was. How crazy I was. He'll make sure they get her. He'll get out eventually and ... she will be his!'

Beth holds up both hands to stop me, grabs me by both shoulders and smiles into my face. 'You're panicking. If he killed you he'd be put away for twenty years! They'd never give her over to his family, especially now they've got criminal records.'

'And what if they never find him?' I'm speaking too fast and too loudly but I can't help myself. 'He knows people everywhere, and he's a good planner. He only has to get her overseas and change his identity.'

'To get overseas you need a passport!'

'Boats? He knows people with boats. Big boats. He'll stow away on a ship!'

'Darling girl.' Beth is half-laughing now, holding me down in my chair, trying to calm me. 'The manhunt would be huge. First he absconds bail for drug charges and then murders the mother of his child! Come on, Tess.'

Even though I'm crying I start laughing too … *darling girl!* I grab her around the waist and she holds me tight. She's right, I'm panicking. It was the sound of gunshots that unnerved me. My head is full of stuff that I can't control.

She pulls my face back and looks into my eyes. 'You really think he would kill you?' she asks doubtfully.

I see then that she doesn't really believe it. She thinks I'm our mother all over again, over-dramatising everything, and a bit crazy. I pull away angrily.

'I don't care if he does kill me. *That* doesn't matter. What I *do* care about is my daughter.'

'Don't say that!' Beth cuts in abruptly.

'All I care about is Nellie,' I say again in a quieter tone. 'I don't want her growing up with them. If they're in jail, their mother will basically be in charge of my *daughter*. Beth, they are horrible people.'

'Okay.' She picks up my hand again, wanting to steady me. 'Believe me, it's just not going to happen.'

'Okay.'

'I will do everything in my power to stop them having anything to do with her.'

'Thank you.'

Everything in your power might not be enough.

I go over to the window and stare out. Rain. It smells like rain. Marly and Jack are back, filling the trailer now with the old bits and pieces on the verandah. I hear their easy laughter and snatches of conversation about their plans to go shooting rabbits that night. But I don't take much in.

When I walk out onto the verandah with the tea in my hand Marly looks over and waves. 'Nellie wants to go to the library?'

'Yeah.'

'We can drop you both off on our way to the tip. Pick you up on the way back.'

'Be good, thanks.'

twenty-five

The library is in the main street of town, built in the same red brick as the post office next door and the courthouse a few doors down. I used to sometimes wait afternoons here for my father when I was in primary school. There were never many people, and the children's books were old and uninviting, but I liked the place. The dramatic atmosphere of the nineteenth-century plasterwork, the long windows and the mustiness appealed to me.

Nellie and I walk up the front steps, through the new sliding glass doors and into the lobby. Once inside, I stand awhile to take it all in. Instead of the one poky room with a few tables, I'm facing a large, airy bright space. The whole back section has been rebuilt with enormous north-facing windows. The floor is now a combination of shining blonde wood and bright red carpet, and the front desk is an oval of curved glossy black. Two women, one smiling and middle-aged with coiffed grey hair and pearls in her ears, and the other a girl about my own age, sit behind it. Both of them are dealing quietly and efficiently with the people lining up for their attention. The look of the younger one fills me with surprise and … envy. *How amazing she looks.* Her purple lipstick and long dark hair streaked with light touches of fluorescent pink, the black nail polish and the bracelets of rose tattoos on her delicate wrists seem bizarre for a country town. I can't see the bottom half of her, but her deep crimson crushed-velvet top is so very nice. I wish I knew how to look like that.

Some school-aged kids are sprinkled among the older people sitting at the tables working on computers. Others sit in easy chairs, reading newspapers and magazines. The quiet buzz of constructive noise thrums along my jumpy nerves. I watch the young librarian with the streaked hair laugh as she runs a book through the scanner.

'I've read it.' She leans towards the middle-aged bald man in the old khaki pants with her punk rock smile. 'You'll love it. I promise.'

A fresh pang of envy jolts through me, leaving me empty and slipping down again into that dead feeling that's been with me pretty much constantly over these last few years. I'm the same age as her. I have long dark hair and smooth skin like hers. How come my life is so different to hers? *What happened to me that I've ended up like this? Who am I?*

Nellie lets go of my hand and makes a run for the children's section at the back of the room.

The tattooed girl turns to watch her race past and gives me a warm smile. 'Someone's keen!'

'Yes.' I smile back nervously.

'You okay?'

'I'm fine, thanks,' I tell her.

I walk to where Nellie is playing. There is a big green plastic tunnel, as well as building blocks and other toys. Two boys about her age are already there, roaring in and out of the tunnel, whooping and laughing. Nellie stands by, watching, too shy to join in.

Suddenly one of them comes over. 'You have to take your boots off,' he tells her solemnly, pointing to her red boots.

Nellie stares back blankly. The boy runs back to his friend and starts playing again. I sit at a nearby table, pick up a magazine and watch her quietly slip off her boots. She edges her way over to the boys. The three of them exchange names, and in a matter of seconds she's part of their game. I flip through the magazine, half-listening to their play.

Nellie runs over and climbs on my knee. 'His name is Oliver,' she tells me breathlessly, pointing at the smaller boy. 'And his name is Hamish and they're *cousins*.'

'Really?' I kiss her hair.

'What is *cousins*?'

'If Beebe had a baby, then the baby would be your cousin,' I say, deciding not to remind her of Jay's brothers' kids.

'Has she got one?'

'No.'

'Can she get one?' Nellie frowns.

'Maybe. One day.'

'Can you make her get one for me?'

'You just got Flash.'

'But I want a cousin too.'

'Well,' I smile. 'Will we go get the books now?'

'Nooooo.' She jumps down. 'I want to keep playing!'

'Okay.' I pull her back and pin her hair back with the clasp from my pocket. 'But Marly is coming by to pick us up soon.'

I get up and go in search of the spot that I used to sit in when I was a kid, delighted to find that the big ugly cupboard alongside the long narrow window has survived the makeover. It still has the battered look I remember well. I used to position myself on the floor under the window to read and daydream and stare out onto the red-brick wall of the post office next door. I quickly slip open the catch on the door to see if my name is still there, and laugh when I see what else I wrote in that same red pen.

Therese Browne actress, millionaire, rock star, bride … All in my big, loopy kid's writing.

So that was what I thought I'd be when I was nine! I close the cupboard and look out the window. The dirt path running down the side of the library is sprinkled with leaves from the branches hanging over the wall. The sky above is heavy, but I love the damp look of recent rain. I remember Dad coming down this path to pick me up one day. He didn't see me watching him as he walked slowly along kicking the leaves. When he was right alongside he looked up and saw me, and we smiled at each other through the glass.

The phone pings in my pocket. Expecting it to be Marly texting me to say they've finished at the tip, I stand up and look over at Nellie as I press the green button. She is sitting with the two cousins on the red beanbag, poring over a big book, the three of them chatting and giggling like old friends. So how am I going to pry her away?

'Tess. It's Harry. You got a minute?'

'Sure,' I tell him. He sounds in a hurry. 'But hang on, I'm in the library. I'll go outside.'

'I'm going just outside the front door,' I tell Nellie, 'to talk to Harry.'

She laughs happily and turns back to her new friends. The bigger cousin is dragging over an even bigger book, with turtles swimming on the front cover.

'Okay for me to go outside a minute?' I ask the girl at the front desk. I point to my phone. 'To take this call?'

She looks down the room at the three small bent heads and smiles. 'I'll keep an eye on her.'

I walk down the steps and flop down on one of the seats in the front of the library.

'Harry,' I say, trying to sound breezy, on top of everything. 'What are you doing? It's such a brilliant day up here.'

'You been to the police yet?'

'No.' His hard tone frightens me. 'I thought I'd wait until—'

'Don't wait for anything,' he cuts in sharply. 'If you don't call them today, then I will.'

I'm momentarily flabbergasted by his tone as much as anything, and don't know what to say.

'Why?' I gulp in a small voice. 'What's happening?'

'Really disturbing stuff left on my phone last night, Tess,' Harry says. 'You've *got* to report it to the police!'

'Oh,' I sigh. 'What is he saying now?'

'That he's coming after both of you,' Harry says. 'That he'll make you watch him … Ah shit, Tess, who knows what he'll do? He is one sick fucker!'

I nod but say nothing.

'Have you still got that number I gave you?'

'Yes, but … I thought with the police after him he'd be so taken up with his own survival that he'd leave us alone!' I burst out defensively. 'I mean …'

'Looks like you might be wrong about that.' Harry's voice is still as hard as nails.

'Okay,' I tell him, 'I'll call as soon as I get back to the farm.'

'Ring the New South Wales police first, and they should organise an appointment with the domestic violence unit in Victoria. Get them in the loop. Let me know when you've got the appointment and I'll meet you there. I'll give them access to my voicemail so they have all this … shit.'

'Okay.'

I click the red button and fight the urge to collapse, to go weak with fear and dread. That's what he's counting on. Me giving in because I'm so afraid. *Please, Jay. Don't touch her. I'll do anything.* That's what he's expecting. I've done it before. *Of course, honey! It's my fault. What was I thinking? I'm an idiot* … I try hard, but there is no compass to find my way through this. It's as if the whole world is tilting and shifting on its axis, and I'm tipping this way and that along with it, with nothing to hang onto. He's in my ear and I hardly know where I am anymore. The clamminess starts in my armpits although my skin is cold. Thoughts come and go, slipping around each other like eels in a bucket, snapping and baring their pointy white teeth. Jay was never one for idle threats. Harry is right. *I need the police. I need my brother. I need Grandpa's gun.*

I pull out my phone and punch in a message to Marly. *We're ready now.* He gets back straight away. *Be there. Ten minutes tops.*

I take a few deep breaths of sweet country air, and gradually the quietness and easy pace of this town works its magic on my frantic thoughts and I start to calm down. The few cars cruising past putter along like lazy oversized beetles. Was it always so quiet here? What would that girl inside find to do on the weekends, with her cool pink hair and tats? I sit on the edge of the wooden seat at the main entrance. People on the street seem to be walking in slow motion. In the distance I hear the roar of a motorbike. Then a lawnmower starts up nearby and sputters out. I take a few more deep breaths and let the raucous chatter of birds on the library lawn fill my head. Two wattlebirds are hanging upside down on the thin branches of a bottlebrush, looking for the last of the summer nectar. The clouds suddenly break, revealing a patch of blue, and a shaft of warm sunlight spills out.

I throw my head back and shut my eyes. The soft sunshine beats into my face so sweetly I can almost taste it. Warm red-and-gold dots dance in the darkness before my eyes. Better go inside now and get Nellie's books before Marly arrives.

There's a sudden movement beside me and then, ever so quickly, a hand covers my eyes. Taken off guard completely, I am unable to even stand up. My shoulders are held in place by two sharp elbows. My first thought is *Marlon!* He used to do this kind of thing to me when I was a kid. *Guess who?* he'd say, blinding me for a moment, cracking up with laughter when I couldn't get free. *Guess who?*

But it isn't Marlon.

The familiar smell of faintly sour breath along with the sharp earthy body odour makes me reel. A prickly cheek presses in hard against my face and I'm hauled up from the seat in a headlock. I struggle, of course, but it gets me nowhere. He drags me across the library entrance, holding my hair tightly with the one hand, almost carrying me. My feet scrabble about trying to kick him, trying to find some leverage on the ground, but I'm like a puppet dancing in mid-air, gasping, trying to yell out, my hands clawing at the arm around my neck.

His grip is as hard and purposeful as a heavy chain.

He pulls me up towards the side of the building and relaxes his hold. I open my mouth to scream and he punches me hard in the side of my head with his right fist, which has the ring on the index finger. My eyes bounce in their sockets and I literally see stars and smell blood. That one punch has punctured my skin. One hard hand grips my throat and he winds my hair around the other fist in an even tighter grip. In this way, we head together further up the side lane. He has yet to utter a word.

About halfway up the side of the building he stops and pushes me hard against the red brick wall, then shoves one knee straight into my groin, making me collapse with pain. The hand holding my hair pulls my head right back as far as it will go. The only part of me that can move is my eyes, and they are on his face. It looms above mine with a grimacing smile, and I smell the hot thick rage of him. The sex. His hand goes down to his belt. *Is he really going to rape me here … in broad daylight?* He releases my hair and then the knee from my groin and pushes himself up hard against me. He puts both hands around my neck and begins to squeeze.

To someone looking on from the street we might be a couple of lovers having a passionate kissing session. I claw at his hands, trying to scratch him, but my nails aren't long. Tighter and tighter until … the air stops altogether and I panic because I can't breathe … *I'm going to die!*

But he's an expert at this. Just as I'm about to black out he releases his hold a bit, allowing me to draw breath.

After the third time I go limp. It's not as though I decide to. It just happens. I feel myself give way and start falling through space. I exist essentially somewhere else where he can't reach me. My mind floats loose as a balloon.

He pulls away a bit. 'Where is she?' he asks in his harsh whisper.

'I … don't—'

He thumps the back of my head hard against the bricks.

'Where is she?' he asks again.

'Please … don't do this.'

He bangs harder. 'Now, where is she?'

'I can't … tell you …'

'Does the guy have her? Or …'

I shake my head and he punches me hard in the stomach. I am gasping and crying now. Snot and blood are pouring from my nose, and blood from my forehead is trickling down into my left eye. When I try to turn my head away he hits it against the wall again and something breaks. Is it my skull, my jaw, or a tooth? But by this stage I'm not feeling a thing. I've moved away from pain. Some part of me is free and I stay intent on that fact. I know that the longer I can stay out here not talking, the better chance she'll have.

'Tell me where she is,' he pants. I think my refusal to talk is surprising him.

'She in there?' He jerks his thumb towards the library.

Maybe the question makes me still, or maybe my eyes give something away, because he releases me a little, keeping one hand on my neck.

'Okay. So here's what's going to happen,' he pants into my face, his eyes wild. 'We're going to go in there together to get her. Nicely, you understand?' He pulls a tissue from his jeans and rubs it roughly over my forehead. 'Quietly. Anyone asks, say you had a fall! The bike is around the back.' He loosens his grip further and waits for me to nod, tell him that I'll play along with what he has in mind. 'And then we go home.'

I pull back and shake my head. 'No.'

The longer I can hold out, the more chance we have. Jack and Marlon will be back soon. One of them will go into the library to look for us. Jay jerks my head around and I stumble and fall into a heap on the stones.

'Leave her alone,' I whisper.

'Leave her alone, you say?' He kicks me viciously in the stomach. 'Leave her alone! Is that what you want? You mad little bitch!'

I murmur something, trying to protect myself from the next kick by curling up into a tight ball.

'I'll make you watch me kill her first!'

My knees are under my chin and I'm trying to hold my broken face with both hands so he can't get it again.

He bends down nearer to me and pulls my hands away. 'You hear that?' He is panting like crazy. 'I'll kill her in front of you.'

'But ... she is your daughter,' I manage to gasp.

'You should have thought of that.' He drags me to my feet again by my hair and then along a few paces, but then seems to change his mind. Maybe I'm more trouble than I'm worth, because he throws me down hard against the wall again and strides off towards the library entrance.

Just before I pass out properly I look straight to the window. And the last thing I see is Nellie's terrified face peering out.

My heart gives way. Both tiny hands are on the glass, raised above her head as though protesting against what is going on. I manage to lift an arm in a weird parody of a wave. And I smile. Or try to, because I want to comfort her. My last thoughts come like lightning strikes, sharp jabs, needles inside the big frothy bubbles.

It's over now. Finished. I'm gone. He won.

twenty-six

'Are you okay?' a young girl's voice asks.

'Of course she's not okay! Fuck! Look at her. Go and get someone.'

'Who is she? Does anyone know who she is?'

'No.'

There is the sound of running footsteps and then nothing. I'm lying somewhere hard. Something is sticking into my back. I try to shift my body into a more comfortable position, but it only digs in deeper. A hand tentatively touches my shoulder.

'Don't worry. We'll get help.'

I don't know how long it takes me to remember where I am and what has happened, but gradually it comes back. I try again to sit up and can't. There are new voices around me – a male and two females – then the clattering of women's shoes on the stones. I manage to open one eye, but my vision is hazy. For some reason I don't immediately understand I can't open the other one. It seems to be stuck closed.

The older woman from the library, the one with the pearls and the nice expression, is kneeling down next to me.

'Oh my goodness.' She bends over my face. 'Oh, you poor girl. Try not to move. We've called the ambulance.'

The librarian's face is bouncing around in front of me. I prop myself up tentatively, my back against the wall. There is a lot of blood in my mouth and my head is spinning wildly; any faster and it's going to explode. I try to swallow the blood, but there is too much, so I spit out to the side and a tooth comes out with all the blood. There is a gasp above me, but I can't look up to see who has made it.

The librarian takes a hanky from her sleeve and wipes my mouth.

'Nellie,' I manage to gasp. 'My little girl?'

My right eye opens wider and I see there are about five or six people surrounding me now. Two of them are girls in school uniform. I have a sudden impulse to tell them that I used to wear that same uniform, but I don't have the energy.

'Who, sweetheart?' the librarian asks, taking my hand.

'My little girl,' I whisper, trying to sit up straighter. But the pain in my head is making me giddy, and waves of nausea have me on the verge of vomiting.

'A little girl,' someone whispers. 'Did anyone see … a little girl?'

There is a lot of conferring about this, and I can't seem to make out what they're saying. I feel myself blacking out again.

'Please, please find her!'

'The person who did this to you,' the librarian says. 'What did he look like?'

'Tall,' I mutter dully through my swollen mouth. 'Dark hair and a ponytail.'

'I saw him come into the library and …' someone says. They go on whispering above me.

I try to keep my eye open. I want to lift my head to see who is talking, but I can't seem to do it.

'I saw him too,' a voice says. 'He went straight past the desk and down to the children's section.'

'Was your child in the library?' the librarian bends to ask me.

'Yes,' I moan dully. 'Nellie. Three years old.'

'Black hair. Red boots?'

I can hear the ambulance siren whining in the distance and I stumble up onto my knees, even though the people around me are trying to make me stay down. I don't want to go in any ambulance! My little girl is out there somewhere and I have to find her, but ... how? I try to get to my feet and topple sideways against the wall.

The young librarian with the wrist tats comes running out. Everyone turns to her.

'My little girl?' I implore her. 'Do you know ...?'

'She's not in there!' She is mortified. 'The little girl isn't there! She asked me to keep an eye ...'

'Shhh ... not your fault,' someone says. 'We're waiting for the ambulance.'

'I don't want an ambulance!' I clutch her hand fiercely. 'I need someone to find her! Where are the police?'

'They'll be here soon. Got to get you checked over first.'

'No!'

I'm not sure what happens after that, because I black out.

When I wake again I'm still lying in the laneway and Marlon is with me. Someone has put a cushion under my head and something soft under me too. The sharp stones are no longer poking into my back, and there is a red blanket covering me.

I don't know how long I've been lying there. There are more people around us and they're all conferring in muted voices.

'What's going on?' I ask the older woman from the library.

She bends down. 'Still waiting, love. There has been an accident out on the highway. The ambulance is out there and so are the local police. So we're just waiting. Won't be long now.'

'So I'm not top priority!' I joke but no one laughs. The whole left side of my face feels ... so numb and swollen. When

I tentatively touch my cheek it's as hard as a piece of wood. The blood in my mouth tastes terrible, as though I've been sucking on a stick of iron. 'What kind of accident?'

'Terrible,' someone above me says.

'Head on,' someone else says.

'Two cars,' a male voice suddenly says to the whole group. 'And a motorbike.'

'A motorbike?' I repeat.

'Yes.'

That takes a moment to sink in, but when it does my mind begins to whirl. *A motorbike? No.* And yet *yes.* Some gut instinct tells me. The panic is racing through me now. *Accident. Motorbike … Nellie.*

But no one can tell me anything except that it was serious and that both local ambulances are at the scene. Another has been called from the next town.

'It's Jay,' I tell Marlon quietly. 'And he's got Nellie with him.'

No one wants me to do what I insist on doing next. Not Marlon or any of the people milling around. The doctor has rung to say he's only five minutes away and that the ambulance isn't too far either. Marlon is torn. I can see it in his face.

'Where is Jack?' I ask.

'She's gone looking for them.'

I stumble to my feet, feeling dizzy, my head spinning. Marlon puts an arm around me and all but carries me down to the main street amid a lot of tut-tutting from the well-meaning crowd of locals.

'It's her daughter,' he keeps trying to explain. 'She has to find her little girl.'

We reach the street and right on cue Grandpa's ute roars into view.

'Couldn't get far,' Jack tells us. 'Bad accident on the highway.'

Marlon manages to get me into the ute and Jack comes around to the other side of me. Someone hands a bottle of water in through the side window. My face is numb, but I'm awake. I guess I'm running on adrenaline.

'Not sure about this, Tess,' Marlon mutters before starting the engine. 'Not sure we should be doing this.'

I don't say anything.

....

The police barriers are set up on the highway at the edge of town. Fluorescent tape is draped across the road and a couple of young officers are holding up blue flashing lights. We pull up behind a few cars. One by one they are redirected.

When it's our turn the young cop leans down to the driver's side to speak to Marlon. 'Turn back, please. There has been a serious accident,' he says curtly. 'The road is closed and traffic diverted.'

'Who?' I ask stupidly.

'There has been a serious accident,' he tells us again, ignoring the question.

'Involving a motorbike?' Marly asks quietly.

The policeman nods shortly. 'Turn back immediately, take the first road off to the right.'

'We think it's her … er, husband on the bike,' Marlon says, jerking his thumb at me.

'No names yet,' the man snaps sourly.

'With a child,' Marlon persists.

The policeman peers into the cabin to take a look at me. 'Your … husband?'

'And child,' I manage to whisper.

'How do you know that?'

'I just do.'

'Hang on.' The young cop moves away to talk into the walkie-talkie pinned to his chest for a couple of minutes. Then he pokes his head into the car. 'You think you can identify the bike rider?'

'Yes,' I say.

'Okay.' He waves us through.

We drive about a hundred metres over the next rise and then stop, the three of us struck mute by what confronts us. We peer through the windscreen.

This terrible scene seems out of a movie. It's so very unreal. The road is a mass of mangled metal, flashing lights and glass, and great puddles of shimmering oil. One vehicle, a small overturned truck, has its top completely smashed in, the road around littered with broken boxes of vegetables and fruit. The other vehicle is an old blue station-wagon, the front end almost severed from the back. Two ambulances sit by the side of the road, lights flashing, in the soft, steady rain.

The terrible dread filling my chest spills over. I feel it flowing through my body and then out the pores of my skin. When I feel myself beginning to lose consciousness Marlon pulls me in close and pours water in my mouth.

'Can't see a bike,' Jack says, peering forward. 'We get out?'

But when I get out of the car, my brain feels as if it's sloshing around in muddy water. I can hardly walk. Marlon and Jack get on either side of me to keep me upright. We edge forward slowly towards the crash site.

Please let her be alive.

Not dead.

Not my sparky little girl … She's only three … Not dead.

I couldn't bear it …

An older male cop accosts Marlon aggressively as we draw nearer to the scene on foot. 'What the hell do you think you're doing here?'

I don't hear them explain, because I can see the bike remnants now, just a mass of twisted metal between two wheels, one of which is twisted almost in two. The split steel panniers have released machinery, paper, plastic folders and broken chains. The indicator lights flick on and off dementedly. The numberplate is buckled up but I can read the first three letters.

I stare at it in disbelief as a flash of memory slides its way into my head. Me, in jeans with my arms bare, careering off into the night *on this very bike* down to the beach. Happy. *In love.* I'm standing between the other two, but my feet are not even touching the ground. I'm weightless.

'It's his bike,' I tell another cop who has come over to us.

He heads over to the older guy. They come back to us together. 'So you know the person who was on the bike?'

I nod.

'And your child was also on the motorbike?' the senior cop asks coldly, as though he doesn't believe it for a second.

I nod but can't speak. Marlon's arm tightens around my shoulders and I almost collapse again.

'Is there any sign,' Marlon's mouth is so tight it barely opens, 'of a three-year-old girl?'

The younger man shares a worried look with his colleague. They head over to another guy and confer quietly while three of us are left to stand there waiting in the rain. A thunderbolt of rage courses through my veins. *How can they just be standing around talking when … How can it be that …* In spite of my injuries I feel as if I could take them both on and win.

Only the senior cop comes back. 'So this guy on the bike definitely had a little girl with him?'

'She is missing,' Marlon says. 'We think he snatched her.'

'You *sure?*'

'Yes,' I say angrily, glad to have found my voice. 'He came and took her!'

He looks at me impassively, as though daring me to say another word.

'You haven't found … her?' Marlon grips my shoulder.

'I'm sorry, but *if* a little girl was with him …' He turns to stare at what is left of the bike. 'With no seatbelt and no helmet, she would have been thrown … some distance.' He shakes his head. 'I'll get a search going in the wider area.'

Just as I'm about to faint, my brother leans in hard to prop me up and Jack does the same on the other side. But we all heard the meaning under the words. *A child of three on this bike wouldn't stand a chance.*

In front of us two people are being lifted into one of the ambulances. I can't see if they're alive or dead but I'm near enough to see patches of blood seeping through the sheet over one of them. Another crew of three is working methodically over a stretcher near the second ambulance.

'The bike rider is over there.' The younger policeman points to the stretcher and pulls out his notebook. 'Can you tell me his name and …'

But I brush off the questions. I seem to have found some new energy, because I've extricated myself from Jack and Marlon and I'm walking by myself now, over towards the stretcher, my feet not even touching the ground.

Jay is lying on his back, eyes closed, his whole body encased in some kind of grey plastic cocoon to keep him still. A thick white collar surrounds his neck.

'Let me through,' I whisper. 'Please.'

'Who the hell is she?' someone mutters, irritated. One of the paramedics finishes securing the wide elastic straps about Jay's body, straightens up and frowns at me.

'Wife,' someone else says quietly.

'Oh.' All three of them pull aside to let me get closer. 'He can't hear you, love,' a young blue-uniformed woman tells me kindly. 'He's unconscious.' But I'm right up close now.

'Where is she?' I scream into his ear. 'Where is she, you bastard!'

The shocked paramedics move in quickly to push me away, but I hang on to the stretcher with both hands. 'He took my little girl!' I scream at them. 'My child!'

It takes two of them to pull me away and by then some cops have come over.

'Listen, you're going to have to calm down.' A plump young cop has one firm arm around my middle as she leads me over to a plastic chair by the side of the police car. Once I'm sitting she takes a hard look at my swollen face.

'Stay here, okay?' she says, quite kindly. 'Someone needs to have a look at you.'

'I want to see him dead first!'

'Okay. Now listen, try to stay calm. You're in shock.'

Who cares if she's right? My whole body is shaking. I point at Jay.

'Don't … let them … save him.' My teeth are chattering uncontrollably. 'I want him dead.'

But the woman is already hurrying back to the stretcher and I don't think she even hears me. It's still raining, just softly. I look around, not sure where Marlon and Jack have got to.

I watch as the paramedics slowly and carefully slide Jay into the back of the ambulance. And I watch one of them jump into the driver's seat. They all turn at one point to look at me. *The nutcase.* I wonder if I'm dreaming. How long ago was it that this man was bashing my head into that wall?

I stare around me. I can see Marlon and Jack in the distance now, roaming the periphery of the crash site. I think of her beautiful, soft body. Those plump little fingers running through my hair. *No seatbelt. No helmet either. Thrown* … My tears mix in with the blood and the snot and the rain and I don't bother to even wipe any of it away. Marlon disappears down the embankment. I know at this point that I will never survive this. Never. *I don't want to survive it.*

The ambulance drives away with Jay in it.

'Where are they taking him?' I ask the woman who comes over with a plastic cup of tea.

'Melbourne. Suspected spinal fracture. Now, I need his name and your connection to him,' she asks, getting out her pad.

I do the best I can. She calls over the senior man when I tell her about Jay being wanted by the New South Wales police. They pull up plastic chairs beside me and make phone calls and ask more questions and meanwhile I'm barely even hearing them. Certainly not taking in anything they're saying. If I answer them, it is by rote. I have no idea what *I'm* saying. The words when they do come just spew out in a garbled rush and I'm not sure if, apart from Jay's name, I've told them anything they want to know. Even so, it's not long before I've had enough. I totter to my feet. *What do I care about drug busts and bail infringements?* But I only manage a few steps before I stumble and have to be helped back into the chair again.

'Tess!'

I look up. Someone has called my name, but I can't see who it is. Then the plump female police officer is hurrying towards me. She reminds me of a teacher we had, always bustling around, with a kind word for everyone. Marlon appears over the top of the embankment and she waves him to us. I watch as they confer. He is throwing his arms around and shouting something. Now they are both running towards me.

'Tess!' the police officer yells again. She is close now and I see that she's excited.

I stand up and she stops abruptly about a metre in front of me.

'What?'

'Found!'

'What?'

'Alive!' She grabs me by both shoulders and laughs in my face. 'Your little girl is safe.'

I wonder if I'm dreaming, and look over at Marlon. But he is doubled over as though he's going to be sick, and then he slumps to his knees.

'Where?' I'm choking now, not daring to believe. *Am I still hallucinating?*

'Back in town.' The woman is still holding me by the shoulders. A couple of the other cops come over to hear the news.

'Back in town?' I whisper.

'But she won't come out until you're there.'

'Out?'

'She's in a cupboard!'

I stare at her, and the feeling that I'm dreaming becomes even stronger. Nothing is clear. Even my brother is blurry and indistinct. Standing upright again now, he doesn't even look like Marlon. His hair is sticking up everywhere; the knees of his pants, his sleeves and both palms are caked in mud. He shouts out to Jack the only word that matters. *'Alive!'* She hurries towards us.

'What cupboard?' I ask the woman.

'Back there in the library. Hiding in a cupboard, she was. All that time! You'd better get back.' She laughs suddenly. 'She's all upset because she peed her pants.'

'Oh.' I try to smile, but my face feels like broken concrete. That cupboard. I know it well. *Actress, millionaire, rock star, bride.* The rain has started again and the cop is busy zipping up her waterproof jacket. I feel a sense of reality click back into place.

'Thank you,' I whisper.

She turns to Marlon. 'Get this one to a doctor quick smart.'

'Yes!' Marlon is pulling me away.

Every bone in my body feels as if it's broken, but I don't care.

Jack is already in the ute waiting for us. She doesn't say a word, but has the biggest smile I've ever seen. Once we're in and the doors are shut she puts both hands over her face and lets out a wild sob of relief.

'Let's go, Jack,' Marlon mumbles.

'Yep.' She gulps and starts the engine.

'The librarian found her. Apparently she got into an old cupboard just before he came into the library and closed the door on herself,' Marlon says.

'But she won't come out?'

'Not until you come!'

a year later

Nellie recognises him first.

I'm holding her hand tightly, scared I'll lose her in the chaos as I try to read the international departures board at Melbourne Airport. Ah! There it is. *Qantas flight 009 to London. Gate 4.* Pulling the handle of my case in one hand and Nellie with the other, I join the long check-in queue. We're not taking too much, just one suitcase full of warm clothes, and a small cabin bag. Nellie's new pink backpack is secured to her back. She sticks close to me, eyes like saucers as she takes in all the people swarming around us. There are Indian women in saris and Muslim women in hijabs, African men in long cotton robes, orthodox Jews in big black hats, and people dressed for the flight in what look to be loose nightclothes. Thankfully, the queue moves quickly, and when it's my turn I lift Nellie up onto the counter so I don't lose her in the crush as I go through the business of checking in. Once that's done we walk out into the lobby again. I look at my watch. We have three hours to fill before the plane leaves.

'Would you like a drink?' I ask.

But she's looking past me to where an escalator is coming up from Arrivals.

'Harry!' she yells excitedly. 'Harry!'

A group of maybe half-a-dozen tousled guys, laughing and talking loudly, are heading down the escalator towards us. Some are carrying musical instrument cases. Nellie shouts his name again and this time Harry sees her.

'Hey!' he yells. He shoves a guitar case into the hands of one of the other guys, and as soon as he's off the escalator he drops to his knees and holds out both arms. 'Nellie!'

Without a moment's hesitation she is running towards him squealing. I laugh as I watch him catch her, then stand to spin her around.

It's been over a year since we've seen him.

'You at school yet?'

'Kinder,' she tells him shyly. 'But not Miss Peters' class.'

'Why not?'

' 'Cause I'm in Miss Nancy's class!'

'She good?'

'Yes.'

He puts her down and walks over to me.

'They wouldn't be able to teach her much, would they?'

We hug awkwardly, then step back to take a look at each other. He is thinner, a bit gaunt, his hair much longer. But the limp is there, and so is the smile.

'Looking good, Tess.'

'Thanks.' I feel myself blush. 'You too.'

Harry turns to wave on the other guys. 'See you outside,' he calls. 'Won't be long.'

They amble off towards the big glass doors.

'So where are you off to?' he asks, steering Nellie and me out of the flow of people over to the windows.

'The UK,' I say shyly. 'And you?'

'We've just come back from there.' He laughs. 'We played a few festivals.'

'We?'

'I'm in a band now.' He shrugs sheepishly, and waves at his disappearing friends. 'Having a lot of fun.'

'Oh. That's … good!' My voice catches in my throat and I have to look away, because it's all flooding back. Being in the car with him. Playing the music. Waking up from the bad dream, talking and not talking. Sniping at each other. Laughing and crying. He got me to the farm … back to my family. I want to thank him all over again and ask the name of the band and what kind of music they play, whether he and Jules worked out or … not? So much I want to know. But the lump in my throat is still there and I don't want to embarrass myself.

'It's so good to see you, Tess,' he tells me quietly.

I look at him then and see that he's remembering too. We smile at each other and together we turn to where Nellie is drawing something on the window with her finger.

'So where are you living now?' he wants to know.

'Sydney. With Salome and Jack in Newtown. But we've been staying down here with Beth for a few days.'

'Salome and Jack!' He grins. 'God! How are they?'

'Good!' I tell him. 'They have a big house with a semi-separate apartment upstairs. Works out well. Next year, when Nellie goes to school, I'm going to study.'

'That's great, Tess,' he says, and then adds softly, 'I've thought of you often. Rang a few times too, but …'

'Sorry. I lost that phone you gave me,' I tell him. 'I didn't get another one.' If we had more time I might explain that I've developed a sort of paranoia about phones. I'll hear a phone ring and fear rips through me. I might also tell him that my feelings towards him ran deep, that I've thought about him a lot over the past year. Instead, I take his damaged hand in my own and take a close look at the fingers, pushing them this way and that.

'I'm playing music, thanks to you,' he laughs, as though he can read my mind. 'The reviews we got in England were good. It was you who gave me the—'

'And I'm walking free because of you,' I shoot straight back.

Harry smiles, and then his face clouds over. 'What about …
him?' he asks grimly.

'The trial starts next month.'

'You have to give evidence?'

'Yeah.'

I would like to tell him how terrified I am about all that too,
but I don't. The last time Harry and I saw each other was when
we went to make my report to the police, soon after the accident.
None of that stuff is his concern anymore.

'So how long you going to be away in the UK?'

'Three weeks. We'll be back in Sydney in three weeks.'

He pulls a wallet out of the back pocket of his jeans and
hands me a red card. I take the card and he grins at me. 'Hey, let's
catch up.'

'Okay.'

He suddenly throws his head back and groans loudly. 'Shit
no! We'll be overseas again when you get back.'

'Where are you going next?'

'We've got a west coast US tour organised.'

'That's exciting, Harry.'

'Yeah.' He looks at his watch and grimaces. 'I've got to go
now, but … what if you lose that card?'

'I won't lose it.'

'I'll take down your details anyway.' He pulls a small black
book out of his jacket pocket, picks the tiny pen out of its spine
and writes down my address. We hug again quickly. Then he picks
up Nellie for a final spin and we promise again to meet when all
the travelling is over.

One last wave and he turns his back and walks over to the
glass doors where his mates are waiting.

For the next couple of hours, Nellie and I wander around
looking at stuff, all the fancy clothes and cosmetics, the magazines

and books and toys. We buy drinks that we don't really need just to fill in the time. By the time our flight is called Nellie is totally over it. It's past her bedtime and she's tired and grumpy. I'm hoping like crazy that she'll fall asleep because her whining is not making me feel any easier. Beth is probably right. Why would I drag my daughter halfway around the world to visit the woman who left us all behind?

When Grandpa died, our mother wrote a brief note addressed to all of us, mainly to tell us that we received Grandpa's inheritance with her blessing. She was glad we were getting it, and she didn't want a cent. At the end of the letter she invited all of us, or any of us who *felt so inclined* to come and visit her village in Scotland.

> *Be warned: it's very remote, the weather is fierce, the seas dangerous, there are only a couple of dozen houses in the whole village and there's nothing to do. But you're welcome to come anyway!*

Beth had sniffed angrily. 'After nine years we're *welcome to come!*' She'd let the letter drift to the floor and slammed out of the room.

I am the only one who decided to take up the invitation. Even Marlon thought I might be asking for trouble. Salome was still at me to change my mind even two days ago. *For what it's worth, I think you're making a big mistake, Tess.*

Thankfully, Nellie's mood picks up when we're strapped in our seats. She has a window seat and is very excited. Her excitement intensifies when the flight attendant brings her a special kids' pack full of puzzles and colouring-in sheets, packets of pencils and small plastic toys.

'Why has that man got hair growing in his ears?' she whispers loudly, pointing. 'Can he hear?'

I rather hope not.

'How big is the plane engine? What do we get to eat? Will your mum like me?' she asks breathlessly as she pulls out a green pencil.

'Yes, of course she will.' I push her hair back from her face.

'But will I be scared of her?'

I'm not quite sure what to say to that. Luckily the plane is gearing up for take-off. When the engines begin to roar, Nellie's face stiffens with fright and she grabs my hand.

'Why has it got so loud?'

'Because it needs those big engines to take us up into the sky.'

There are three hundred and fifty people on board this flight, I hear one of the attendants tell a man near us. When it begins its fast scream down the runway I think of all those lives, as precious and complex as mine and Nellie's, all of us packed so tightly within this big steel machine and I feel a bit terrified too. Nellie hides her face in my side.

'I want to get off,' she moans.

'It's okay, baby,' I try to soothe her.

'It's going too fast.'

'We'll be up in the air soon,' I tell her. 'And everything is going to be okay.' I think of Harry's red card tucked into my purse and somehow its presence calms my nerves.

As soon as the plane has levelled out in the sky Nellie comes out from behind her hands, and within about a minute she's cheerful again. When the meal comes and she finds chicken nuggets and chips under the silver-foiled dishes on her tray, her joy knows no bounds. 'How did they know this was my favourite?' she asks, slurping down the orange juice and reverently dipping her nugget into a plastic container of tomato sauce. 'Maybe Jack told them,' she adds happily.

When her tray has been collected and the flight attendant has brought her an ice-cream she turns to me excitedly. 'Is eating up in the sky magic?'

'Yes, it is.' I kiss her head.

'We're not scared of anything now, are we, Mamma?'

'No,' I whisper in her ear, wishing it were true. 'We're not scared of anything.'

He is still here, of course, in my head and my dreams. But I live with it. I wake up occasionally, breathless with fear that he's found us, that she is gone and I'm under his spell again. The two broken legs and the spinal injuries from that bike accident were never enough to quell it. He might be in remand and his prospects dim, but he breathes and so … I fear.

At last Nellie's off to sleep, curled up like a beautiful little kitten. Most of her curly dark hair has escaped its clasp and cascades around her face like soft lace. I keep one hand on her as I stare out into the pitch-dark night outside. When I lean across her I can see the occasional star. After a while I sit back and close my own eyes for a few minutes, hoping to nod off too. No such luck.

Yesterday was my great-grandparents' wedding anniversary.

I still see Tess sometimes. Just glimpses. It usually happens in the late afternoon or early evening. I might be walking through the park on the way home from somewhere, when the dark is settling in around the trees and the house like the folds of a skirt. I walk outside into the back garden. It's the time of the day when even dogs know anything can happen. They shift about, smelling the danger in the fading light, barking every now and again, howling and whining. *Waiting* …

I see her and yet ... I don't.

A slightly built woman appears at the edge of my vision, dressed in a long, ill-fitting dress of indeterminate colour, faded blue, grey or fawn, material that might have started off cream or white but has been washed too many times in the big industrial machines. There were only two sizes in the asylum, small and large. I've learnt not to turn sharply or look too hard. I don't want to frighten her. Her feet are bare. Cold. Mostly she is calm, but sometimes she seems agitated and opens her mouth to cry out. At such times I stop what I'm doing and wait, holding my breath for the sound that never comes, waiting for all the terrible things to gather themselves together into one shriek, or a cry of protest perhaps, or a low, keening lament for a life gone too soon. I almost hear it and yet I don't.

Come back! I hear it in the breeze, in the creak and bend of a branch stretching beyond itself in the surrounding darkness. *Come back, my sister ... children ... life!*

She is refusing to simply fade away into the long-distant past. She won't stay dead. Or she can't. And at such times I can barely breathe, I feel her distress so keenly, and yet ... what can I do? There's nothing to do except tell her story, and I'm so ill-equipped to do it. I don't have Beth's quick sharp brain, or Salome's nose for a story, or Marlon's calm reflective nature, or my mother's force of personality, or my father's philosophical bent that would give gravity and depth to the subject matter. They are, all of them, so much more able than me. And yet it is to me she turns ...

I saw things and heard things that I couldn't have possibly seen or heard. But even during the worst times some part of me knew to hang on. That if I was brave and lucky enough, I might just make it to a new life.

I reach up to the luggage hold and pull out my bag. I unzip it and feel inside for the slim silver laptop Salome gave me last

Christmas. *Top of the range*, she told me proudly. At first I was almost too scared to open it, because in all those years with Jay I'd never so much as sent an email, and I'd forgotten everything I'd ever known about computers. Salome sat me down, showed me how things had changed. One day, a whole new world had opened up.

Around me, people are settling down with their airline cushions and eye shields to sleep. The lights are dimmed and the cabin becomes dark. The flight attendant hovers about collecting rubbish and getting drinks of water. We're making good time, the pilot tells us. All being well, we'll be touching down in Singapore in seven hours for the three-hour stopover. The older woman across the aisle is already asleep.

I pull down my tray table and open the laptop. The translucent blue screen glows back at me like a friendly ghost.

I click to the page where I left off two days ago, and feel all my uneasiness about what I'm doing fade away.

Being here with my daughter, travelling to the other side of the world, is the best way to begin.

acknowledgements

This book was written with the generous assistance of the Australia Council for the Arts.

I would also like to thank my publishers Erica Wagner and Susannah Chambers at Allen & Unwin, who were at all times supportive and enthusiastic. And many thanks to Sophie Splatt who took over the meticulous work of editing the manuscript at a later crucial stage.

My warm thanks to three writer friends: Kirsty Murray who has at all times been so encouraging about my work; and Jacqui Ross and Kate Ryan, with whom I shared a work space at the Abbotsford Convent last year, both so enthusiastic and generous with their time during the writing of this novel. And to my two sisters, Michaela and Patrice: thank you for your interest, kindness and support for the project.

I never knew my paternal grandmother, Lillian Josephine McCarthy, but her life and her sad, untimely death at the Kew Asylum in 1924 was the initial inspiration for this work. I dedicate the book to her and to all women, past and present, who have been deemed 'mad' when they were only reacting to their lives: to intolerable grief and distress and, too often, mental and physical abuse.

Life is better now. In so many ways!

Also by Maureen McCarthy

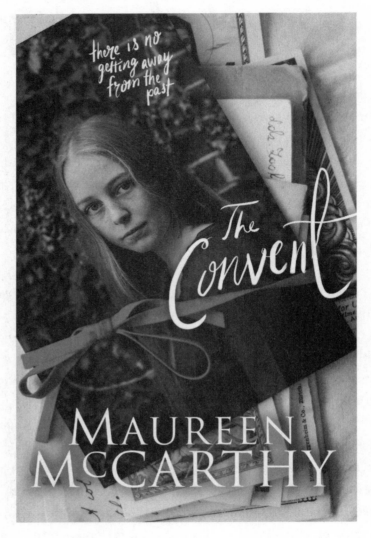

When Peach takes a summer job at a cafe in the old convent, her idea of who she is takes a sharp turn into the past. The nuns, orphans and fallen women are long gone, but her own connection to the place jolts her out of her comfort zone.

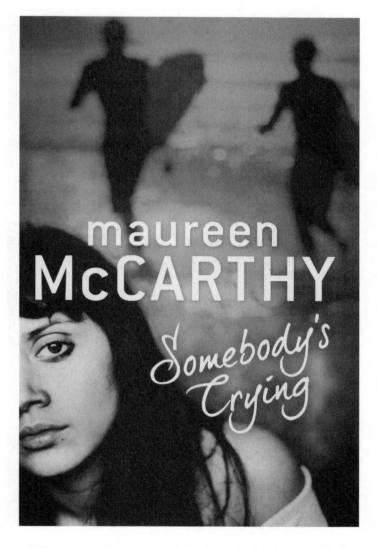

maureen
McCARTHY

Somebody's
Crying

Three years have passed since the murder of Alice's
mother, but still the killer is unknown. Alice, her
cousin Jonty and his friend Tom are drawn together
by the mystery, but what are they hiding?
Will their secrets bind them even tighter or tear
everything apart?

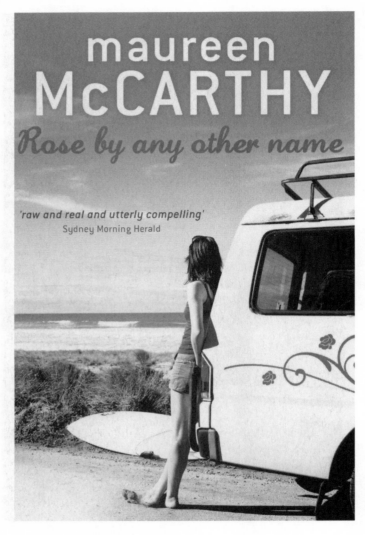

maureen
McCARTHY

Rose by any other name

'raw and real and utterly compelling'
Sydney Morning Herald

Rose is all packed up. She's got a van full of petrol
and a stack of CDs. She's got a surfboard in the back
and a secret that won't go away. But that's okay. She
also has enough attitude to light up the night sky.
Then her mother decides to come along … and
Rose's road trip takes an unplanned U-turn,
straight to the heart of last summer.

Queen Kat, Carmel & St. Jude Get a Life

MAUREEN McCARTHY

Carmel, Jude and Katerina come from the same
country town, but they couldn't be more different. So
when they all move into the same inner-city house
in their first university year, sparks fly. But this year is
a time to re-invent themselves, a time to square up to
the world. Time to get a life.

about the author

Maureen McCarthy is the ninth of ten children and grew up on a farm near Yea in Victoria. After working for a while as an art teacher, Maureen became a full-time writer. Her novels for young adults include *The Convent*, *Somebody's Crying*, *Rose by any other name*, and her much-loved bestseller *Queen Kat, Carmel and St Jude Get a Life*, which was made into a highly successful four-part mini-series for ABC TV. Her books for children include *Careful what you wish for* and *Flash Jack*.